GIANT DAYS

VOLUME SEVEN

BOOM! BOX

GIANT DAYS Volume Seven, March 2018. Published by BOOM! Box, a division of Boom Entertainment, Inc. Giant Days is ™ & © 2018 John Allison. Originally published in single magazine form as GIANT DAYS No. 25-28. ™ & © 2016, 2017 John Allison. All rights reserved. BOOM! Box™ and the BOOM! Box logo are trademarks of Boom Entertainment, Inc., registered in various countries and categories. All characters, events, and institutions depicted herein are fictional. Any similarity between any of the names, characters, persons, events, and/or institutions in this publication to actual names, characters, and persons, whether living or dead, events, and/or institutions is unintended and purely coincidental. BOOM! Box does not read or accept unsolicited submissions of ideas, stories, or artwork.

For information regarding the CPSIA on this printed material, call: (203) 595-3636 and provide reference #RICH – 771146.

BOOM! Studios, 5670 Wilshire Boulevard, Suite 400, Los Angeles, CA 90036-5679. Printed in USA. First Printing.

ISBN: 978-1-68415-131-8, eISBN: 978-1-61398-870-1

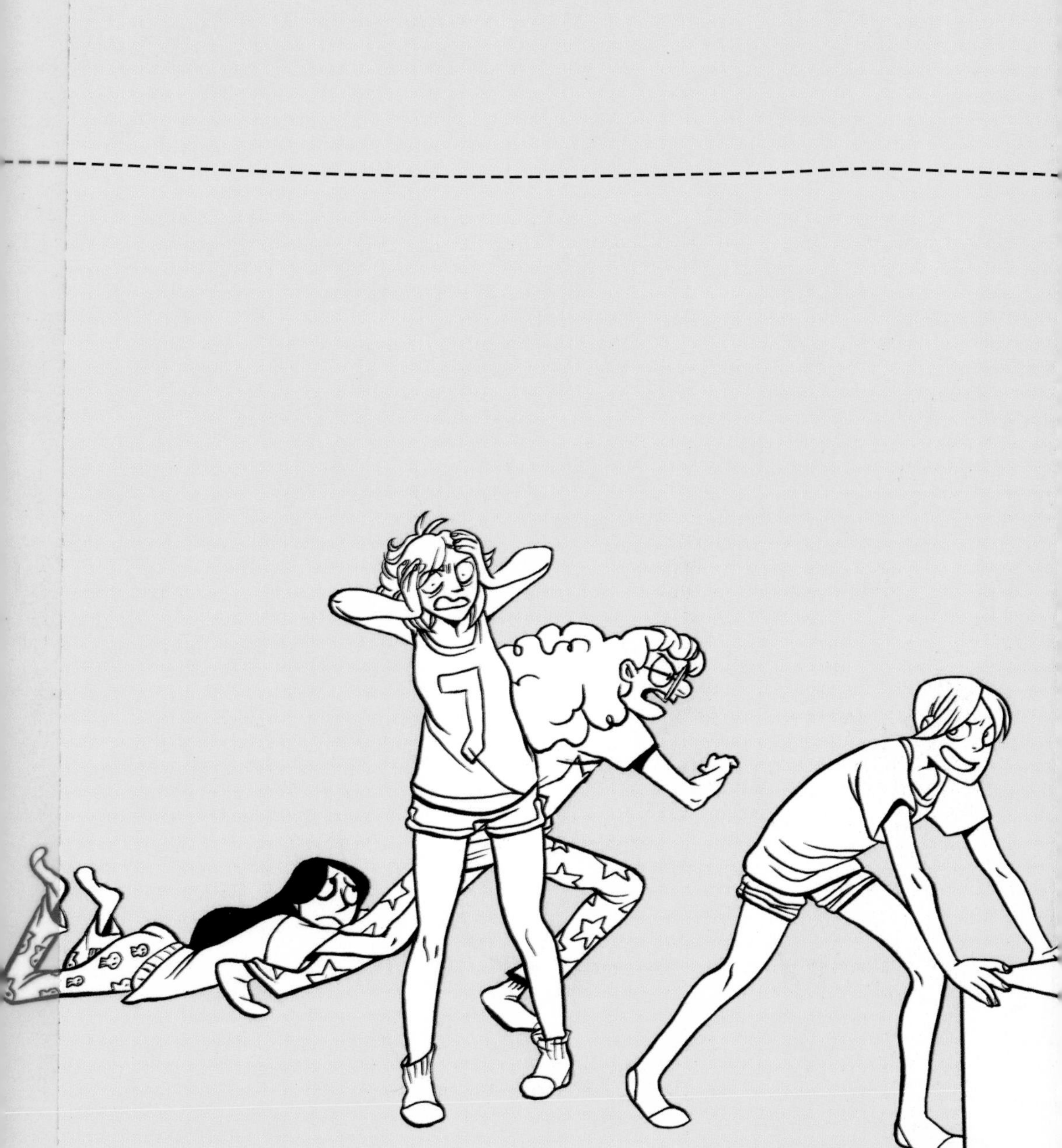

GIANT DAYS ™

CREATED & WRITTEN BY
JOHN ALLISON

ILLUSTRATED BY
MAX SARIN

INKS BY
LIZ FLEMING

COLORS BY
WHITNEY COGAR

LETTERS BY
JIM CAMPBELL

COVER BY
LISSA TREIMAN

DESIGNER
MICHELLE ANKLEY

ASSISTANT EDITOR
SOPHIE PHILIPS-ROBERTS

EDITOR
SHANNON WATTERS

SPECIAL THANKS TO JASMINE AMIRI

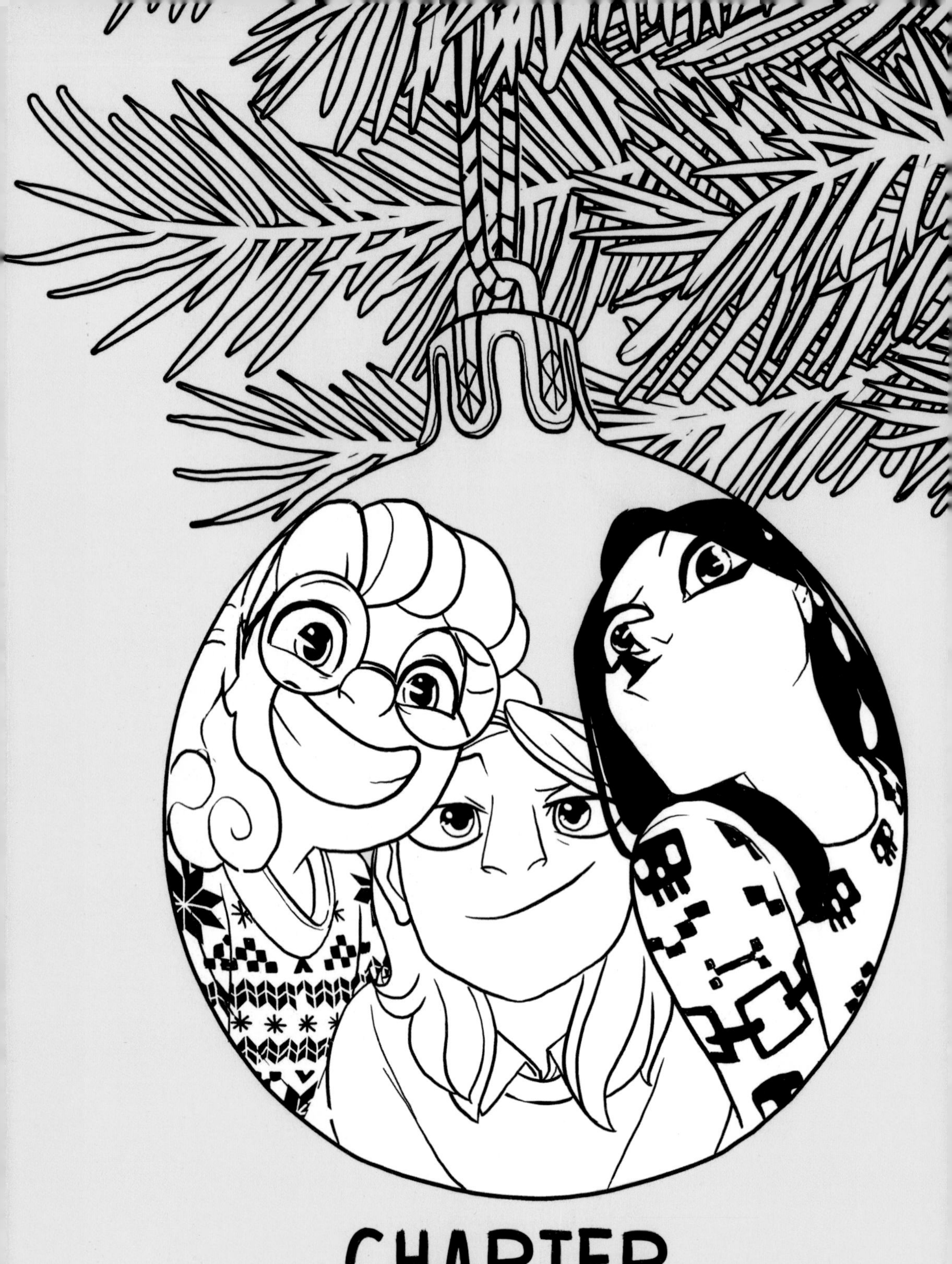

CHAPTER TWENTY FIVE

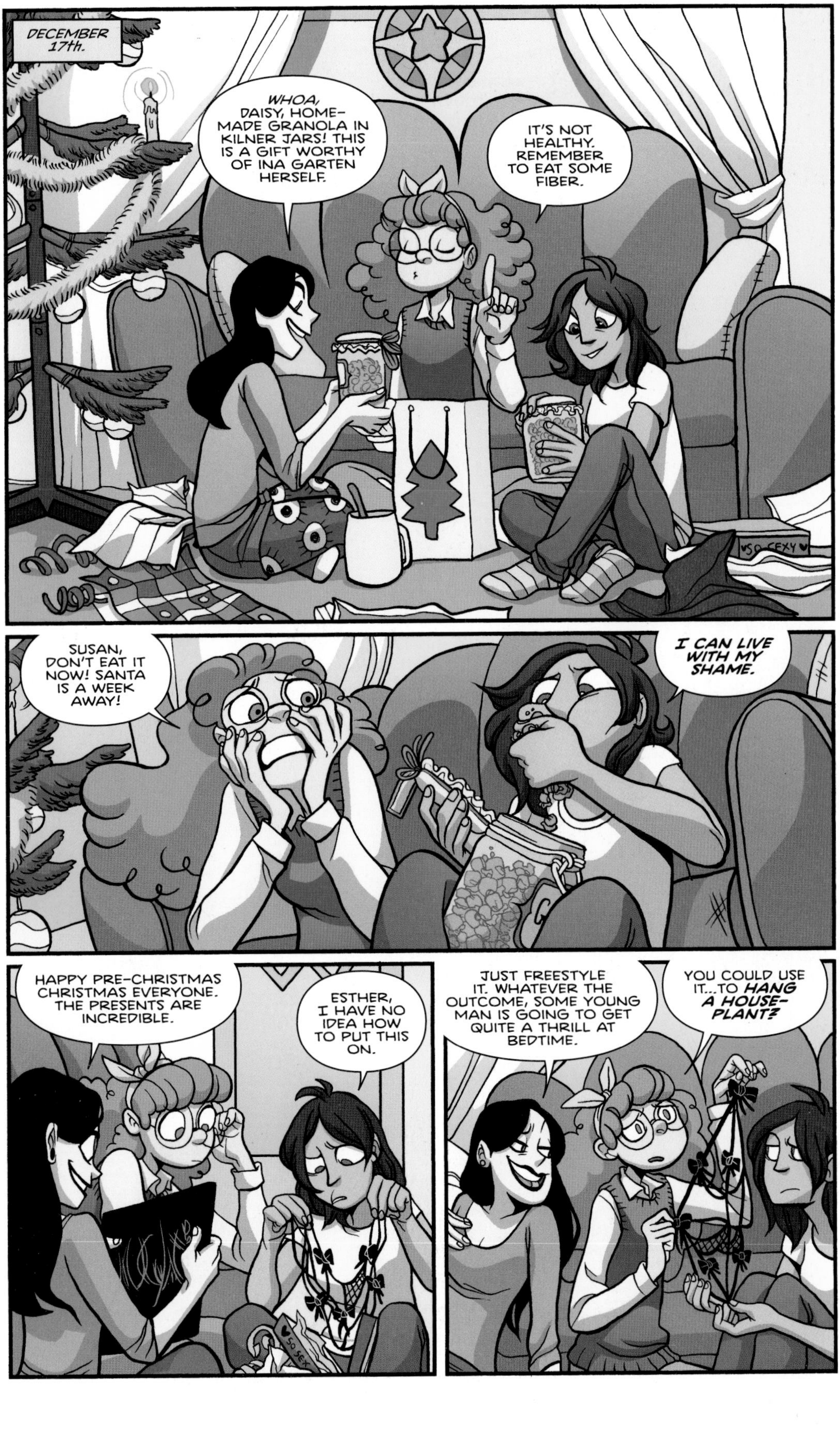
DECEMBER 17th.
WHOA, DAISY, HOME-MADE GRANOLA IN KILNER JARS! THIS IS A GIFT WORTHY OF INA GARTEN HERSELF.
IT'S NOT HEALTHY. REMEMBER TO EAT SOME FIBER.
SO SEXY
SUSAN, DON'T EAT IT NOW! SANTA IS A WEEK AWAY!
I CAN LIVE WITH MY SHAME.
HAPPY PRE-CHRISTMAS CHRISTMAS EVERYONE. THE PRESENTS ARE INCREDIBLE.
ESTHER, I HAVE NO IDEA HOW TO PUT THIS ON.
JUST FREESTYLE IT. WHATEVER THE OUTCOME, SOME YOUNG MAN IS GOING TO GET QUITE A THRILL AT BEDTIME.
YOU COULD USE IT...TO HANG A HOUSE-PLANT?

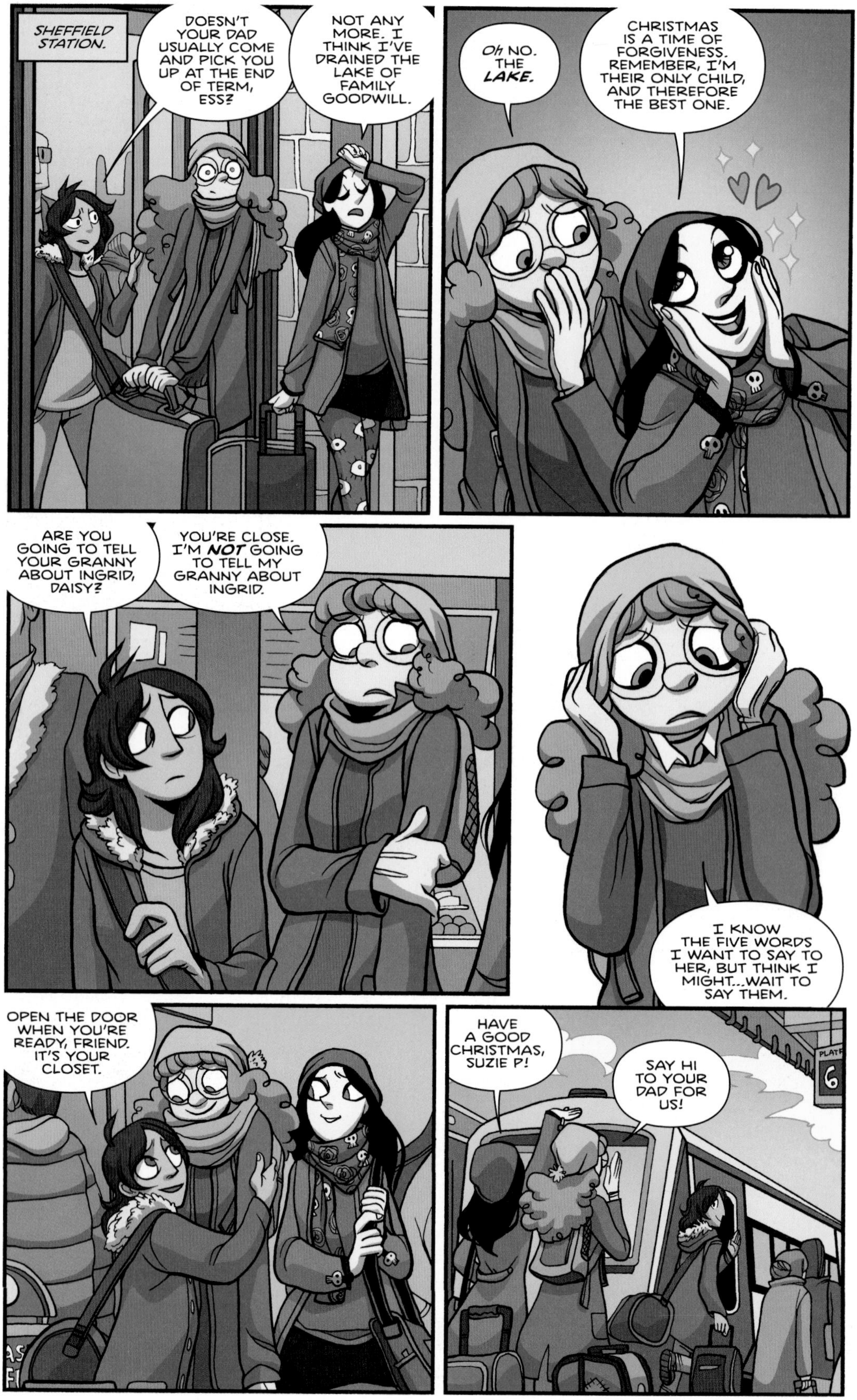
SHEFFIELD STATION.
DOESN'T YOUR DAD USUALLY COME AND PICK YOU UP AT THE END OF TERM, ESS?
NOT ANY MORE. I THINK I'VE DRAINED THE LAKE OF FAMILY GOODWILL.
Oh NO. THE LAKE.
CHRISTMAS IS A TIME OF FORGIVENESS. REMEMBER, I'M THEIR ONLY CHILD, AND THEREFORE THE BEST ONE.
ARE YOU GOING TO TELL YOUR GRANNY ABOUT INGRID, DAISY?
YOU'RE CLOSE. I'M NOT GOING TO TELL MY GRANNY ABOUT INGRID.
I KNOW THE FIVE WORDS I WANT TO SAY TO HER, BUT THINK I MIGHT...WAIT TO SAY THEM.
OPEN THE DOOR WHEN YOU'RE READY, FRIEND. IT'S YOUR CLOSET.
HAVE A GOOD CHRISTMAS, SUZIE P!
SAY HI TO YOUR DAD FOR US!

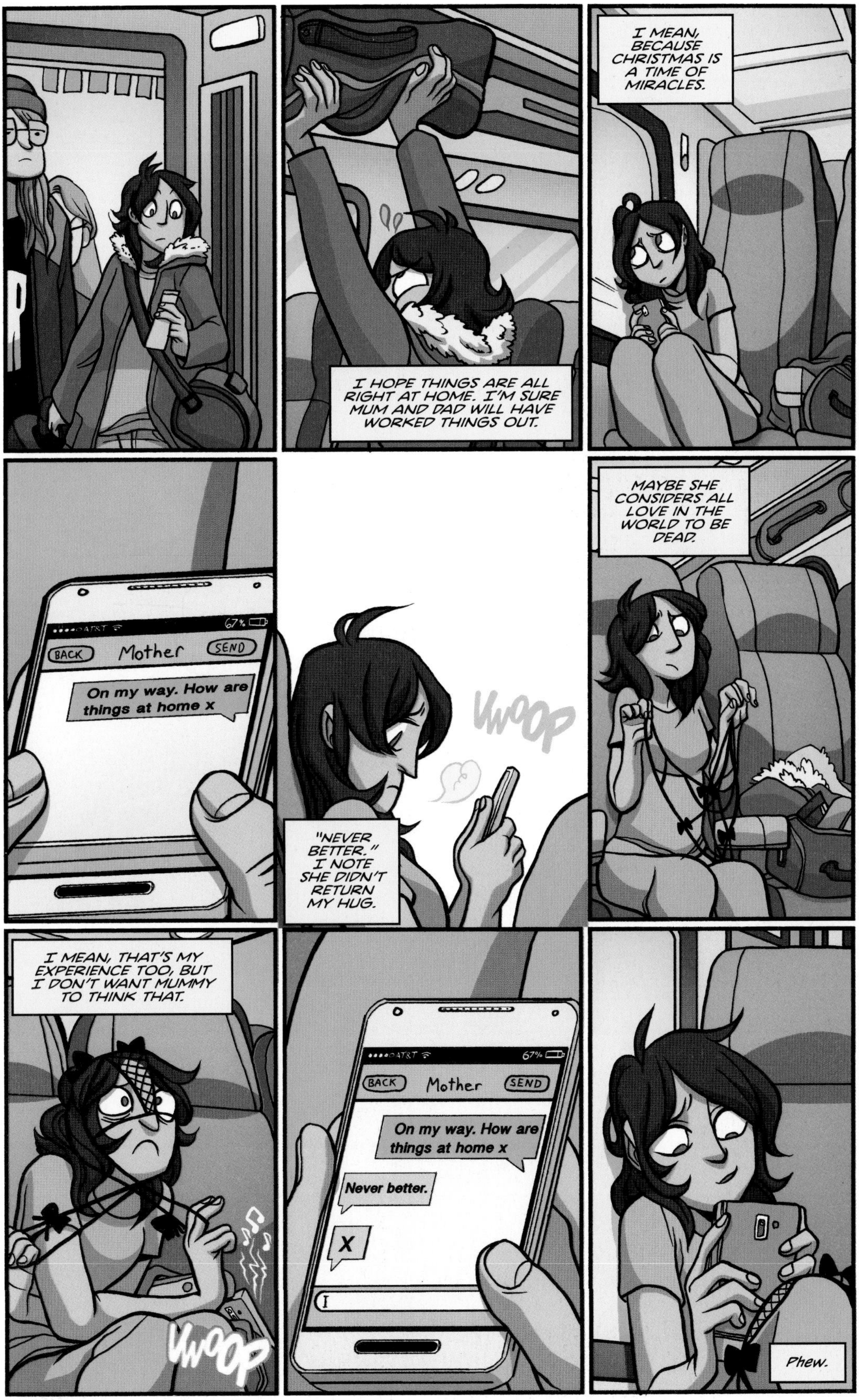
I HOPE THINGS ARE ALL RIGHT AT HOME. I'M SURE MUM AND DAD WILL HAVE WORKED THINGS OUT.
I MEAN, BECAUSE CHRISTMAS IS A TIME OF MIRACLES.
Mother
BACK
SEND
67%
On my way. How are things at home x
VWOOP
"NEVER BETTER." I NOTE SHE DIDN'T RETURN MY HUG.
MAYBE SHE CONSIDERS ALL LOVE IN THE WORLD TO BE DEAD.
I MEAN, THAT'S MY EXPERIENCE TOO, BUT I DON'T WANT MUMMY TO THINK THAT.
VWOOP
Mother
BACK
SEND
67%
On my way. How are things at home x
Never better.
X
Phew.

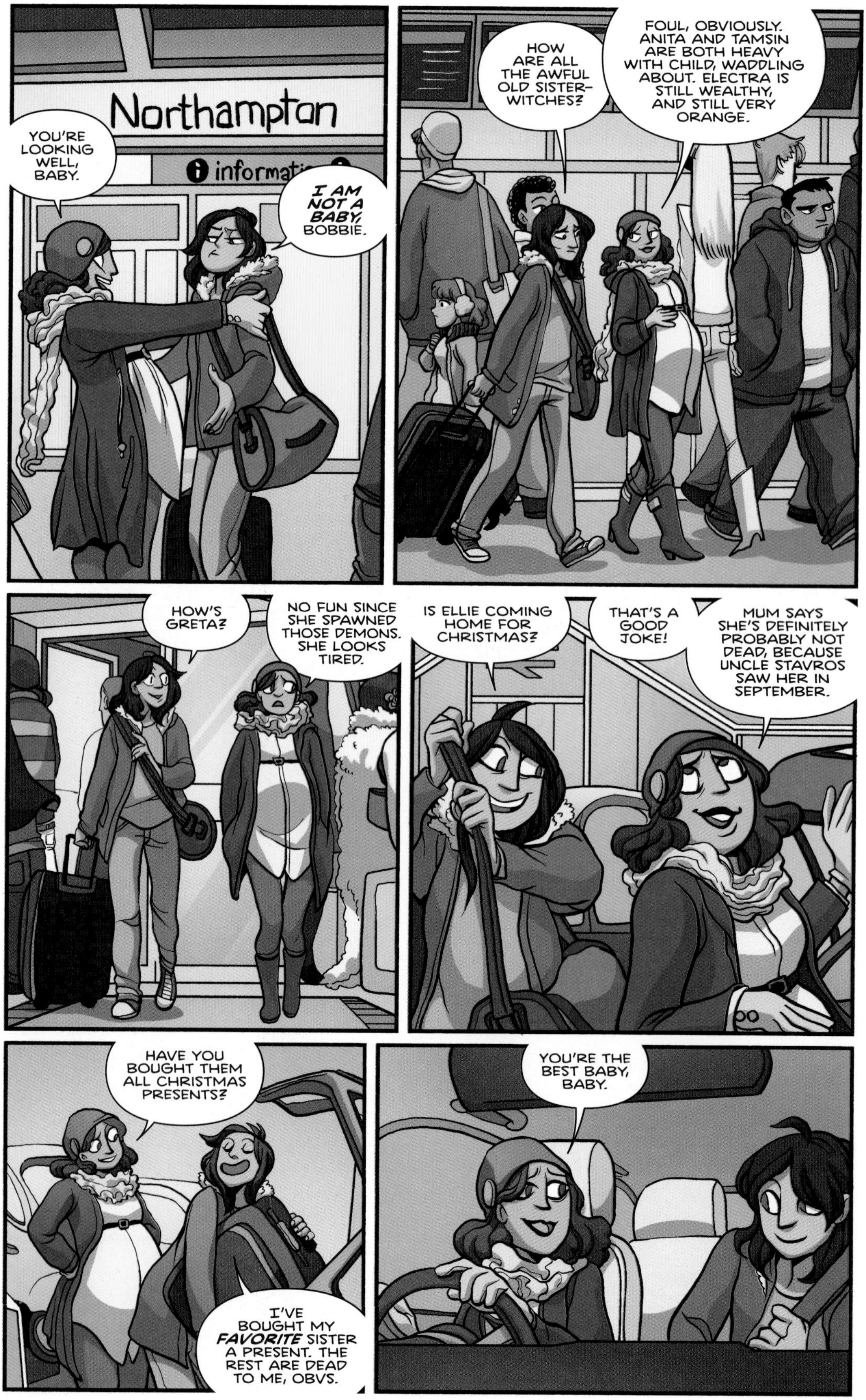
Northampton
information
YOU'RE LOOKING WELL, BABY.
I AM NOT A BABY, BOBBIE.
HOW ARE ALL THE AWFUL OLD SISTER-WITCHES?
FOUL, OBVIOUSLY. ANITA AND TAMSIN ARE BOTH HEAVY WITH CHILD, WADDLING ABOUT. ELECTRA IS STILL WEALTHY, AND STILL VERY ORANGE.
HOW'S GRETA?
NO FUN SINCE SHE SPAWNED THOSE DEMONS. SHE LOOKS TIRED.
IS ELLIE COMING HOME FOR CHRISTMAS?
THAT'S A GOOD JOKE!
MUM SAYS SHE'S DEFINITELY PROBABLY NOT DEAD, BECAUSE UNCLE STAVROS SAW HER IN SEPTEMBER.
HAVE YOU BOUGHT THEM ALL CHRISTMAS PRESENTS?
I'VE BOUGHT MY FAVORITE SISTER A PRESENT. THE REST ARE DEAD TO ME, OBVS.
YOU'RE THE BEST BABY, BABY.

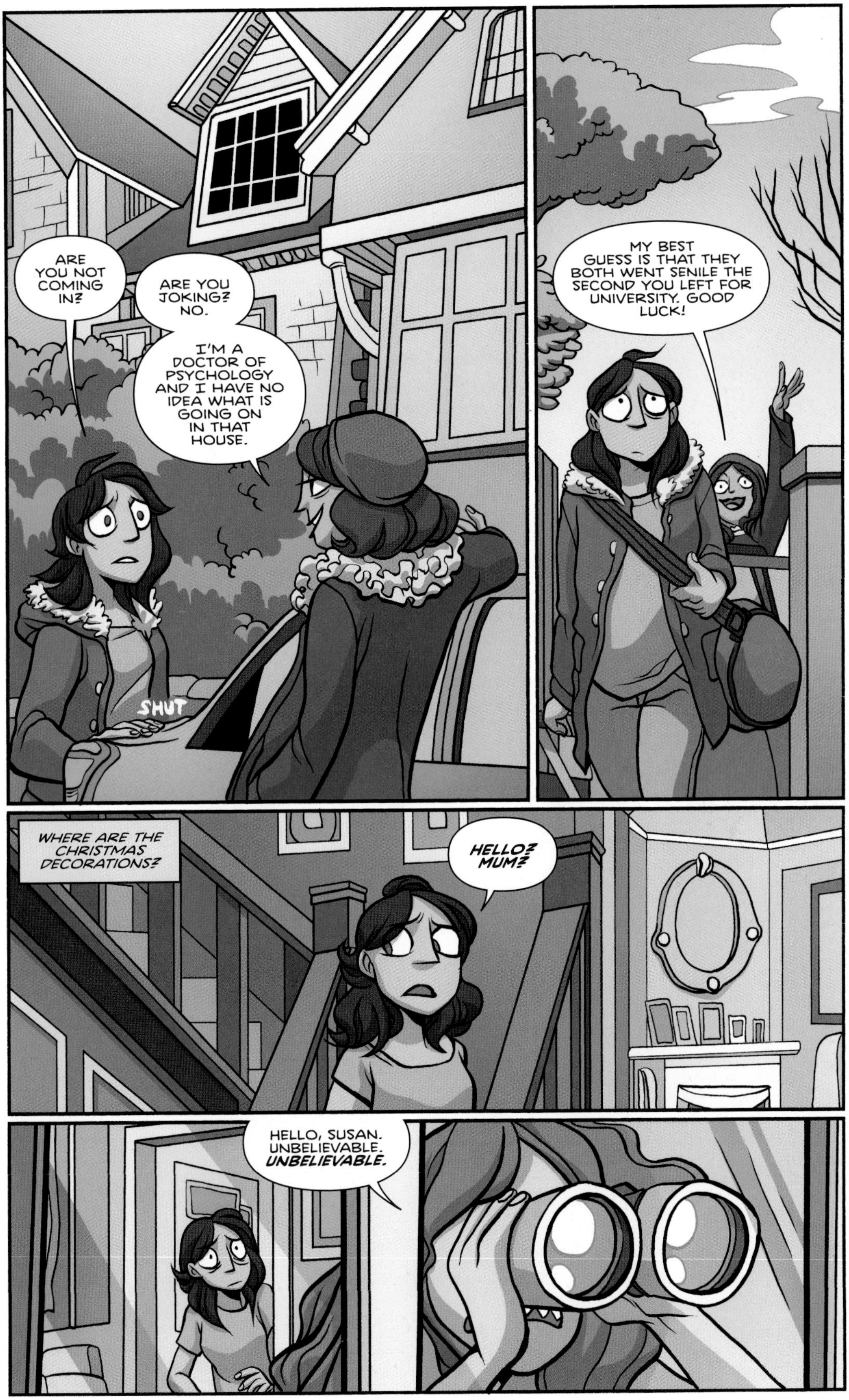
ARE YOU NOT COMING IN?
ARE YOU JOKING? NO.
I'M A DOCTOR OF PSYCHOLOGY AND I HAVE NO IDEA WHAT IS GOING ON IN THAT HOUSE.
SHUT
MY BEST GUESS IS THAT THEY BOTH WENT SENILE THE SECOND YOU LEFT FOR UNIVERSITY. GOOD LUCK!
WHERE ARE THE CHRISTMAS DECORATIONS?
HELLO? MUM?
HELLO, SUSAN. UNBELIEVABLE. UNBELIEVABLE.

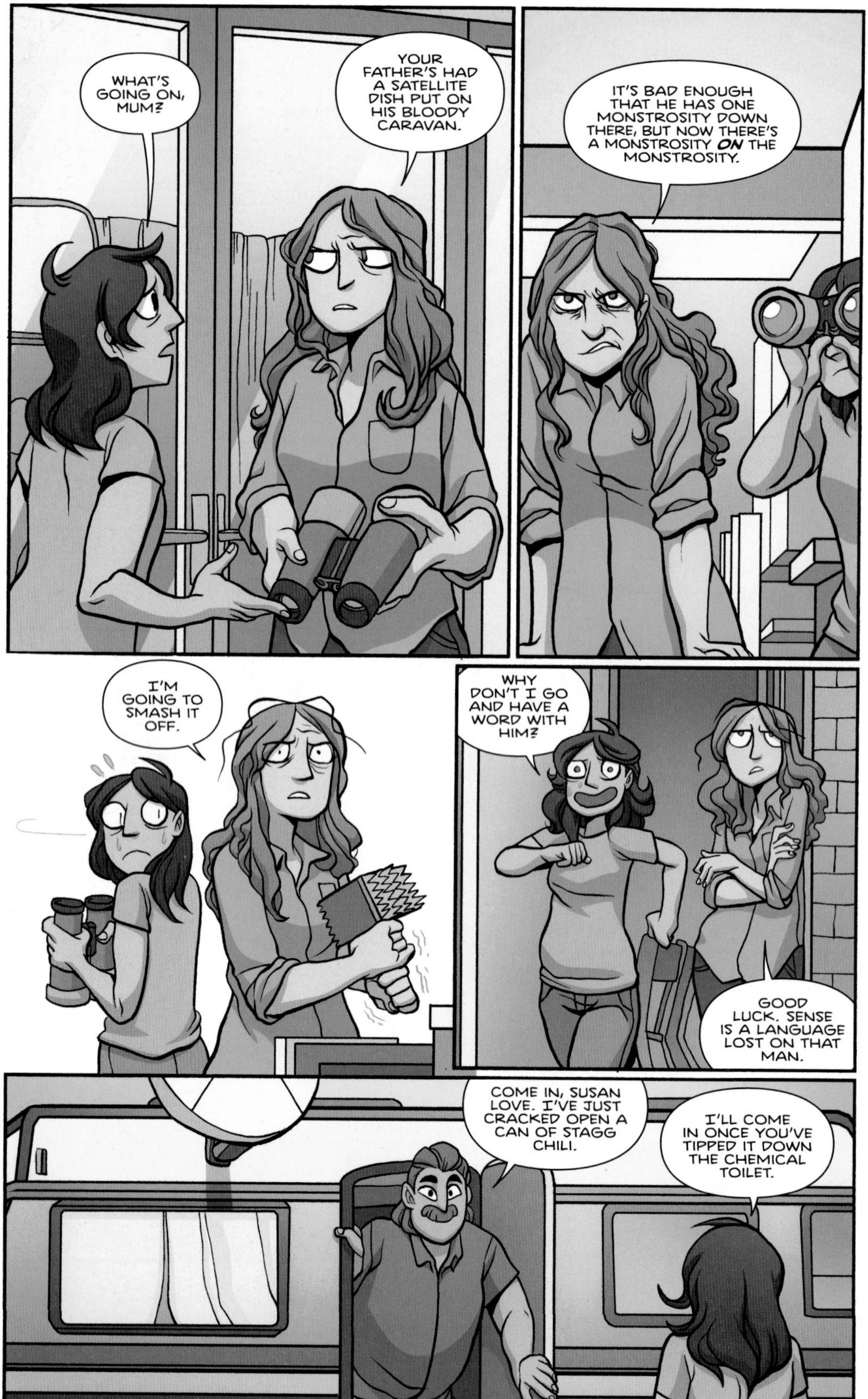
WHAT'S GOING ON, MUM?
YOUR FATHER'S HAD A SATELLITE DISH PUT ON HIS BLOODY CARAVAN.
IT'S BAD ENOUGH THAT HE HAS ONE MONSTROSITY DOWN THERE, BUT NOW THERE'S A MONSTROSITY ***ON*** THE MONSTROSITY.
I'M GOING TO SMASH IT OFF.
WHY DON'T I GO AND HAVE A WORD WITH HIM?
GOOD LUCK. SENSE IS A LANGUAGE LOST ON THAT MAN.
COME IN, SUSAN LOVE. I'VE JUST CRACKED OPEN A CAN OF STAGG CHILI.
I'LL COME IN ONCE YOU'VE TIPPED IT DOWN THE CHEMICAL TOILET.

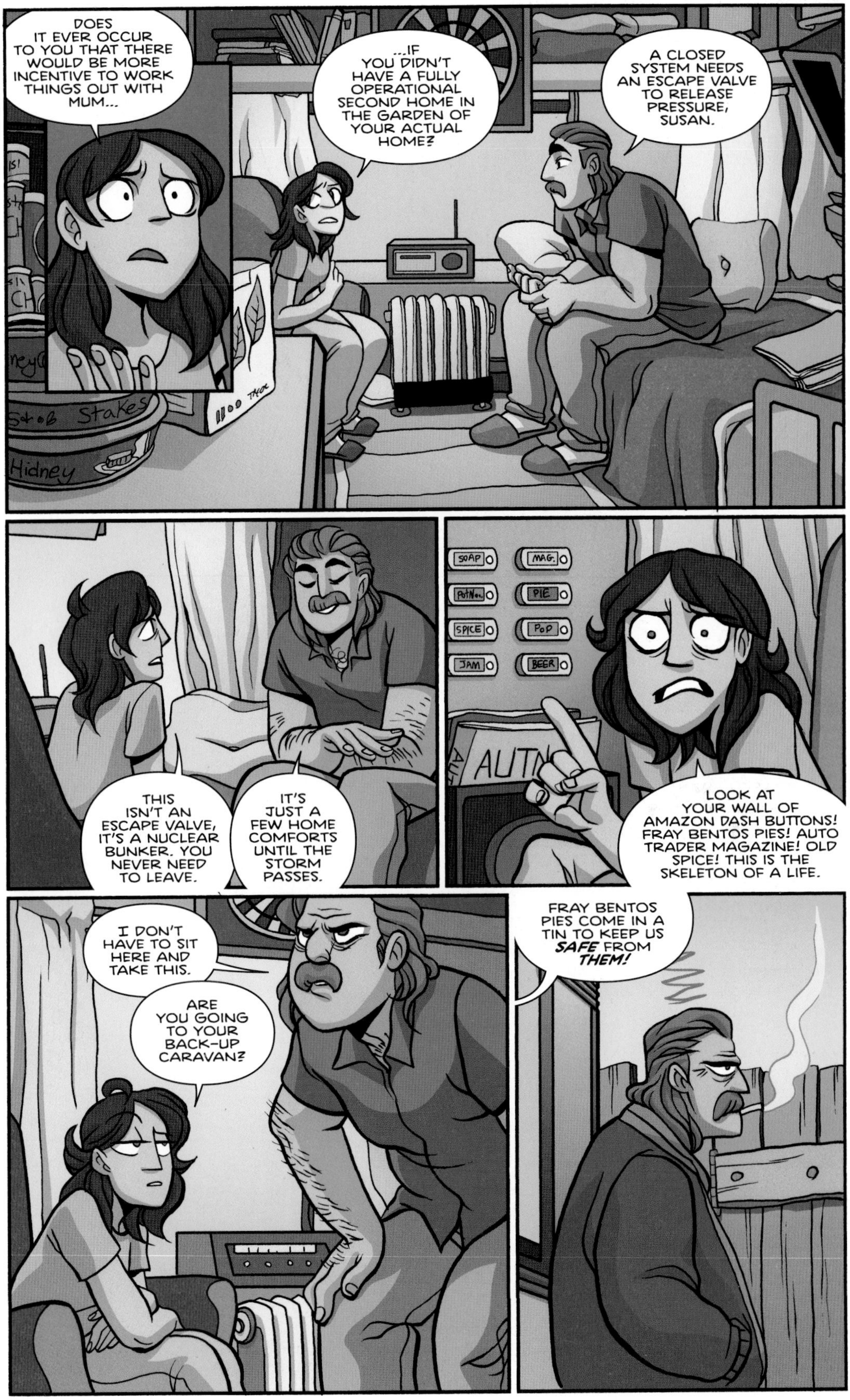
DOES IT EVER OCCUR TO YOU THAT THERE WOULD BE MORE INCENTIVE TO WORK THINGS OUT WITH MUM...
...IF YOU DIDN'T HAVE A FULLY OPERATIONAL SECOND HOME IN THE GARDEN OF YOUR ACTUAL HOME?
A CLOSED SYSTEM NEEDS AN ESCAPE VALVE TO RELEASE PRESSURE, SUSAN.
THIS ISN'T AN ESCAPE VALVE, IT'S A NUCLEAR BUNKER. YOU NEVER NEED TO LEAVE.
IT'S JUST A FEW HOME COMFORTS UNTIL THE STORM PASSES.
SOAP
MAG.
PotNoo
PIE
SPICE
PoP
JAM
BEER
LOOK AT YOUR WALL OF AMAZON DASH BUTTONS! FRAY BENTOS PIES! AUTO TRADER MAGAZINE! OLD SPICE! THIS IS THE SKELETON OF A LIFE.
I DON'T HAVE TO SIT HERE AND TAKE THIS.
ARE YOU GOING TO YOUR BACK-UP CARAVAN?
FRAY BENTOS PIES COME IN A TIN TO KEEP US *SAFE* FROM *THEM!*

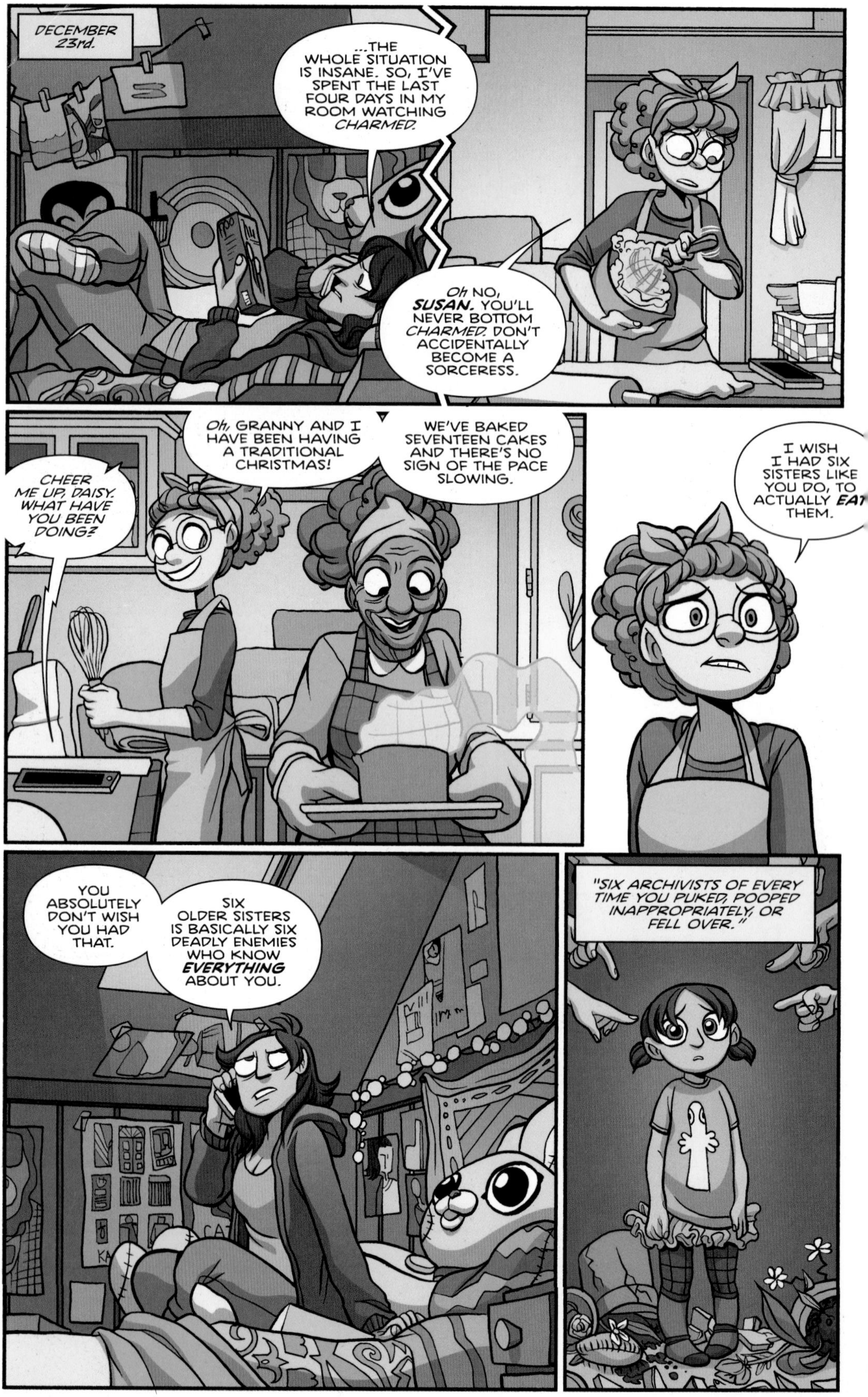
DECEMBER 23rd.
...THE WHOLE SITUATION IS INSANE. SO, I'VE SPENT THE LAST FOUR DAYS IN MY ROOM WATCHING *CHARMED*.
Oh NO, **SUSAN.** YOU'LL NEVER BOTTOM *CHARMED*. DON'T ACCIDENTALLY BECOME A SORCERESS.
CHEER ME UP, DAISY. WHAT HAVE YOU BEEN DOING?
Oh, GRANNY AND I HAVE BEEN HAVING A TRADITIONAL CHRISTMAS!
WE'VE BAKED SEVENTEEN CAKES AND THERE'S NO SIGN OF THE PACE SLOWING.
I WISH I HAD SIX SISTERS LIKE YOU DO, TO ACTUALLY **EAT** THEM.
YOU ABSOLUTELY DON'T WISH YOU HAD THAT.
SIX OLDER SISTERS IS BASICALLY SIX DEADLY ENEMIES WHO KNOW **EVERYTHING** ABOUT YOU.
"SIX ARCHIVISTS OF EVERY TIME YOU PUKED, POOPED INAPPROPRIATELY, OR FELL OVER."

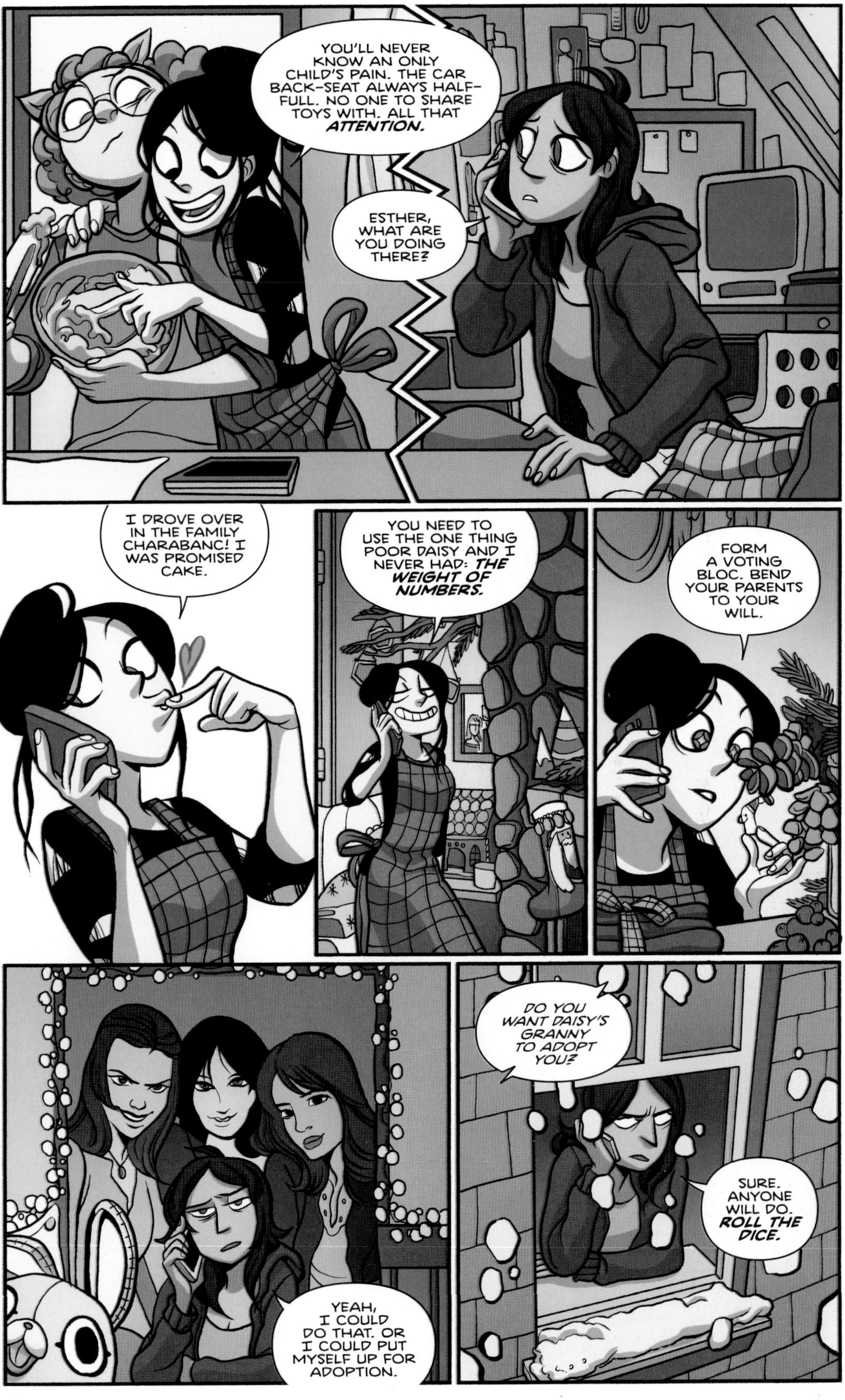
YOU'LL NEVER KNOW AN ONLY CHILD'S PAIN. THE CAR BACK-SEAT ALWAYS HALF-FULL. NO ONE TO SHARE TOYS WITH. ALL THAT *ATTENTION.*
ESTHER, WHAT ARE YOU DOING THERE?
I DROVE OVER IN THE FAMILY CHARABANC! I WAS PROMISED CAKE.
YOU NEED TO USE THE ONE THING POOR DAISY AND I NEVER HAD: ***THE WEIGHT OF NUMBERS.***
FORM A VOTING BLOC. BEND YOUR PARENTS TO YOUR WILL.
YEAH, I COULD DO THAT. OR I COULD PUT MYSELF UP FOR ADOPTION.
DO YOU WANT DAISY'S GRANNY TO ADOPT YOU?
SURE. ANYONE WILL DO. ***ROLL THE DICE.***

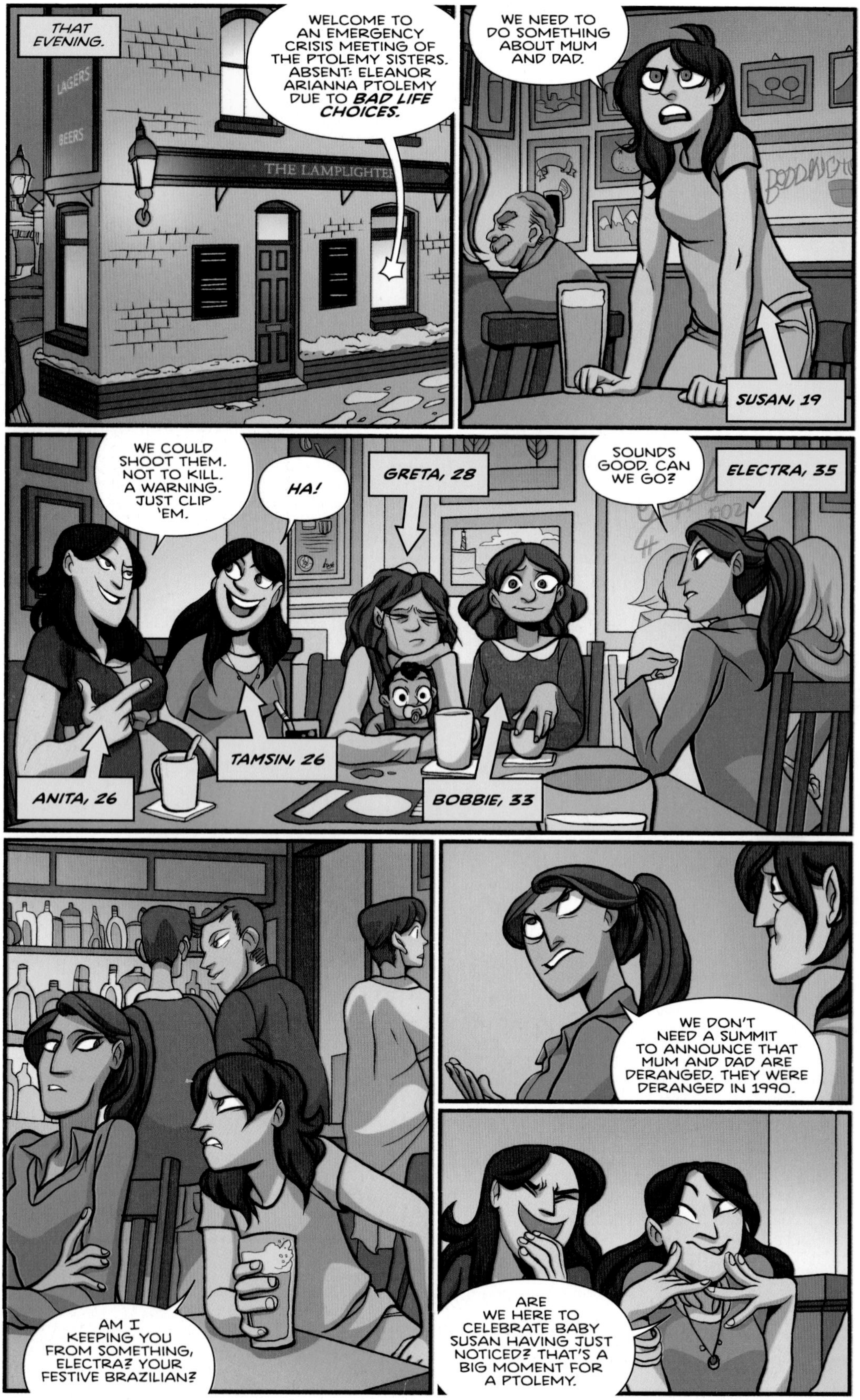

THAT EVENING.
LAGERS
BEERS
THE LAMPLIGHTER
WELCOME TO AN EMERGENCY CRISIS MEETING OF THE PTOLEMY SISTERS. ABSENT: ELEANOR ARIANNA PTOLEMY DUE TO ***BAD LIFE CHOICES.***
WE NEED TO DO SOMETHING ABOUT MUM AND DAD.
SUSAN, 19
WE COULD SHOOT THEM. NOT TO KILL. A WARNING. JUST CLIP 'EM.
HA!
GRETA, 28
SOUNDS GOOD. CAN WE GO?
ELECTRA, 35
ANITA, 26
TAMSIN, 26
BOBBIE, 33
AM I KEEPING YOU FROM SOMETHING, ELECTRA? YOUR FESTIVE BRAZILIAN?
WE DON'T NEED A SUMMIT TO ANNOUNCE THAT MUM AND DAD ARE DERANGED. THEY WERE DERANGED IN 1990.
ARE WE HERE TO CELEBRATE BABY SUSAN HAVING JUST NOTICED? THAT'S A BIG MOMENT FOR A PTOLEMY.

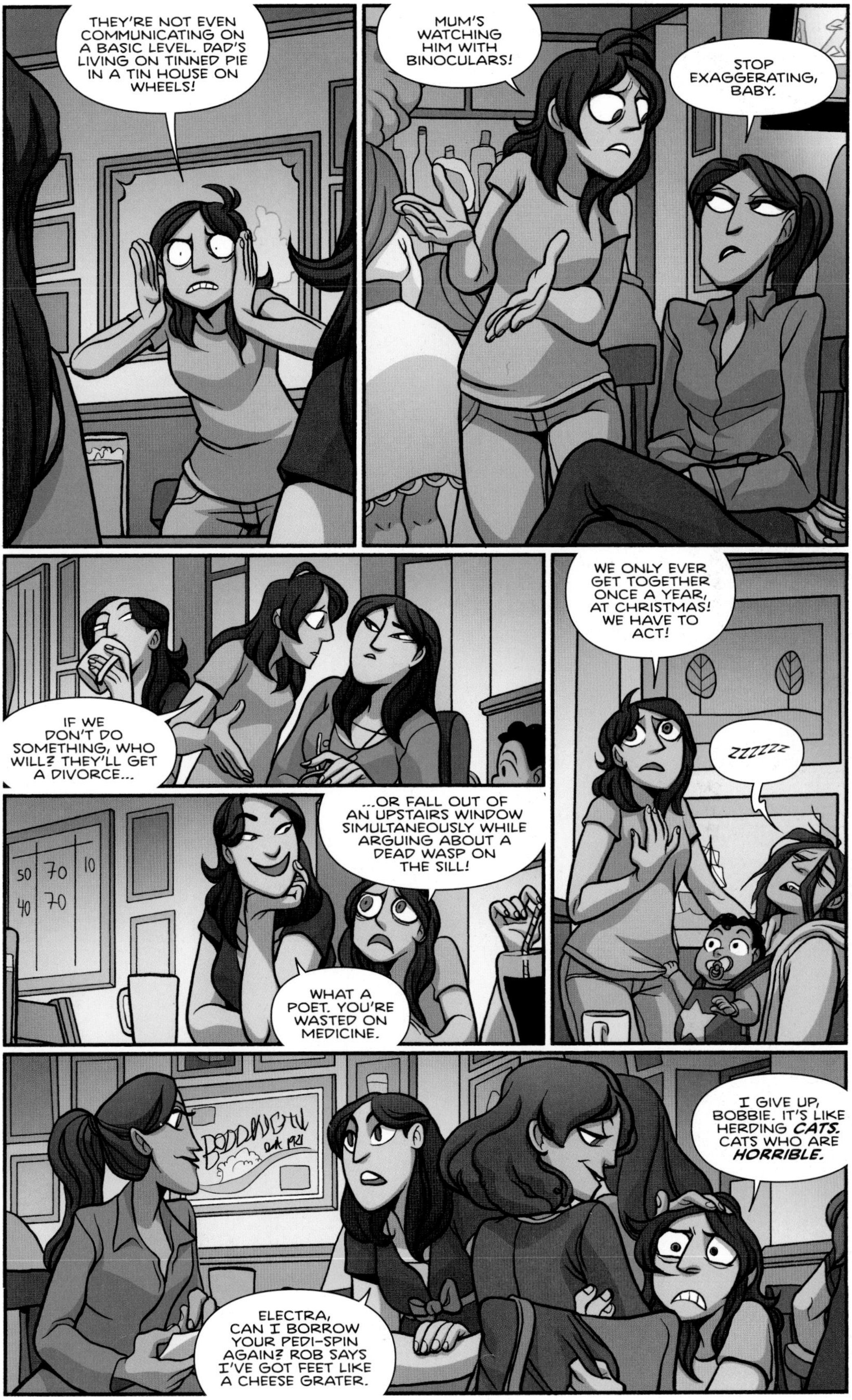
THEY'RE NOT EVEN COMMUNICATING ON A BASIC LEVEL. DAD'S LIVING ON TINNED PIE IN A TIN HOUSE ON WHEELS!
MUM'S WATCHING HIM WITH BINOCULARS!
STOP EXAGGERATING, BABY.
IF WE DON'T DO SOMETHING, WHO WILL? THEY'LL GET A DIVORCE...
...OR FALL OUT OF AN UPSTAIRS WINDOW SIMULTANEOUSLY WHILE ARGUING ABOUT A DEAD WASP ON THE SILL!
WHAT A POET. YOU'RE WASTED ON MEDICINE.
WE ONLY EVER GET TOGETHER ONCE A YEAR, AT CHRISTMAS! WE HAVE TO ACT!
ZZZZZZ
I GIVE UP, BOBBIE. IT'S LIKE HERDING CATS. CATS WHO ARE HORRIBLE.
ELECTRA, CAN I BORROW YOUR PEDI-SPIN AGAIN? ROB SAYS I'VE GOT FEET LIKE A CHEESE GRATER.

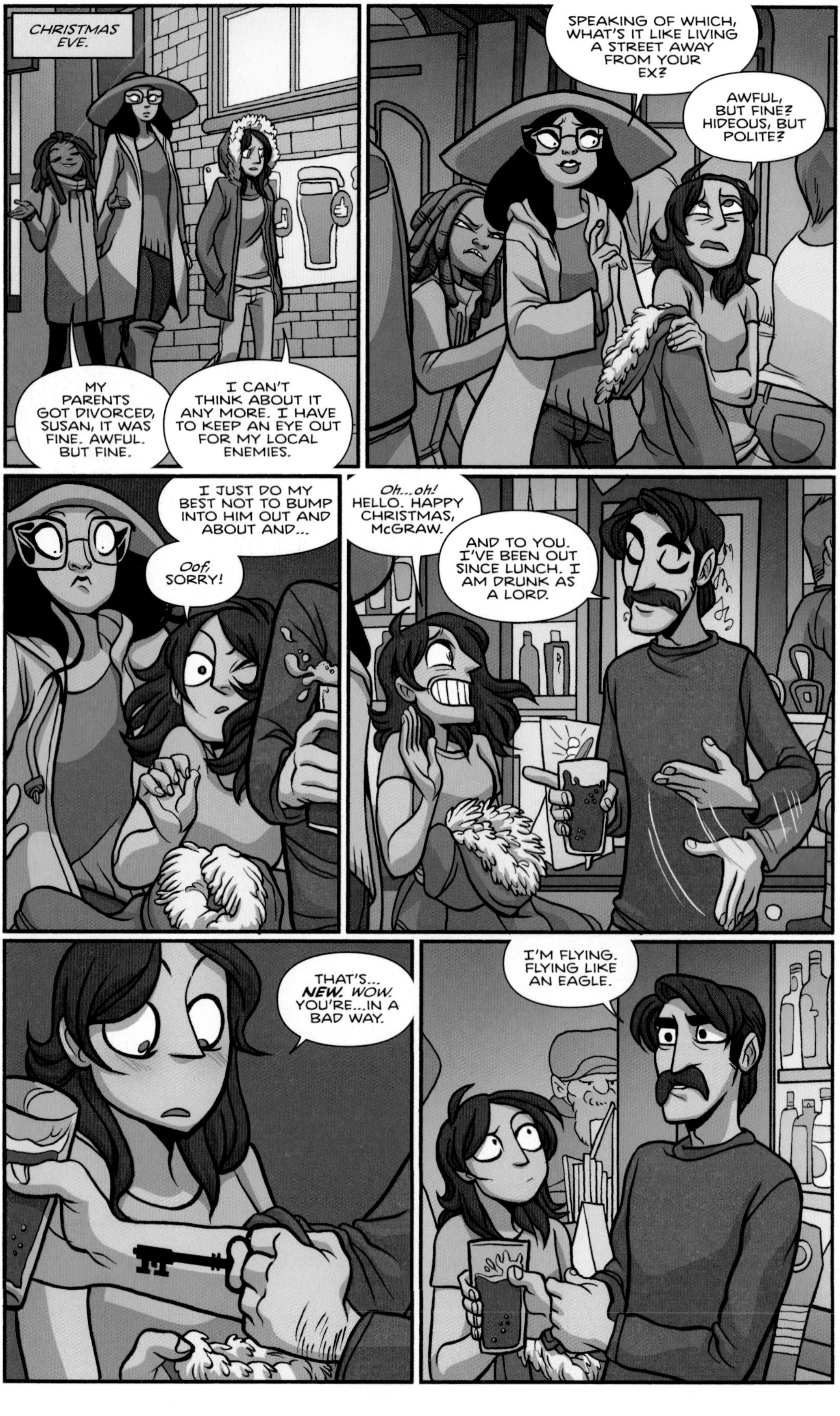
CHRISTMAS EVE.
MY PARENTS GOT DIVORCED, SUSAN, IT WAS FINE. AWFUL. BUT FINE.
I CAN'T THINK ABOUT IT ANY MORE. I HAVE TO KEEP AN EYE OUT FOR MY LOCAL ENEMIES.
SPEAKING OF WHICH, WHAT'S IT LIKE LIVING A STREET AWAY FROM YOUR EX?
AWFUL, BUT FINE? HIDEOUS, BUT POLITE?
I JUST DO MY BEST NOT TO BUMP INTO HIM OUT AND ABOUT AND...
Oof, SORRY!
Oh...oh! HELLO. HAPPY CHRISTMAS, McGRAW.
AND TO YOU. I'VE BEEN OUT SINCE LUNCH. I AM DRUNK AS A LORD.
THAT'S... NEW. WOW. YOU'RE...IN A BAD WAY.
I'M FLYING. FLYING LIKE AN EAGLE.

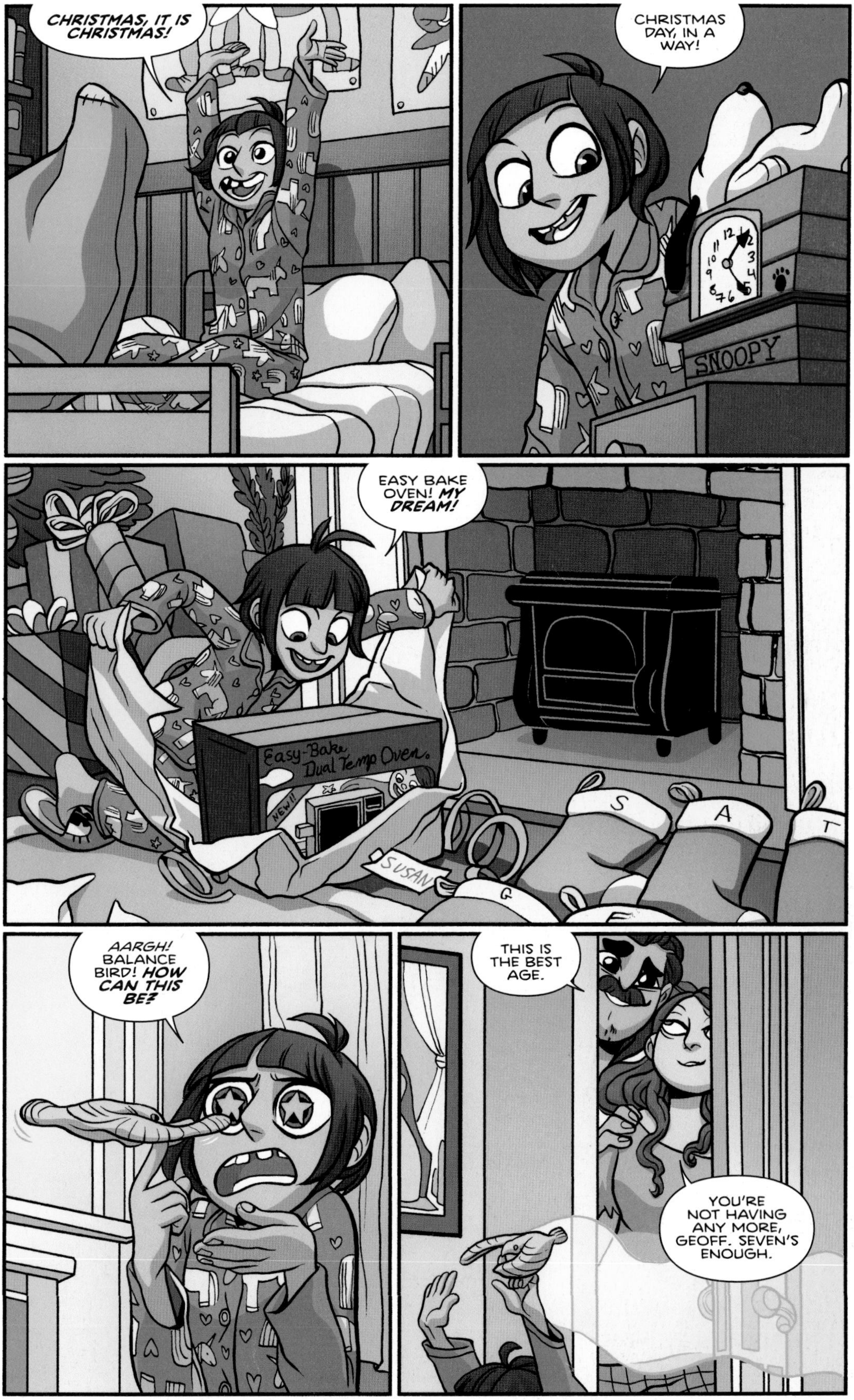
CHRISTMAS, IT IS CHRISTMAS!
CHRISTMAS DAY, IN A WAY!
SNOOPY
EASY BAKE OVEN! MY DREAM!
Easy-Bake Dual Temp Oven.
NEW!!
SUSAN
S
A
T
G
AARGH! BALANCE BIRD! HOW CAN THIS BE?
THIS IS THE BEST AGE.
YOU'RE NOT HAVING ANY MORE, GEOFF. SEVEN'S ENOUGH.

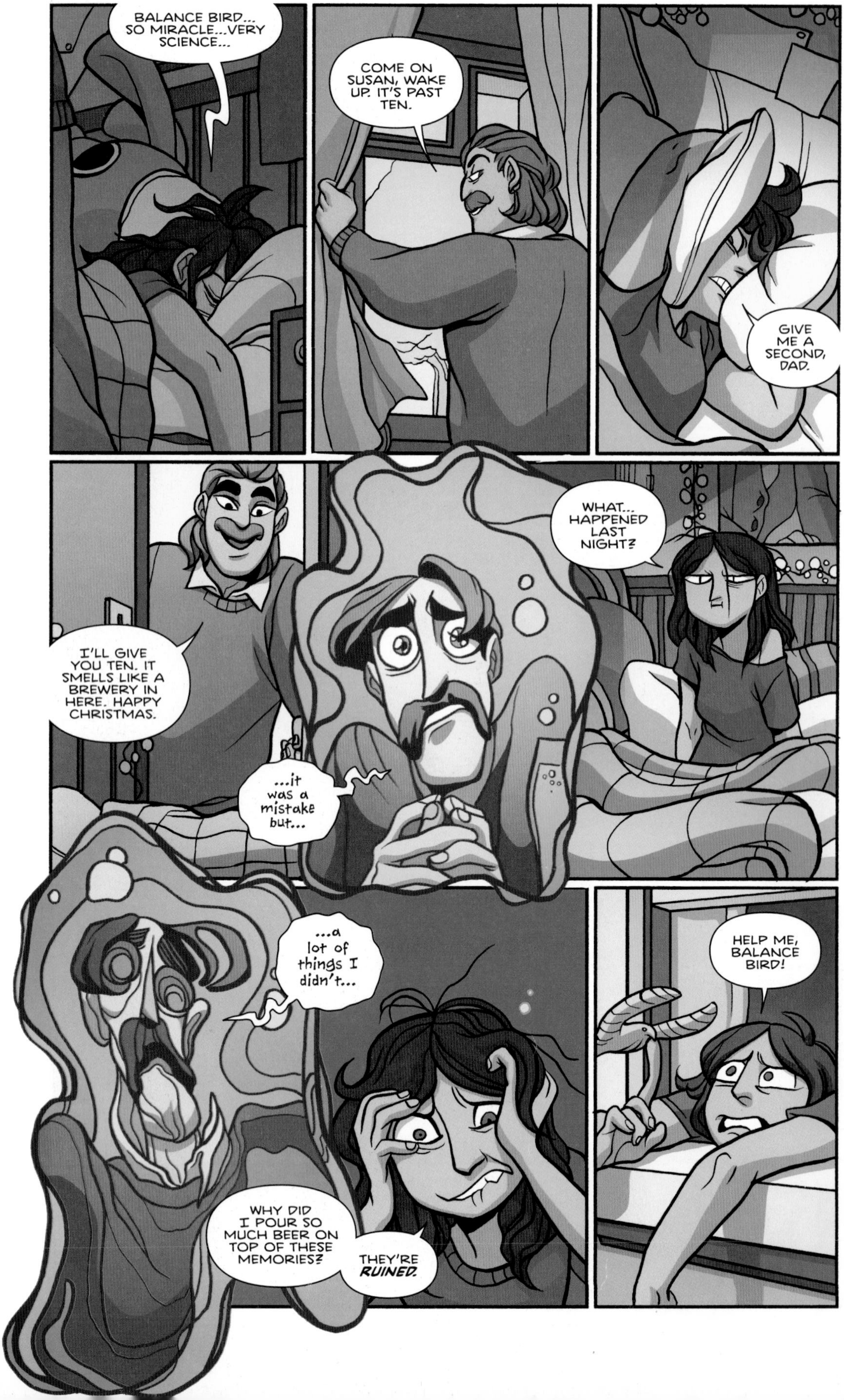
BALANCE BIRD... SO MIRACLE...VERY SCIENCE...
COME ON SUSAN, WAKE UP. IT'S PAST TEN.
GIVE ME A SECOND, DAD.
I'LL GIVE YOU TEN. IT SMELLS LIKE A BREWERY IN HERE. HAPPY CHRISTMAS.
WHAT... HAPPENED LAST NIGHT?
...it was a mistake but...
...a lot of things I didn't...
WHY DID I POUR SO MUCH BEER ON TOP OF THESE MEMORIES?
THEY'RE *RUINED.*
HELP ME, BALANCE BIRD!

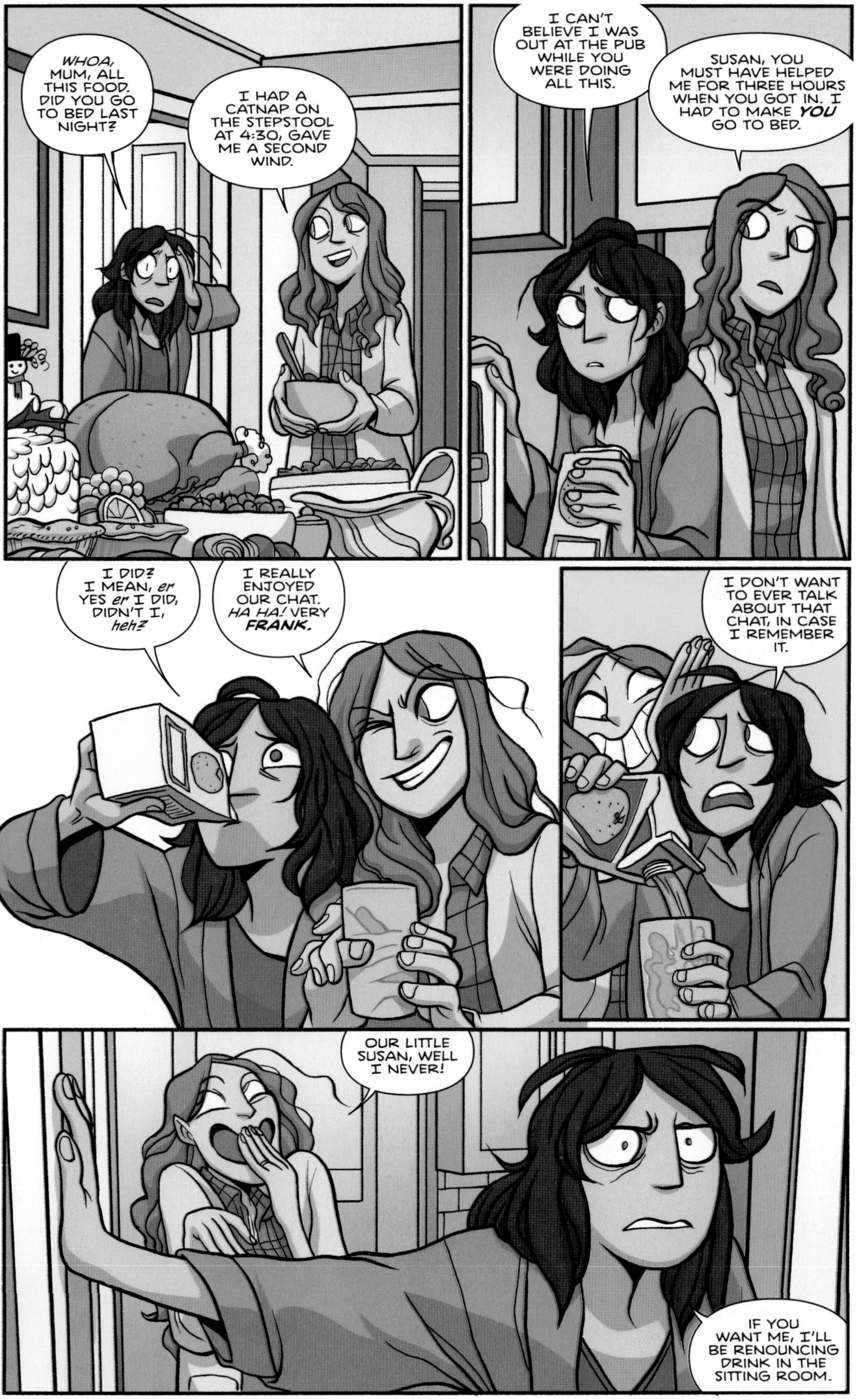
WHOA, MUM, ALL THIS FOOD. DID YOU GO TO BED LAST NIGHT?
I HAD A CATNAP ON THE STEPSTOOL AT 4:30, GAVE ME A SECOND WIND.
I CAN'T BELIEVE I WAS OUT AT THE PUB WHILE YOU WERE DOING ALL THIS.
SUSAN, YOU MUST HAVE HELPED ME FOR THREE HOURS WHEN YOU GOT IN. I HAD TO MAKE *YOU* GO TO BED.
I DID? I MEAN, *er* YES *er* I DID, DIDN'T I, *heh?*
I REALLY ENJOYED OUR CHAT. *HA HA!* VERY **FRANK.**
I DON'T WANT TO EVER TALK ABOUT THAT CHAT, IN CASE I REMEMBER IT.
OUR LITTLE SUSAN, WELL I NEVER!
IF YOU WANT ME, I'LL BE RENOUNCING DRINK IN THE SITTING ROOM.

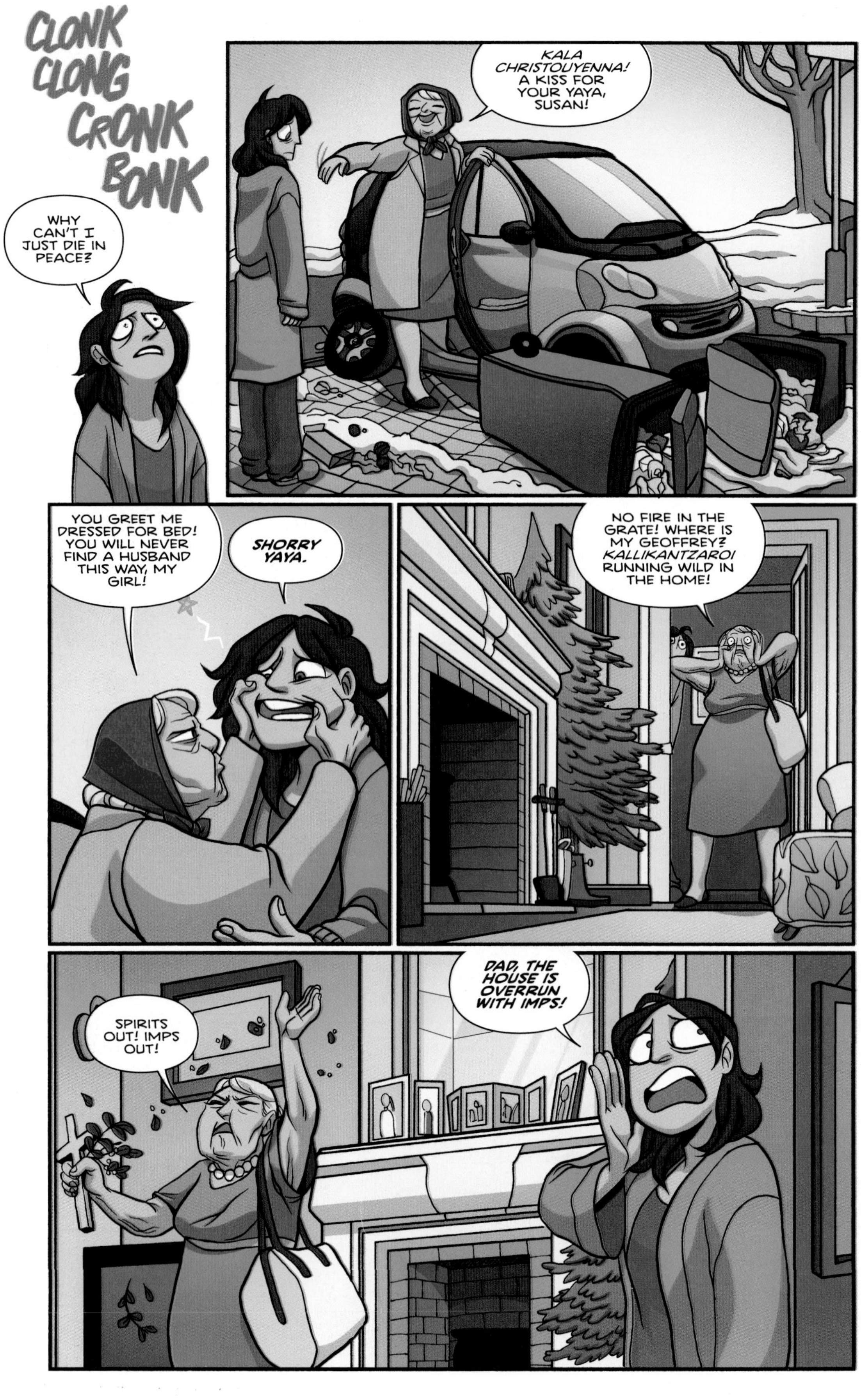

CLONK
CLONG
CRONK
BONK
WHY CAN'T I JUST DIE IN PEACE?
KALA CHRISTOUYENNA! A KISS FOR YOUR YAYA, SUSAN!
YOU GREET ME DRESSED FOR BED! YOU WILL NEVER FIND A HUSBAND THIS WAY, MY GIRL!
SHORRY YAYA.
NO FIRE IN THE GRATE! WHERE IS MY GEOFFREY? KALLIKANTZAROI RUNNING WILD IN THE HOME!
SPIRITS OUT! IMPS OUT!
DAD, THE HOUSE IS OVERRUN WITH IMPS!

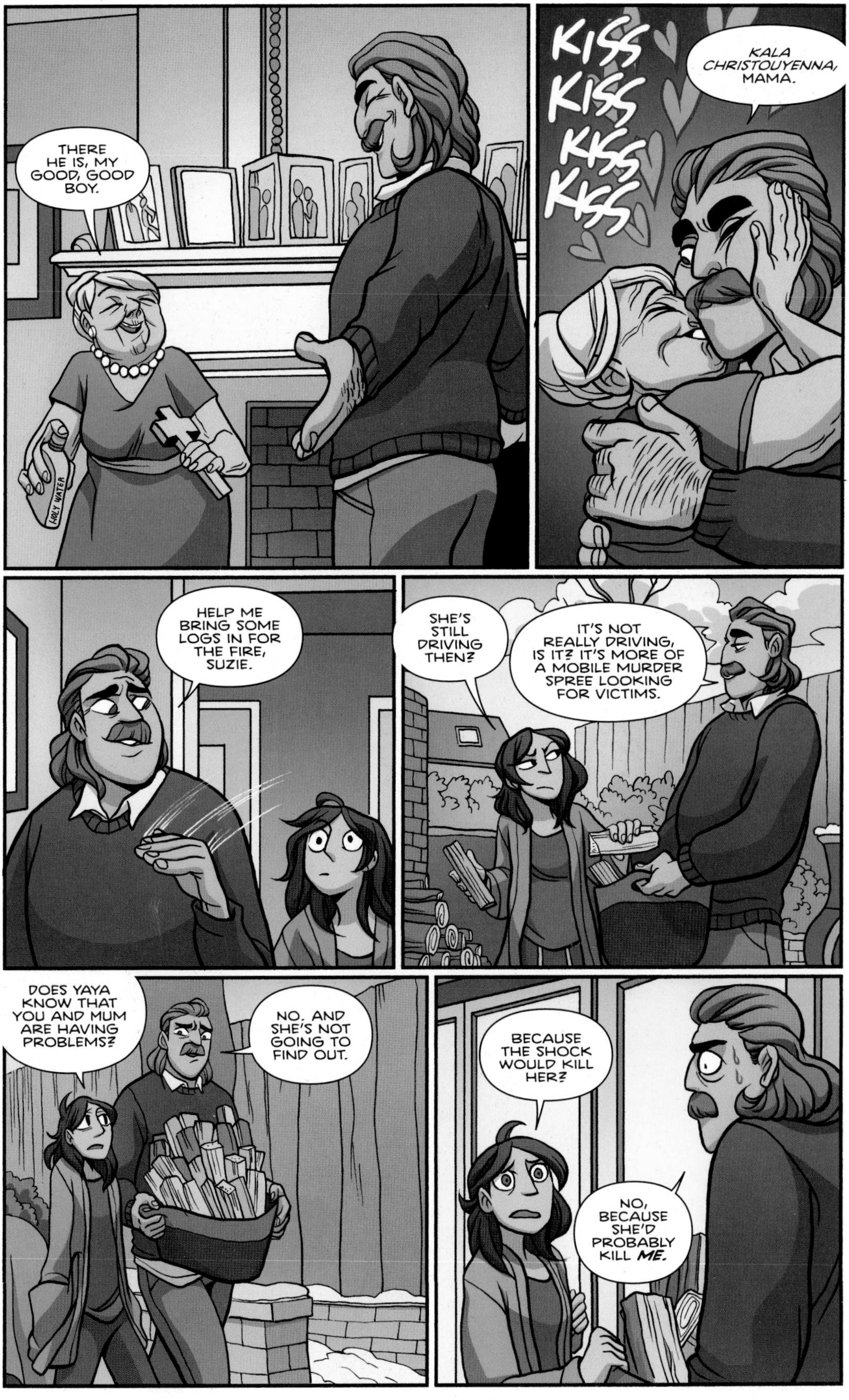

THERE HE IS, MY GOOD, GOOD BOY.
HOLY WATER
KISS KISS KISS KISS
KALA CHRISTOUYENNA, MAMA.
HELP ME BRING SOME LOGS IN FOR THE FIRE, SUZIE.
SHE'S STILL DRIVING THEN?
IT'S NOT REALLY DRIVING, IS IT? IT'S MORE OF A MOBILE MURDER SPREE LOOKING FOR VICTIMS.
DOES YAYA KNOW THAT YOU AND MUM ARE HAVING PROBLEMS?
NO. AND SHE'S NOT GOING TO FIND OUT.
BECAUSE THE SHOCK WOULD KILL HER?
NO, BECAUSE SHE'D PROBABLY KILL *ME.*

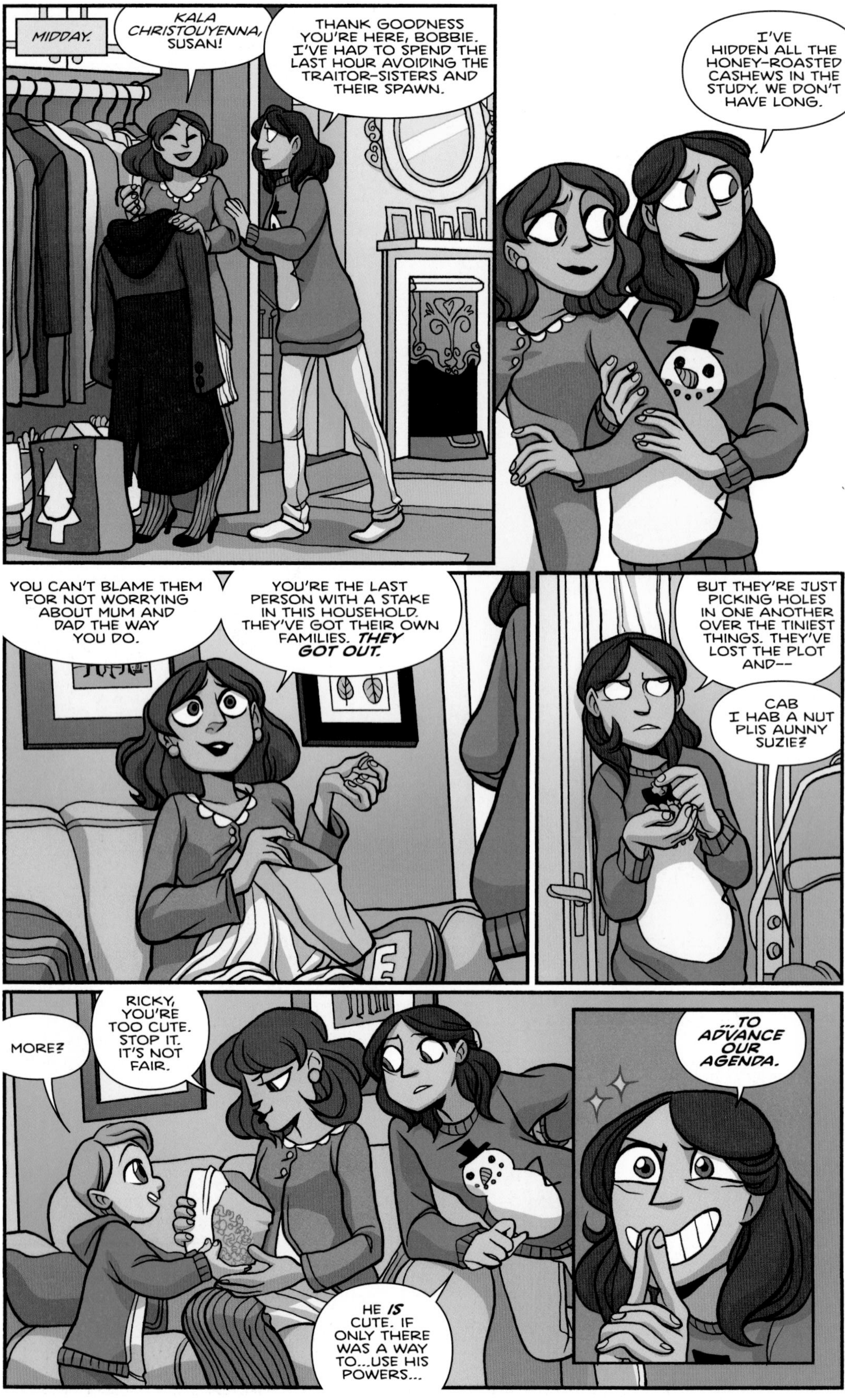
MIDDAY.
KALA CHRISTOUYENNA, SUSAN!
THANK GOODNESS YOU'RE HERE, BOBBIE. I'VE HAD TO SPEND THE LAST HOUR AVOIDING THE TRAITOR-SISTERS AND THEIR SPAWN.
I'VE HIDDEN ALL THE HONEY-ROASTED CASHEWS IN THE STUDY. WE DON'T HAVE LONG.
YOU CAN'T BLAME THEM FOR NOT WORRYING ABOUT MUM AND DAD THE WAY YOU DO.
YOU'RE THE LAST PERSON WITH A STAKE IN THIS HOUSEHOLD. THEY'VE GOT THEIR OWN FAMILIES. *THEY GOT OUT.*
BUT THEY'RE JUST PICKING HOLES IN ONE ANOTHER OVER THE TINIEST THINGS. THEY'VE LOST THE PLOT AND--
CAB I HAB A NUT PLIS AUNNY SUZIE?
MORE?
RICKY, YOU'RE TOO CUTE. STOP IT. IT'S NOT FAIR.
HE *IS* CUTE. IF ONLY THERE WAS A WAY TO...USE HIS POWERS...
...TO ADVANCE OUR AGENDA.

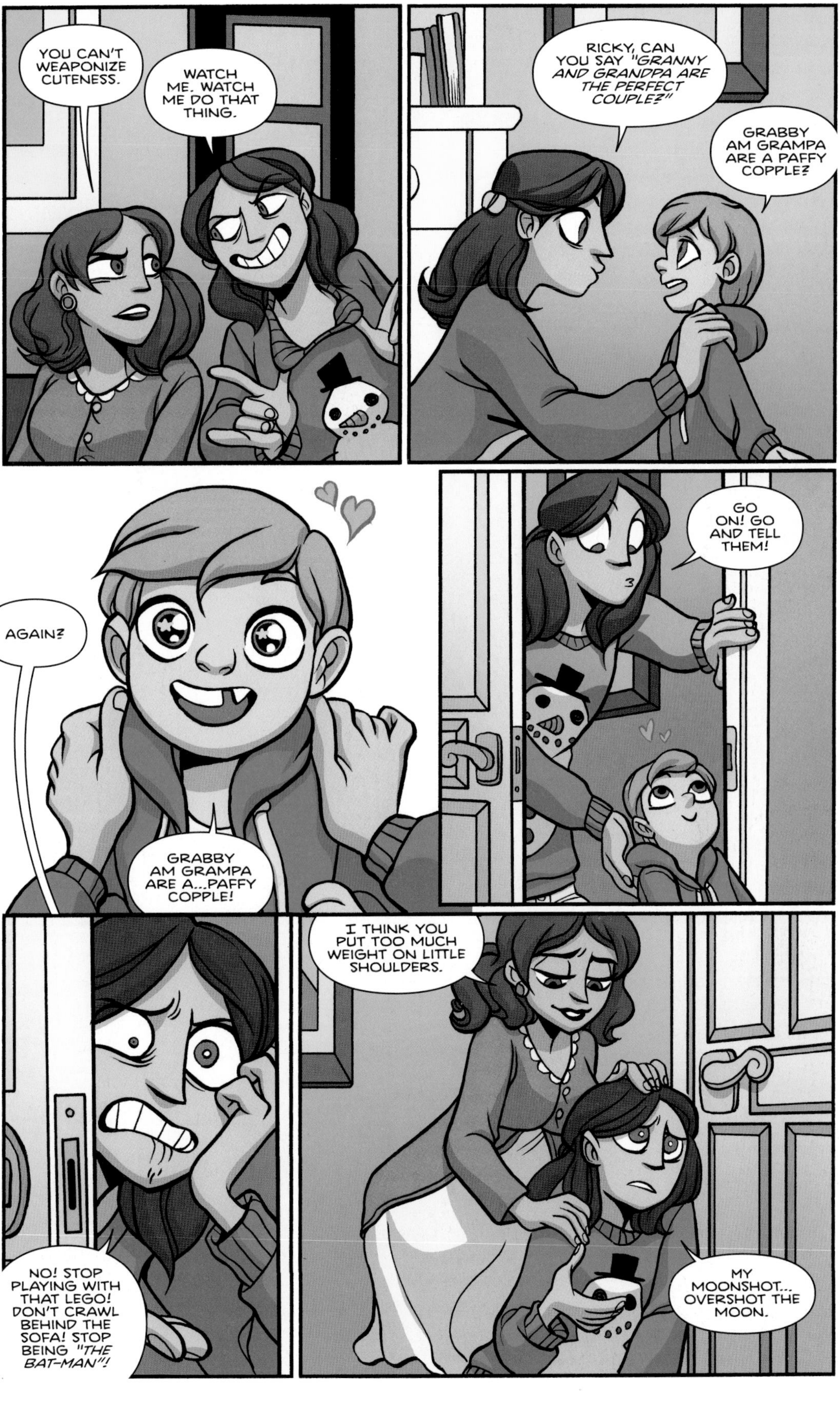

YOU CAN'T WEAPONIZE CUTENESS.
WATCH ME. WATCH ME DO THAT THING.
RICKY, CAN YOU SAY *"GRANNY AND GRANDPA ARE THE PERFECT COUPLE?"*
GRABBY AM GRAMPA ARE A PAFFY COPPLE?
AGAIN?
GRABBY AM GRAMPA ARE A...PAFFY COPPLE!
GO ON! GO AND TELL THEM!
NO! STOP PLAYING WITH THAT LEGO! DON'T CRAWL BEHIND THE SOFA! STOP BEING *"THE BAT-MAN"*!
I THINK YOU PUT TOO MUCH WEIGHT ON LITTLE SHOULDERS.
MY MOONSHOT... OVERSHOT THE MOON.

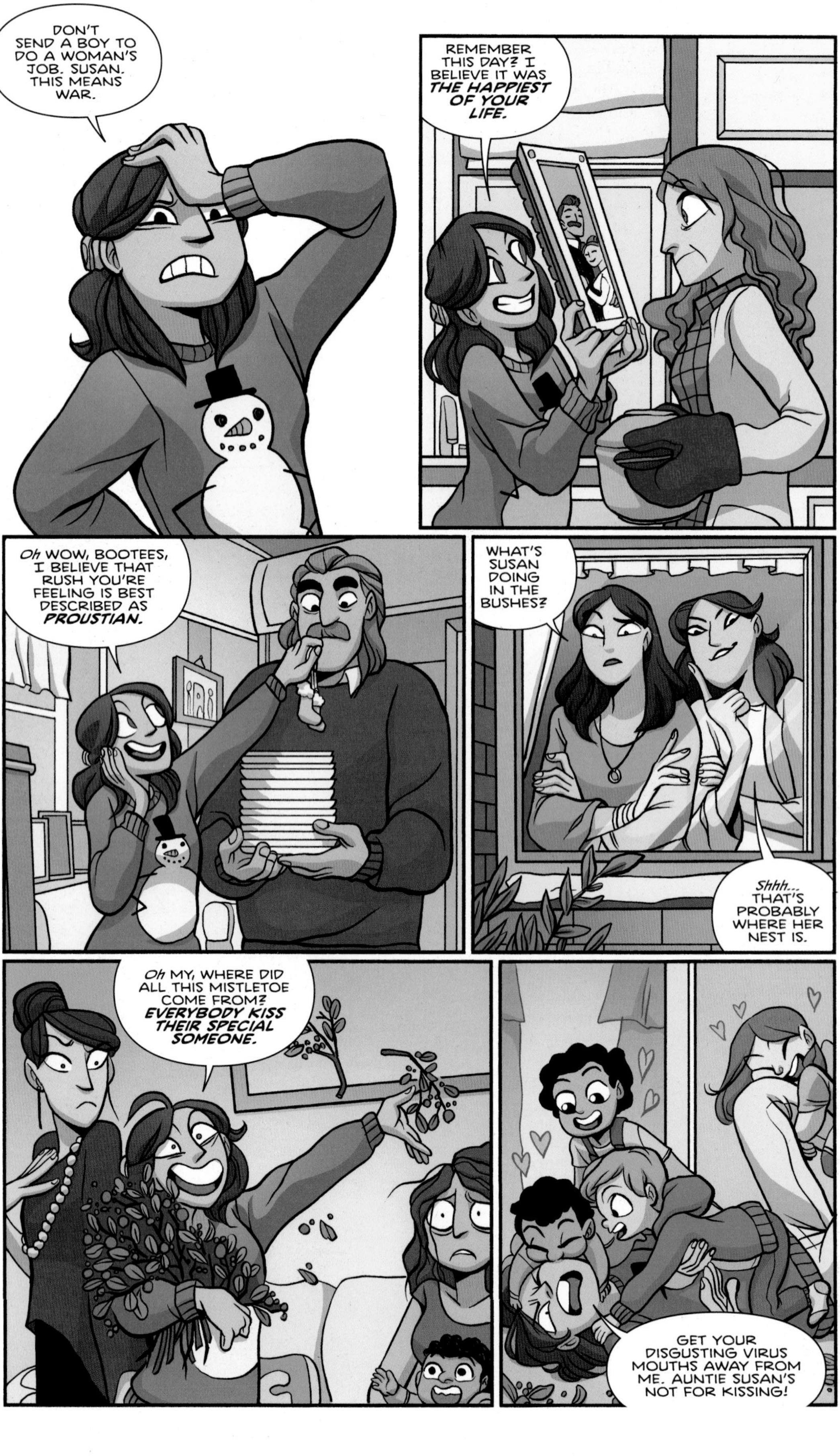
DON'T SEND A BOY TO DO A WOMAN'S JOB. SUSAN. THIS MEANS WAR.
REMEMBER THIS DAY? I BELIEVE IT WAS ***THE HAPPIEST OF YOUR LIFE.***
Oh WOW, BOOTEES, I BELIEVE THAT RUSH YOU'RE FEELING IS BEST DESCRIBED AS ***PROUSTIAN.***
WHAT'S SUSAN DOING IN THE BUSHES?
Shhh... THAT'S PROBABLY WHERE HER NEST IS.
Oh MY, WHERE DID ALL THIS MISTLETOE COME FROM? ***EVERYBODY KISS THEIR SPECIAL SOMEONE.***
GET YOUR DISGUSTING VIRUS MOUTHS AWAY FROM ME. AUNTIE SUSAN'S NOT FOR KISSING!

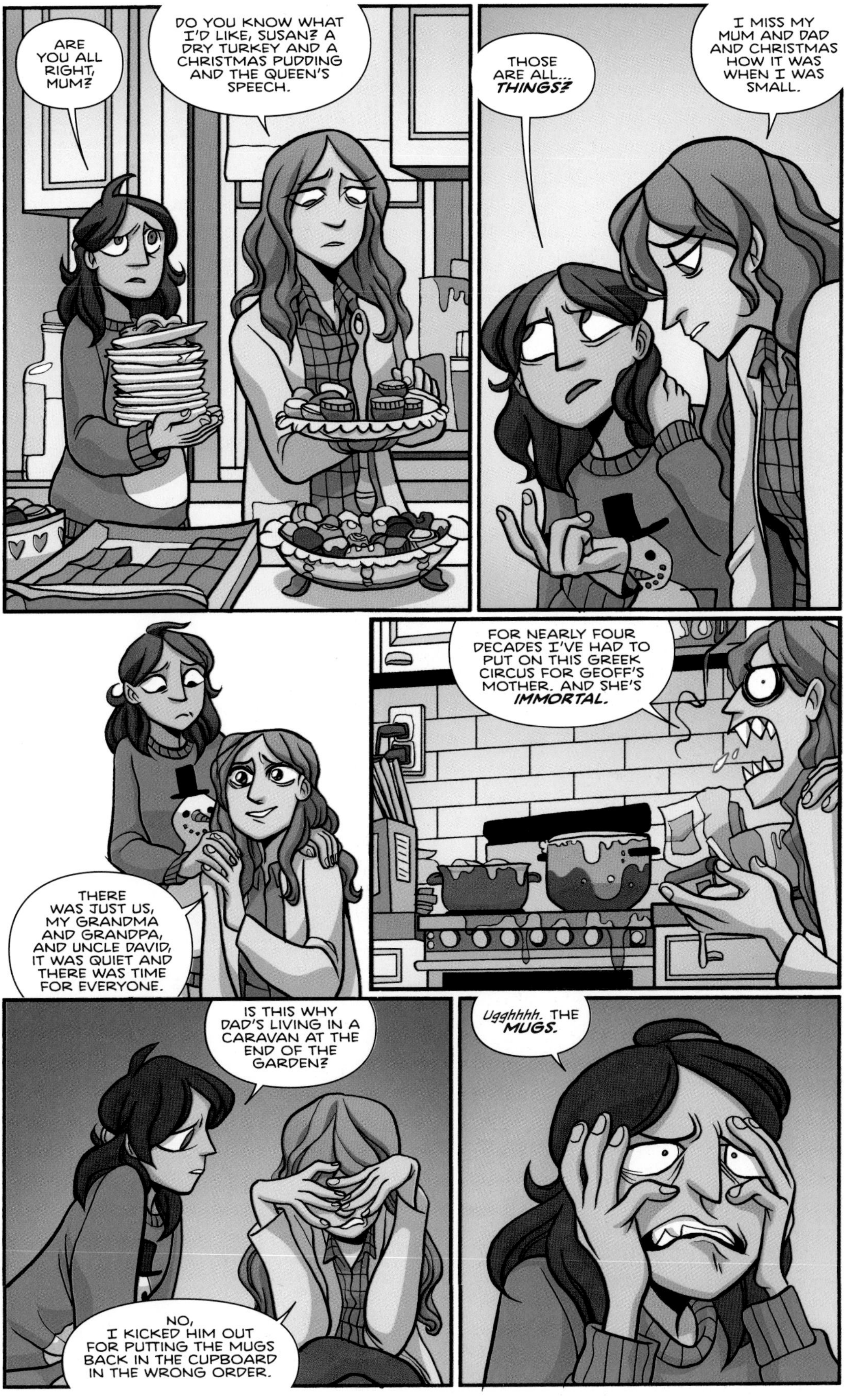
ARE YOU ALL RIGHT, MUM?
DO YOU KNOW WHAT I'D LIKE, SUSAN? A DRY TURKEY AND A CHRISTMAS PUDDING AND THE QUEEN'S SPEECH.
THOSE ARE ALL... THINGS?
I MISS MY MUM AND DAD AND CHRISTMAS HOW IT WAS WHEN I WAS SMALL.
THERE WAS JUST US, MY GRANDMA AND GRANDPA, AND UNCLE DAVID, IT WAS QUIET AND THERE WAS TIME FOR EVERYONE.
FOR NEARLY FOUR DECADES I'VE HAD TO PUT ON THIS GREEK CIRCUS FOR GEOFF'S MOTHER. AND SHE'S IMMORTAL.
IS THIS WHY DAD'S LIVING IN A CARAVAN AT THE END OF THE GARDEN?
NO, I KICKED HIM OUT FOR PUTTING THE MUGS BACK IN THE CUPBOARD IN THE WRONG ORDER.
Ugghhhh. THE MUGS.

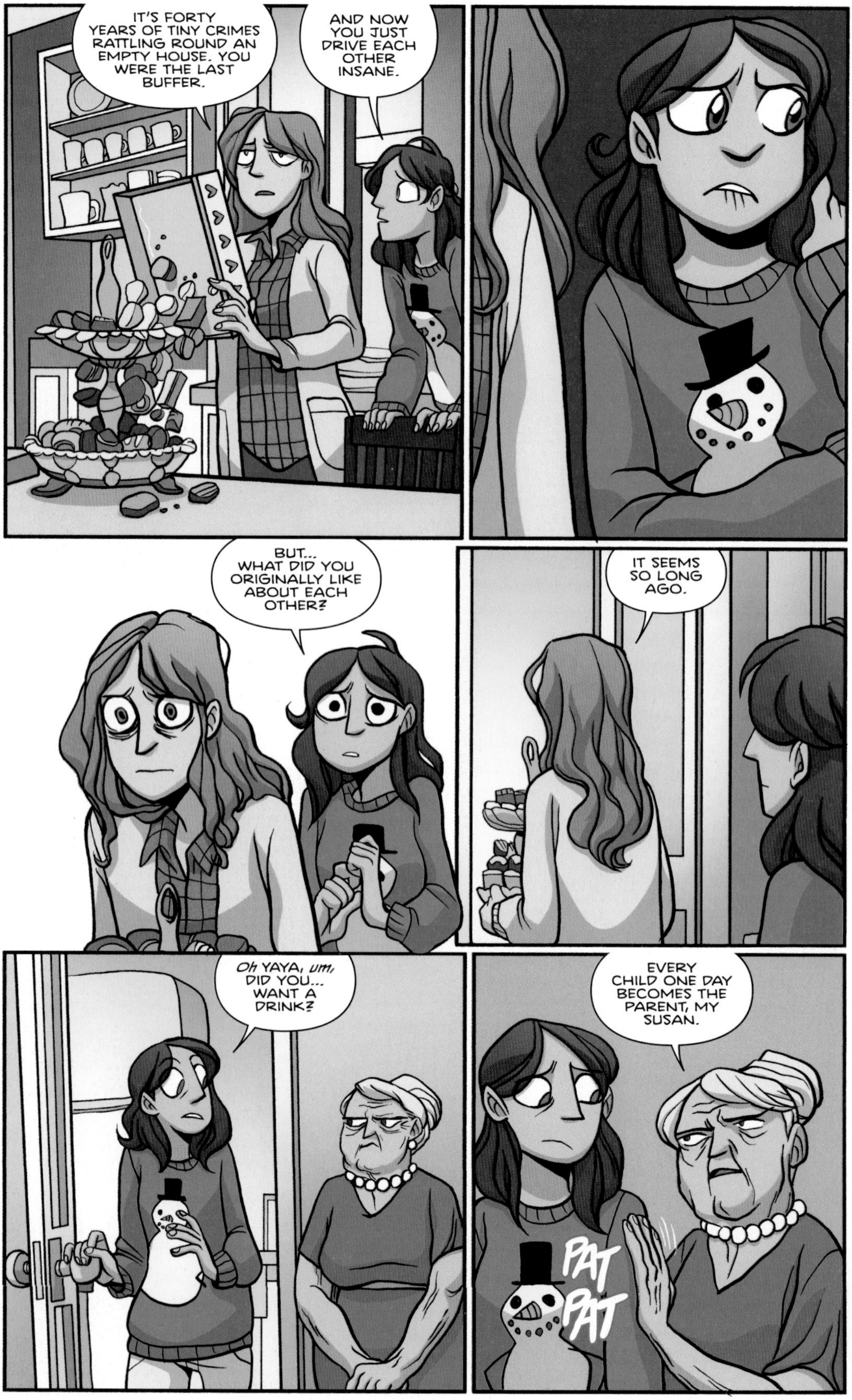
IT'S FORTY YEARS OF TINY CRIMES RATTLING ROUND AN EMPTY HOUSE. YOU WERE THE LAST BUFFER.
AND NOW YOU JUST DRIVE EACH OTHER INSANE.
BUT... WHAT DID YOU ORIGINALLY LIKE ABOUT EACH OTHER?
IT SEEMS SO LONG AGO.
Oh YAYA, *um*, DID YOU... WANT A DRINK?
EVERY CHILD ONE DAY BECOMES THE PARENT, MY SUSAN.
PAT
PAT

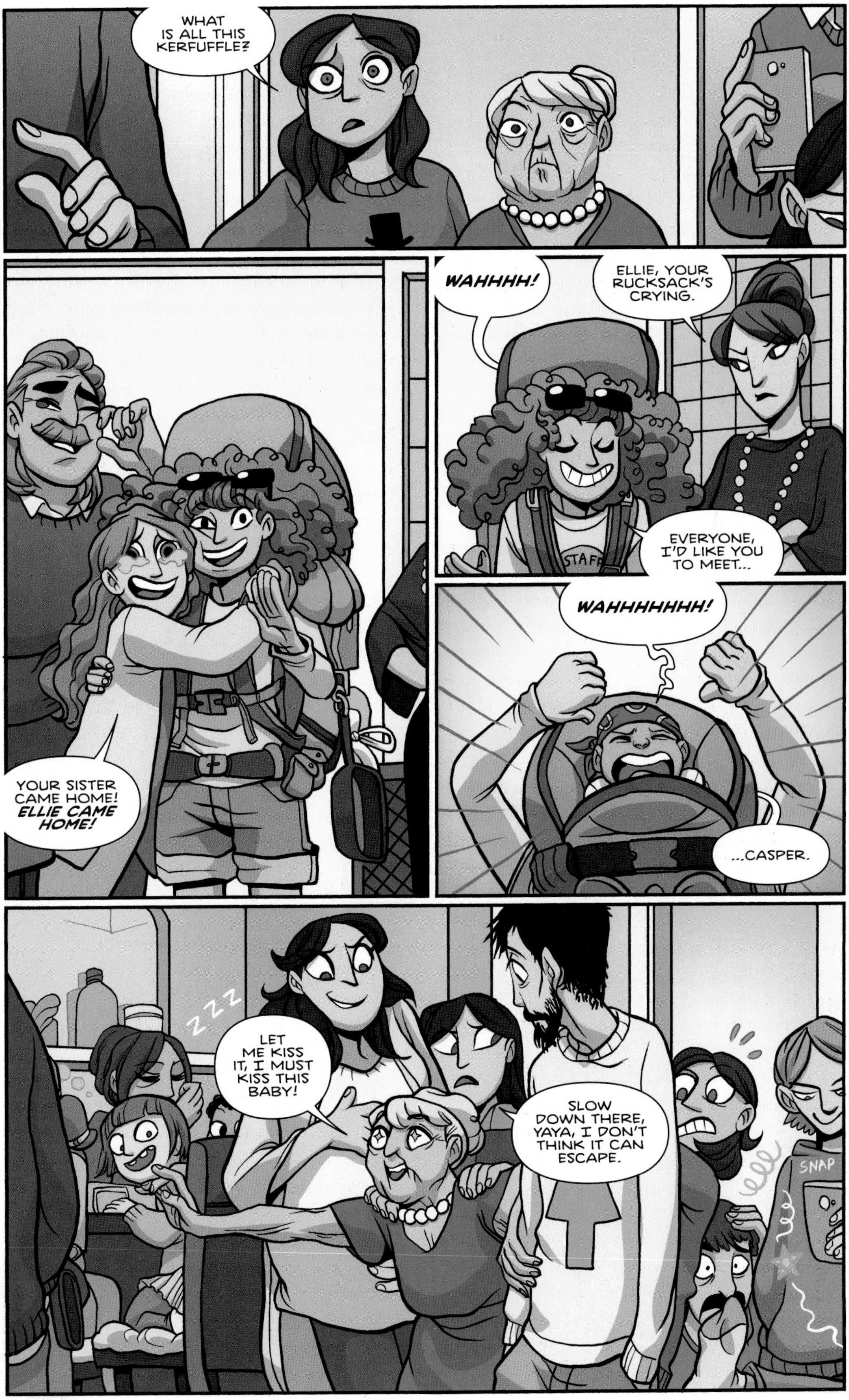
WHAT IS ALL THIS KERFUFFLE?
YOUR SISTER CAME HOME! ELLIE CAME HOME!
WAHHHH!
ELLIE, YOUR RUCKSACK'S CRYING.
STAFF
EVERYONE, I'D LIKE YOU TO MEET...
WAHHHHHHH!
...CASPER.
ZZZ
LET ME KISS IT, I MUST KISS THIS BABY!
SLOW DOWN THERE, YAYA, I DON'T THINK IT CAN ESCAPE.
SNAP

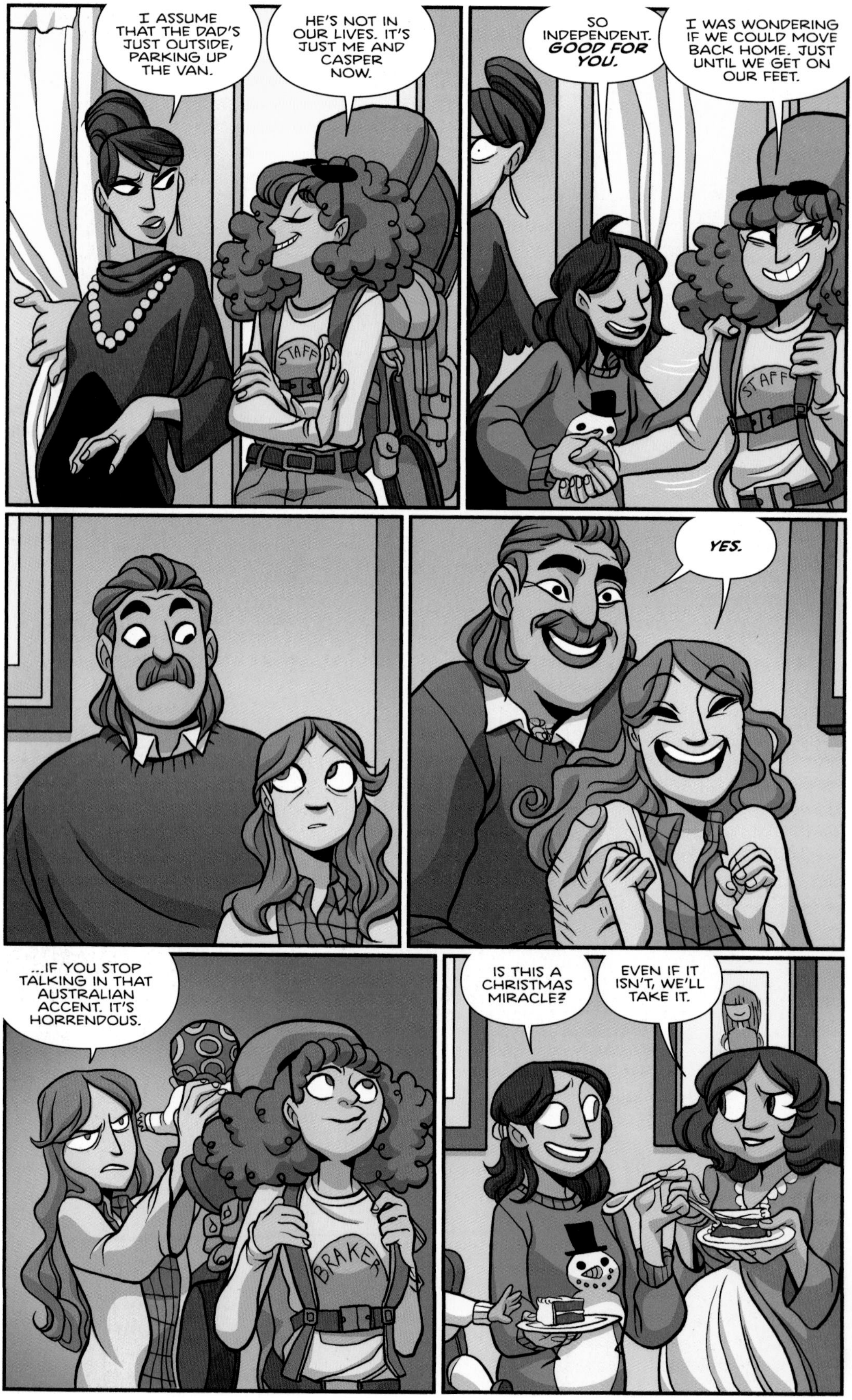

I ASSUME THAT THE DAD'S JUST OUTSIDE, PARKING UP THE VAN.
HE'S NOT IN OUR LIVES. IT'S JUST ME AND CASPER NOW.
SO INDEPENDENT. GOOD FOR YOU.
I WAS WONDERING IF WE COULD MOVE BACK HOME. JUST UNTIL WE GET ON OUR FEET.
STAFF
STAFF
YES.
...IF YOU STOP TALKING IN THAT AUSTRALIAN ACCENT. IT'S HORRENDOUS.
BRAKER
IS THIS A CHRISTMAS MIRACLE?
EVEN IF IT ISN'T, WE'LL TAKE IT.

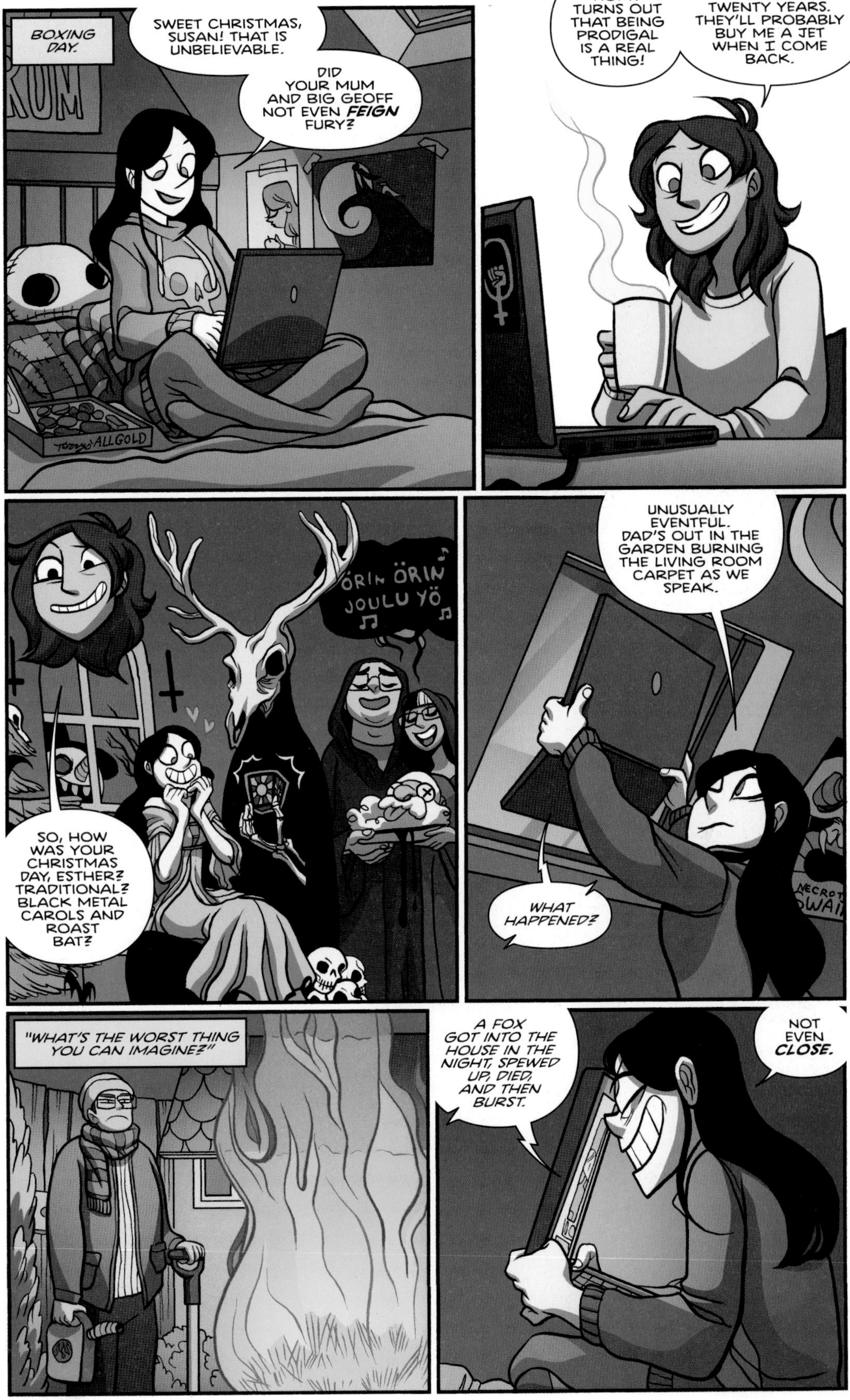
BOXING DAY.
SWEET CHRISTMAS, SUSAN! THAT IS UNBELIEVABLE.
DID YOUR MUM AND BIG GEOFF NOT EVEN FEIGN FURY?
TORRY'S ALLGOLD
NO! IT TURNS OUT THAT BEING PRODIGAL IS A REAL THING!
I'M GOING TO LEAVE FOR TWENTY YEARS. THEY'LL PROBABLY BUY ME A JET WHEN I COME BACK.
ÖRIN ÖRIN JOULU YÖ
SO, HOW WAS YOUR CHRISTMAS DAY, ESTHER? TRADITIONAL? BLACK METAL CAROLS AND ROAST BAT?
WHAT HAPPENED?
UNUSUALLY EVENTFUL. DAD'S OUT IN THE GARDEN BURNING THE LIVING ROOM CARPET AS WE SPEAK.
"WHAT'S THE WORST THING YOU CAN IMAGINE?"
A FOX GOT INTO THE HOUSE IN THE NIGHT, SPEWED UP, DIED, AND THEN BURST.
NOT EVEN CLOSE.

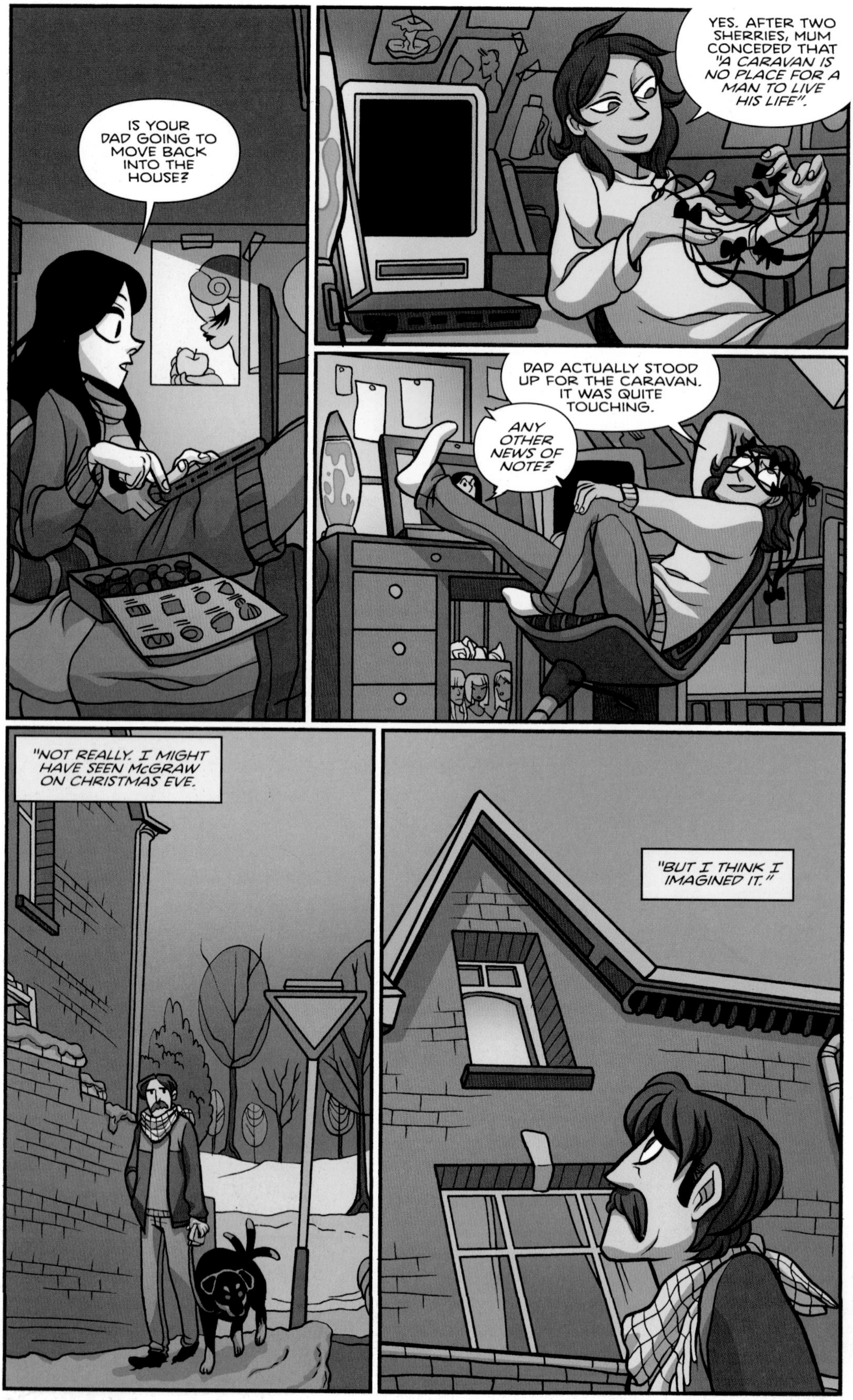

IS YOUR DAD GOING TO MOVE BACK INTO THE HOUSE?
YES. AFTER TWO SHERRIES, MUM CONCEDED THAT "A CARAVAN IS NO PLACE FOR A MAN TO LIVE HIS LIFE".
DAD ACTUALLY STOOD UP FOR THE CARAVAN. IT WAS QUITE TOUCHING.
ANY OTHER NEWS OF NOTE?
"NOT REALLY. I MIGHT HAVE SEEN McGRAW ON CHRISTMAS EVE.
"BUT I THINK I IMAGINED IT."

CHAPTER TWENTY SIX

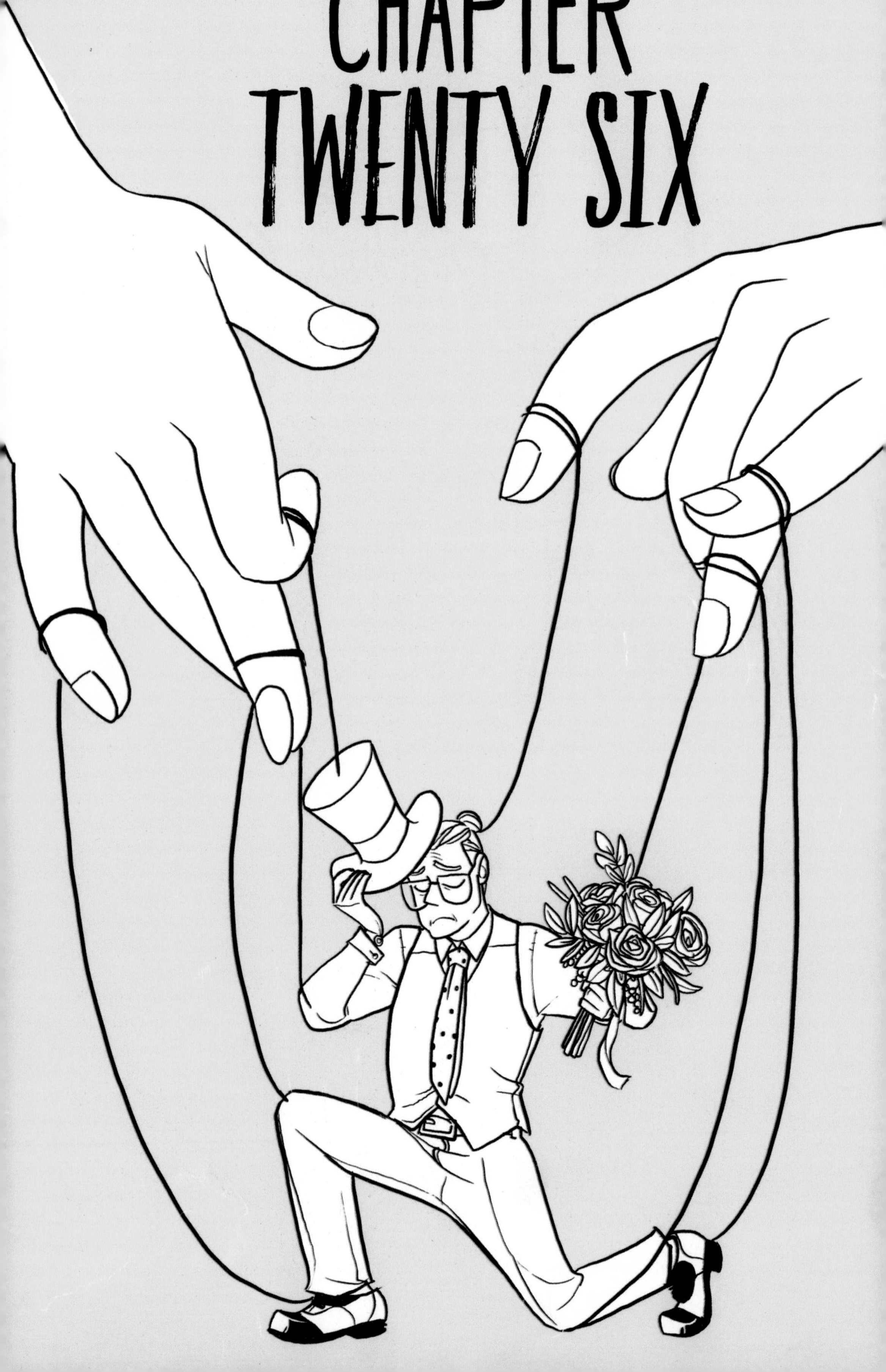

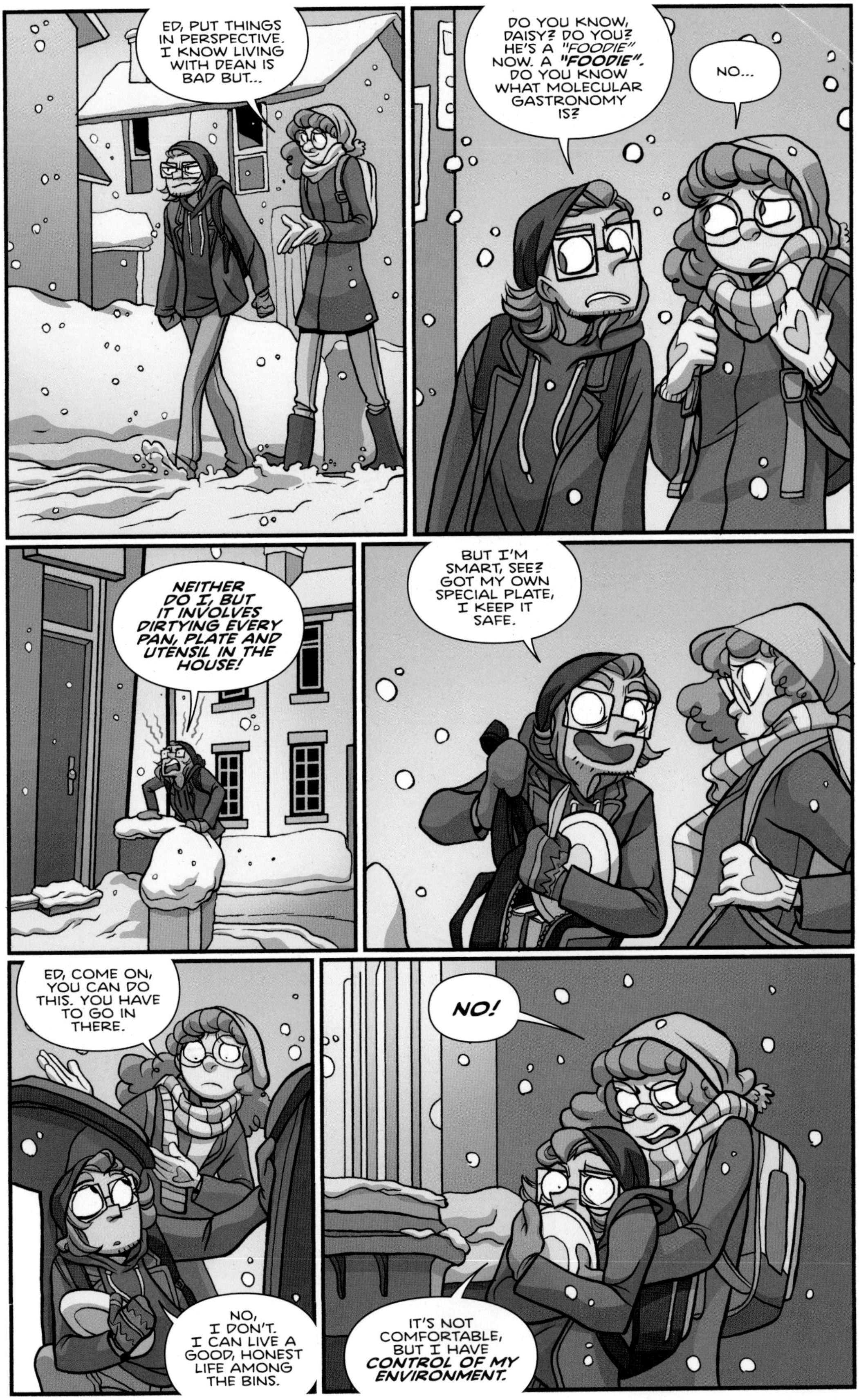

ED, PUT THINGS IN PERSPECTIVE. I KNOW LIVING WITH DEAN IS BAD BUT...
DO YOU KNOW, DAISY? DO YOU? HE'S A "FOODIE" NOW. A "FOODIE". DO YOU KNOW WHAT MOLECULAR GASTRONOMY IS?
NO...
NEITHER DO I, BUT IT INVOLVES DIRTYING EVERY PAN, PLATE AND UTENSIL IN THE HOUSE!
BUT I'M SMART, SEE? GOT MY OWN SPECIAL PLATE, I KEEP IT SAFE.
ED, COME ON, YOU CAN DO THIS. YOU HAVE TO GO IN THERE.
NO, I DON'T. I CAN LIVE A GOOD, HONEST LIFE AMONG THE BINS.
NO!
IT'S NOT COMFORTABLE, BUT I HAVE CONTROL OF MY ENVIRONMENT.

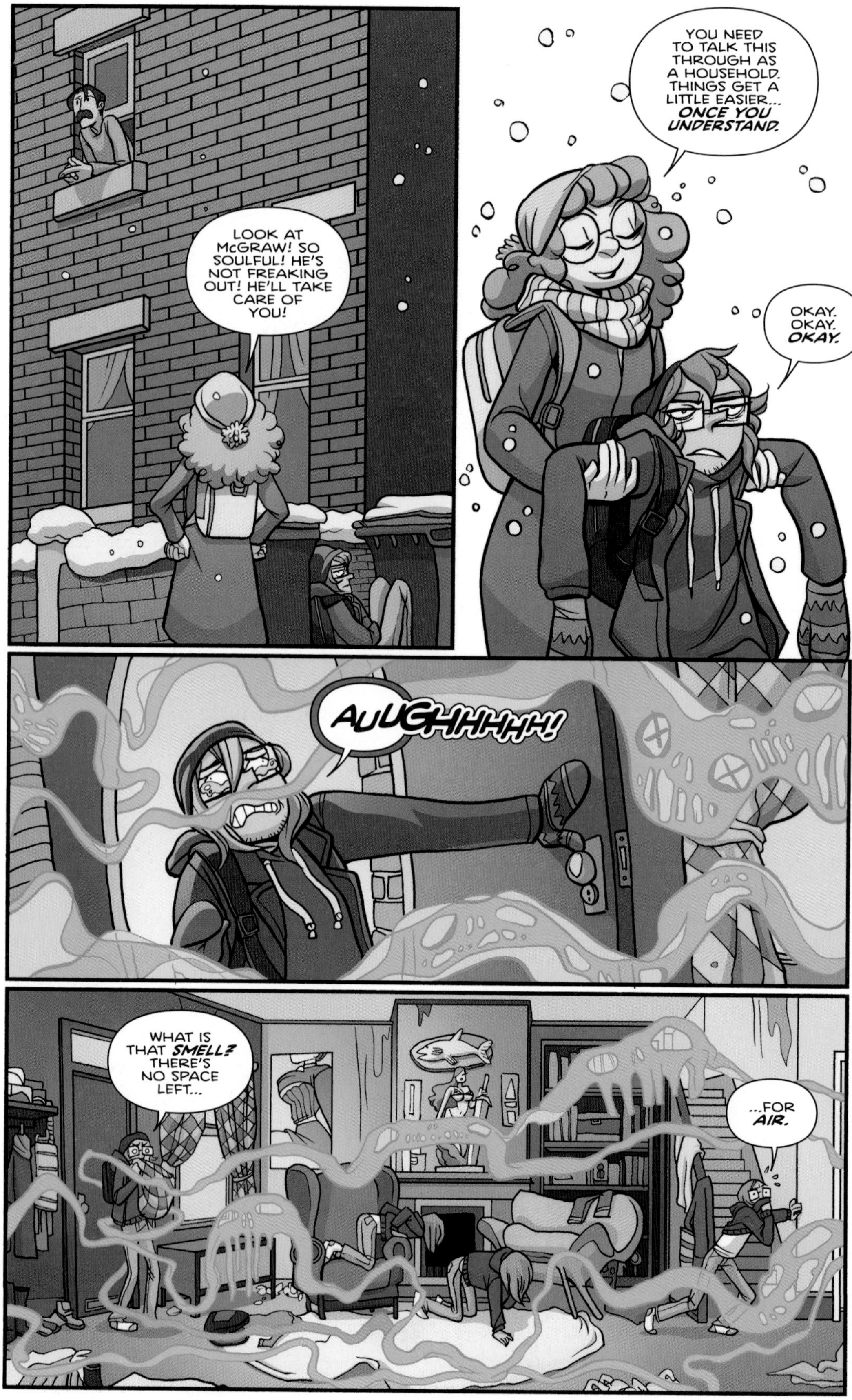
LOOK AT McGRAW! SO SOULFUL! HE'S NOT FREAKING OUT! HE'LL TAKE CARE OF YOU!
YOU NEED TO TALK THIS THROUGH AS A HOUSEHOLD. THINGS GET A LITTLE EASIER... ONCE YOU UNDERSTAND.
OKAY. OKAY. OKAY.
AUUGHHHHH!
WHAT IS THAT SMELL? THERE'S NO SPACE LEFT...
...FOR AIR.

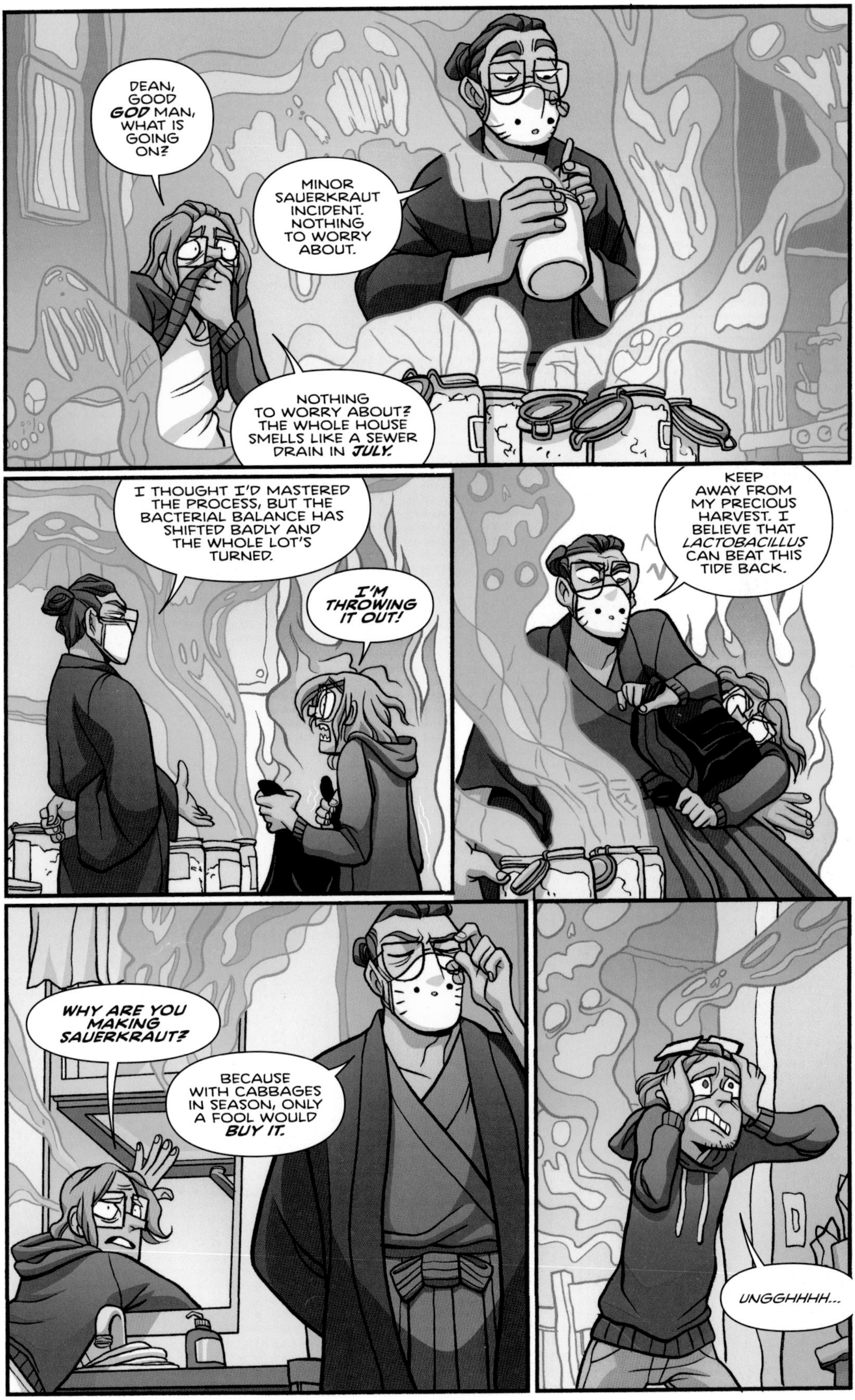
DEAN, GOOD *GOD* MAN, WHAT IS GOING ON?
MINOR SAUERKRAUT INCIDENT. NOTHING TO WORRY ABOUT.
NOTHING TO WORRY ABOUT? THE WHOLE HOUSE SMELLS LIKE A SEWER DRAIN IN *JULY.*
I THOUGHT I'D MASTERED THE PROCESS, BUT THE BACTERIAL BALANCE HAS SHIFTED BADLY AND THE WHOLE LOT'S TURNED.
I'M THROWING IT OUT!
KEEP AWAY FROM MY PRECIOUS HARVEST. I BELIEVE THAT *LACTOBACILLUS* CAN BEAT THIS TIDE BACK.
WHY ARE YOU MAKING SAUERKRAUT?
BECAUSE WITH CABBAGES IN SEASON, ONLY A FOOL WOULD *BUY IT.*
UNGGHHHH...

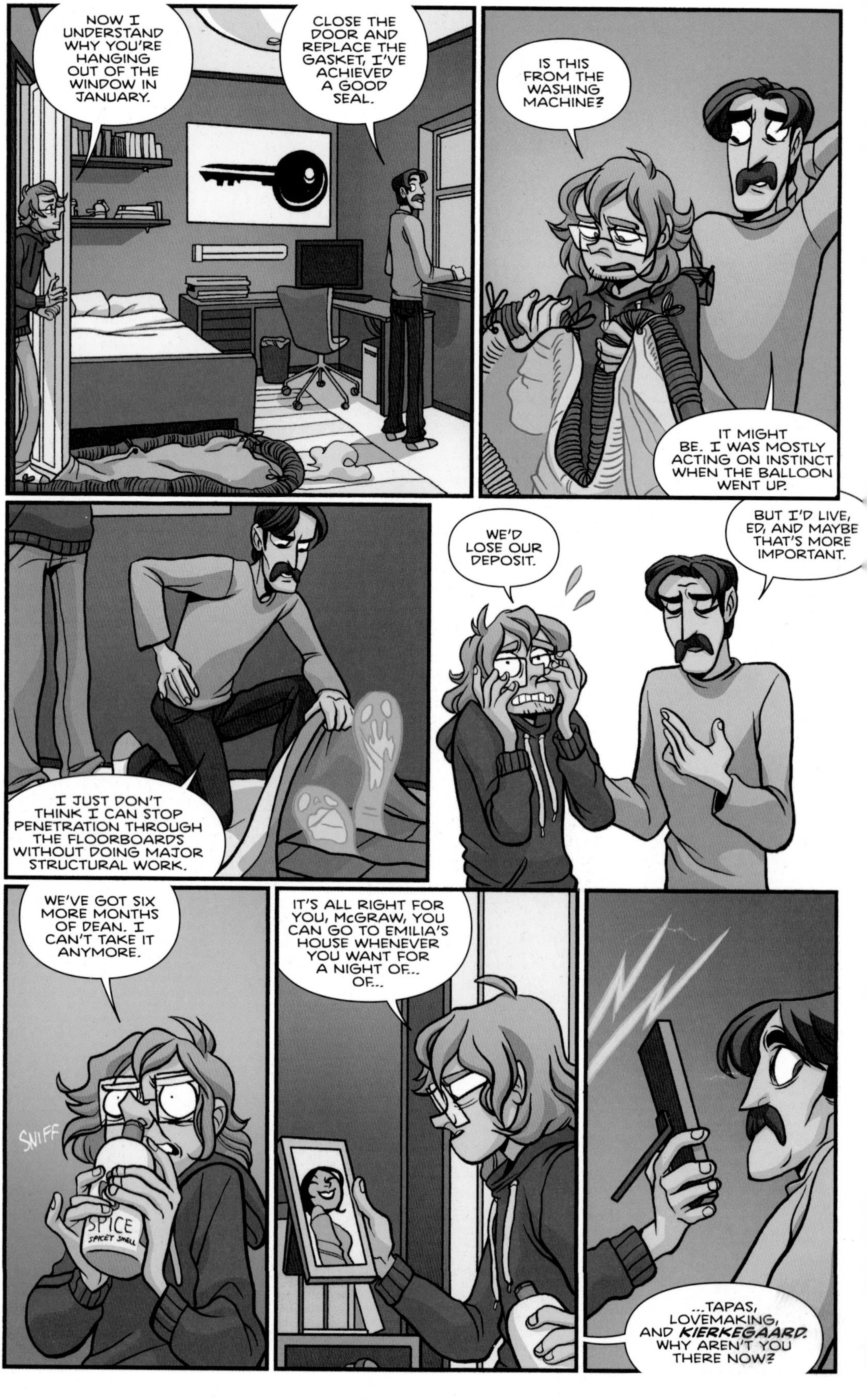
NOW I UNDERSTAND WHY YOU'RE HANGING OUT OF THE WINDOW IN JANUARY.
CLOSE THE DOOR AND REPLACE THE GASKET, I'VE ACHIEVED A GOOD SEAL.
IS THIS FROM THE WASHING MACHINE?
IT MIGHT BE. I WAS MOSTLY ACTING ON INSTINCT WHEN THE BALLOON WENT UP.
I JUST DON'T THINK I CAN STOP PENETRATION THROUGH THE FLOORBOARDS WITHOUT DOING MAJOR STRUCTURAL WORK.
WE'D LOSE OUR DEPOSIT.
BUT I'D LIVE, ED, AND MAYBE THAT'S MORE IMPORTANT.
WE'VE GOT SIX MORE MONTHS OF DEAN. I CAN'T TAKE IT ANYMORE.
SNIFF
SPICE
SPICEY SMELL
IT'S ALL RIGHT FOR YOU, McGRAW, YOU CAN GO TO EMILIA'S HOUSE WHENEVER YOU WANT FOR A NIGHT OF... OF...
...TAPAS, LOVEMAKING, AND KIERKEGAARD. WHY AREN'T YOU THERE NOW?

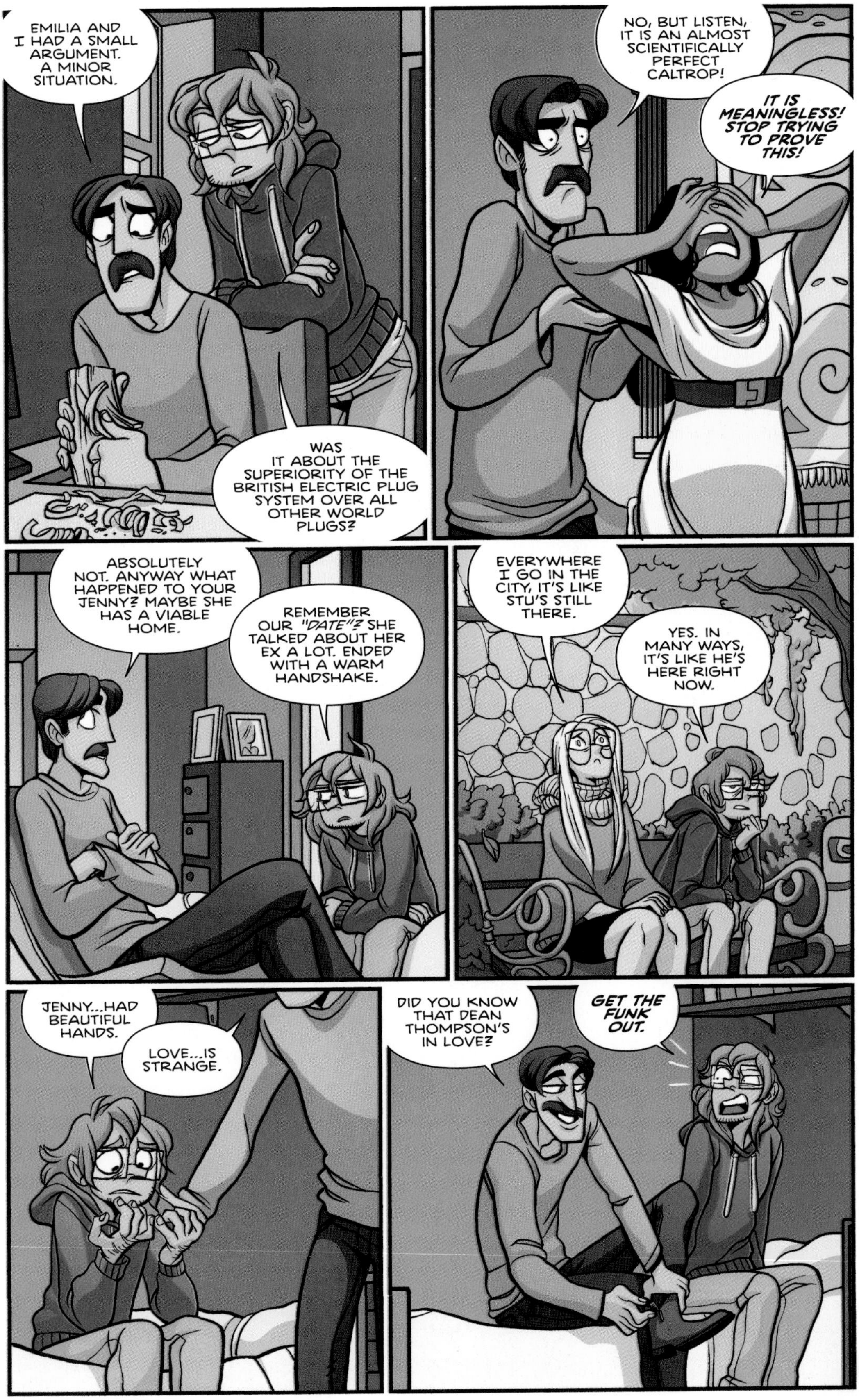

EMILIA AND I HAD A SMALL ARGUMENT. A MINOR SITUATION.
WAS IT ABOUT THE SUPERIORITY OF THE BRITISH ELECTRIC PLUG SYSTEM OVER ALL OTHER WORLD PLUGS?
NO, BUT LISTEN, IT IS AN ALMOST SCIENTIFICALLY PERFECT CALTROP!
IT IS MEANINGLESS! STOP TRYING TO PROVE THIS!
ABSOLUTELY NOT. ANYWAY WHAT HAPPENED TO YOUR JENNY? MAYBE SHE HAS A VIABLE HOME.
REMEMBER OUR "DATE"? SHE TALKED ABOUT HER EX A LOT. ENDED WITH A WARM HANDSHAKE.
EVERYWHERE I GO IN THE CITY, IT'S LIKE STU'S STILL THERE.
YES. IN MANY WAYS, IT'S LIKE HE'S HERE RIGHT NOW.
JENNY...HAD BEAUTIFUL HANDS.
LOVE...IS STRANGE.
DID YOU KNOW THAT DEAN THOMPSON'S IN LOVE?
GET THE FUNK OUT.

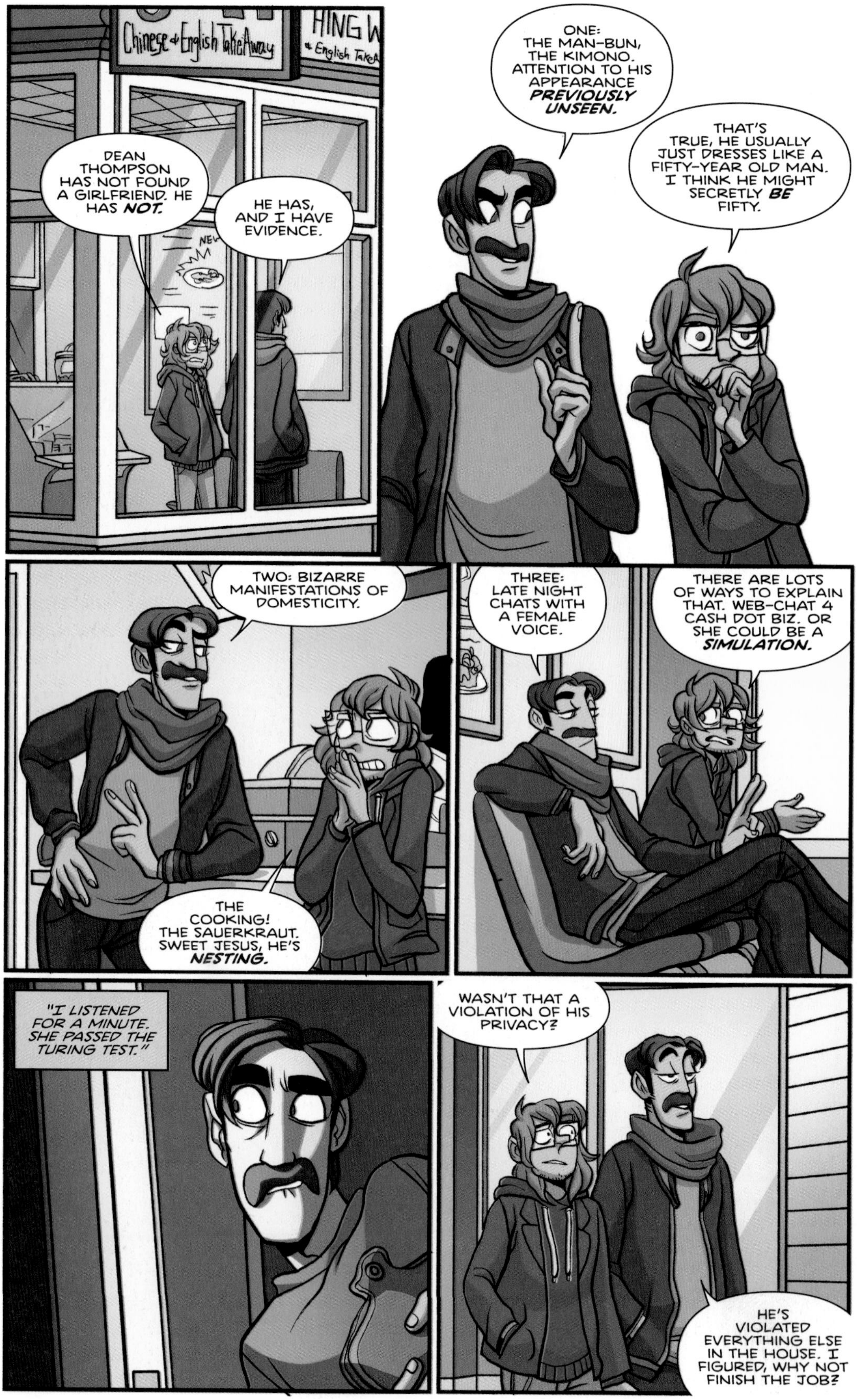
Chinese & English TakeAway
HING W
& English TakeA
DEAN THOMPSON HAS NOT FOUND A GIRLFRIEND. HE HAS *NOT.*
HE HAS, AND I HAVE EVIDENCE.
ONE: THE MAN-BUN, THE KIMONO. ATTENTION TO HIS APPEARANCE *PREVIOUSLY UNSEEN.*
THAT'S TRUE, HE USUALLY JUST DRESSES LIKE A FIFTY-YEAR OLD MAN. I THINK HE MIGHT SECRETLY *BE* FIFTY.
TWO: BIZARRE MANIFESTATIONS OF DOMESTICITY.
THE COOKING! THE SAUERKRAUT. SWEET JESUS, HE'S *NESTING.*
THREE: LATE NIGHT CHATS WITH A FEMALE VOICE.
THERE ARE LOTS OF WAYS TO EXPLAIN THAT. WEB-CHAT 4 CASH DOT BIZ. OR SHE COULD BE A *SIMULATION.*
"I LISTENED FOR A MINUTE. SHE PASSED THE TURING TEST."
WASN'T THAT A VIOLATION OF HIS PRIVACY?
HE'S VIOLATED EVERYTHING ELSE IN THE HOUSE. I FIGURED, WHY NOT FINISH THE JOB?

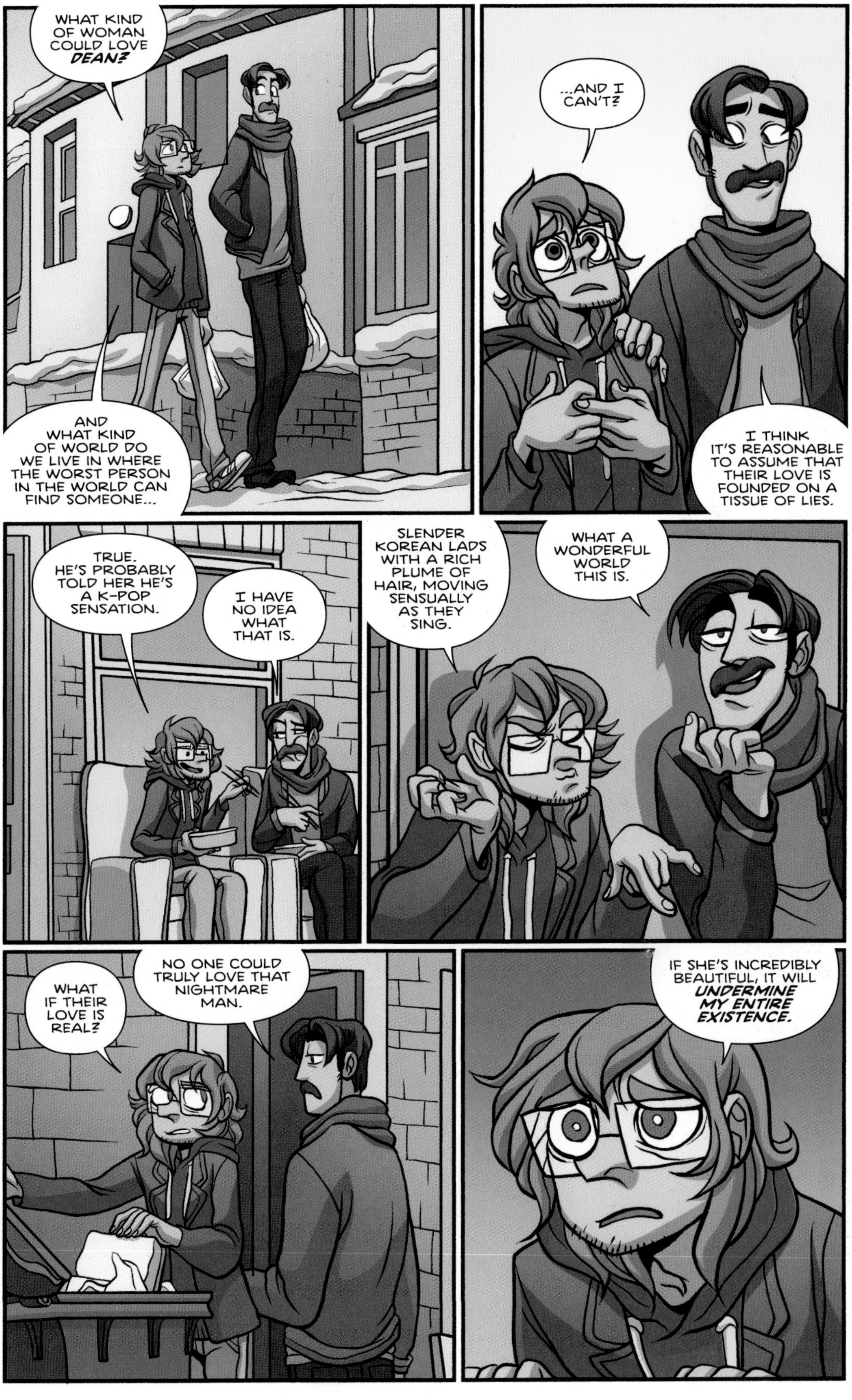

WHAT KIND OF WOMAN COULD LOVE DEAN?
AND WHAT KIND OF WORLD DO WE LIVE IN WHERE THE WORST PERSON IN THE WORLD CAN FIND SOMEONE...
...AND I CAN'T?
I THINK IT'S REASONABLE TO ASSUME THAT THEIR LOVE IS FOUNDED ON A TISSUE OF LIES.
TRUE. HE'S PROBABLY TOLD HER HE'S A K-POP SENSATION.
I HAVE NO IDEA WHAT THAT IS.
SLENDER KOREAN LADS WITH A RICH PLUME OF HAIR, MOVING SENSUALLY AS THEY SING.
WHAT A WONDERFUL WORLD THIS IS.
WHAT IF THEIR LOVE IS REAL?
NO ONE COULD TRULY LOVE THAT NIGHTMARE MAN.
IF SHE'S INCREDIBLY BEAUTIFUL, IT WILL *UNDERMINE MY ENTIRE EXISTENCE.*

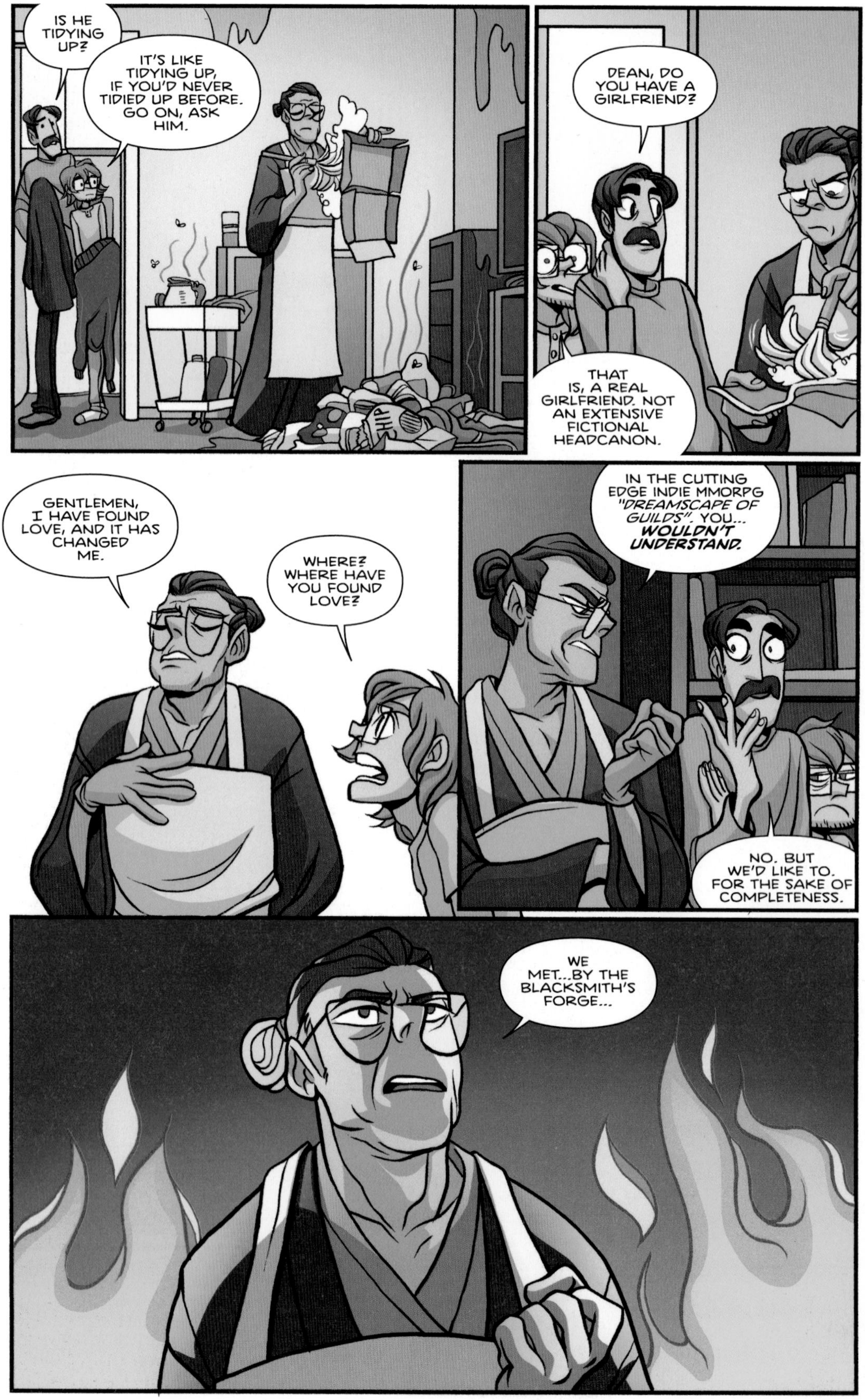
IS HE TIDYING UP?
IT'S LIKE TIDYING UP, IF YOU'D NEVER TIDIED UP BEFORE. GO ON, ASK HIM.
DEAN, DO YOU HAVE A GIRLFRIEND?
THAT IS, A REAL GIRLFRIEND. NOT AN EXTENSIVE FICTIONAL HEADCANON.
GENTLEMEN, I HAVE FOUND LOVE, AND IT HAS CHANGED ME.
WHERE? WHERE HAVE YOU FOUND LOVE?
IN THE CUTTING EDGE INDIE MMORPG *"DREAMSCAPE OF GUILDS"*. YOU... ***WOULDN'T UNDERSTAND.***
NO. BUT WE'D LIKE TO. FOR THE SAKE OF COMPLETENESS.
WE MET...BY THE BLACKSMITH'S FORGE...

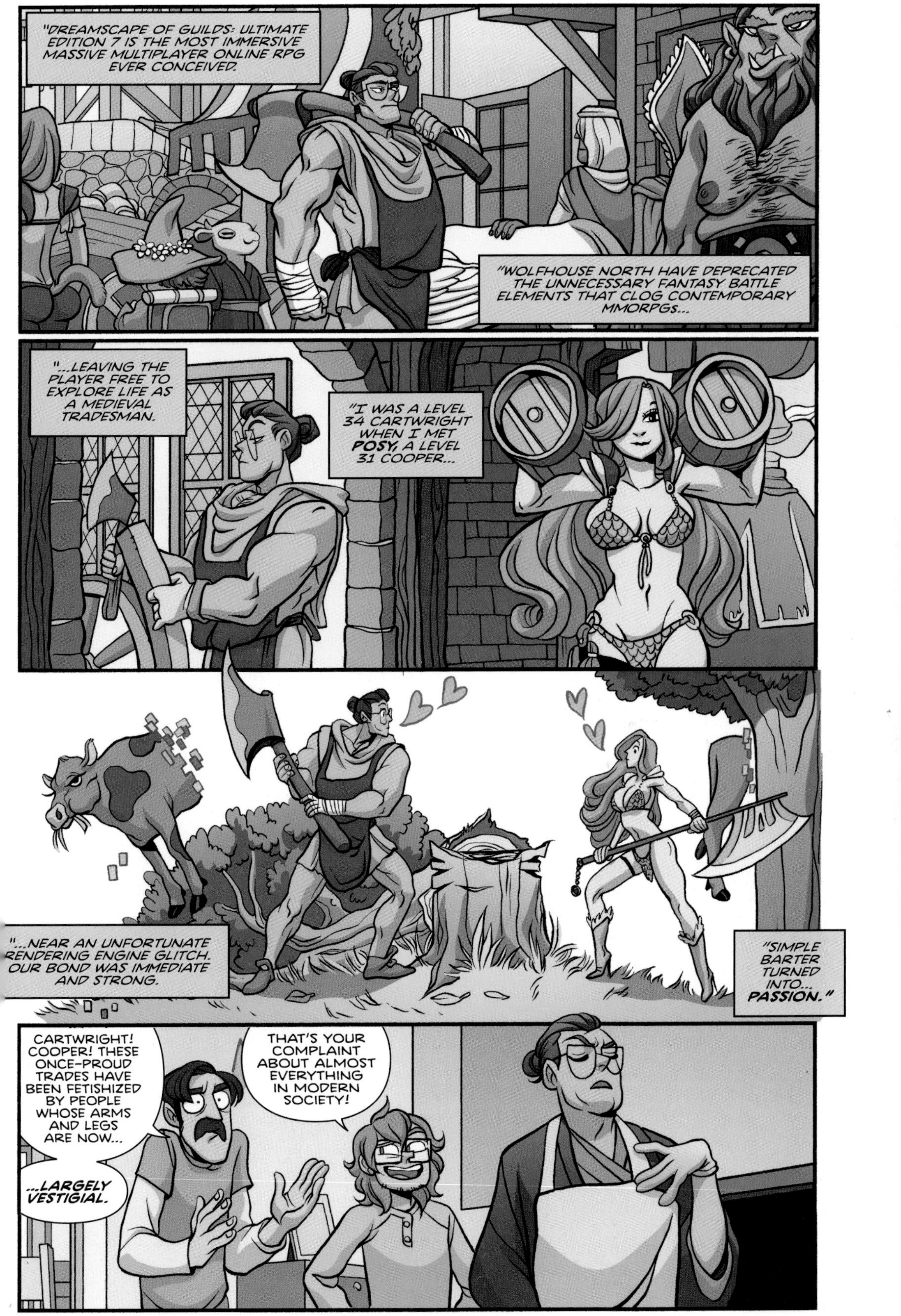
"DREAMSCAPE OF GUILDS: ULTIMATE EDITION 7 IS THE MOST IMMERSIVE MASSIVE MULTIPLAYER ONLINE RPG EVER CONCEIVED.
"WOLFHOUSE NORTH HAVE DEPRECATED THE UNNECESSARY FANTASY BATTLE ELEMENTS THAT CLOG CONTEMPORARY MMORPGS...
"...LEAVING THE PLAYER FREE TO EXPLORE LIFE AS A MEDIEVAL TRADESMAN.
"I WAS A LEVEL 34 CARTWRIGHT WHEN I MET POSY, A LEVEL 31 COOPER...
"...NEAR AN UNFORTUNATE RENDERING ENGINE GLITCH. OUR BOND WAS IMMEDIATE AND STRONG.
"SIMPLE BARTER TURNED INTO... PASSION."
CARTWRIGHT! COOPER! THESE ONCE-PROUD TRADES HAVE BEEN FETISHIZED BY PEOPLE WHOSE ARMS AND LEGS ARE NOW...
...LARGELY VESTIGIAL.
THAT'S YOUR COMPLAINT ABOUT ALMOST EVERYTHING IN MODERN SOCIETY!

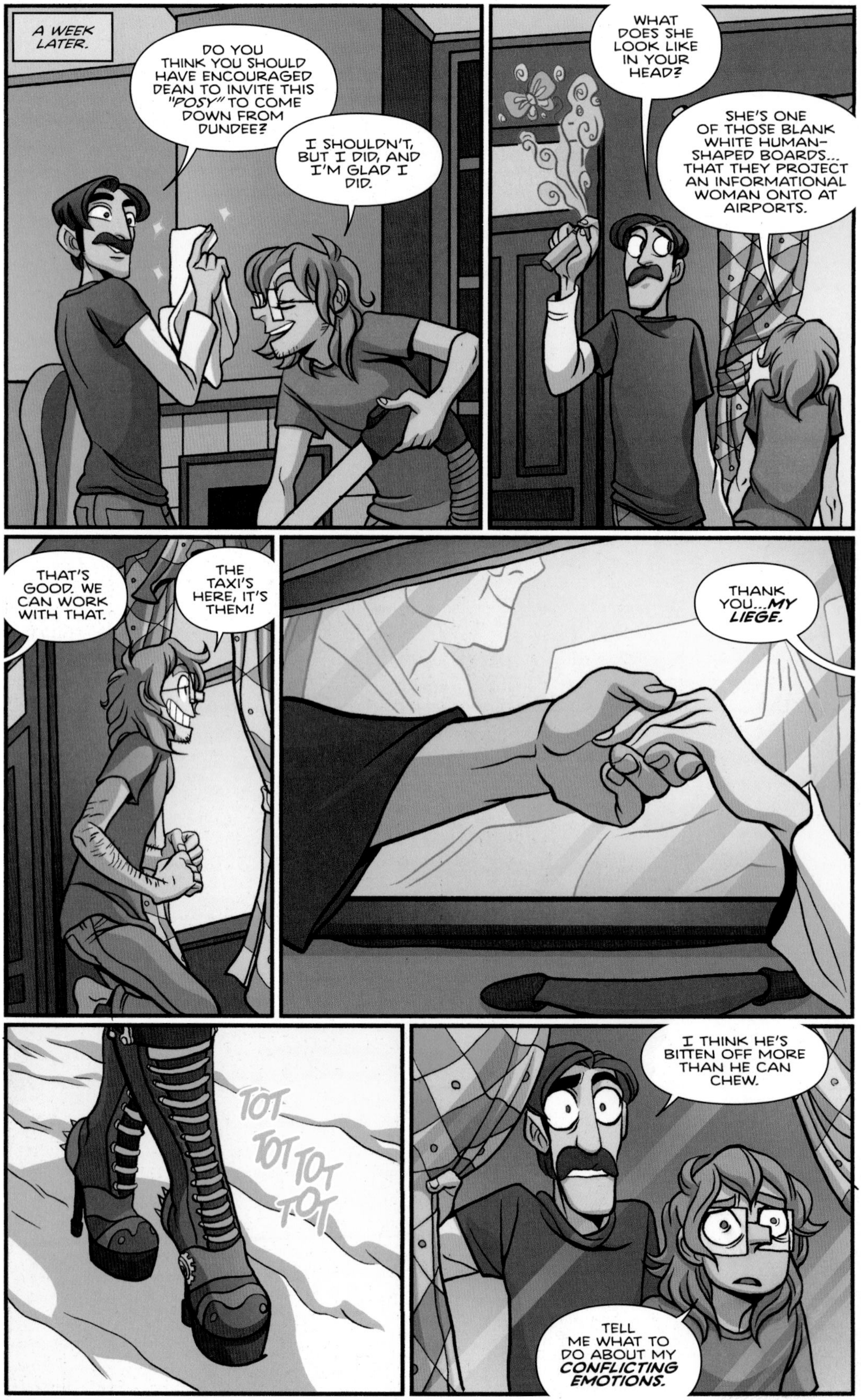
A WEEK LATER.
DO YOU THINK YOU SHOULD HAVE ENCOURAGED DEAN TO INVITE THIS "POSY" TO COME DOWN FROM DUNDEE?
I SHOULDN'T, BUT I DID, AND I'M GLAD I DID.
WHAT DOES SHE LOOK LIKE IN YOUR HEAD?
SHE'S ONE OF THOSE BLANK WHITE HUMAN-SHAPED BOARDS... THAT THEY PROJECT AN INFORMATIONAL WOMAN ONTO AT AIRPORTS.
THAT'S GOOD. WE CAN WORK WITH THAT.
THE TAXI'S HERE, IT'S THEM!
THANK YOU... ***MY LIEGE.***
TOT TOT TOT TOT
I THINK HE'S BITTEN OFF MORE THAN HE CAN CHEW.
TELL ME WHAT TO DO ABOUT MY ***CONFLICTING EMOTIONS.***

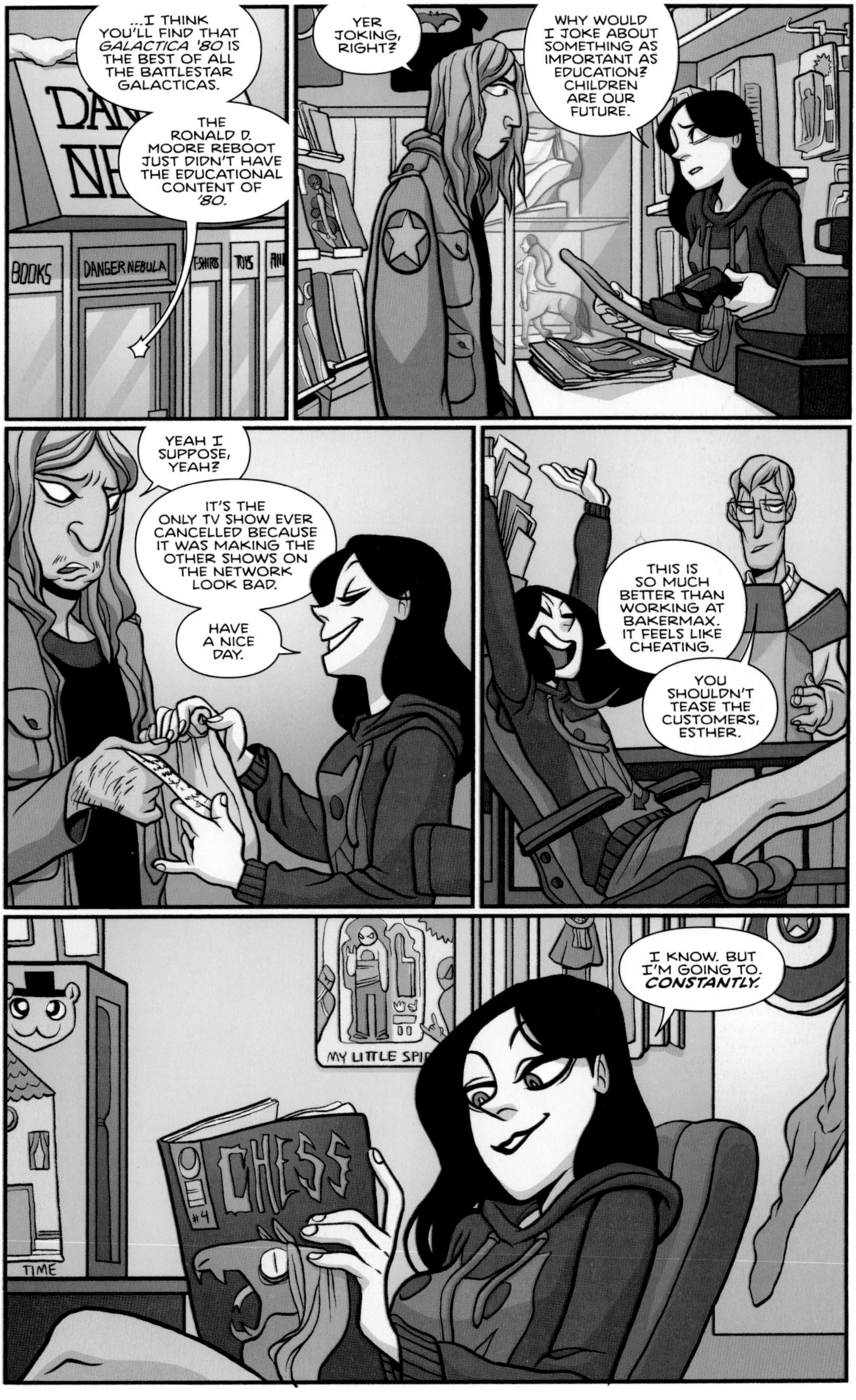
DAN
NE
BOOKS
DANGER NEBULA
T-SHIRTS
TOYS
...I THINK YOU'LL FIND THAT *GALACTICA '80* IS THE BEST OF ALL THE BATTLESTAR GALACTICAS.
THE RONALD D. MOORE REBOOT JUST DIDN'T HAVE THE EDUCATIONAL CONTENT OF *'80*.
YER JOKING, RIGHT?
WHY WOULD I JOKE ABOUT SOMETHING AS IMPORTANT AS EDUCATION? CHILDREN ARE OUR FUTURE.
YEAH I SUPPOSE, YEAH?
IT'S THE ONLY TV SHOW EVER CANCELLED BECAUSE IT WAS MAKING THE OTHER SHOWS ON THE NETWORK LOOK BAD.
HAVE A NICE DAY.
THIS IS SO MUCH BETTER THAN WORKING AT BAKERMAX. IT FEELS LIKE CHEATING.
YOU SHOULDN'T TEASE THE CUSTOMERS, ESTHER.
MY LITTLE SPI
TIME
CHESS
#4
I KNOW. BUT I'M GOING TO. ***CONSTANTLY.***

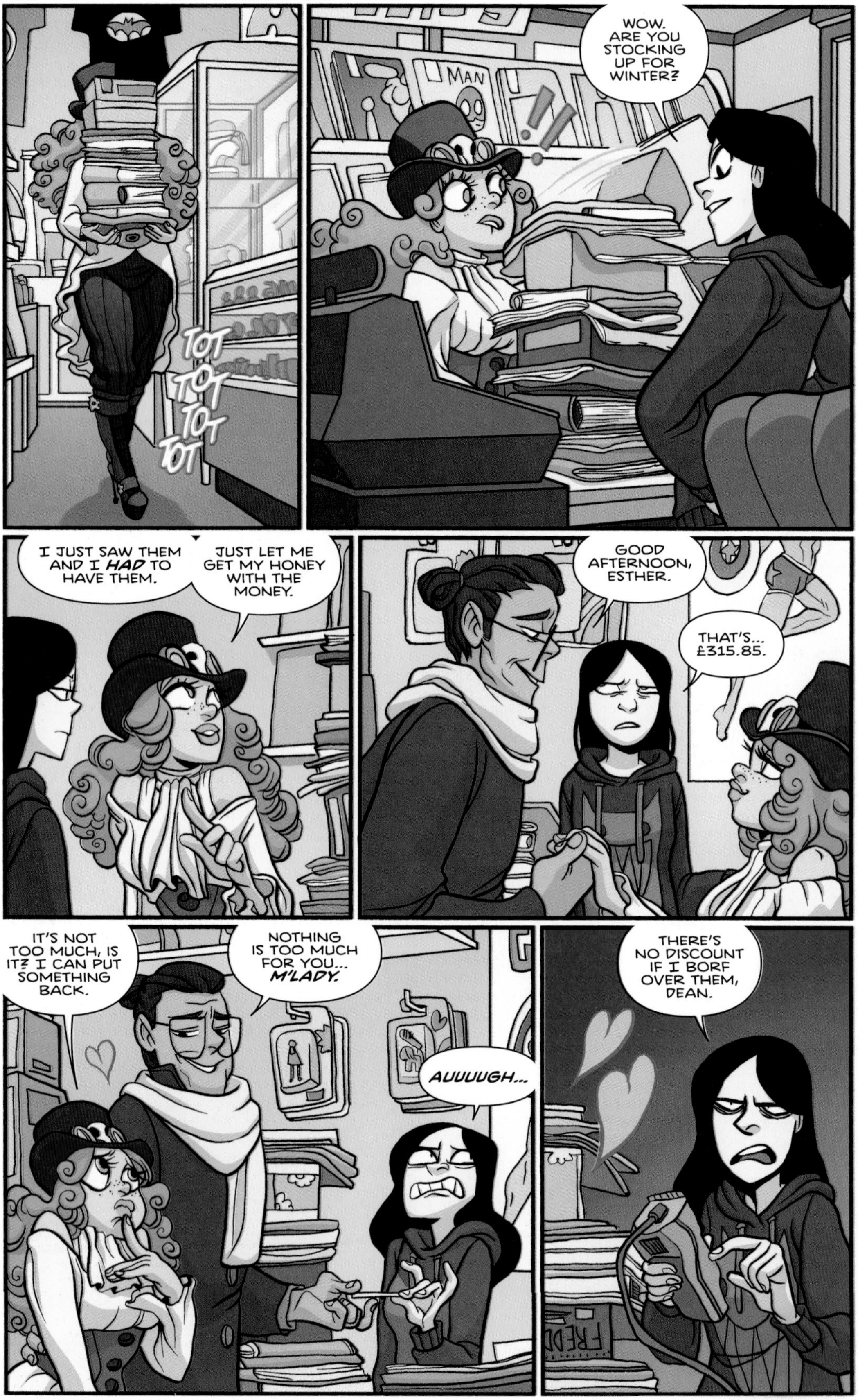
TOT TOT TOT TOT
WOW. ARE YOU STOCKING UP FOR WINTER?
I JUST SAW THEM AND I HAD TO HAVE THEM.
JUST LET ME GET MY HONEY WITH THE MONEY.
GOOD AFTERNOON, ESTHER.
THAT'S... £315.85.
IT'S NOT TOO MUCH, IS IT? I CAN PUT SOMETHING BACK.
NOTHING IS TOO MUCH FOR YOU... M'LADY.
AUUUUGH...
THERE'S NO DISCOUNT IF I BORF OVER THEM, DEAN.

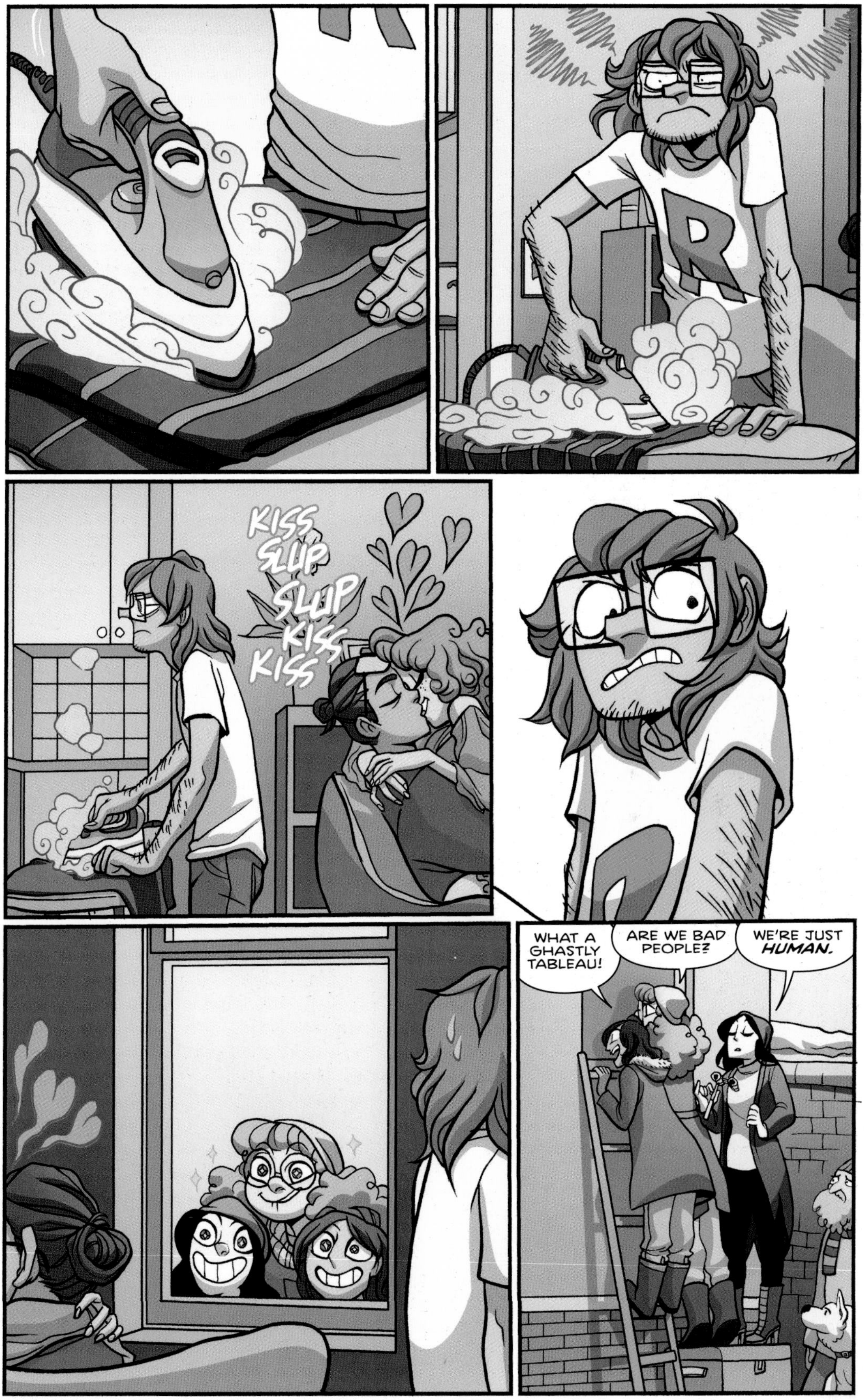
KISS
SLUP
SLUP
KISS
KISS
WHAT A GHASTLY TABLEAU!
ARE WE BAD PEOPLE?
WE'RE JUST *HUMAN.*

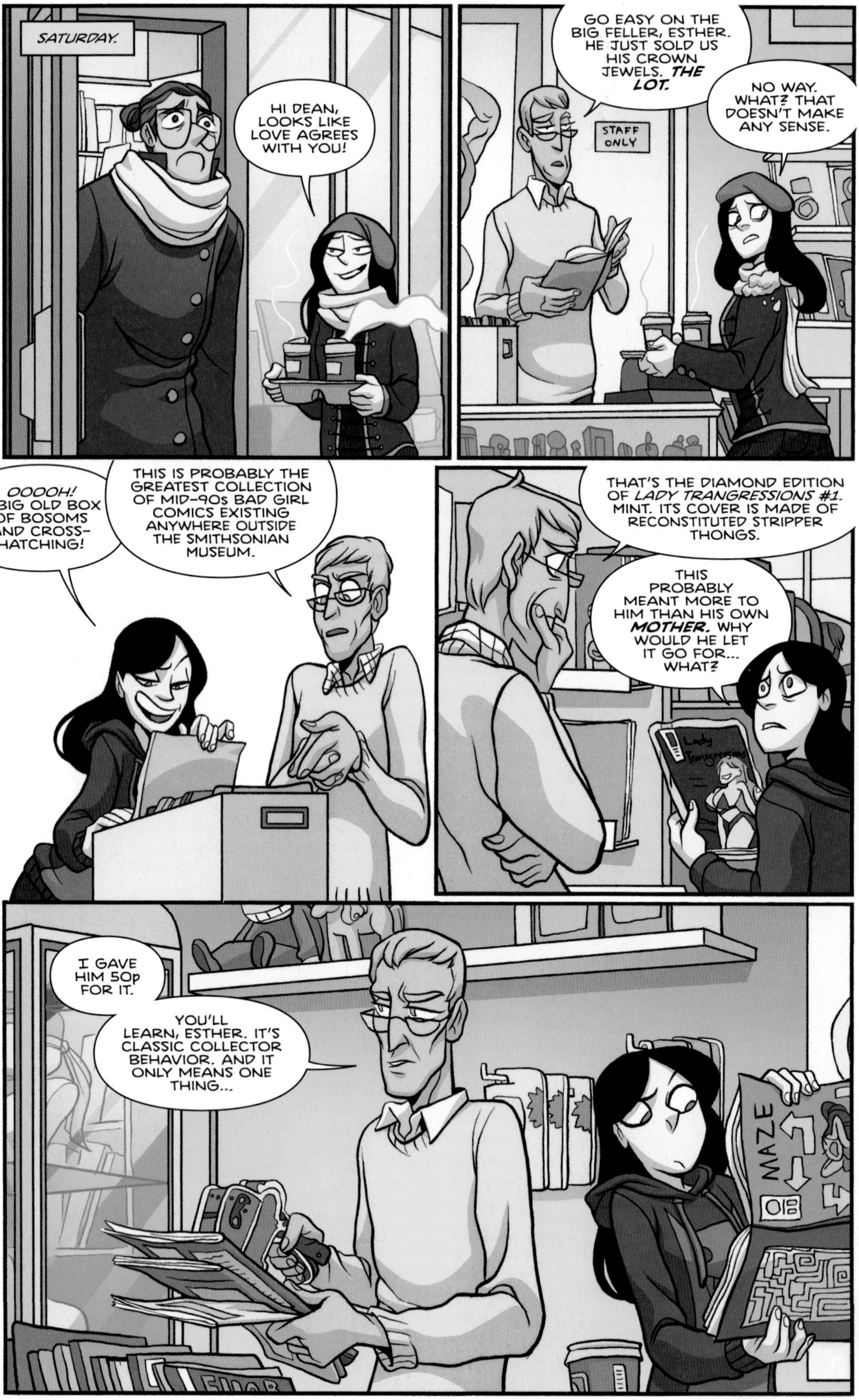
SATURDAY.
HI DEAN, LOOKS LIKE LOVE AGREES WITH YOU!
GO EASY ON THE BIG FELLER, ESTHER. HE JUST SOLD US HIS CROWN JEWELS. ***THE LOT.***
STAFF ONLY
NO WAY. WHAT? THAT DOESN'T MAKE ANY SENSE.
OOOOH! A BIG OLD BOX OF BOSOMS AND CROSS-HATCHING!
THIS IS PROBABLY THE GREATEST COLLECTION OF MID-90s BAD GIRL COMICS EXISTING ANYWHERE OUTSIDE THE SMITHSONIAN MUSEUM.
THAT'S THE DIAMOND EDITION OF *LADY TRANGRESSIONS #1.* MINT. ITS COVER IS MADE OF RECONSTITUTED STRIPPER THONGS.
THIS PROBABLY MEANT MORE TO HIM THAN HIS OWN ***MOTHER.*** WHY WOULD HE LET IT GO FOR... WHAT?
Lady Transgressions
I GAVE HIM 50p FOR IT.
YOU'LL LEARN, ESTHER. IT'S CLASSIC COLLECTOR BEHAVIOR. AND IT ONLY MEANS ONE THING...
MAZE

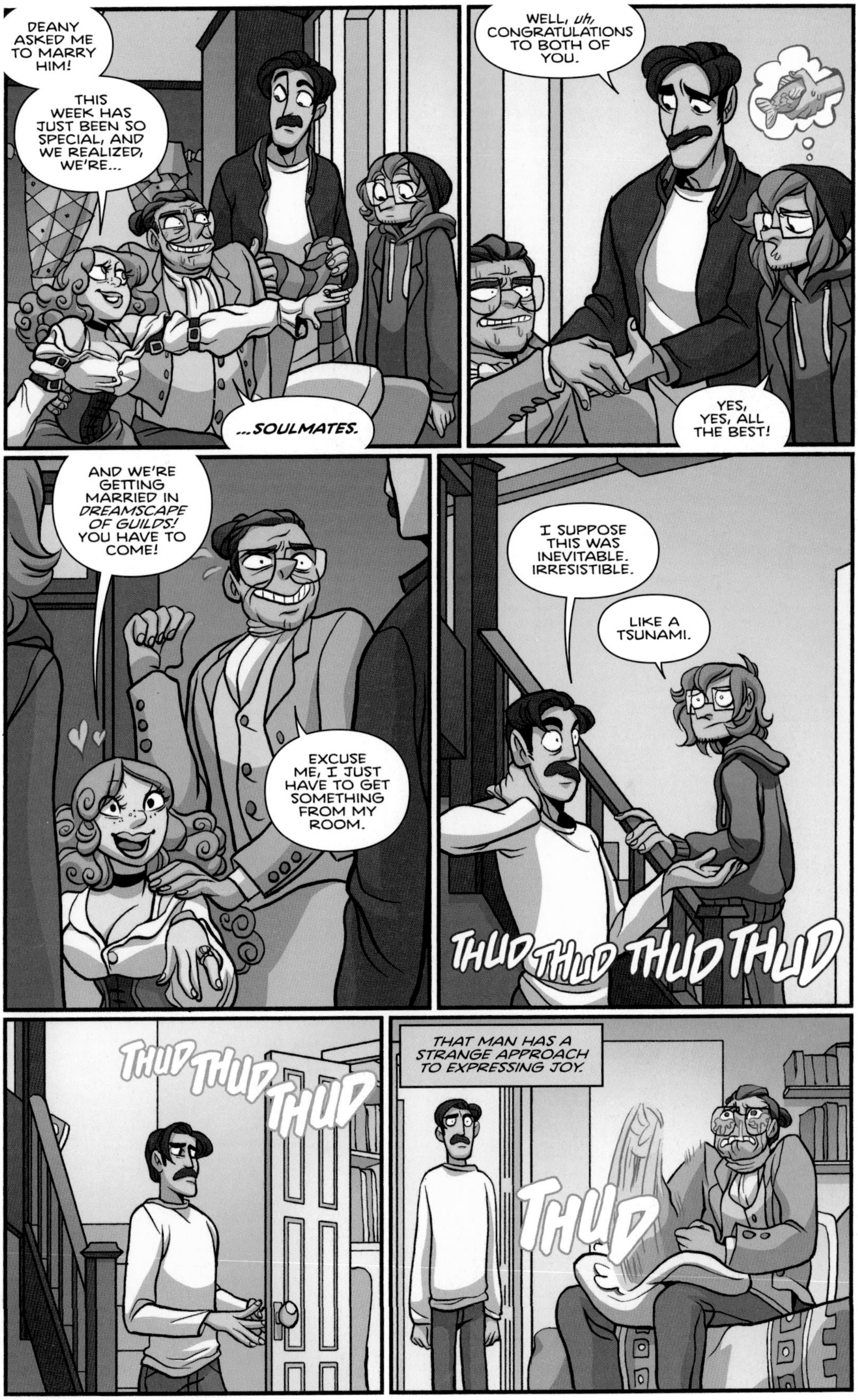
DEANY ASKED ME TO MARRY HIM!
THIS WEEK HAS JUST BEEN SO SPECIAL, AND WE REALIZED, WE'RE...
...SOULMATES.
WELL, *uh*, CONGRATULATIONS TO BOTH OF YOU.
YES, YES, ALL THE BEST!
AND WE'RE GETTING MARRIED IN *DREAMSCAPE OF GUILDS!* YOU HAVE TO COME!
EXCUSE ME, I JUST HAVE TO GET SOMETHING FROM MY ROOM.
I SUPPOSE THIS WAS INEVITABLE. IRRESISTIBLE.
LIKE A TSUNAMI.
THUD THUD THUD THUD
THUD THUD THUD
THAT MAN HAS A STRANGE APPROACH TO EXPRESSING JOY.
THUD

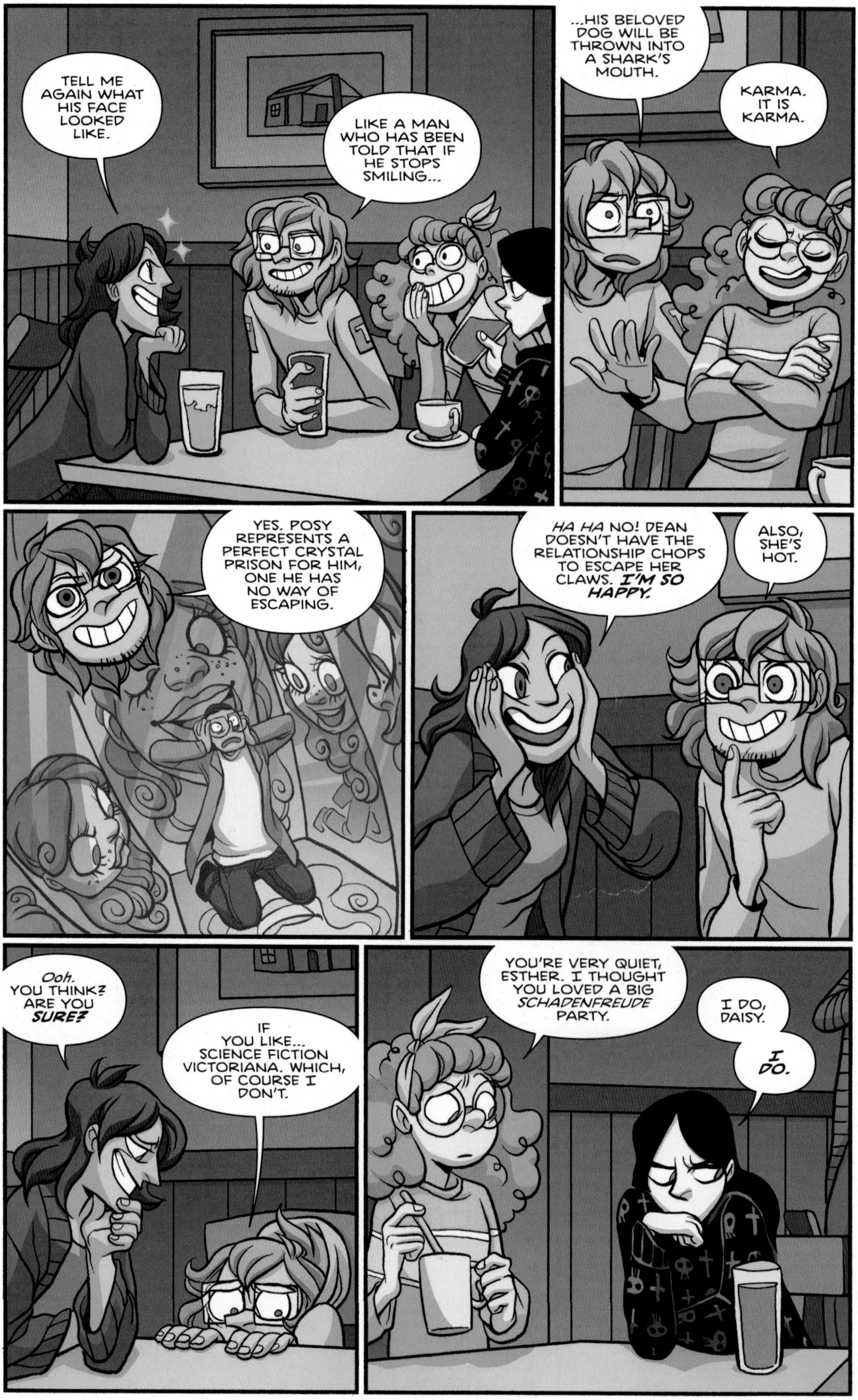
TELL ME AGAIN WHAT HIS FACE LOOKED LIKE.
LIKE A MAN WHO HAS BEEN TOLD THAT IF HE STOPS SMILING...
...HIS BELOVED DOG WILL BE THROWN INTO A SHARK'S MOUTH.
KARMA. IT IS KARMA.
YES. POSY REPRESENTS A PERFECT CRYSTAL PRISON FOR HIM, ONE HE HAS NO WAY OF ESCAPING.
HA HA NO! DEAN DOESN'T HAVE THE RELATIONSHIP CHOPS TO ESCAPE HER CLAWS. ***I'M SO HAPPY.***
ALSO, SHE'S HOT.
Ooh. YOU THINK? ARE YOU ***SURE?***
IF YOU LIKE... SCIENCE FICTION VICTORIANA. WHICH, OF COURSE I DON'T.
YOU'RE VERY QUIET, ESTHER. I THOUGHT YOU LOVED A BIG *SCHADENFREUDE* PARTY.
I DO, DAISY.
I DO.

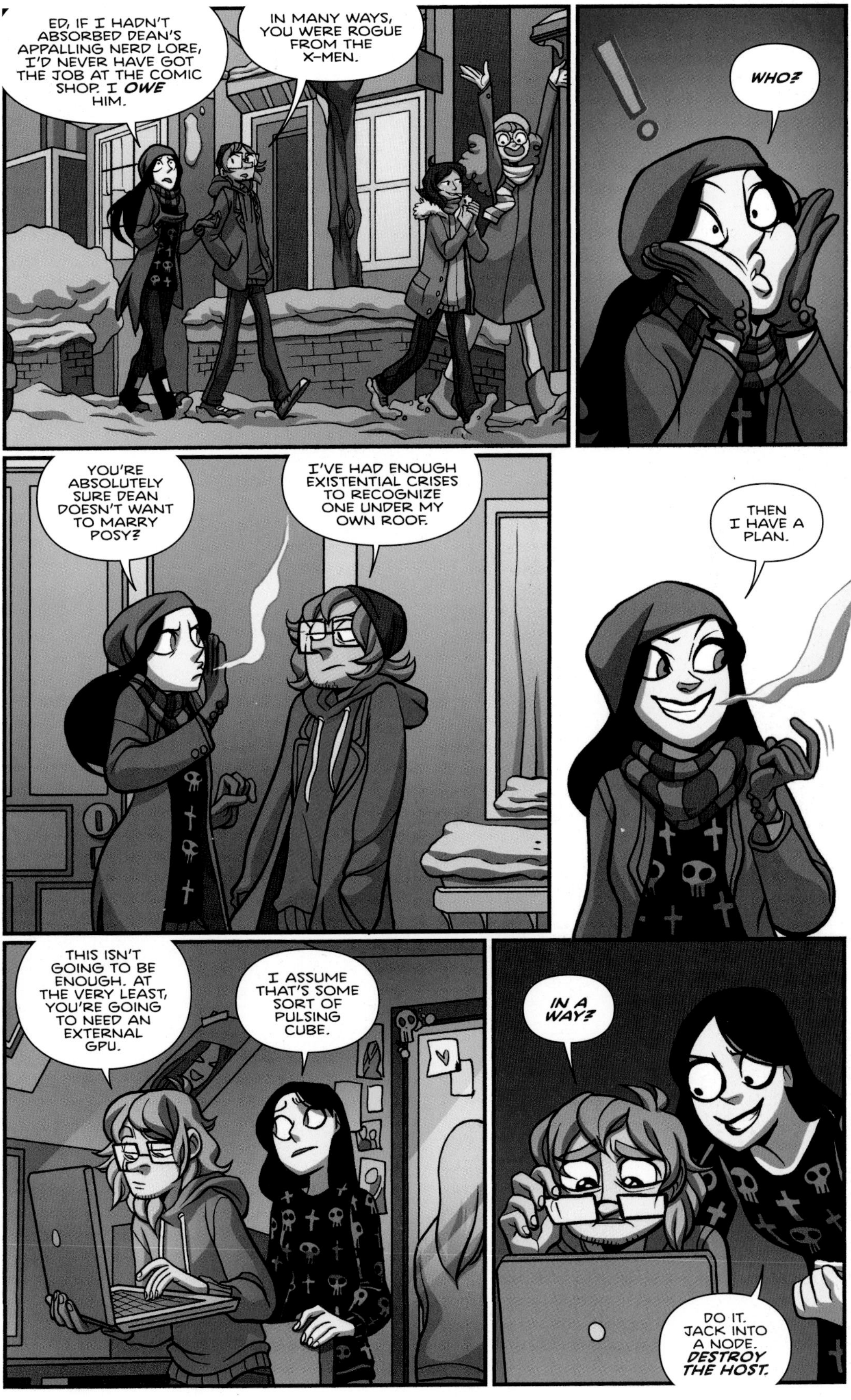
ED, IF I HADN'T ABSORBED DEAN'S APPALLING NERD LORE, I'D NEVER HAVE GOT THE JOB AT THE COMIC SHOP. I OWE HIM.
IN MANY WAYS, YOU WERE ROGUE FROM THE X-MEN.
!
WHO?
YOU'RE ABSOLUTELY SURE DEAN DOESN'T WANT TO MARRY POSY?
I'VE HAD ENOUGH EXISTENTIAL CRISES TO RECOGNIZE ONE UNDER MY OWN ROOF.
THEN I HAVE A PLAN.
THIS ISN'T GOING TO BE ENOUGH. AT THE VERY LEAST, YOU'RE GOING TO NEED AN EXTERNAL GPU.
I ASSUME THAT'S SOME SORT OF PULSING CUBE.
IN A WAY?
DO IT. JACK INTO A NODE. DESTROY THE HOST.

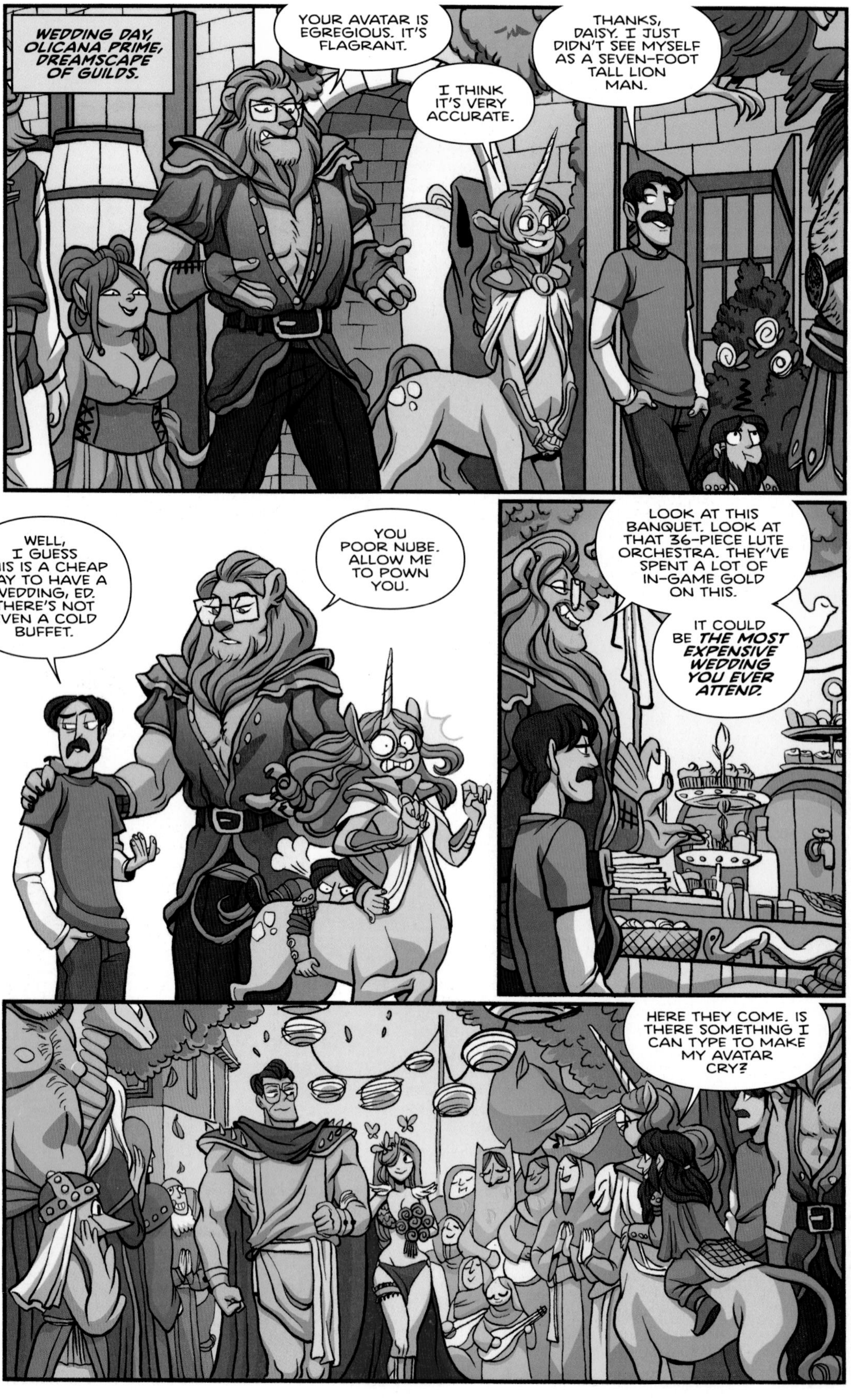
WEDDING DAY, OLICANA PRIME, DREAMSCAPE OF GUILDS.
YOUR AVATAR IS EGREGIOUS. IT'S FLAGRANT.
I THINK IT'S VERY ACCURATE.
THANKS, DAISY. I JUST DIDN'T SEE MYSELF AS A SEVEN-FOOT TALL LION MAN.
WELL, I GUESS THIS IS A CHEAP WAY TO HAVE A WEDDING, ED. THERE'S NOT EVEN A COLD BUFFET.
YOU POOR NUBE. ALLOW ME TO POWN YOU.
LOOK AT THIS BANQUET. LOOK AT THAT 36-PIECE LUTE ORCHESTRA. THEY'VE SPENT A LOT OF IN-GAME GOLD ON THIS.
IT COULD BE *THE MOST EXPENSIVE WEDDING YOU EVER ATTEND.*
HERE THEY COME. IS THERE SOMETHING I CAN TYPE TO MAKE MY AVATAR CRY?

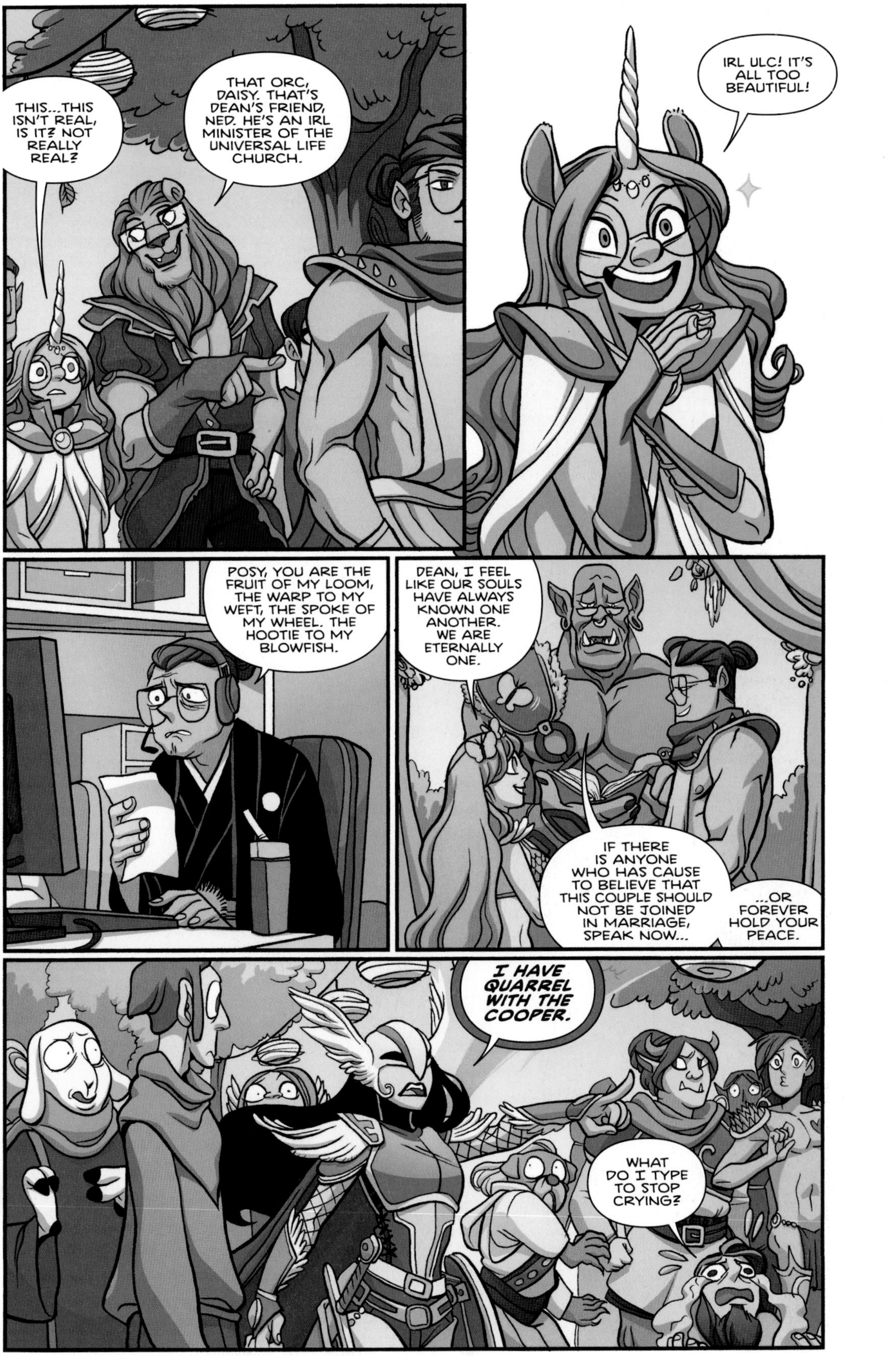

THIS...THIS ISN'T REAL, IS IT? NOT REALLY REAL?
THAT ORC, DAISY. THAT'S DEAN'S FRIEND, NED. HE'S AN IRL MINISTER OF THE UNIVERSAL LIFE CHURCH.
IRL ULC! IT'S ALL TOO BEAUTIFUL!
POSY, YOU ARE THE FRUIT OF MY LOOM, THE WARP TO MY WEFT, THE SPOKE OF MY WHEEL. THE HOOTIE TO MY BLOWFISH.
DEAN, I FEEL LIKE OUR SOULS HAVE ALWAYS KNOWN ONE ANOTHER. WE ARE ETERNALLY ONE.
IF THERE IS ANYONE WHO HAS CAUSE TO BELIEVE THAT THIS COUPLE SHOULD NOT BE JOINED IN MARRIAGE, SPEAK NOW...
...OR FOREVER HOLD YOUR PEACE.
I HAVE QUARREL WITH THE COOPER.
WHAT DO I TYPE TO STOP CRYING?

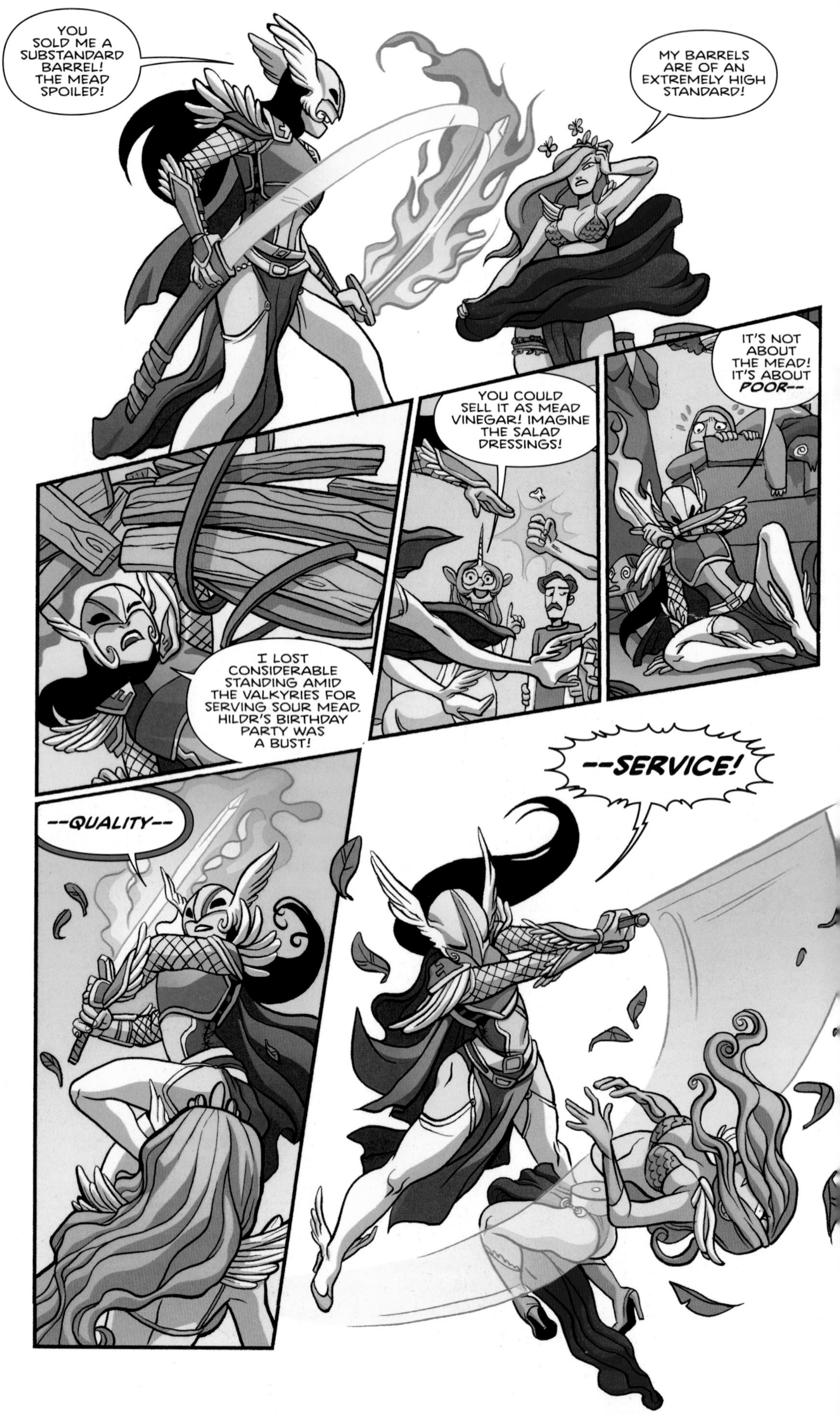
YOU SOLD ME A SUBSTANDARD BARREL! THE MEAD SPOILED!
MY BARRELS ARE OF AN EXTREMELY HIGH STANDARD!
I LOST CONSIDERABLE STANDING AMID THE VALKYRIES FOR SERVING SOUR MEAD. HILDR'S BIRTHDAY PARTY WAS A BUST!
YOU COULD SELL IT AS MEAD VINEGAR! IMAGINE THE SALAD DRESSINGS!
IT'S NOT ABOUT THE MEAD! IT'S ABOUT POOR--
--QUALITY--
--SERVICE!

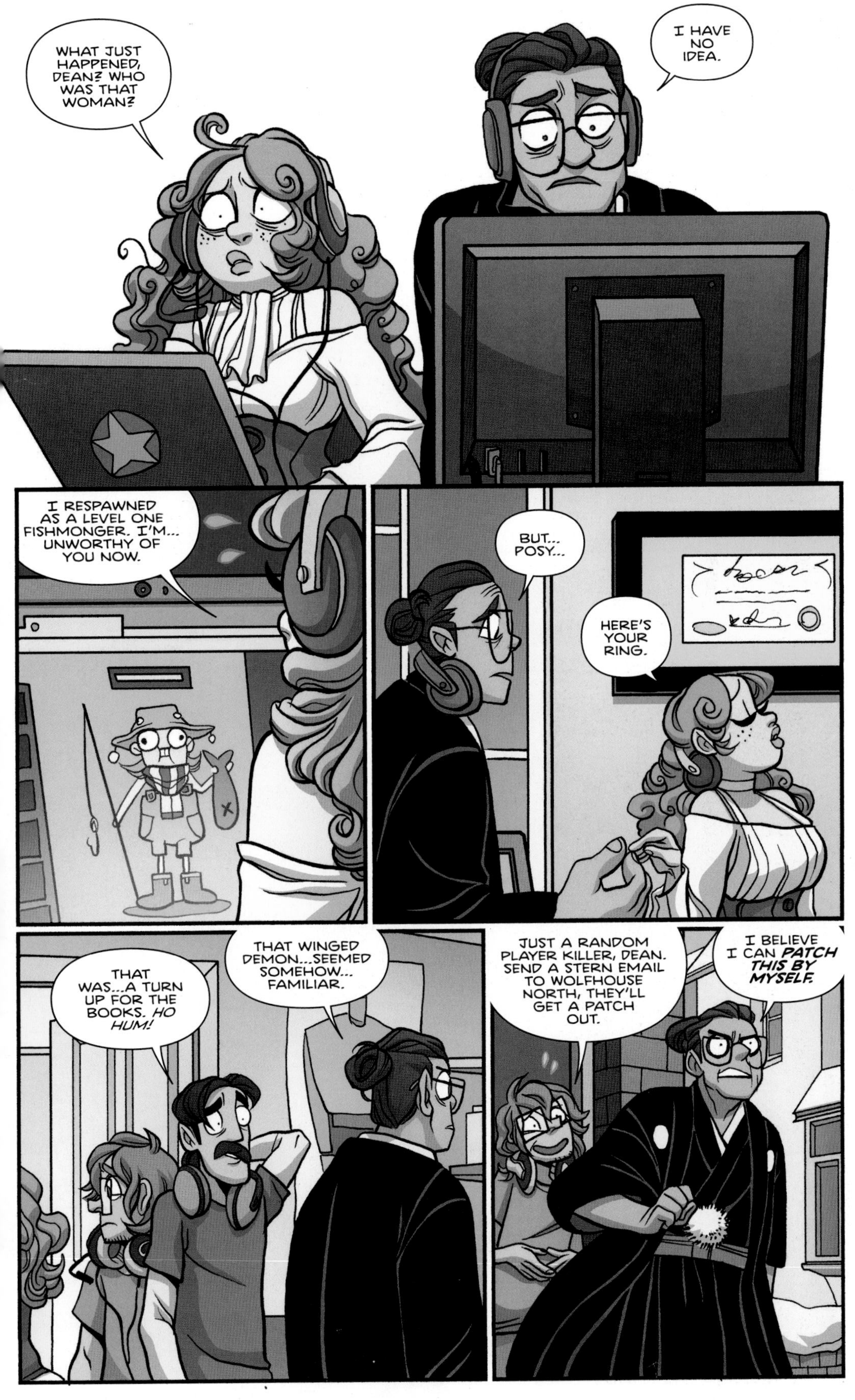
WHAT JUST HAPPENED, DEAN? WHO WAS THAT WOMAN?
I HAVE NO IDEA.
I RESPAWNED AS A LEVEL ONE FISHMONGER. I'M... UNWORTHY OF YOU NOW.
BUT... POSY...
HERE'S YOUR RING.
THAT WAS...A TURN UP FOR THE BOOKS. HO HUM!
THAT WINGED DEMON...SEEMED SOMEHOW... FAMILIAR.
JUST A RANDOM PLAYER KILLER, DEAN. SEND A STERN EMAIL TO WOLFHOUSE NORTH, THEY'LL GET A PATCH OUT.
I BELIEVE I CAN PATCH THIS BY MYSELF.

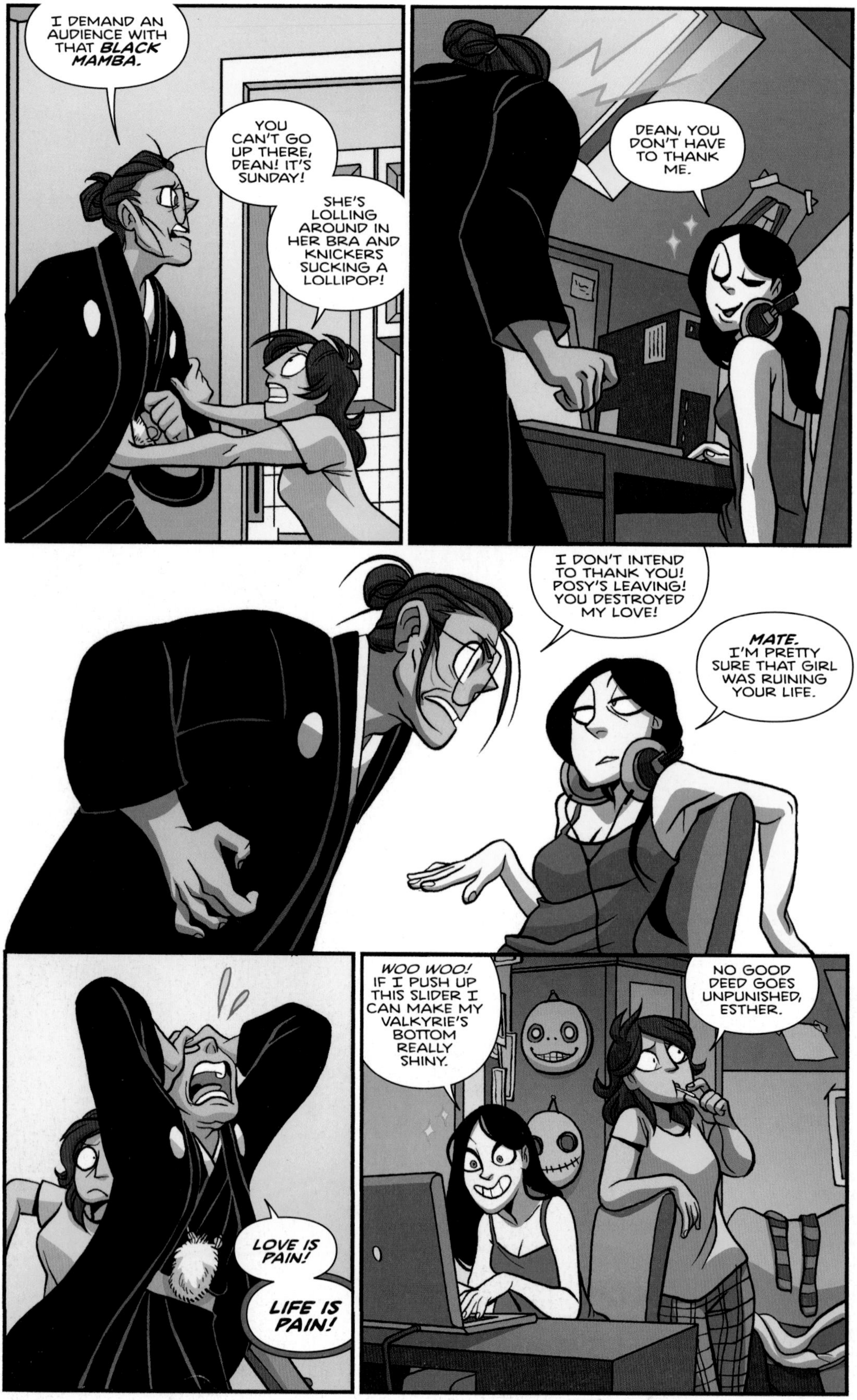
I DEMAND AN AUDIENCE WITH THAT *BLACK MAMBA.*
YOU CAN'T GO UP THERE, DEAN! IT'S SUNDAY!
SHE'S LOLLING AROUND IN HER BRA AND KNICKERS SUCKING A LOLLIPOP!
DEAN, YOU DON'T HAVE TO THANK ME.
I DON'T INTEND TO THANK YOU! POSY'S LEAVING! YOU DESTROYED MY LOVE!
MATE. I'M PRETTY SURE THAT GIRL WAS RUINING YOUR LIFE.
LOVE IS PAIN!
LIFE IS PAIN!
WOO WOO! IF I PUSH UP THIS SLIDER I CAN MAKE MY VALKYRIE'S BOTTOM REALLY SHINY.
NO GOOD DEED GOES UNPUNISHED, ESTHER.

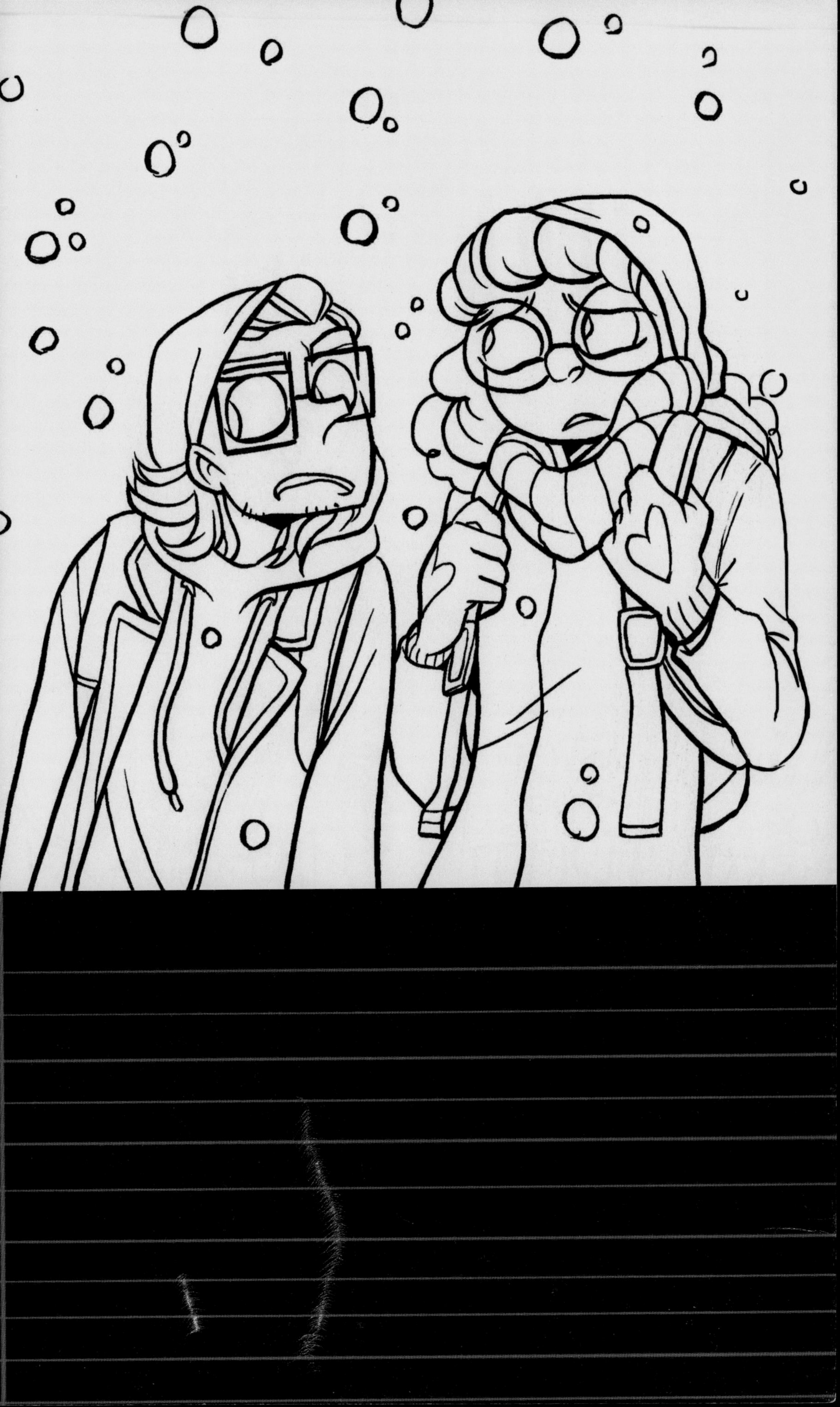

CHAPTER TWENTY SEVEN

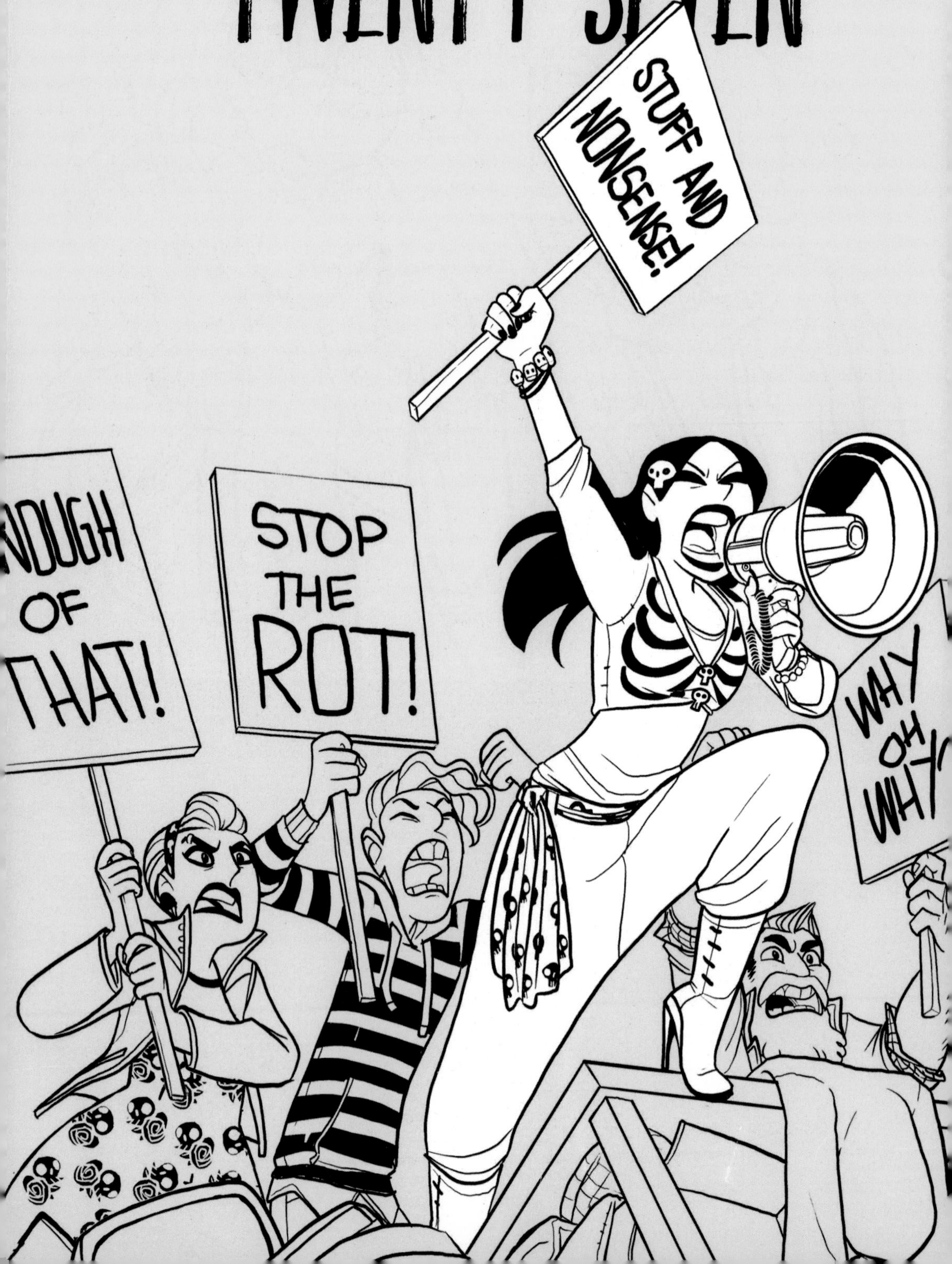
STUFF AND NONSENSE!
NOUGH OF THAT!
STOP THE ROT!
WHY OH WH

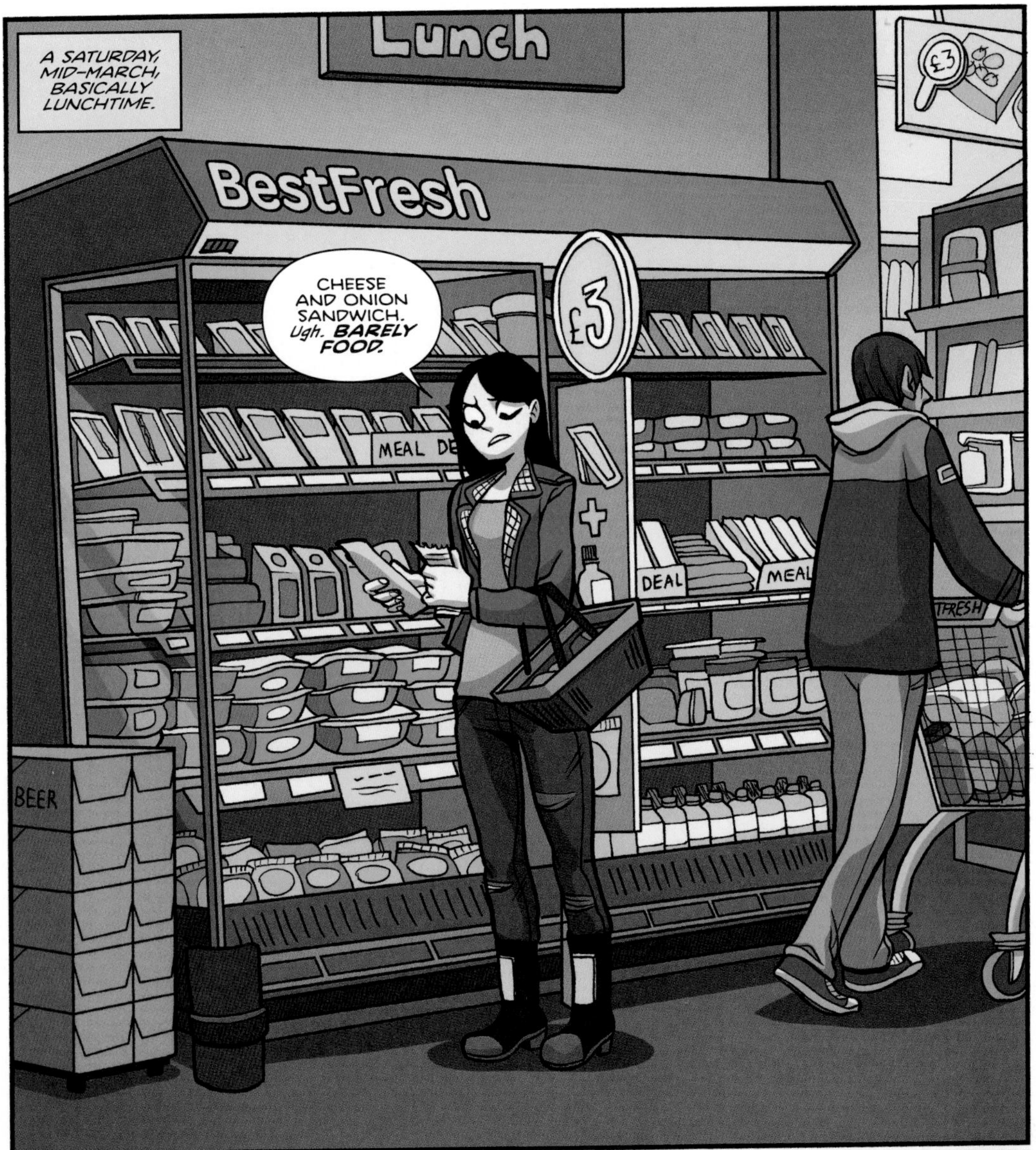
A SATURDAY, MID-MARCH, BASICALLY LUNCHTIME.
Lunch
BestFresh
£3
CHEESE AND ONION SANDWICH. Ugh. BARELY FOOD.
MEAL DE
DEAL
MEAL
BEER

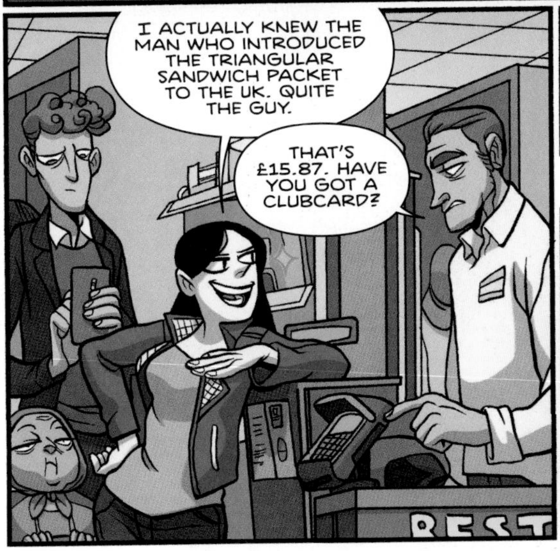
I ACTUALLY KNEW THE MAN WHO INTRODUCED THE TRIANGULAR SANDWICH PACKET TO THE UK. QUITE THE GUY.
THAT'S £15.87. HAVE YOU GOT A CLUBCARD?
BEST

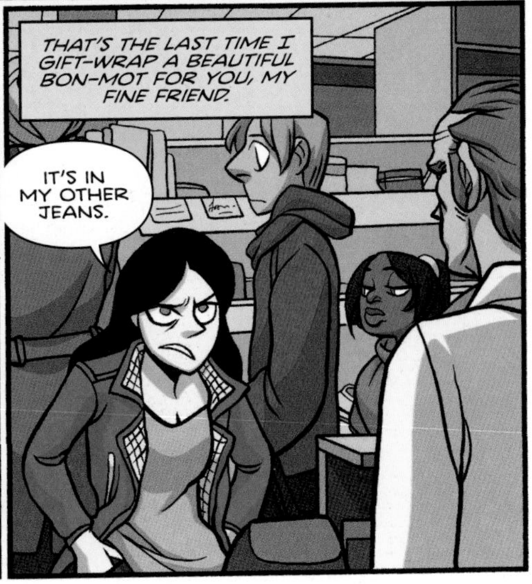
THAT'S THE LAST TIME I GIFT-WRAP A BEAUTIFUL BON-MOT FOR YOU, MY FINE FRIEND.
IT'S IN MY OTHER JEANS.

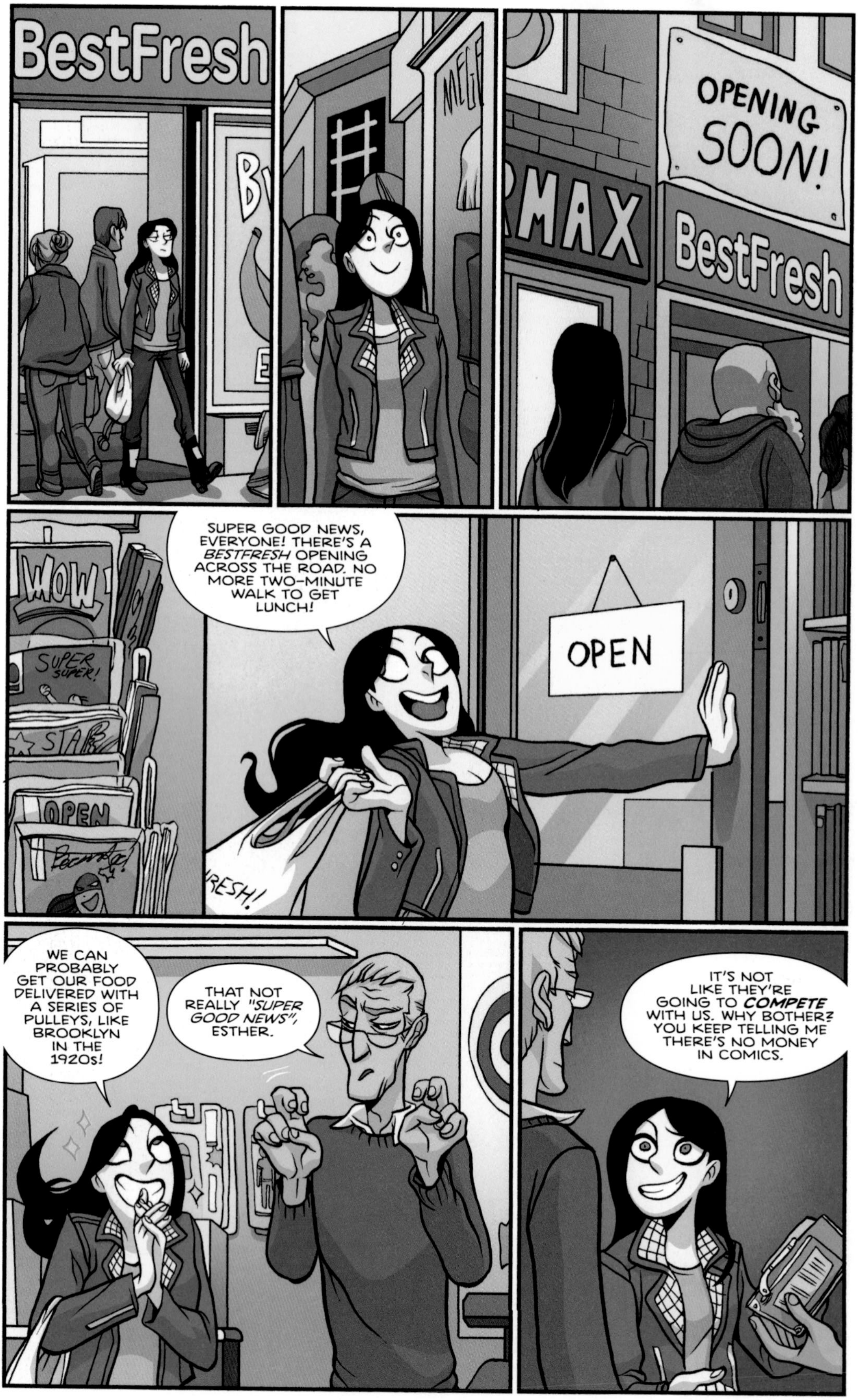
BestFresh
OPENING SOON!
BestFresh
SUPER GOOD NEWS, EVERYONE! THERE'S A BESTFRESH OPENING ACROSS THE ROAD. NO MORE TWO-MINUTE WALK TO GET LUNCH!
OPEN
WE CAN PROBABLY GET OUR FOOD DELIVERED WITH A SERIES OF PULLEYS, LIKE BROOKLYN IN THE 1920s!
THAT NOT REALLY "SUPER GOOD NEWS", ESTHER.
IT'S NOT LIKE THEY'RE GOING TO COMPETE WITH US. WHY BOTHER? YOU KEEP TELLING ME THERE'S NO MONEY IN COMICS.

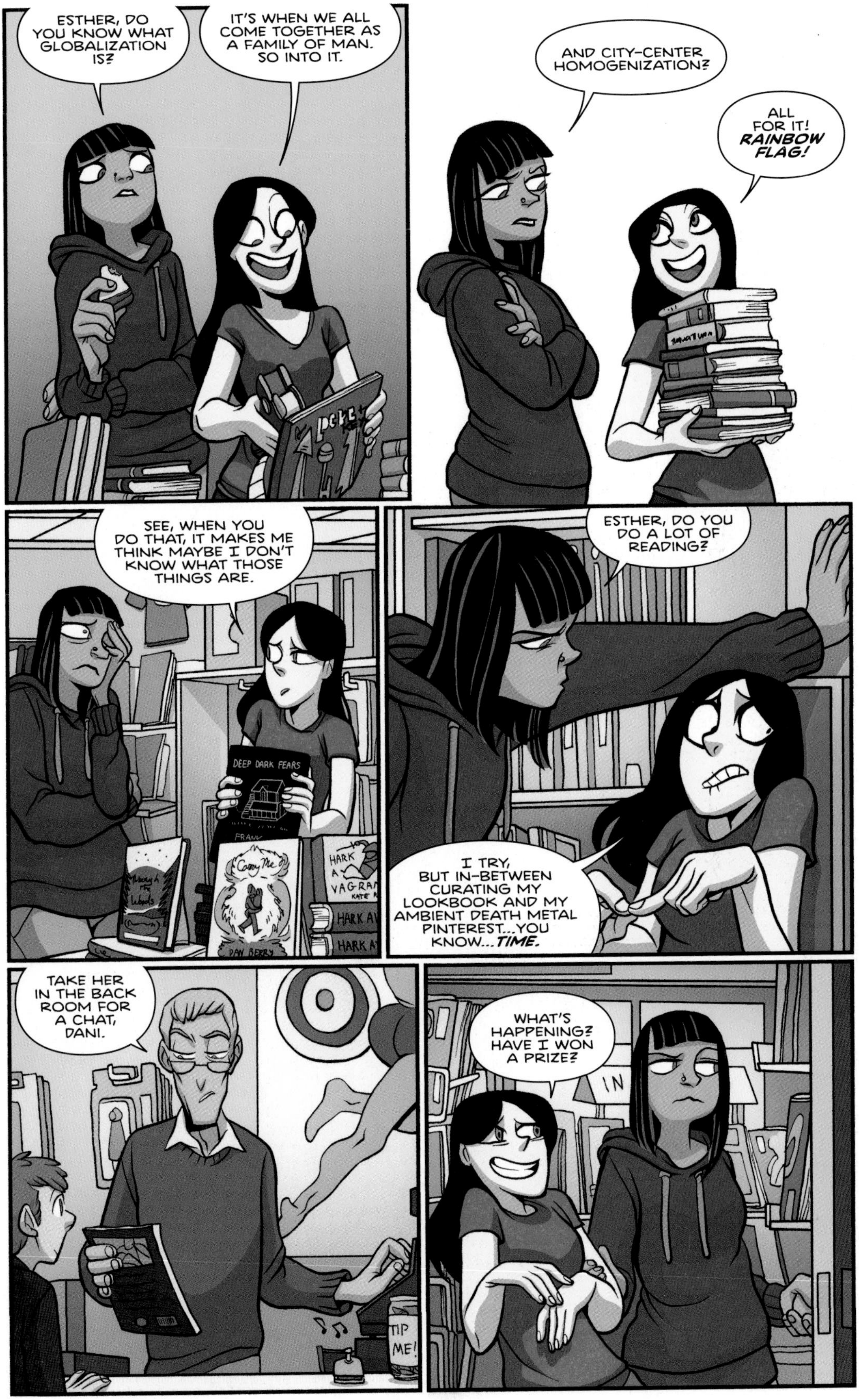
ESTHER, DO YOU KNOW WHAT GLOBALIZATION IS?
IT'S WHEN WE ALL COME TOGETHER AS A FAMILY OF MAN. SO INTO IT.
AND CITY-CENTER HOMOGENIZATION?
ALL FOR IT! RAINBOW FLAG!
SEE, WHEN YOU DO THAT, IT MAKES ME THINK MAYBE I DON'T KNOW WHAT THOSE THINGS ARE.
DEEP DARK FEARS
HARK A VAGRANT
DAN BERRY
ESTHER, DO YOU DO A LOT OF READING?
I TRY, BUT IN-BETWEEN CURATING MY LOOKBOOK AND MY AMBIENT DEATH METAL PINTEREST... YOU KNOW... TIME.
TAKE HER IN THE BACK ROOM FOR A CHAT, DANI.
TIP ME!
WHAT'S HAPPENING? HAVE I WON A PRIZE?
IN

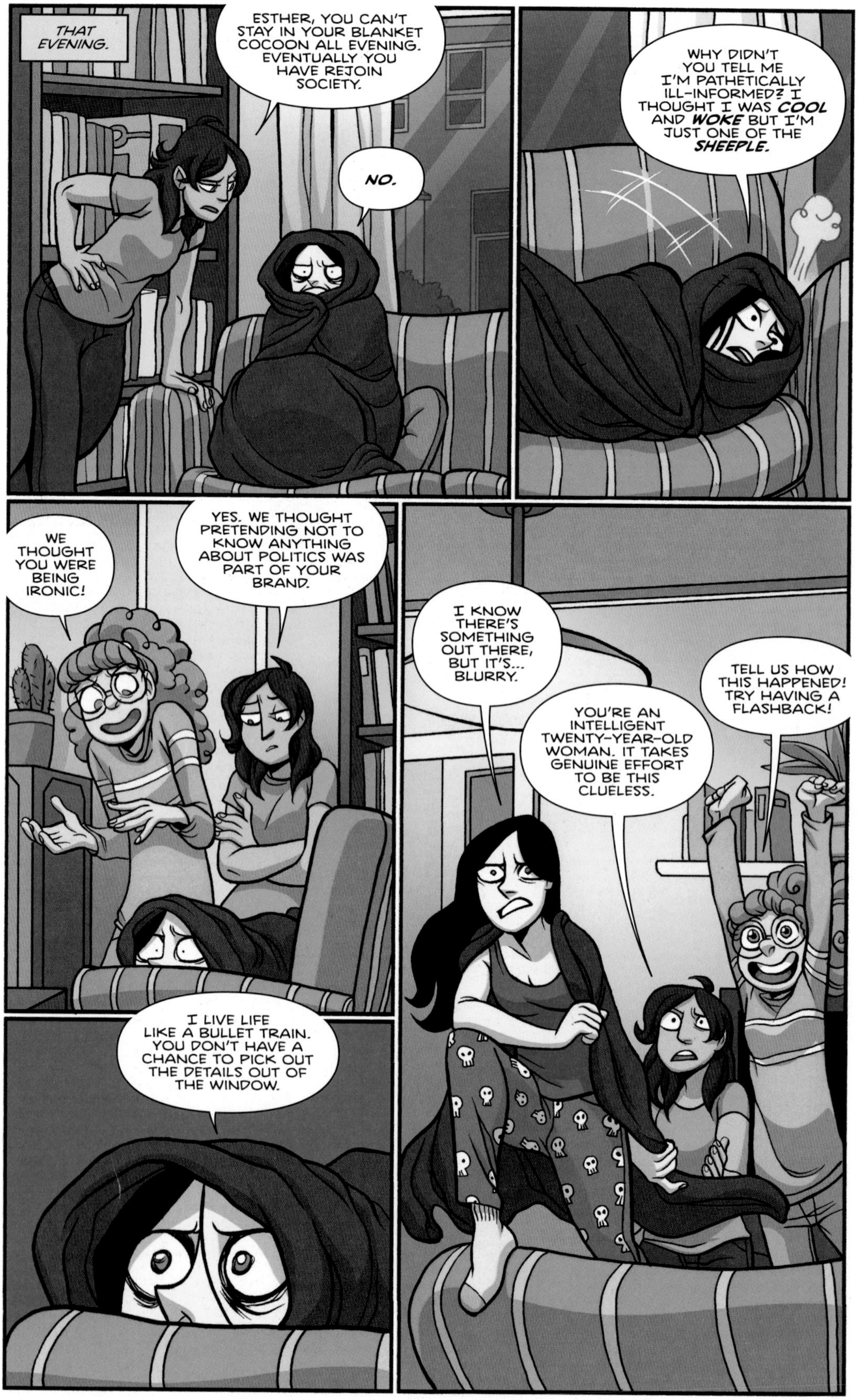
THAT EVENING.
ESTHER, YOU CAN'T STAY IN YOUR BLANKET COCOON ALL EVENING. EVENTUALLY YOU HAVE REJOIN SOCIETY.
NO.
WHY DIDN'T YOU TELL ME I'M PATHETICALLY ILL-INFORMED? I THOUGHT I WAS COOL AND WOKE BUT I'M JUST ONE OF THE SHEEPLE.
WE THOUGHT YOU WERE BEING IRONIC!
YES. WE THOUGHT PRETENDING NOT TO KNOW ANYTHING ABOUT POLITICS WAS PART OF YOUR BRAND.
I LIVE LIFE LIKE A BULLET TRAIN. YOU DON'T HAVE A CHANCE TO PICK OUT THE DETAILS OUT OF THE WINDOW.
I KNOW THERE'S SOMETHING OUT THERE, BUT IT'S... BLURRY.
YOU'RE AN INTELLIGENT TWENTY-YEAR-OLD WOMAN. IT TAKES GENUINE EFFORT TO BE THIS CLUELESS.
TELL US HOW THIS HAPPENED! TRY HAVING A FLASHBACK!

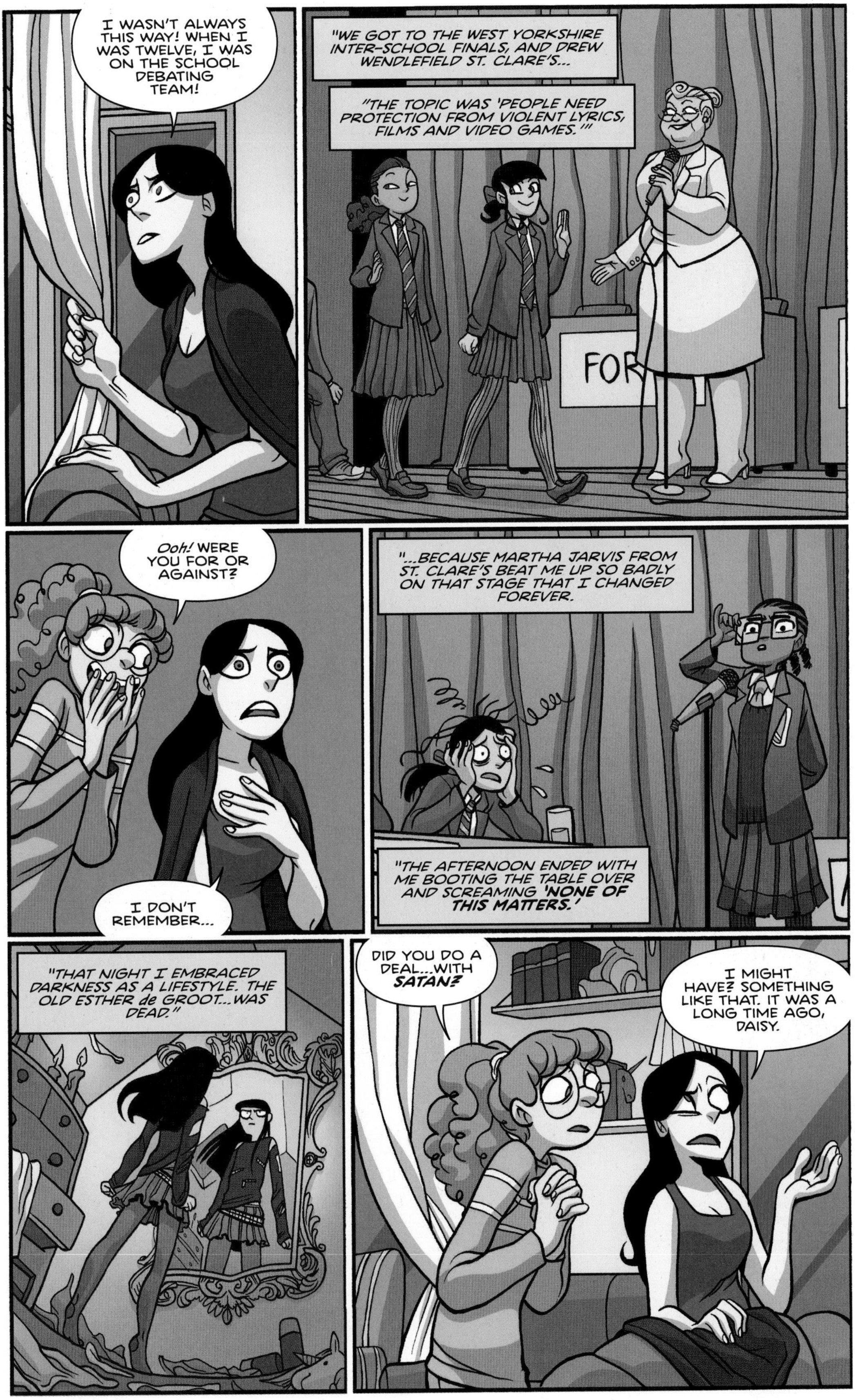

I WASN'T ALWAYS THIS WAY! WHEN I WAS TWELVE, I WAS ON THE SCHOOL DEBATING TEAM!
"WE GOT TO THE WEST YORKSHIRE INTER-SCHOOL FINALS, AND DREW WENDLEFIELD ST. CLARE'S...
"THE TOPIC WAS 'PEOPLE NEED PROTECTION FROM VIOLENT LYRICS, FILMS AND VIDEO GAMES.'"
FOR
Ooh! WERE YOU FOR OR AGAINST?
I DON'T REMEMBER...
"...BECAUSE MARTHA JARVIS FROM ST. CLARE'S BEAT ME UP SO BADLY ON THAT STAGE THAT I CHANGED FOREVER.
"THE AFTERNOON ENDED WITH ME BOOTING THE TABLE OVER AND SCREAMING 'NONE OF THIS MATTERS.'
"THAT NIGHT I EMBRACED DARKNESS AS A LIFESTYLE. THE OLD ESTHER de GROOT...WAS DEAD."
DID YOU DO A DEAL...WITH SATAN?
I MIGHT HAVE? SOMETHING LIKE THAT. IT WAS A LONG TIME AGO, DAISY.

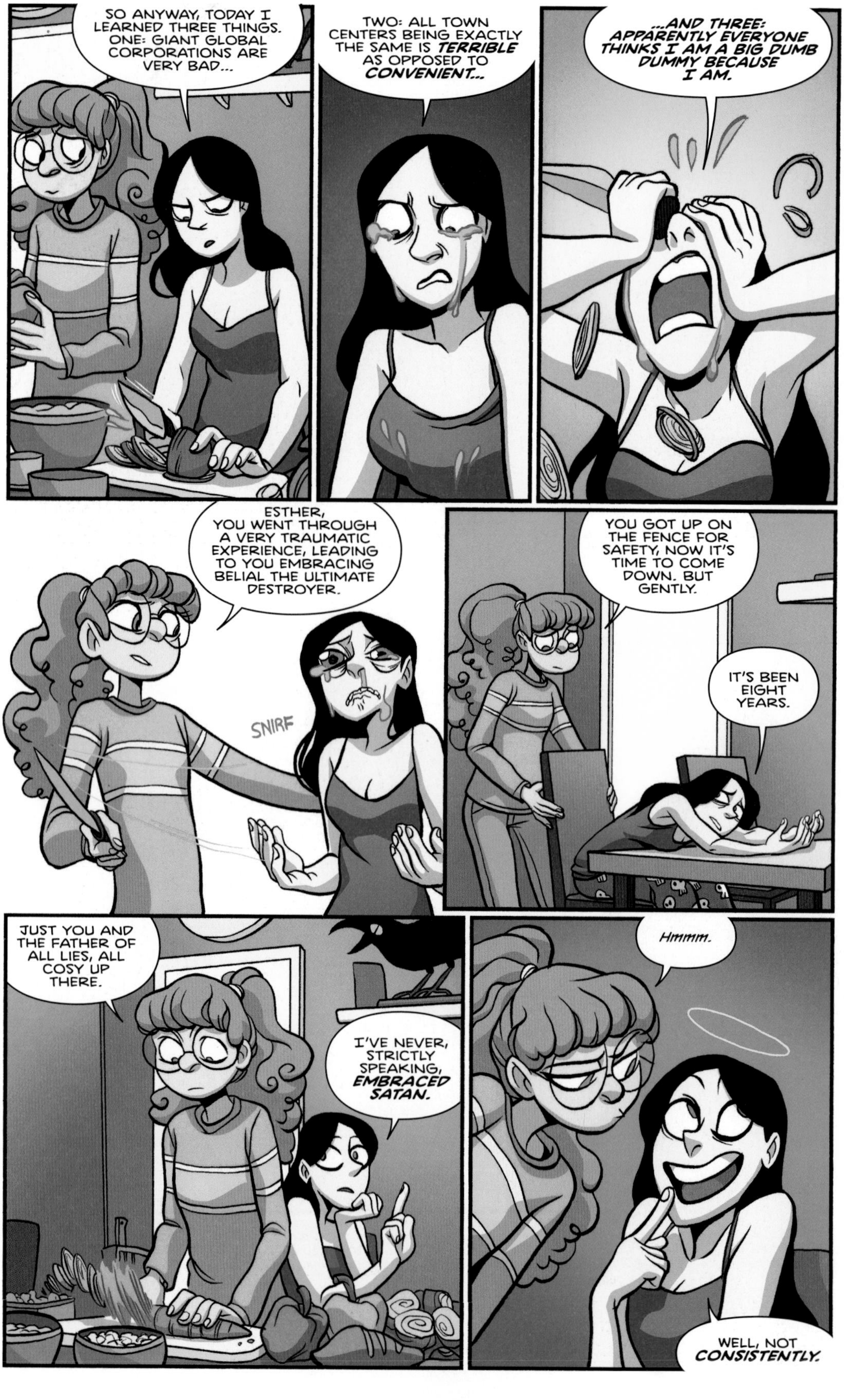
SO ANYWAY, TODAY I LEARNED THREE THINGS. ONE: GIANT GLOBAL CORPORATIONS ARE VERY BAD...
TWO: ALL TOWN CENTERS BEING EXACTLY THE SAME IS *TERRIBLE* AS OPPOSED TO *CONVENIENT...*
...AND THREE: APPARENTLY EVERYONE THINKS I AM A BIG DUMB DUMMY BECAUSE I AM.
ESTHER, YOU WENT THROUGH A VERY TRAUMATIC EXPERIENCE, LEADING TO YOU EMBRACING BELIAL THE ULTIMATE DESTROYER.
SNIRF
YOU GOT UP ON THE FENCE FOR SAFETY, NOW IT'S TIME TO COME DOWN. BUT GENTLY.
IT'S BEEN EIGHT YEARS.
JUST YOU AND THE FATHER OF ALL LIES, ALL COSY UP THERE.
I'VE NEVER, STRICTLY SPEAKING, *EMBRACED SATAN.*
Hmmm.
WELL, NOT *CONSISTENTLY.*

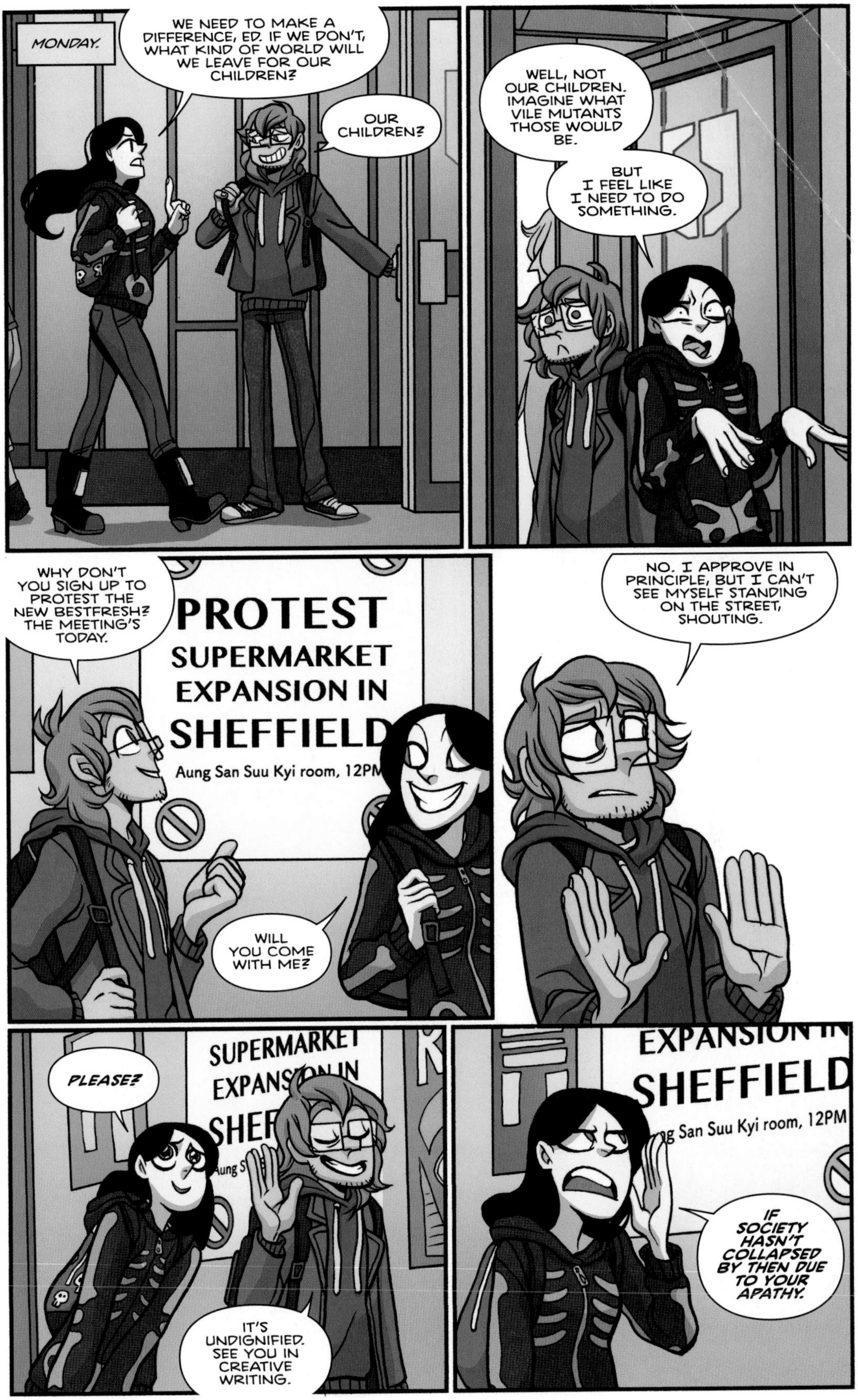

MONDAY.
WE NEED TO MAKE A DIFFERENCE, ED. IF WE DON'T, WHAT KIND OF WORLD WILL WE LEAVE FOR OUR CHILDREN?
OUR CHILDREN?
WELL, NOT OUR CHILDREN. IMAGINE WHAT VILE MUTANTS THOSE WOULD BE.
BUT I FEEL LIKE I NEED TO DO SOMETHING.
WHY DON'T YOU SIGN UP TO PROTEST THE NEW BESTFRESH? THE MEETING'S TODAY.
PROTEST
SUPERMARKET
EXPANSION IN
SHEFFIELD
Aung San Suu Kyi room, 12PM
WILL YOU COME WITH ME?
NO. I APPROVE IN PRINCIPLE, BUT I CAN'T SEE MYSELF STANDING ON THE STREET, SHOUTING.
PLEASE?
IT'S UNDIGNIFIED. SEE YOU IN CREATIVE WRITING.
IF SOCIETY HASN'T COLLAPSED BY THEN DUE TO YOUR APATHY.

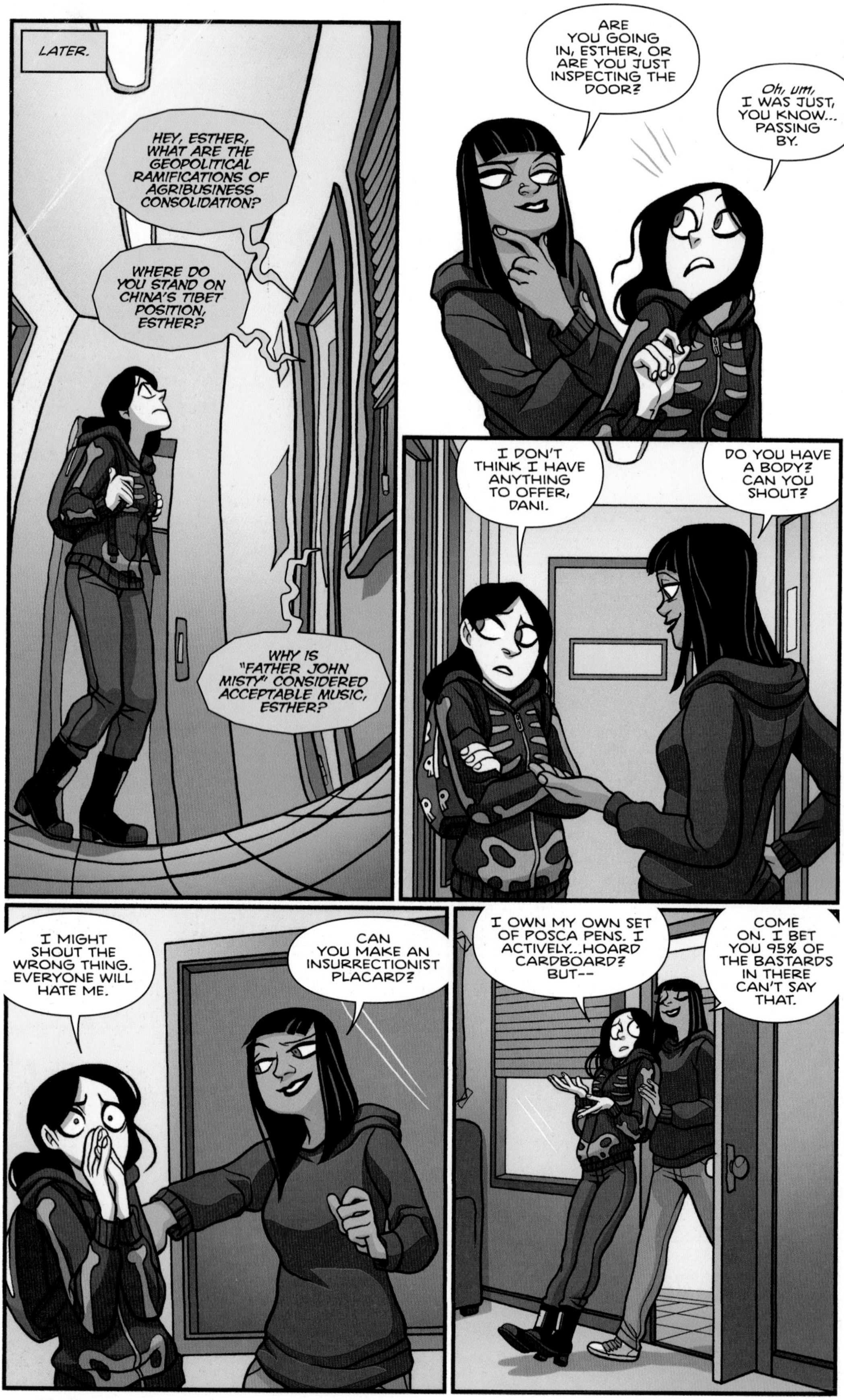
LATER.
HEY, ESTHER, WHAT ARE THE GEOPOLITICAL RAMIFICATIONS OF AGRIBUSINESS CONSOLIDATION?
WHERE DO YOU STAND ON CHINA'S TIBET POSITION, ESTHER?
WHY IS "FATHER JOHN MISTY" CONSIDERED ACCEPTABLE MUSIC, ESTHER?
ARE YOU GOING IN, ESTHER, OR ARE YOU JUST INSPECTING THE DOOR?
Oh, um, I WAS JUST, YOU KNOW... PASSING BY.
I DON'T THINK I HAVE ANYTHING TO OFFER, DANI.
DO YOU HAVE A BODY? CAN YOU SHOUT?
I MIGHT SHOUT THE WRONG THING. EVERYONE WILL HATE ME.
CAN YOU MAKE AN INSURRECTIONIST PLACARD?
I OWN MY OWN SET OF POSCA PENS. I ACTIVELY...HOARD CARDBOARD? BUT--
COME ON. I BET YOU 95% OF THE BASTARDS IN THERE CAN'T SAY THAT.

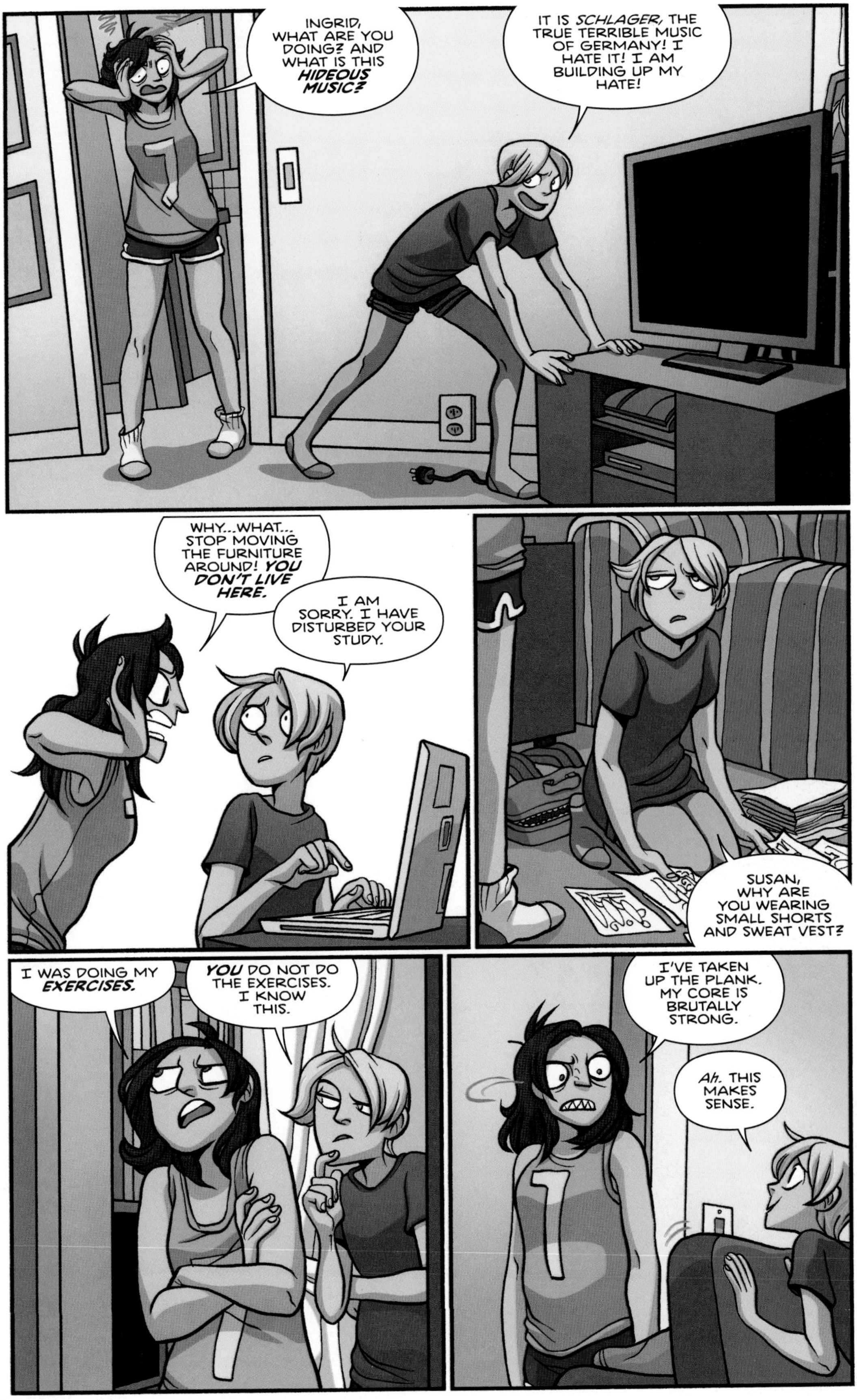

INGRID, WHAT ARE YOU DOING? AND WHAT IS THIS ***HIDEOUS MUSIC?***
IT IS *SCHLAGER,* THE TRUE TERRIBLE MUSIC OF GERMANY! I HATE IT! I AM BUILDING UP MY HATE!
WHY...WHAT... STOP MOVING THE FURNITURE AROUND! ***YOU DON'T LIVE HERE.***
I AM SORRY. I HAVE DISTURBED YOUR STUDY.
SUSAN, WHY ARE YOU WEARING SMALL SHORTS AND SWEAT VEST?
I WAS DOING MY ***EXERCISES.***
YOU DO NOT DO THE EXERCISES. I KNOW THIS.
I'VE TAKEN UP THE PLANK. MY CORE IS BRUTALLY STRONG.
Ah. THIS MAKES SENSE.

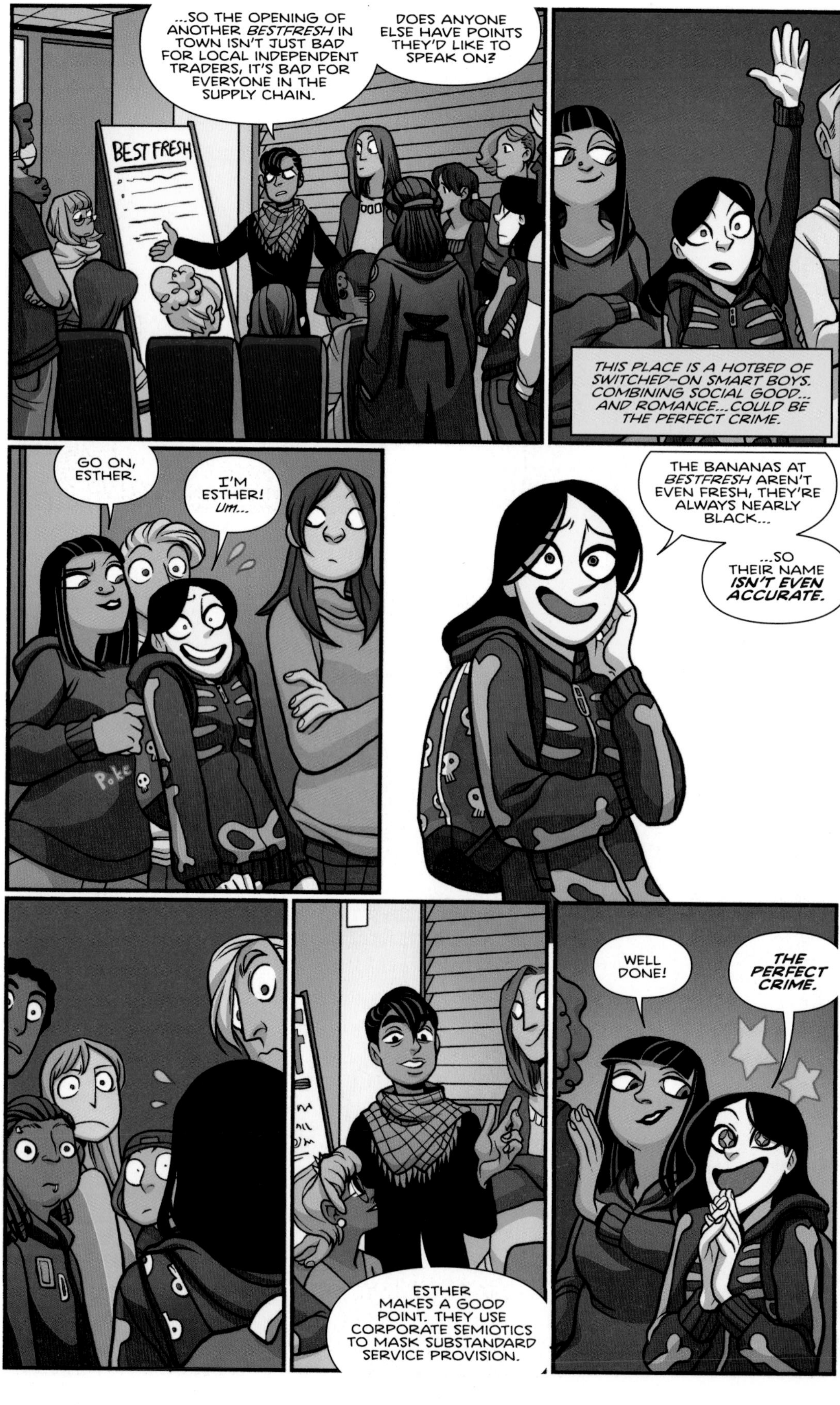

...SO THE OPENING OF ANOTHER *BESTFRESH* IN TOWN ISN'T JUST BAD FOR LOCAL INDEPENDENT TRADERS, IT'S BAD FOR EVERYONE IN THE SUPPLY CHAIN.
DOES ANYONE ELSE HAVE POINTS THEY'D LIKE TO SPEAK ON?
BEST FRESH
THIS PLACE IS A HOTBED OF SWITCHED-ON SMART BOYS. COMBINING SOCIAL GOOD... AND ROMANCE...COULD BE THE PERFECT CRIME.
GO ON, ESTHER.
I'M ESTHER! *UM...*
Poke
THE BANANAS AT *BESTFRESH* AREN'T EVEN FRESH, THEY'RE ALWAYS NEARLY BLACK...
...SO THEIR NAME ***ISN'T EVEN ACCURATE.***
ESTHER MAKES A GOOD POINT. THEY USE CORPORATE SEMIOTICS TO MASK SUBSTANDARD SERVICE PROVISION.
WELL DONE!
THE PERFECT CRIME.

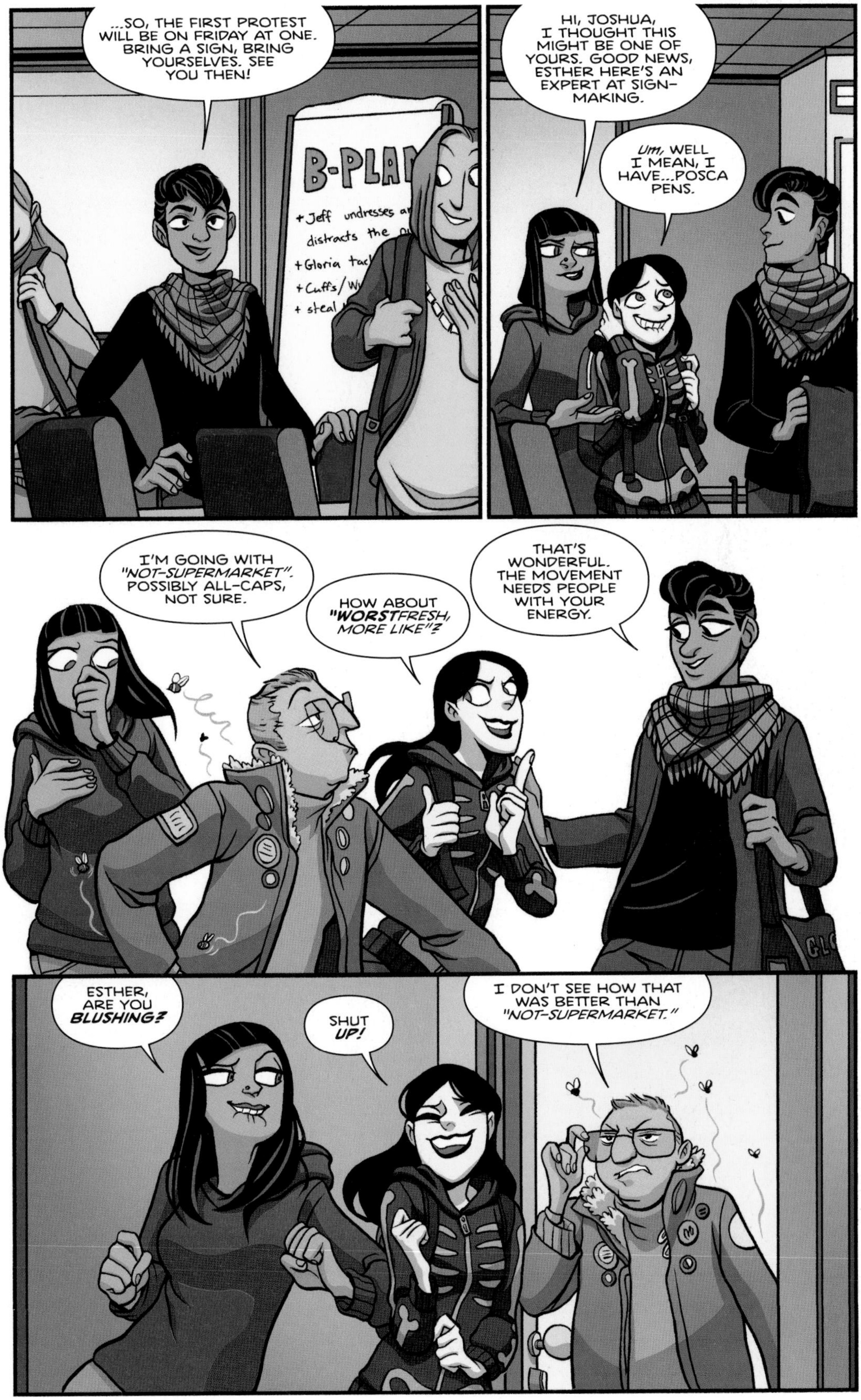

...SO, THE FIRST PROTEST WILL BE ON FRIDAY AT ONE. BRING A SIGN, BRING YOURSELVES. SEE YOU THEN!
B-PLAN
+ Jeff undresses a
distracts the
+ Gloria tac
+ Cuffs/
+ steal
HI, JOSHUA, I THOUGHT THIS MIGHT BE ONE OF YOURS. GOOD NEWS, ESTHER HERE'S AN EXPERT AT SIGN-MAKING.
UM, WELL I MEAN, I HAVE...POSCA PENS.
I'M GOING WITH *"NOT-SUPERMARKET"*. POSSIBLY ALL-CAPS, NOT SURE.
HOW ABOUT ***"WORST****FRESH, MORE LIKE"*?
THAT'S WONDERFUL. THE MOVEMENT NEEDS PEOPLE WITH YOUR ENERGY.
ESTHER, ARE YOU ***BLUSHING?***
SHUT ***UP!***
I DON'T SEE HOW THAT WAS BETTER THAN *"NOT-SUPERMARKET."*

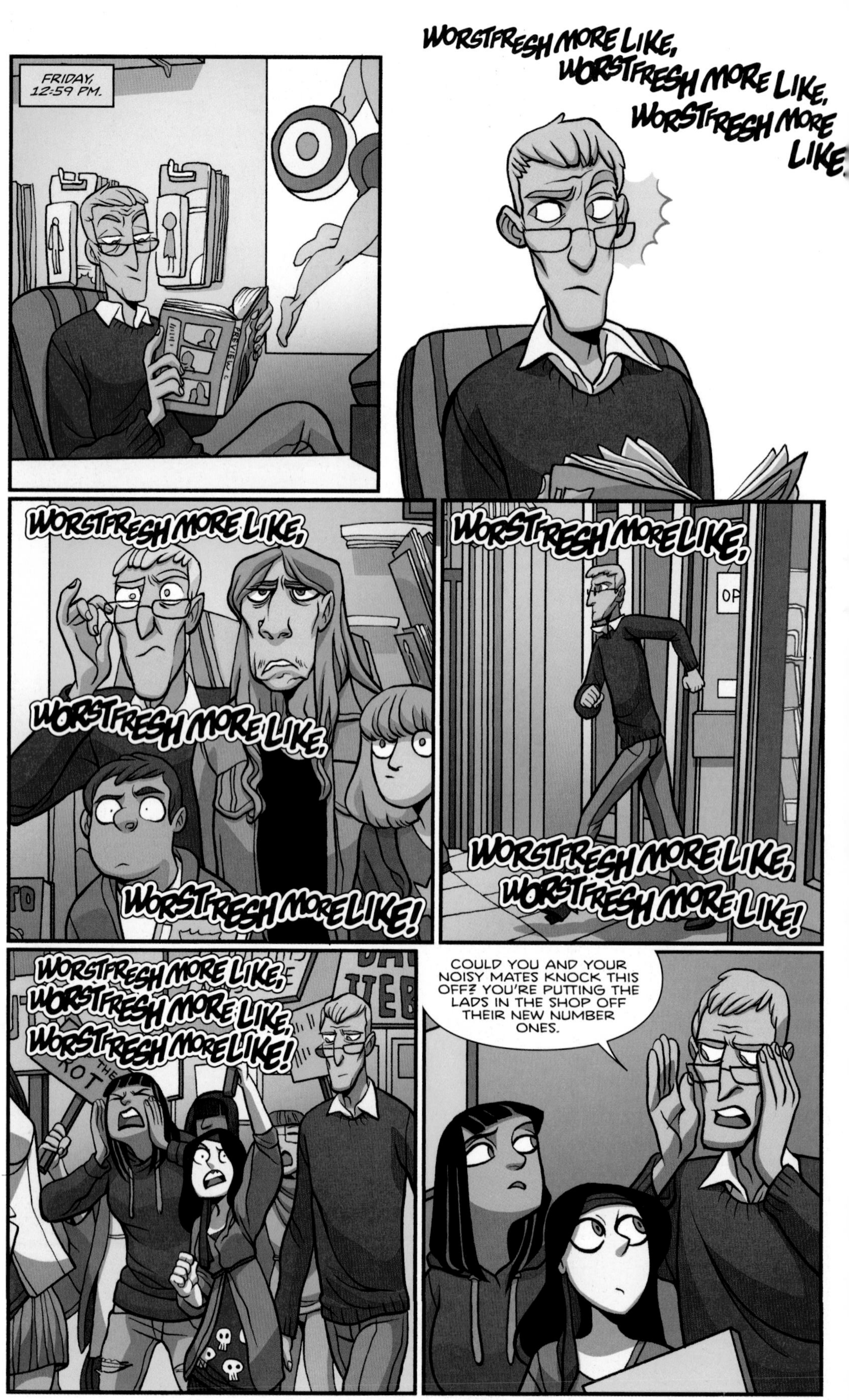
FRIDAY, 12:59 PM.
PREVIEWS
WORSTFRESH MORE LIKE,
WORSTFRESH MORE LIKE,
WORSTFRESH MORE LIKE.
WORSTFRESH MORE LIKE,
WORSTFRESH MORE LIKE,
WORSTFRESH MORE LIKE!
WORSTFRESH MORE LIKE,
WORSTFRESH MORE LIKE,
WORSTFRESH MORE LIKE!
WORSTFRESH MORE LIKE,
WORSTFRESH MORE LIKE,
WORSTFRESH MORE LIKE!
COULD YOU AND YOUR NOISY MATES KNOCK THIS OFF? YOU'RE PUTTING THE LADS IN THE SHOP OFF THEIR NEW NUMBER ONES.

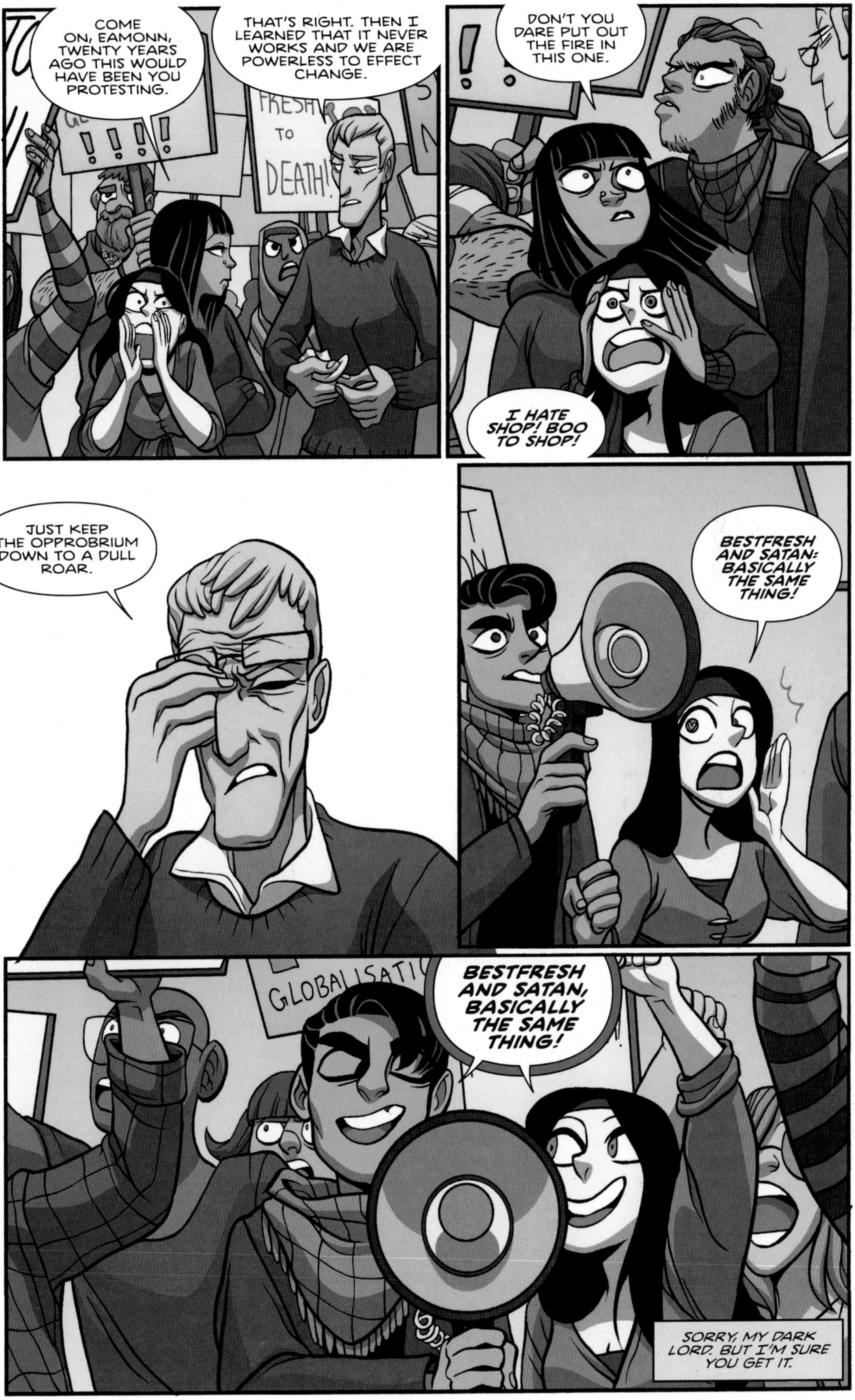
COME ON, EAMONN, TWENTY YEARS AGO THIS WOULD HAVE BEEN YOU PROTESTING.
THAT'S RIGHT. THEN I LEARNED THAT IT NEVER WORKS AND WE ARE POWERLESS TO EFFECT CHANGE.
FRESH TO DEATH!
DON'T YOU DARE PUT OUT THE FIRE IN THIS ONE.
I HATE SHOP! BOO TO SHOP!
JUST KEEP THE OPPROBRIUM DOWN TO A DULL ROAR.
BESTFRESH AND SATAN: BASICALLY THE SAME THING!
GLOBALISATI
BESTFRESH AND SATAN, BASICALLY THE SAME THING!
SORRY, MY DARK LORD. BUT I'M SURE YOU GET IT.

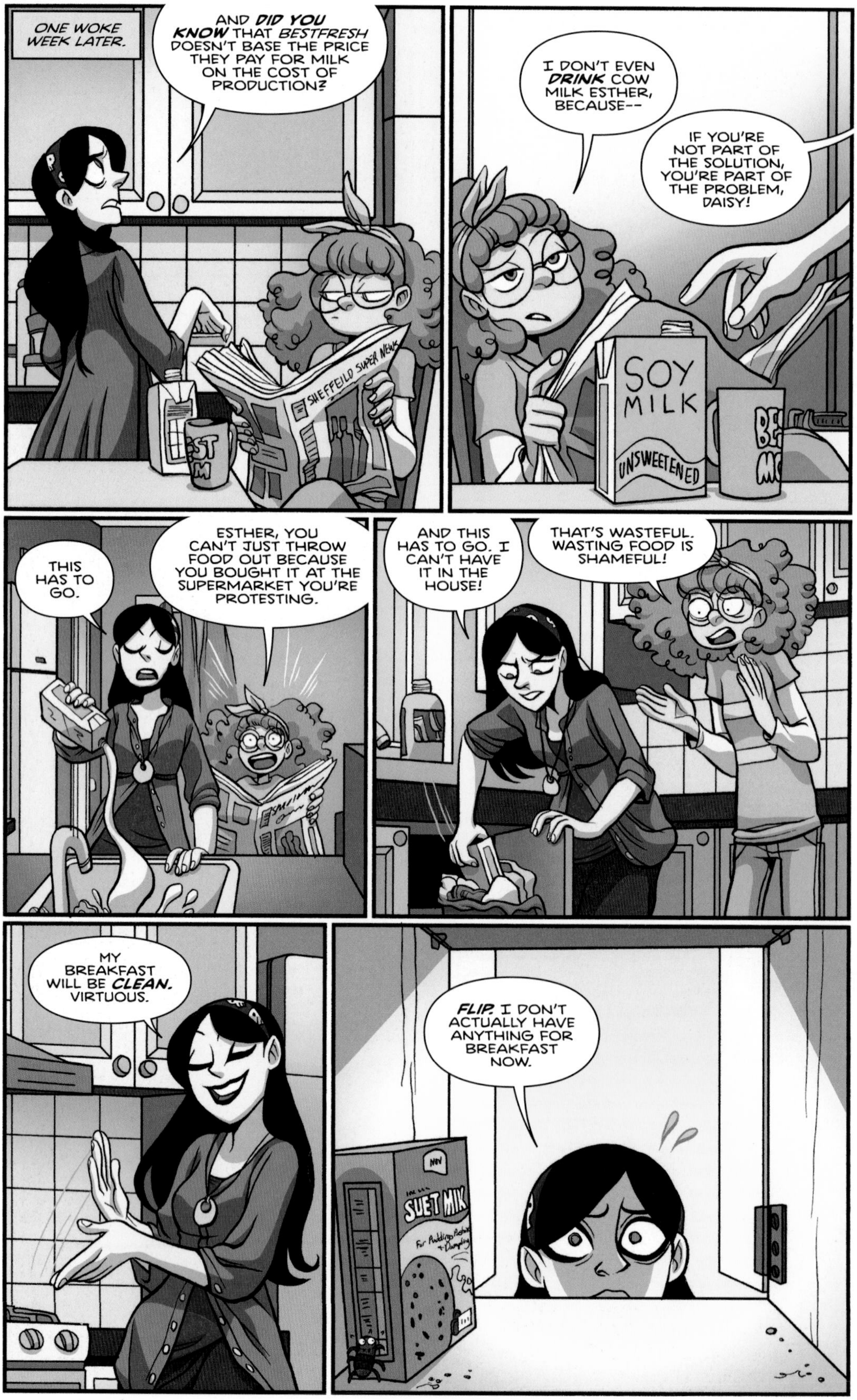
ONE WOKE WEEK LATER.
AND DID YOU KNOW THAT BESTFRESH DOESN'T BASE THE PRICE THEY PAY FOR MILK ON THE COST OF PRODUCTION?
SHEFFEILD SUPER NEWS
I DON'T EVEN DRINK COW MILK ESTHER, BECAUSE--
IF YOU'RE NOT PART OF THE SOLUTION, YOU'RE PART OF THE PROBLEM, DAISY!
SOY MILK
UNSWEETENED
THIS HAS TO GO.
ESTHER, YOU CAN'T JUST THROW FOOD OUT BECAUSE YOU BOUGHT IT AT THE SUPERMARKET YOU'RE PROTESTING.
AND THIS HAS TO GO. I CAN'T HAVE IT IN THE HOUSE!
THAT'S WASTEFUL. WASTING FOOD IS SHAMEFUL!
MY BREAKFAST WILL BE CLEAN. VIRTUOUS.
FLIP. I DON'T ACTUALLY HAVE ANYTHING FOR BREAKFAST NOW.
SUET MIX

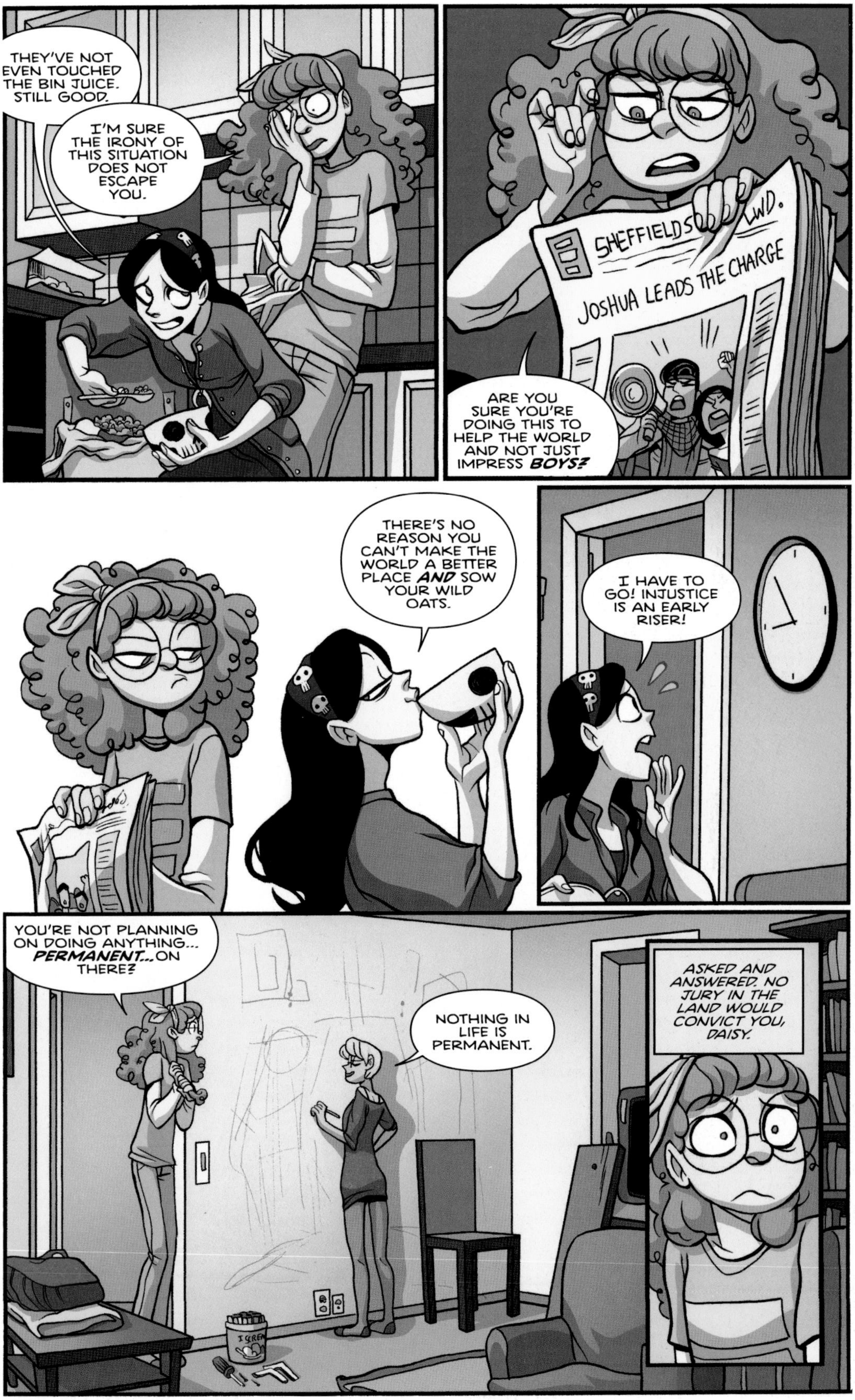
THEY'VE NOT EVEN TOUCHED THE BIN JUICE. STILL GOOD.
I'M SURE THE IRONY OF THIS SITUATION DOES NOT ESCAPE YOU.
SHEFFIELDS
LWD.
JOSHUA LEADS THE CHARGE
ARE YOU SURE YOU'RE DOING THIS TO HELP THE WORLD AND NOT JUST IMPRESS BOYS?
THERE'S NO REASON YOU CAN'T MAKE THE WORLD A BETTER PLACE AND SOW YOUR WILD OATS.
I HAVE TO GO! INJUSTICE IS AN EARLY RISER!
YOU'RE NOT PLANNING ON DOING ANYTHING... PERMANENT...ON THERE?
NOTHING IN LIFE IS PERMANENT.
ASKED AND ANSWERED. NO JURY IN THE LAND WOULD CONVICT YOU, DAISY.

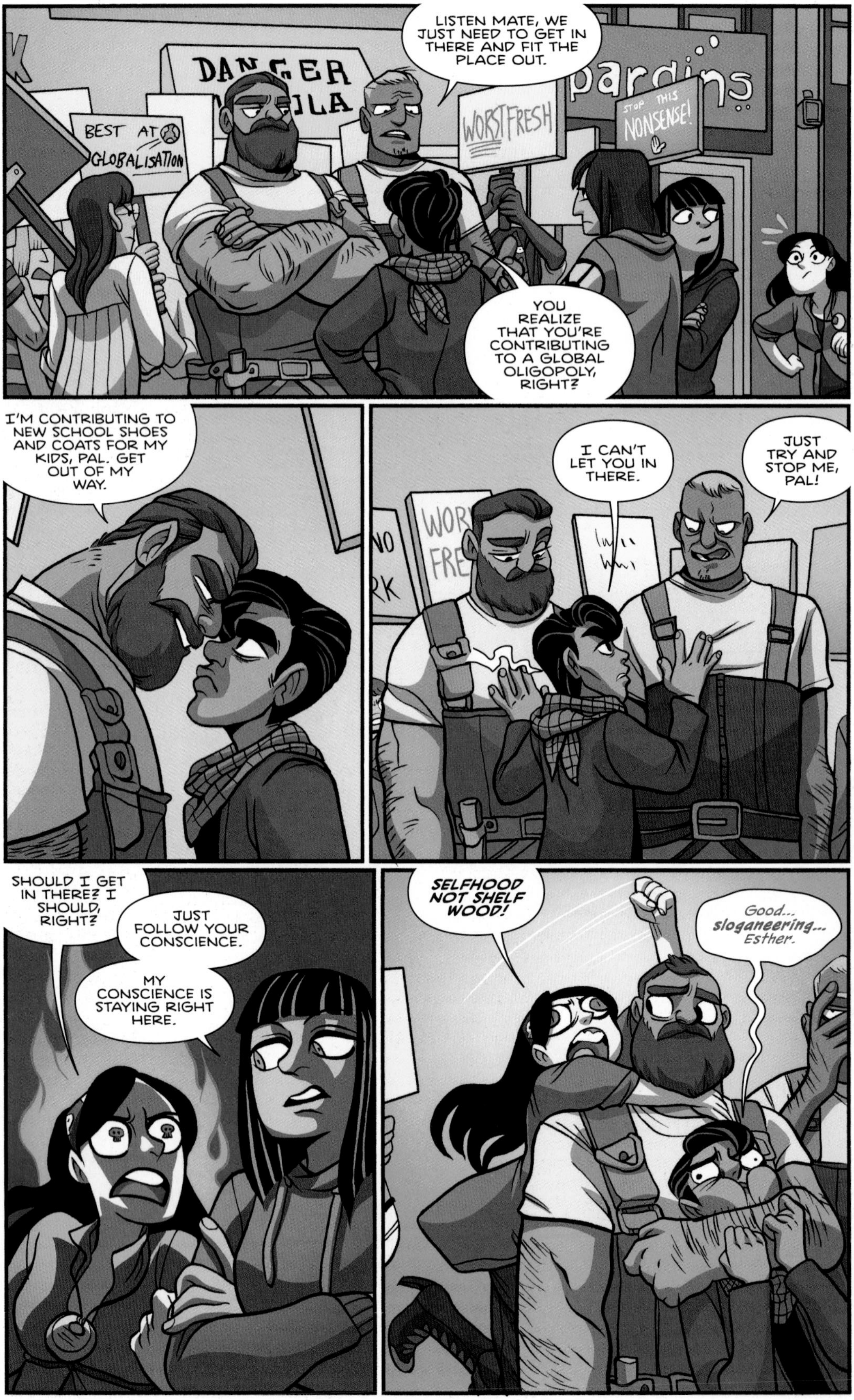

DANGER
BEST AT GLOBALISATION
WORSTFRESH
STOP THIS NONSENSE!
LISTEN MATE, WE JUST NEED TO GET IN THERE AND FIT THE PLACE OUT.
YOU REALIZE THAT YOU'RE CONTRIBUTING TO A GLOBAL OLIGOPOLY, RIGHT?
I'M CONTRIBUTING TO NEW SCHOOL SHOES AND COATS FOR MY KIDS, PAL. GET OUT OF MY WAY.
I CAN'T LET YOU IN THERE.
JUST TRY AND STOP ME, PAL!
SHOULD I GET IN THERE? I SHOULD, RIGHT?
JUST FOLLOW YOUR CONSCIENCE.
MY CONSCIENCE IS STAYING RIGHT HERE.
SELFHOOD NOT SHELF WOOD!
Good... sloganeering... Esther.

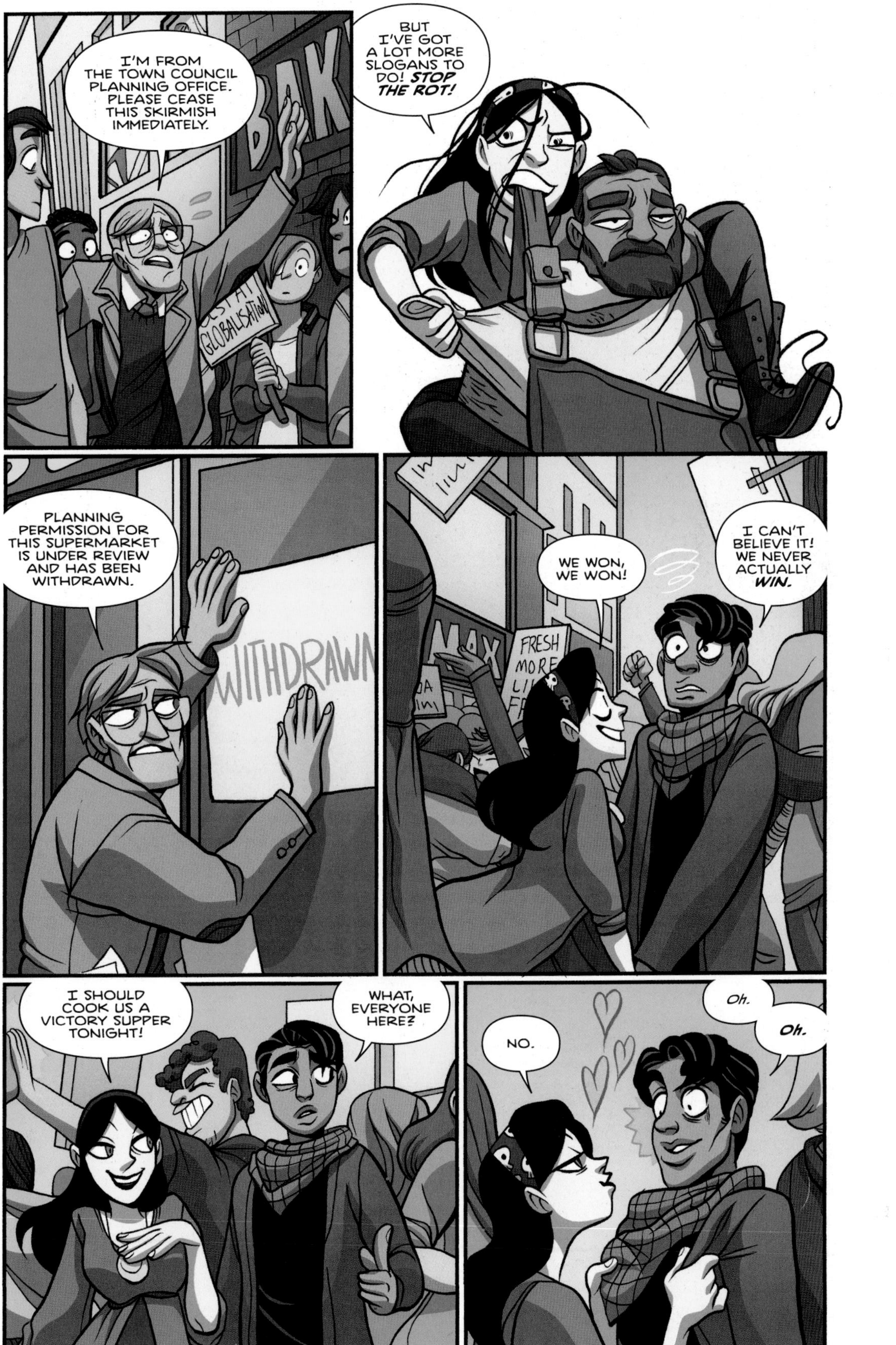
I'M FROM THE TOWN COUNCIL PLANNING OFFICE. PLEASE CEASE THIS SKIRMISH IMMEDIATELY.
BAK
GLOBALISATION
BUT I'VE GOT A LOT MORE SLOGANS TO DO! *STOP THE ROT!*
PLANNING PERMISSION FOR THIS SUPERMARKET IS UNDER REVIEW AND HAS BEEN WITHDRAWN.
WITHDRAWN
WE WON, WE WON!
I CAN'T BELIEVE IT! WE NEVER ACTUALLY *WIN.*
MAX
FRESH MORE
I SHOULD COOK US A VICTORY SUPPER TONIGHT!
WHAT, EVERYONE HERE?
NO.
Oh.
Oh.

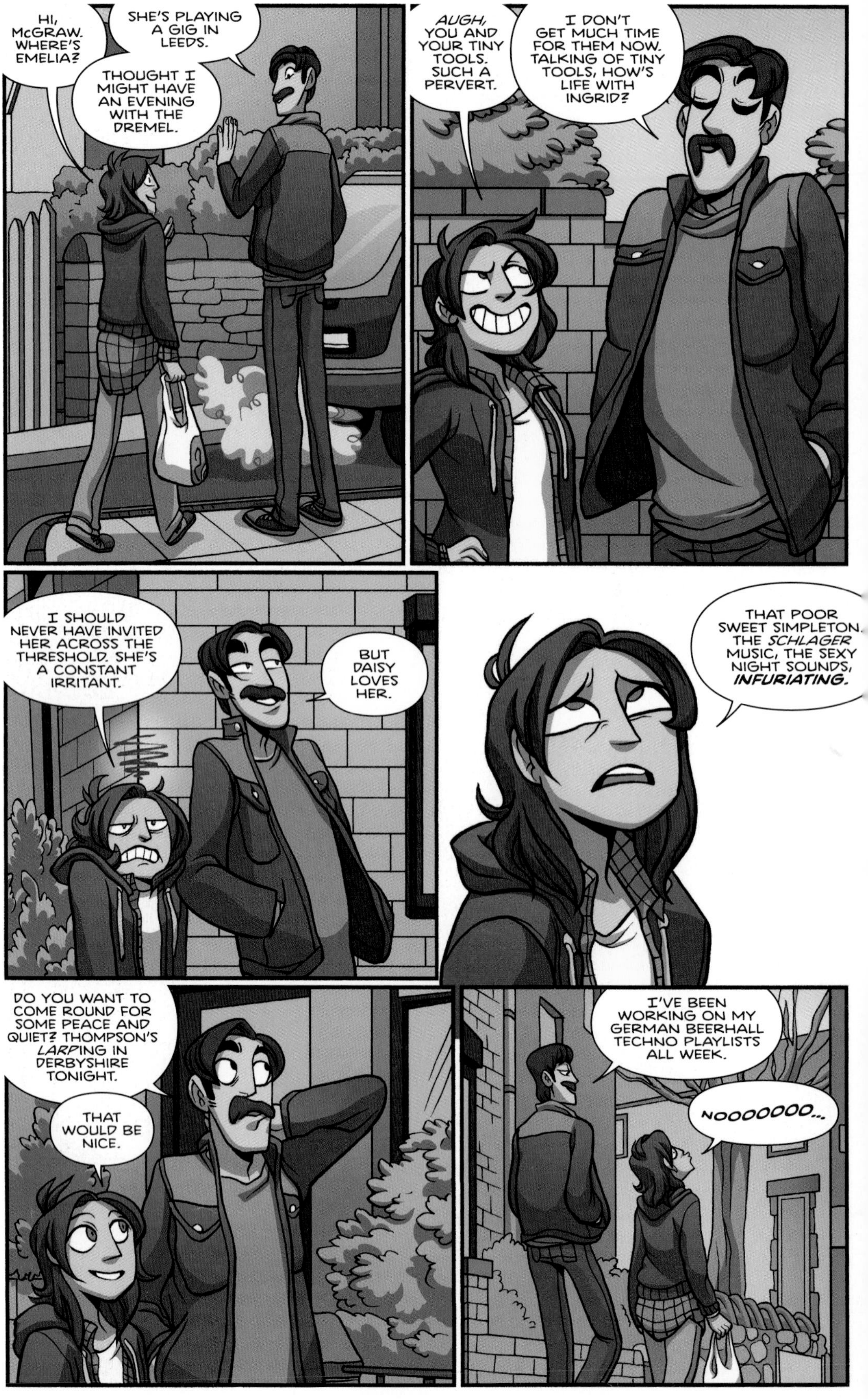
HI, McGRAW. WHERE'S EMELIA?
SHE'S PLAYING A GIG IN LEEDS.
THOUGHT I MIGHT HAVE AN EVENING WITH THE DREMEL.
AUGH, YOU AND YOUR TINY TOOLS. SUCH A PERVERT.
I DON'T GET MUCH TIME FOR THEM NOW. TALKING OF TINY TOOLS, HOW'S LIFE WITH INGRID?
I SHOULD NEVER HAVE INVITED HER ACROSS THE THRESHOLD. SHE'S A CONSTANT IRRITANT.
BUT DAISY LOVES HER.
THAT POOR SWEET SIMPLETON. THE *SCHLAGER* MUSIC, THE SEXY NIGHT SOUNDS, ***INFURIATING.***
DO YOU WANT TO COME ROUND FOR SOME PEACE AND QUIET? THOMPSON'S *LARP*ING IN DERBYSHIRE TONIGHT.
THAT WOULD BE NICE.
I'VE BEEN WORKING ON MY GERMAN BEERHALL TECHNO PLAYLISTS ALL WEEK.
NOOOOOOO...

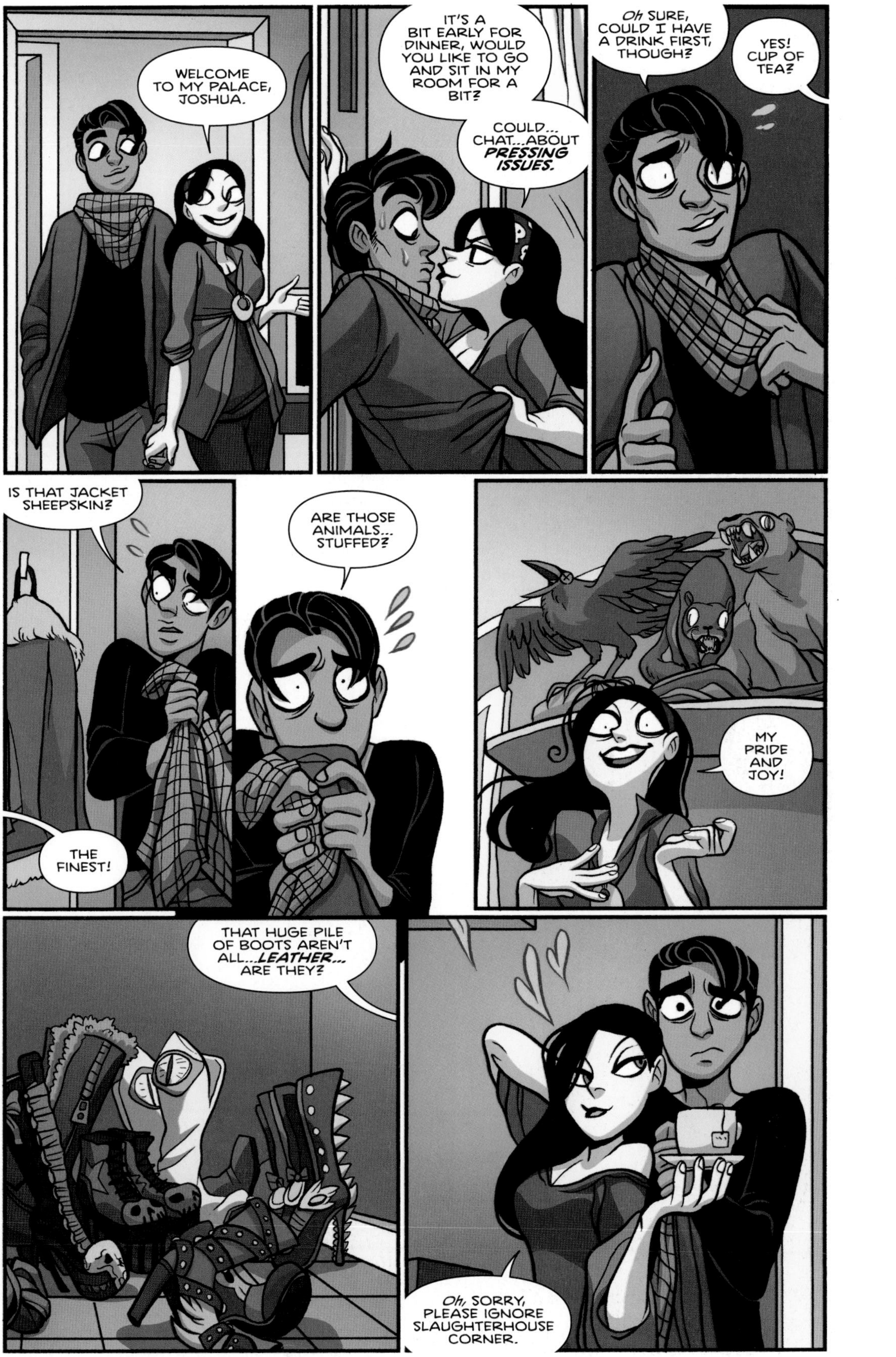
WELCOME TO MY PALACE, JOSHUA.
IT'S A BIT EARLY FOR DINNER, WOULD YOU LIKE TO GO AND SIT IN MY ROOM FOR A BIT?
COULD... CHAT...ABOUT *PRESSING ISSUES.*
Oh SURE, COULD I HAVE A DRINK FIRST, THOUGH?
YES! CUP OF TEA?
IS THAT JACKET SHEEPSKIN?
THE FINEST!
ARE THOSE ANIMALS... STUFFED?
MY PRIDE AND JOY!
THAT HUGE PILE OF BOOTS AREN'T ALL...*LEATHER...* ARE THEY?
Oh, SORRY, PLEASE IGNORE SLAUGHTERHOUSE CORNER.

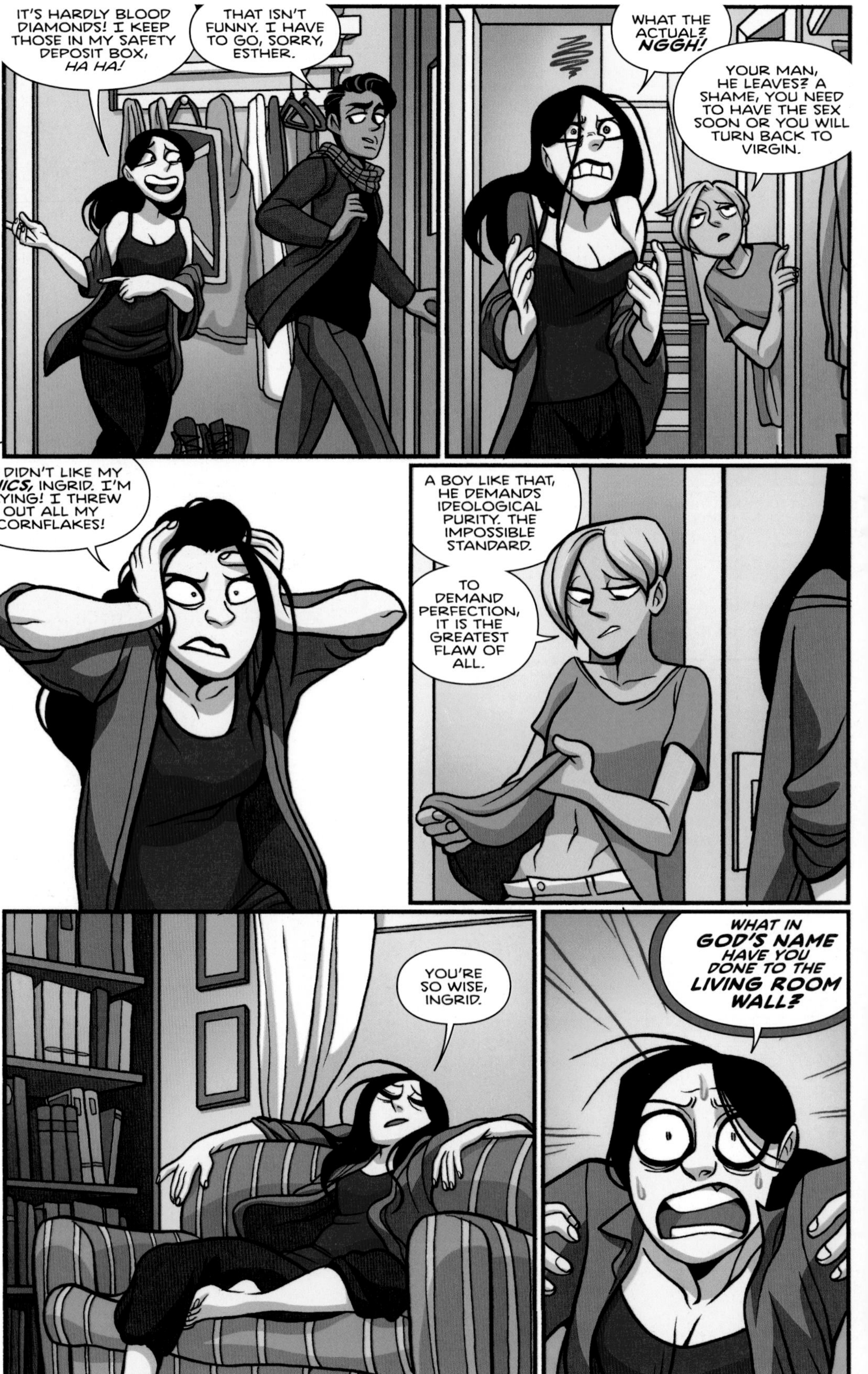
IT'S HARDLY BLOOD DIAMONDS! I KEEP THOSE IN MY SAFETY DEPOSIT BOX, *HA HA!*
THAT ISN'T FUNNY. I HAVE TO GO, SORRY, ESTHER.
WHAT THE ACTUAL? ***NGGH!***
YOUR MAN, HE LEAVES? A SHAME, YOU NEED TO HAVE THE SEX SOON OR YOU WILL TURN BACK TO VIRGIN.
HE DIDN'T LIKE MY ***ETHICS,*** INGRID. I'M TRYING! I THREW OUT ALL MY CORNFLAKES!
A BOY LIKE THAT, HE DEMANDS IDEOLOGICAL PURITY. THE IMPOSSIBLE STANDARD.
TO DEMAND PERFECTION, IT IS THE GREATEST FLAW OF ALL.
YOU'RE SO WISE, INGRID.
WHAT IN GOD'S NAME HAVE YOU DONE TO THE LIVING ROOM WALL?

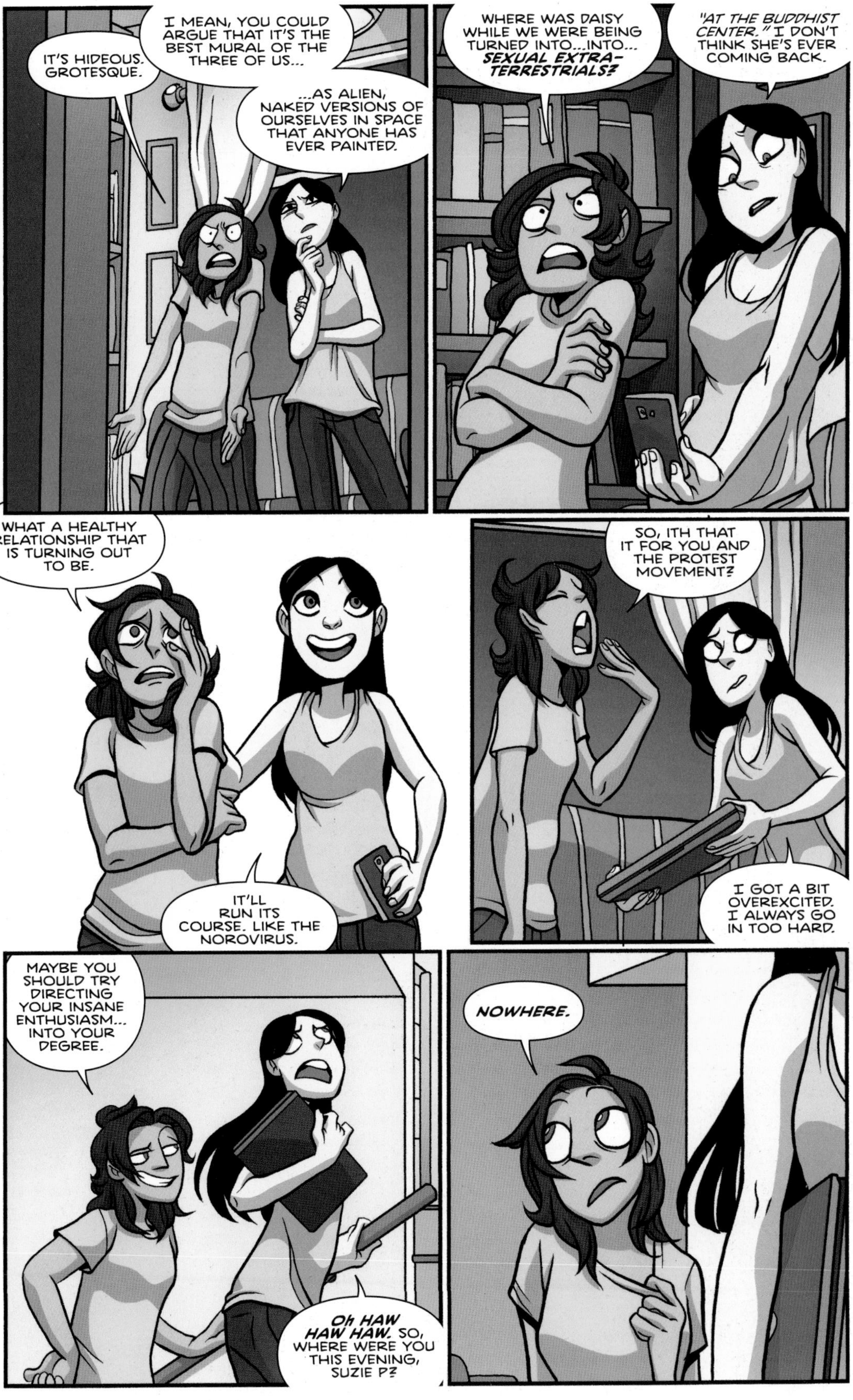
IT'S HIDEOUS. GROTESQUE.
I MEAN, YOU COULD ARGUE THAT IT'S THE BEST MURAL OF THE THREE OF US...
...AS ALIEN, NAKED VERSIONS OF OURSELVES IN SPACE THAT ANYONE HAS EVER PAINTED.
WHERE WAS DAISY WHILE WE WERE BEING TURNED INTO...INTO... SEXUAL EXTRA-TERRESTRIALS?
"AT THE BUDDHIST CENTER." I DON'T THINK SHE'S EVER COMING BACK.
WHAT A HEALTHY RELATIONSHIP THAT IS TURNING OUT TO BE.
IT'LL RUN ITS COURSE. LIKE THE NOROVIRUS.
SO, ITH THAT IT FOR YOU AND THE PROTEST MOVEMENT?
I GOT A BIT OVEREXCITED. I ALWAYS GO IN TOO HARD.
MAYBE YOU SHOULD TRY DIRECTING YOUR INSANE ENTHUSIASM... INTO YOUR DEGREE.
Oh HAW HAW HAW. SO, WHERE WERE YOU THIS EVENING, SUZIE P?
NOWHERE.

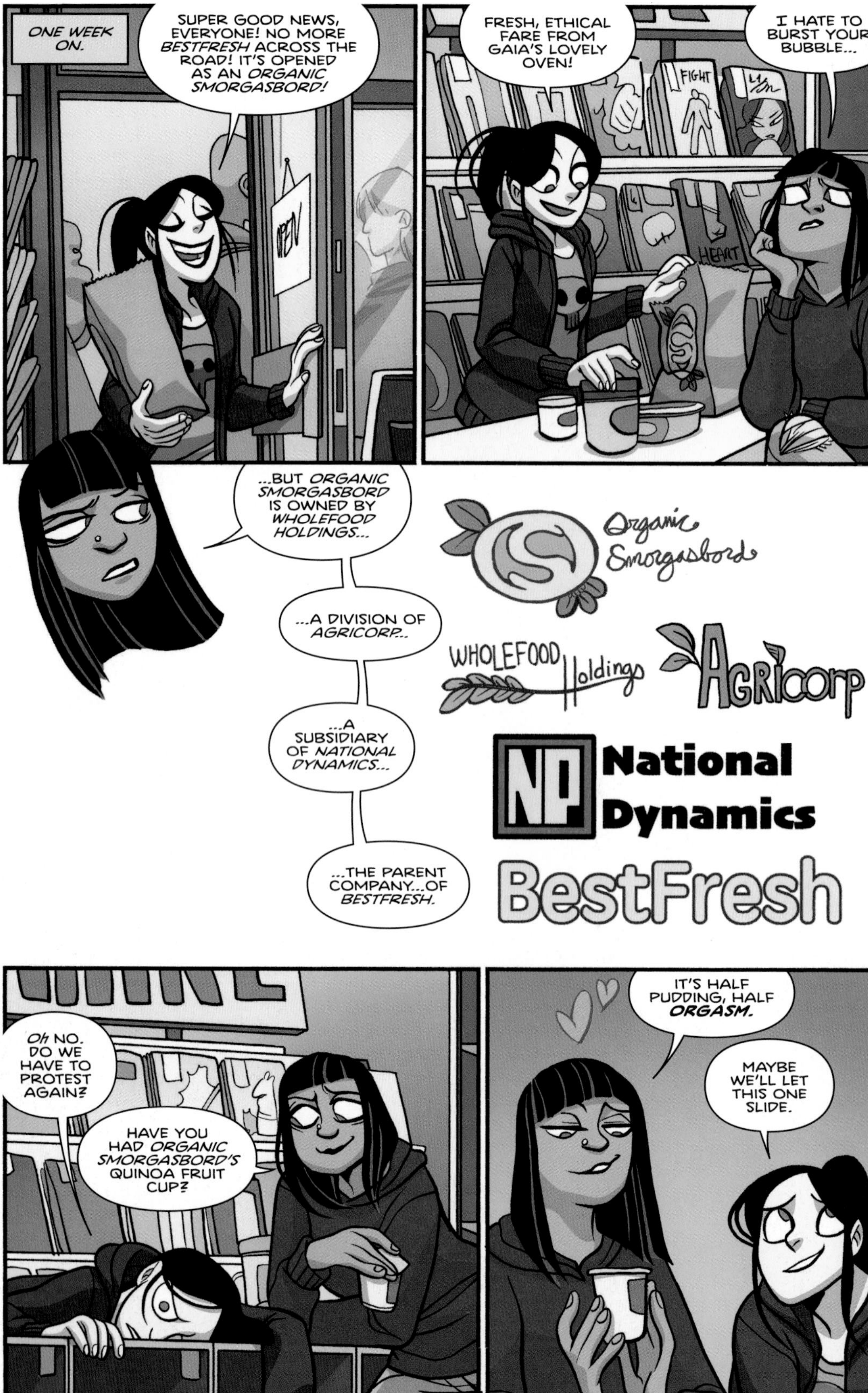

ONE WEEK ON.
SUPER GOOD NEWS, EVERYONE! NO MORE BESTFRESH ACROSS THE ROAD! IT'S OPENED AS AN ORGANIC SMORGASBORD!
OPEN
FRESH, ETHICAL FARE FROM GAIA'S LOVELY OVEN!
I HATE TO BURST YOUR BUBBLE...
FIGHT
HEART
...BUT ORGANIC SMORGASBORD IS OWNED BY WHOLEFOOD HOLDINGS...
...A DIVISION OF AGRICORP...
...A SUBSIDIARY OF NATIONAL DYNAMICS...
...THE PARENT COMPANY...OF BESTFRESH.
Organic Smorgasbord
WHOLEFOOD Holdings
AGRIcorp
ND National Dynamics
BestFresh
Oh NO. DO WE HAVE TO PROTEST AGAIN?
HAVE YOU HAD ORGANIC SMORGASBORD'S QUINOA FRUIT CUP?
IT'S HALF PUDDING, HALF ORGASM.
MAYBE WE'LL LET THIS ONE SLIDE.

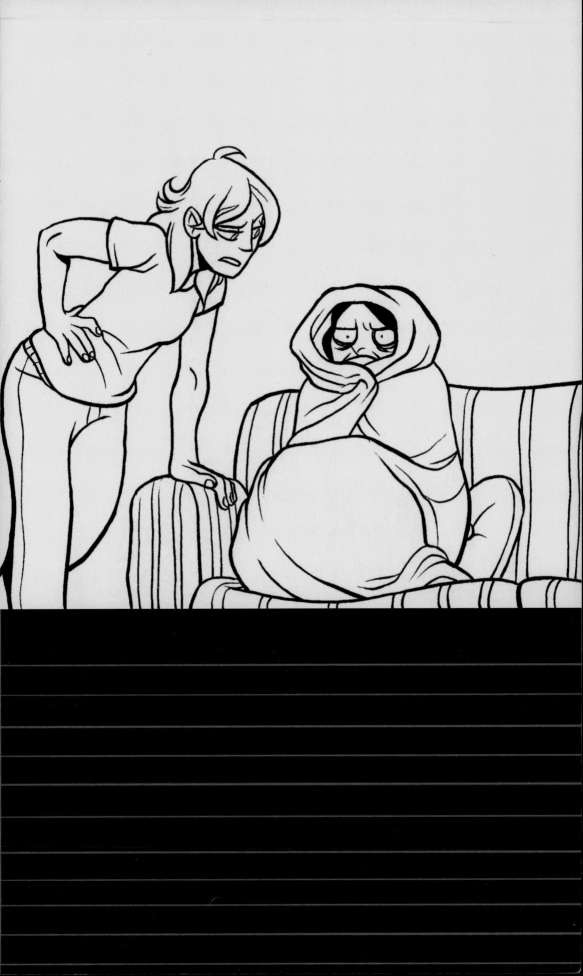

CHAPTER TWENTY EIGHT

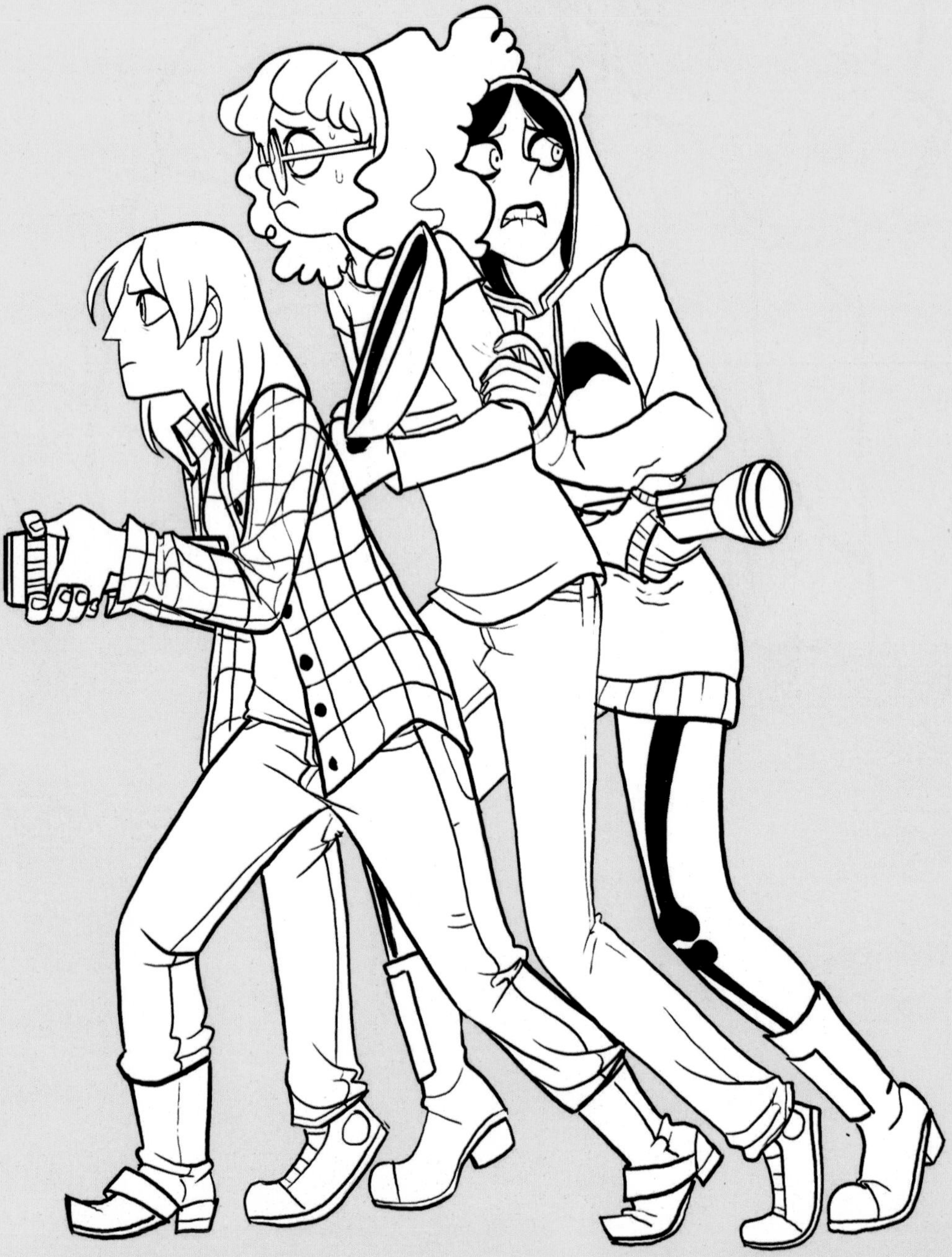

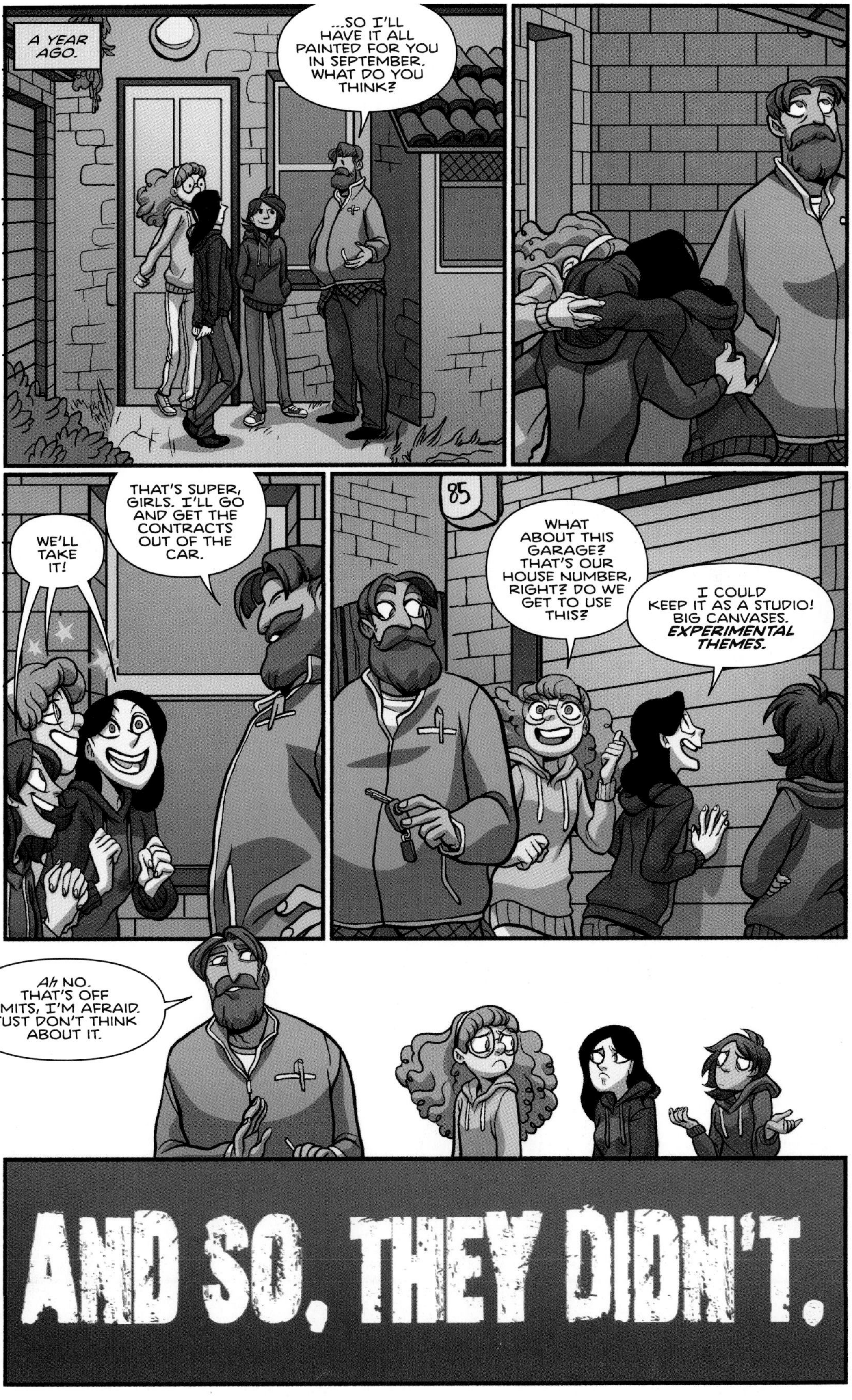
A YEAR AGO.
...SO I'LL HAVE IT ALL PAINTED FOR YOU IN SEPTEMBER. WHAT DO YOU THINK?
WE'LL TAKE IT!
THAT'S SUPER, GIRLS. I'LL GO AND GET THE CONTRACTS OUT OF THE CAR.
85
WHAT ABOUT THIS GARAGE? THAT'S OUR HOUSE NUMBER, RIGHT? DO WE GET TO USE THIS?
I COULD KEEP IT AS A STUDIO! BIG CANVASES. EXPERIMENTAL THEMES.
Ah NO. THAT'S OFF LIMITS, I'M AFRAID. JUST DON'T THINK ABOUT IT.
AND SO, THEY DIDN'T.

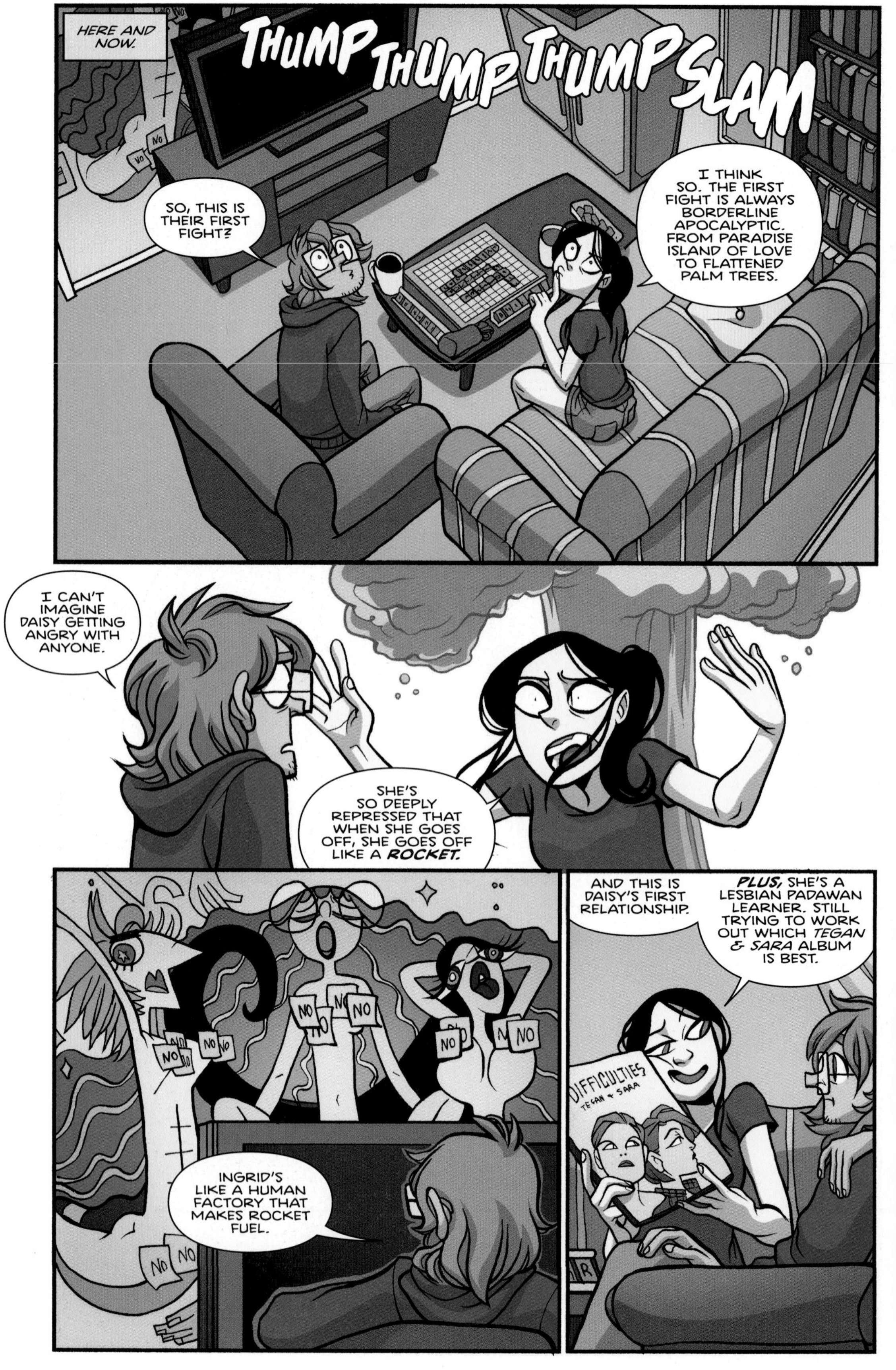
HERE AND NOW.
THUMP THUMP THUMP SLAM
SO, THIS IS THEIR FIRST FIGHT?
I THINK SO. THE FIRST FIGHT IS ALWAYS BORDERLINE APOCALYPTIC. FROM PARADISE ISLAND OF LOVE TO FLATTENED PALM TREES.
I CAN'T IMAGINE DAISY GETTING ANGRY WITH ANYONE.
SHE'S SO DEEPLY REPRESSED THAT WHEN SHE GOES OFF, SHE GOES OFF LIKE A ROCKET.
NO
INGRID'S LIKE A HUMAN FACTORY THAT MAKES ROCKET FUEL.
AND THIS IS DAISY'S FIRST RELATIONSHIP.
PLUS, SHE'S A LESBIAN PADAWAN LEARNER. STILL TRYING TO WORK OUT WHICH TEGAN & SARA ALBUM IS BEST.
DIFFICULTIES
TEGAN & SARA

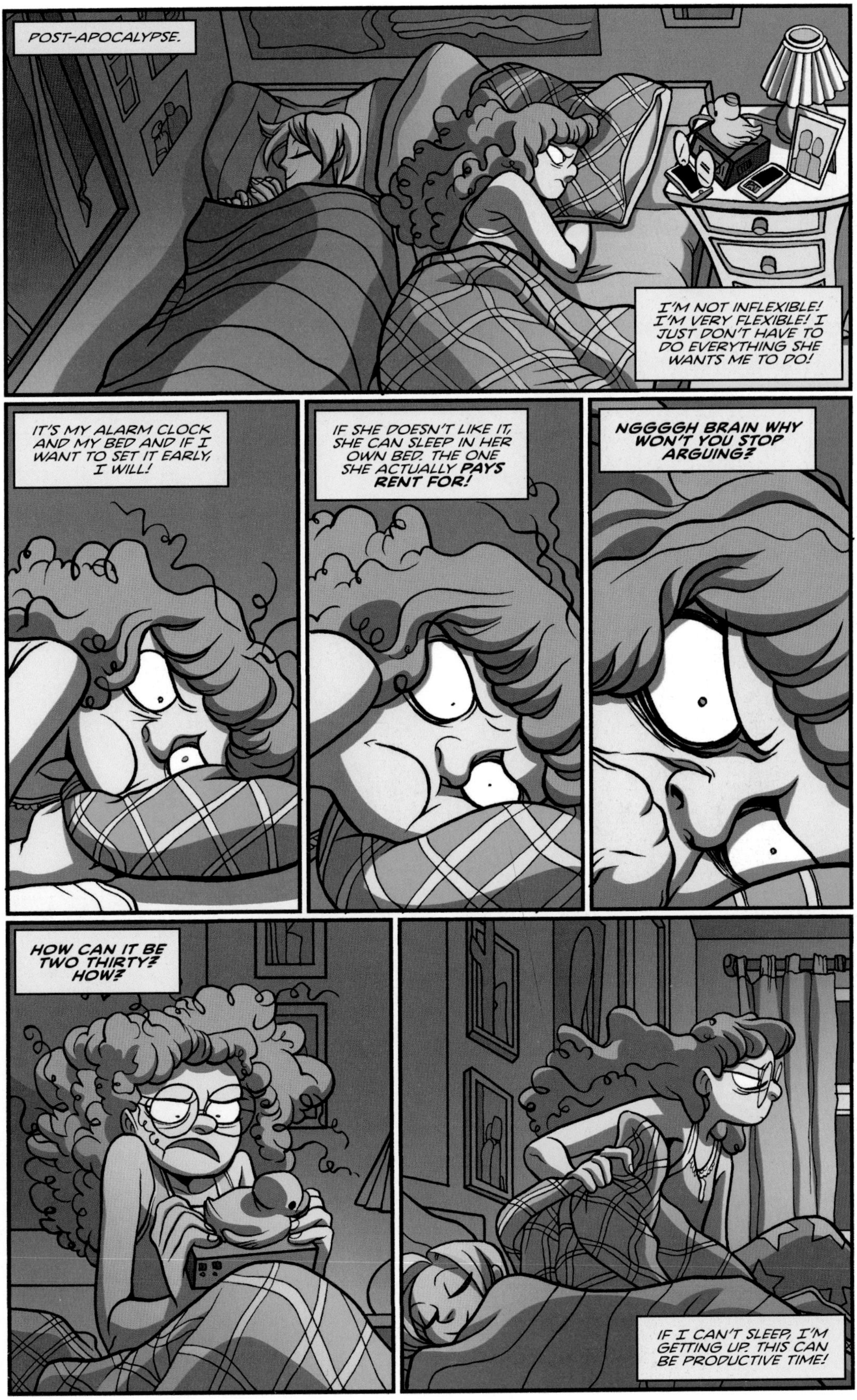
POST-APOCALYPSE.
I'M NOT INFLEXIBLE! I'M VERY FLEXIBLE! I JUST DON'T HAVE TO DO EVERYTHING SHE WANTS ME TO DO!
IT'S MY ALARM CLOCK AND MY BED AND IF I WANT TO SET IT EARLY, I WILL!
IF SHE DOESN'T LIKE IT, SHE CAN SLEEP IN HER OWN BED. THE ONE SHE ACTUALLY PAYS RENT FOR!
NGGGGH BRAIN WHY WON'T YOU STOP ARGUING?
HOW CAN IT BE TWO THIRTY? HOW?
IF I CAN'T SLEEP, I'M GETTING UP. THIS CAN BE PRODUCTIVE TIME!

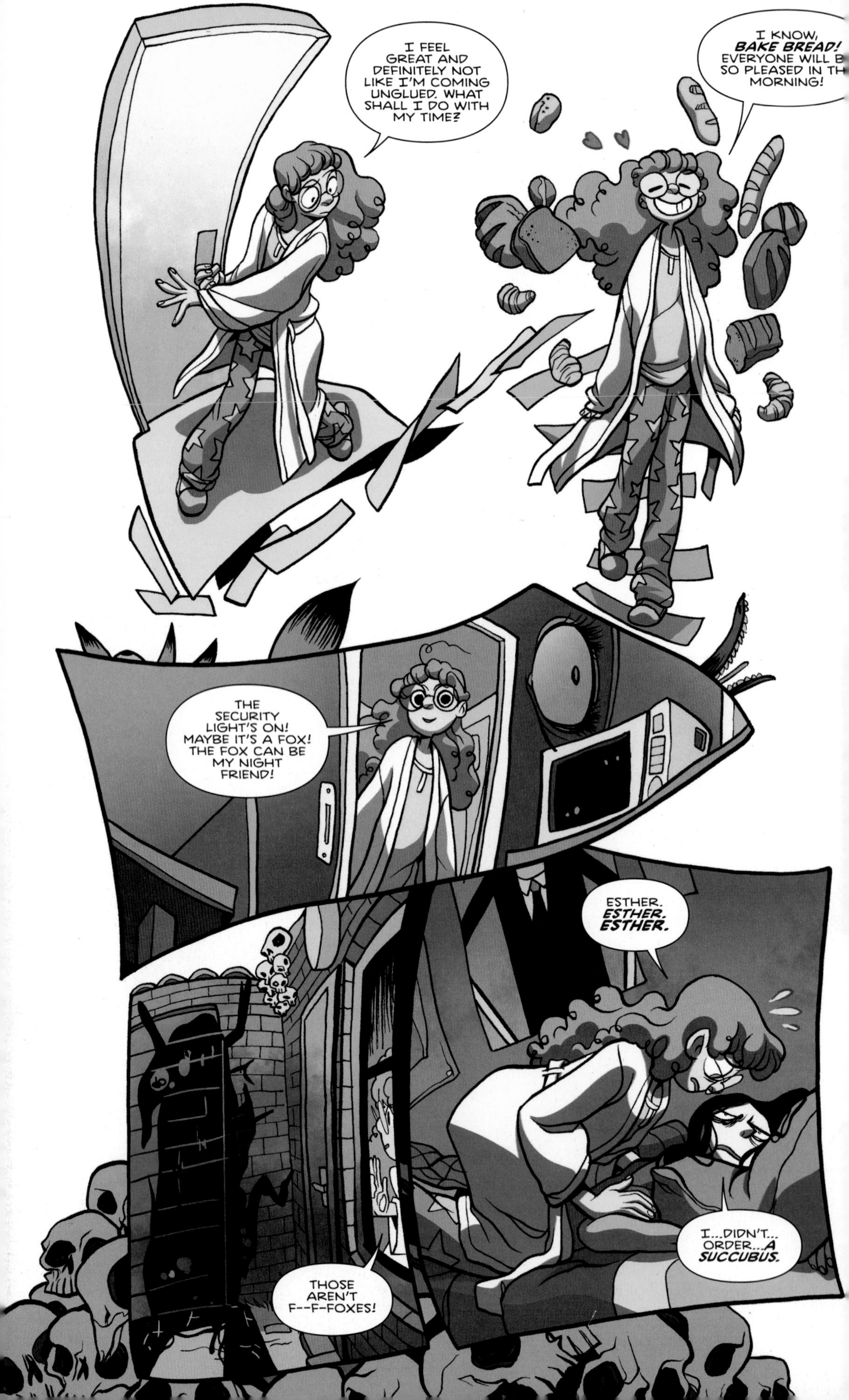
I FEEL GREAT AND DEFINITELY NOT LIKE I'M COMING UNGLUED. WHAT SHALL I DO WITH MY TIME?
I KNOW, **BAKE BREAD!** EVERYONE WILL B SO PLEASED IN TH MORNING!
THE SECURITY LIGHT'S ON! MAYBE IT'S A FOX! THE FOX CAN BE MY NIGHT FRIEND!
ESTHER. **ESTHER. ESTHER.**
I...DIDN'T... ORDER...**A SUCCUBUS.**
THOSE AREN'T F--F-FOXES!

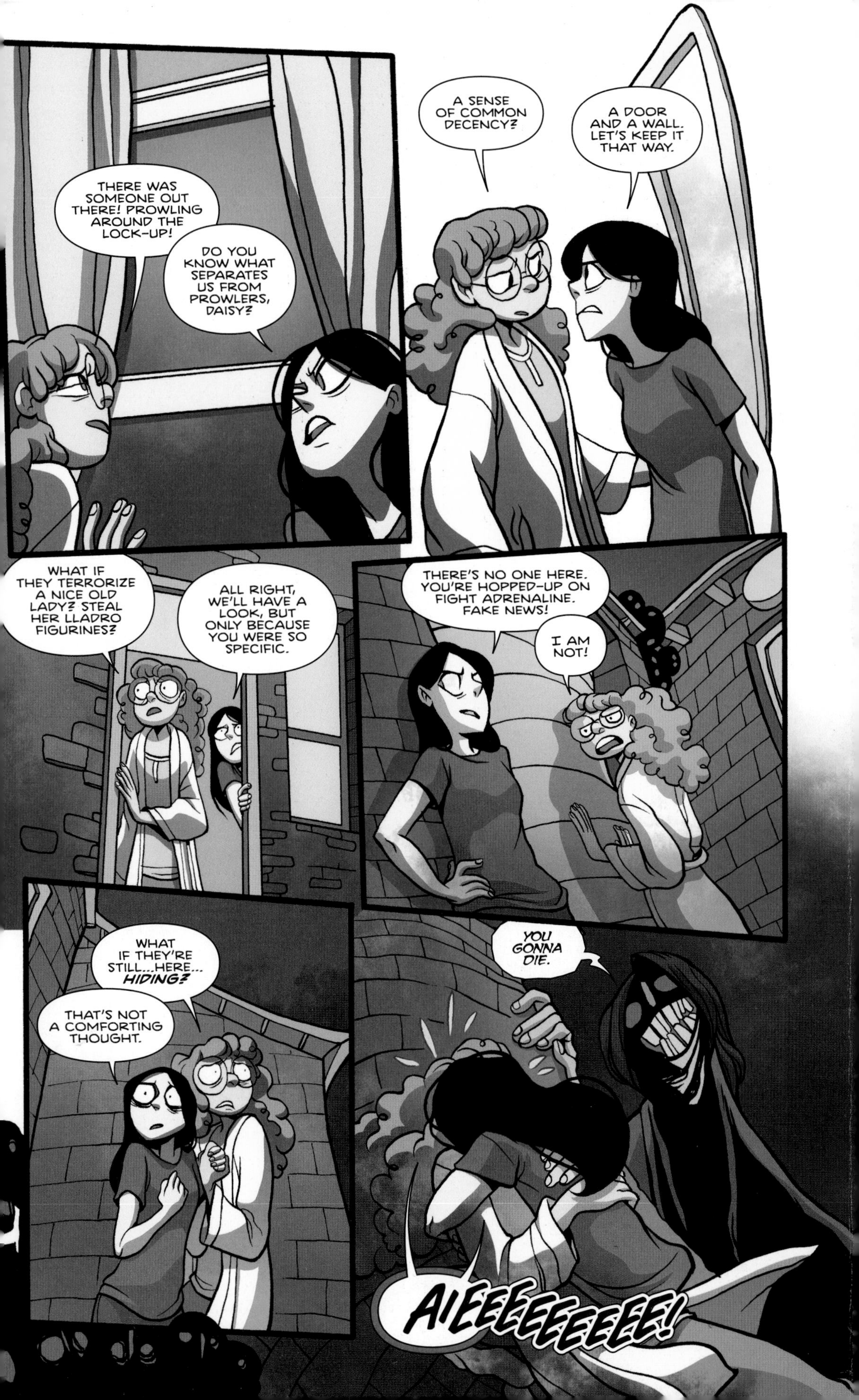
THERE WAS SOMEONE OUT THERE! PROWLING AROUND THE LOCK-UP!
DO YOU KNOW WHAT SEPARATES US FROM PROWLERS, DAISY?
A SENSE OF COMMON DECENCY?
A DOOR AND A WALL. LET'S KEEP IT THAT WAY.
WHAT IF THEY TERRORIZE A NICE OLD LADY? STEAL HER LLADRO FIGURINES?
ALL RIGHT, WE'LL HAVE A LOOK, BUT ONLY BECAUSE YOU WERE SO SPECIFIC.
THERE'S NO ONE HERE. YOU'RE HOPPED-UP ON FIGHT ADRENALINE. FAKE NEWS!
I AM NOT!
WHAT IF THEY'RE STILL...HERE... *HIDING?*
THAT'S NOT A COMFORTING THOUGHT.
YOU GONNA DIE.
AIEEEEEEEEEE!

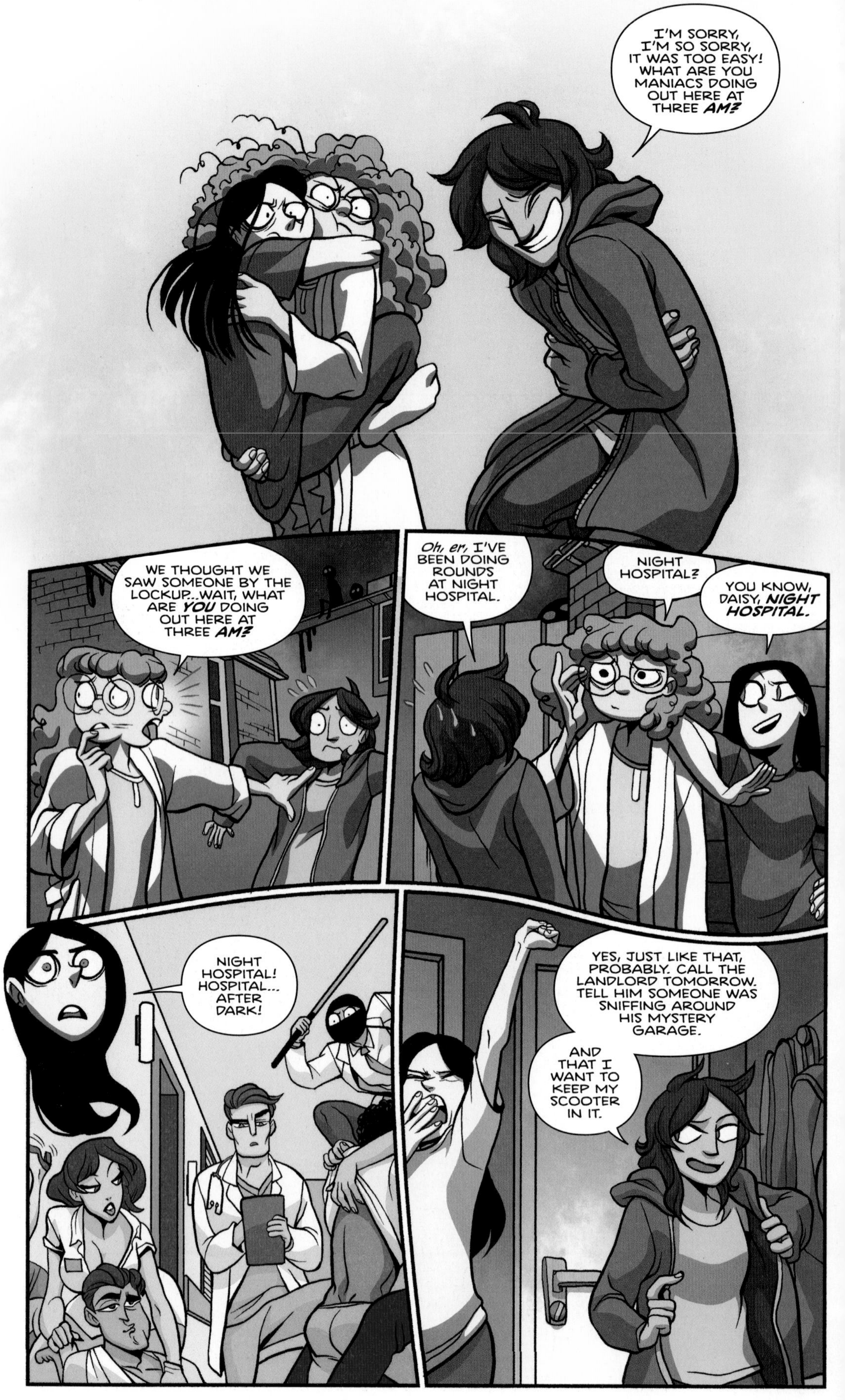

I'M SORRY, I'M SO SORRY, IT WAS TOO EASY! WHAT ARE YOU MANIACS DOING OUT HERE AT THREE AM?
WE THOUGHT WE SAW SOMEONE BY THE LOCKUP...WAIT, WHAT ARE YOU DOING OUT HERE AT THREE AM?
Oh, er, I'VE BEEN DOING ROUNDS AT NIGHT HOSPITAL.
NIGHT HOSPITAL?
YOU KNOW, DAISY, NIGHT HOSPITAL.
NIGHT HOSPITAL! HOSPITAL... AFTER DARK!
YES, JUST LIKE THAT, PROBABLY. CALL THE LANDLORD TOMORROW. TELL HIM SOMEONE WAS SNIFFING AROUND HIS MYSTERY GARAGE.
AND THAT I WANT TO KEEP MY SCOOTER IN IT.

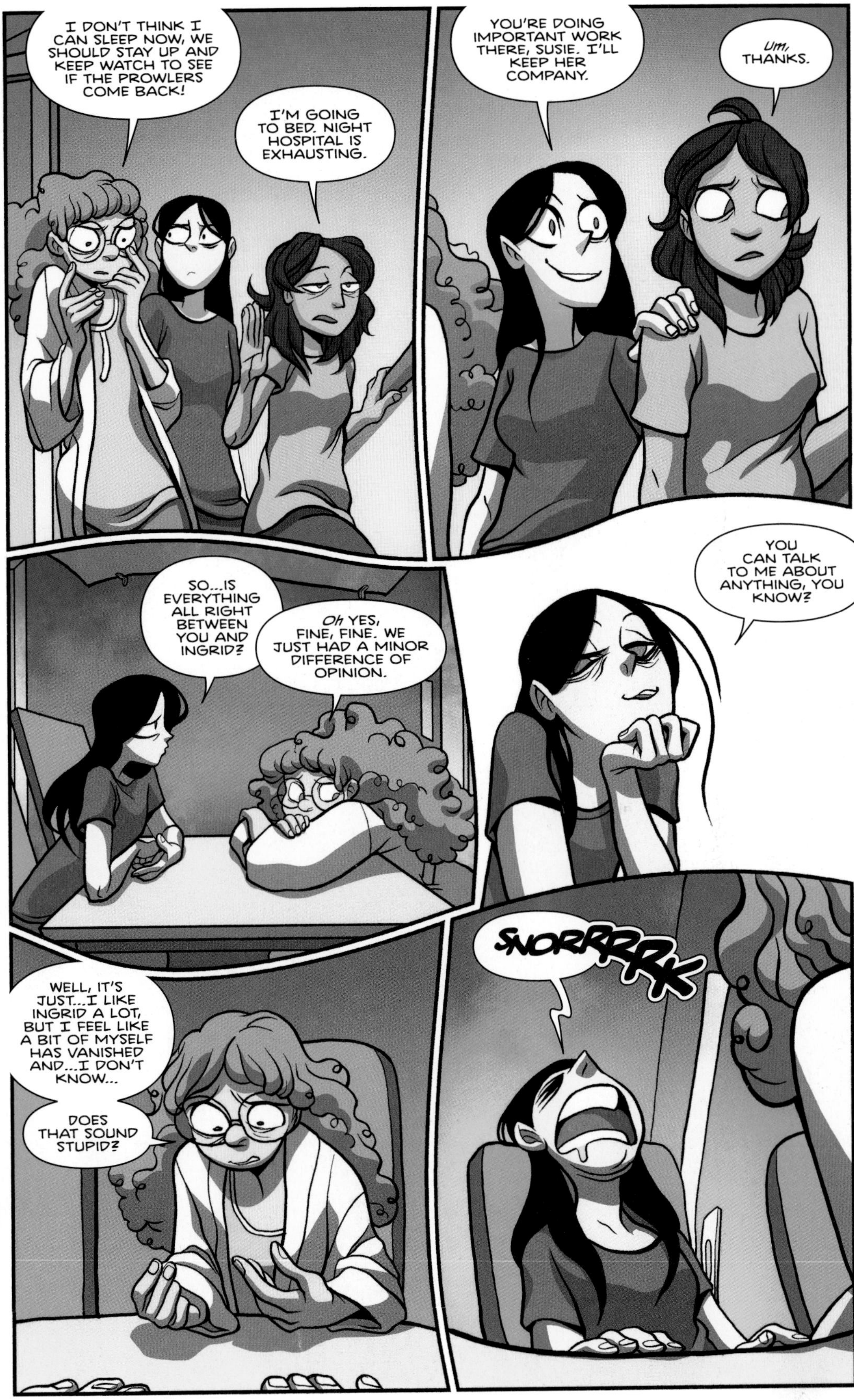
I DON'T THINK I CAN SLEEP NOW, WE SHOULD STAY UP AND KEEP WATCH TO SEE IF THE PROWLERS COME BACK!
I'M GOING TO BED. NIGHT HOSPITAL IS EXHAUSTING.
YOU'RE DOING IMPORTANT WORK THERE, SUSIE. I'LL KEEP HER COMPANY.
UM, THANKS.
SO...IS EVERYTHING ALL RIGHT BETWEEN YOU AND INGRID?
OH YES, FINE, FINE. WE JUST HAD A MINOR DIFFERENCE OF OPINION.
YOU CAN TALK TO ME ABOUT ANYTHING, YOU KNOW?
WELL, IT'S JUST...I LIKE INGRID A LOT, BUT I FEEL LIKE A BIT OF MYSELF HAS VANISHED AND...I DON'T KNOW...
DOES THAT SOUND STUPID?
SNORRRRRK

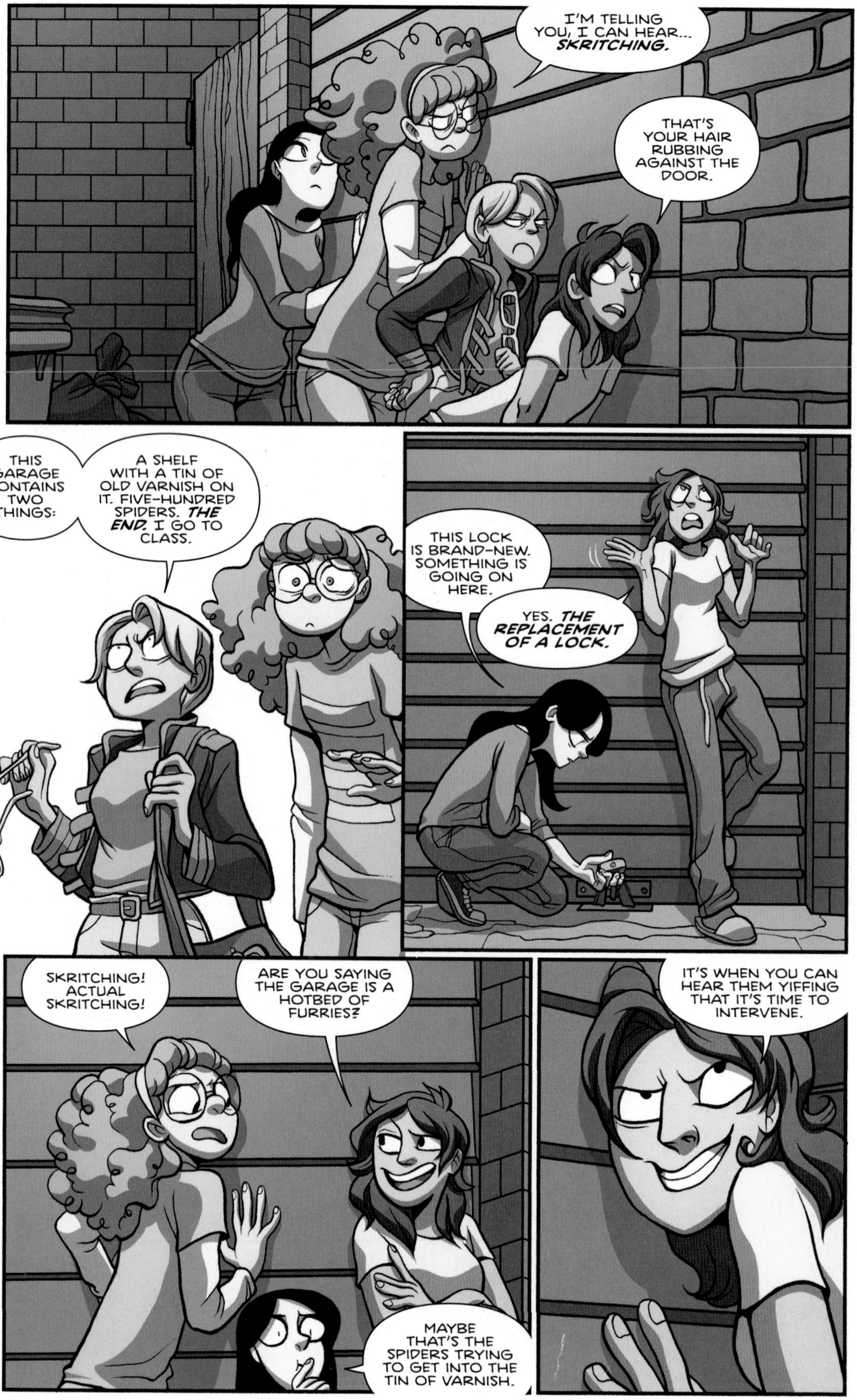
I'M TELLING YOU, I CAN HEAR... SKRITCHING.
THAT'S YOUR HAIR RUBBING AGAINST THE DOOR.
THIS GARAGE CONTAINS TWO THINGS:
A SHELF WITH A TIN OF OLD VARNISH ON IT. FIVE-HUNDRED SPIDERS. THE END. I GO TO CLASS.
THIS LOCK IS BRAND-NEW. SOMETHING IS GOING ON HERE.
YES. THE REPLACEMENT OF A LOCK.
SKRITCHING! ACTUAL SKRITCHING!
ARE YOU SAYING THE GARAGE IS A HOTBED OF FURRIES?
MAYBE THAT'S THE SPIDERS TRYING TO GET INTO THE TIN OF VARNISH.
IT'S WHEN YOU CAN HEAR THEM YIFFING THAT IT'S TIME TO INTERVENE.

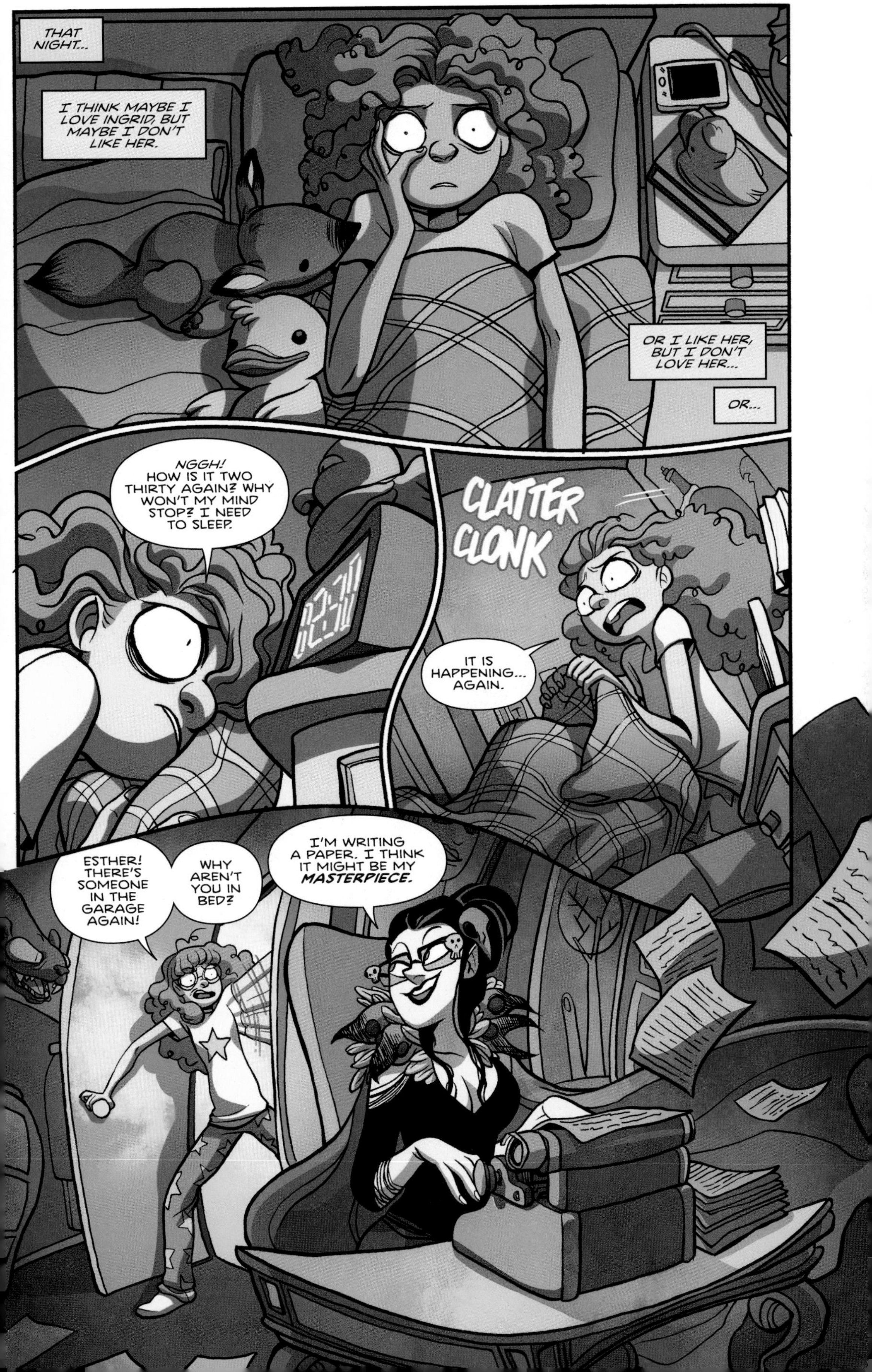
THAT NIGHT...
I THINK MAYBE I LOVE INGRID, BUT MAYBE I DON'T LIKE HER.
OR I LIKE HER, BUT I DON'T LOVE HER...
OR...
NGGH! HOW IS IT TWO THIRTY AGAIN? WHY WON'T MY MIND STOP? I NEED TO SLEEP.
02:30
CLATTER
CLONK
IT IS HAPPENING... AGAIN.
ESTHER! THERE'S SOMEONE IN THE GARAGE AGAIN!
WHY AREN'T YOU IN BED?
I'M WRITING A PAPER. I THINK IT MIGHT BE MY MASTERPIECE.

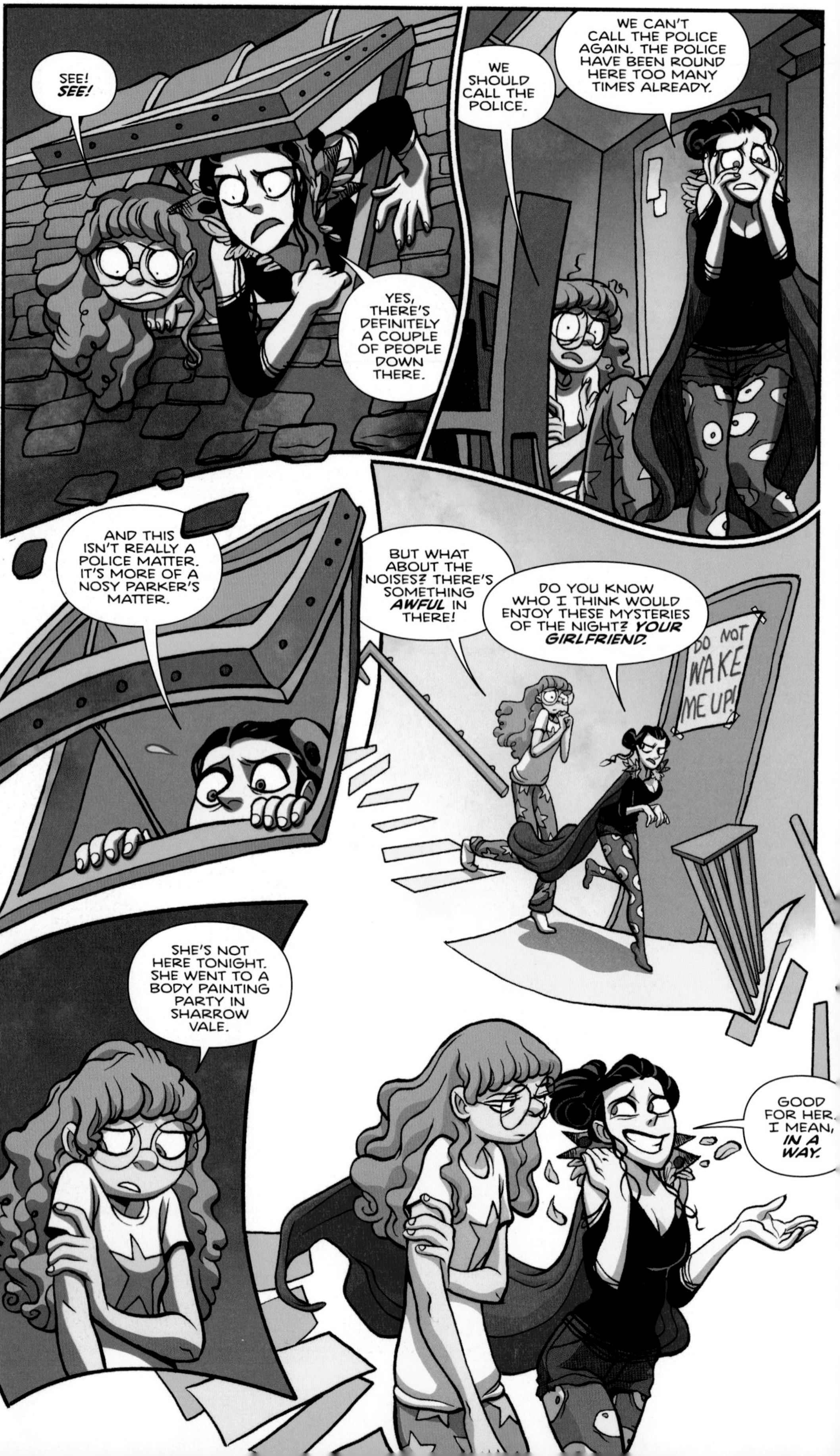
SEE! SEE!
YES, THERE'S DEFINITELY A COUPLE OF PEOPLE DOWN THERE.
WE SHOULD CALL THE POLICE.
WE CAN'T CALL THE POLICE AGAIN. THE POLICE HAVE BEEN ROUND HERE TOO MANY TIMES ALREADY.
AND THIS ISN'T REALLY A POLICE MATTER. IT'S MORE OF A NOSY PARKER'S MATTER.
BUT WHAT ABOUT THE NOISES? THERE'S SOMETHING AWFUL IN THERE!
DO YOU KNOW WHO I THINK WOULD ENJOY THESE MYSTERIES OF THE NIGHT? YOUR GIRLFRIEND.
DO NOT WAKE ME UP!
SHE'S NOT HERE TONIGHT. SHE WENT TO A BODY PAINTING PARTY IN SHARROW VALE.
GOOD FOR HER. I MEAN, IN A WAY.

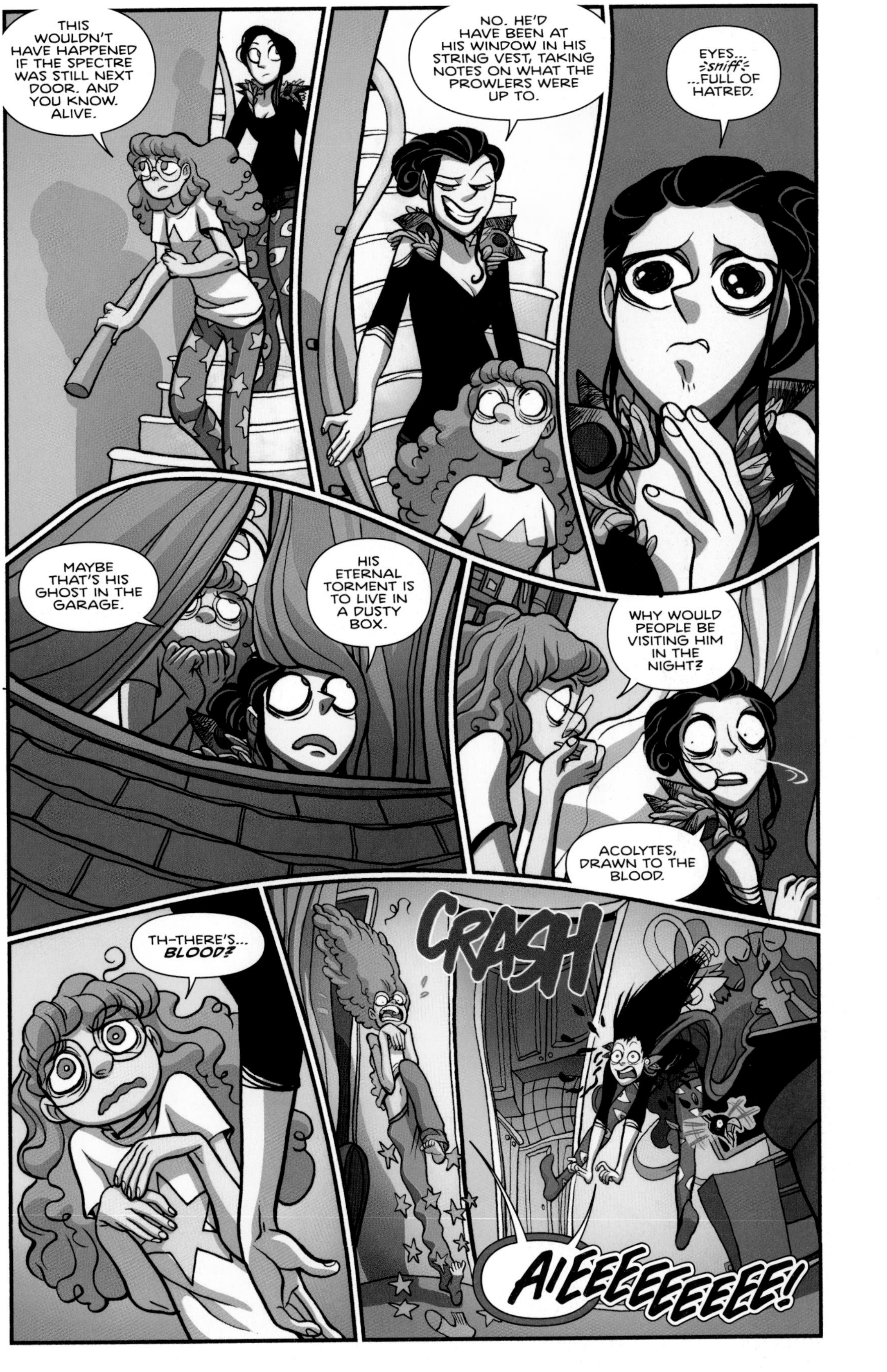
THIS WOULDN'T HAVE HAPPENED IF THE SPECTRE WAS STILL NEXT DOOR. AND YOU KNOW. ALIVE.
NO. HE'D HAVE BEEN AT HIS WINDOW IN HIS STRING VEST, TAKING NOTES ON WHAT THE PROWLERS WERE UP TO.
EYES... *sniff* ...FULL OF HATRED.
MAYBE THAT'S HIS GHOST IN THE GARAGE.
HIS ETERNAL TORMENT IS TO LIVE IN A DUSTY BOX.
WHY WOULD PEOPLE BE VISITING HIM IN THE NIGHT?
ACOLYTES, DRAWN TO THE BLOOD.
TH-THERE'S... BLOOD?
CRASH
AIEEEEEEEEEE!

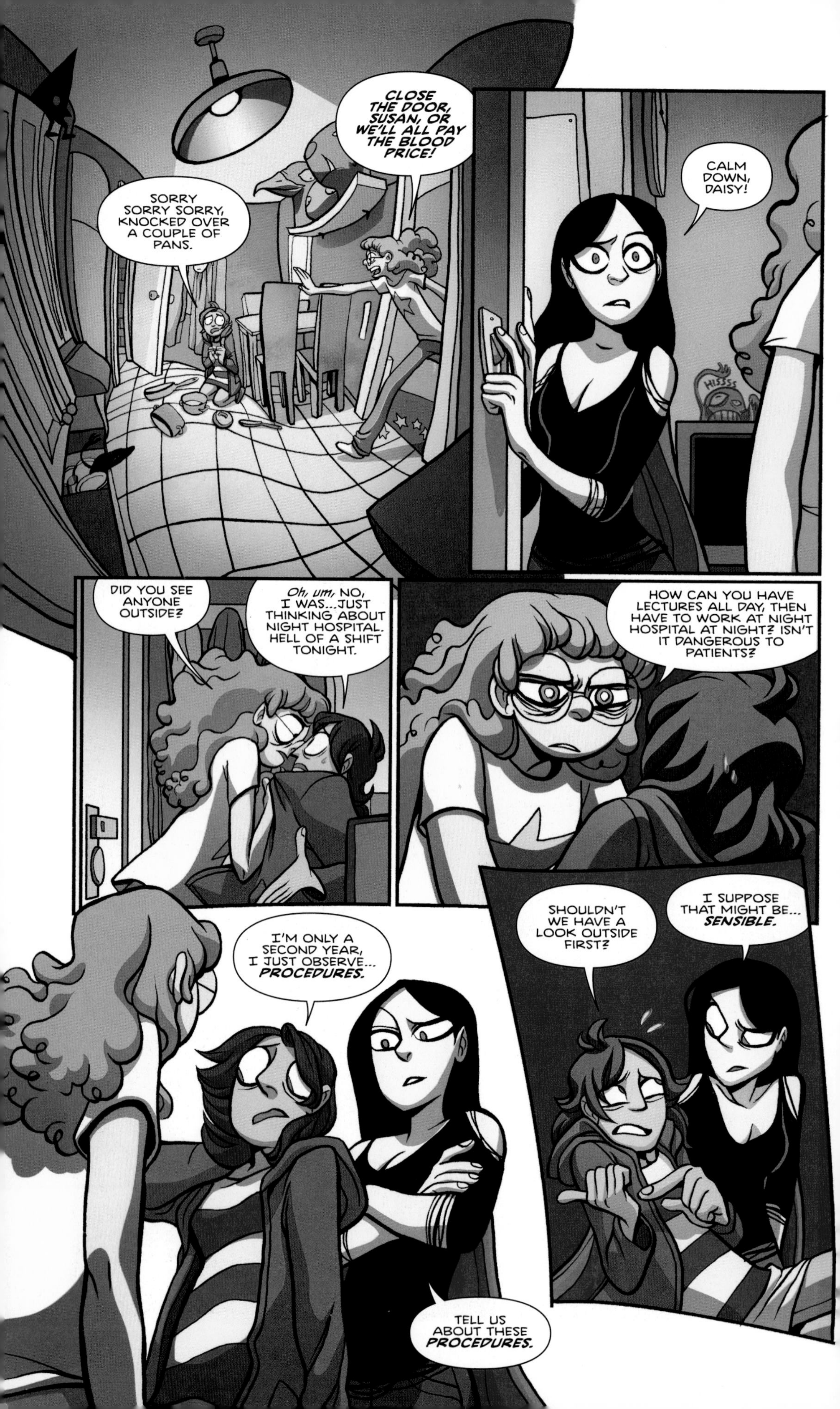
CLOSE THE DOOR, SUSAN, OR WE'LL ALL PAY THE BLOOD PRICE!
SORRY SORRY SORRY, KNOCKED OVER A COUPLE OF PANS.
CALM DOWN, DAISY!
HISSSS
DID YOU SEE ANYONE OUTSIDE?
Oh, um, NO, I WAS... JUST THINKING ABOUT NIGHT HOSPITAL. HELL OF A SHIFT TONIGHT.
HOW CAN YOU HAVE LECTURES ALL DAY, THEN HAVE TO WORK AT NIGHT HOSPITAL AT NIGHT? ISN'T IT DANGEROUS TO PATIENTS?
I'M ONLY A SECOND YEAR, I JUST OBSERVE... PROCEDURES.
TELL US ABOUT THESE PROCEDURES.
SHOULDN'T WE HAVE A LOOK OUTSIDE FIRST?
I SUPPOSE THAT MIGHT BE... SENSIBLE.

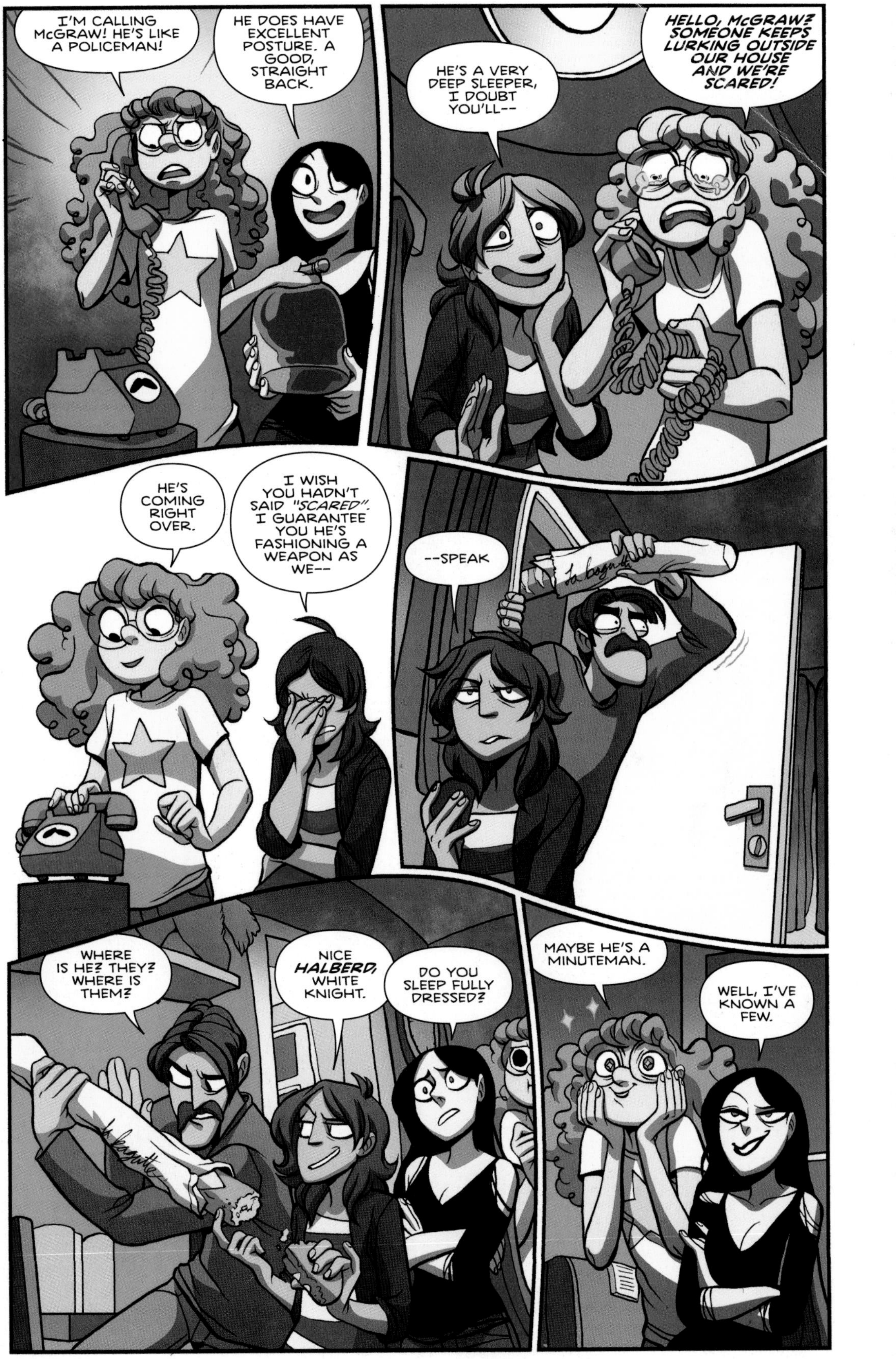

I'M CALLING McGRAW! HE'S LIKE A POLICEMAN!
HE DOES HAVE EXCELLENT POSTURE. A GOOD, STRAIGHT BACK.
HE'S A VERY DEEP SLEEPER, I DOUBT YOU'LL--
HELLO, McGRAW? SOMEONE KEEPS LURKING OUTSIDE OUR HOUSE AND WE'RE SCARED!
HE'S COMING RIGHT OVER.
I WISH YOU HADN'T SAID "SCARED". I GUARANTEE YOU HE'S FASHIONING A WEAPON AS WE--
--SPEAK
WHERE IS HE? THEY? WHERE IS THEM?
NICE HALBERD, WHITE KNIGHT.
DO YOU SLEEP FULLY DRESSED?
MAYBE HE'S A MINUTEMAN.
WELL, I'VE KNOWN A FEW.

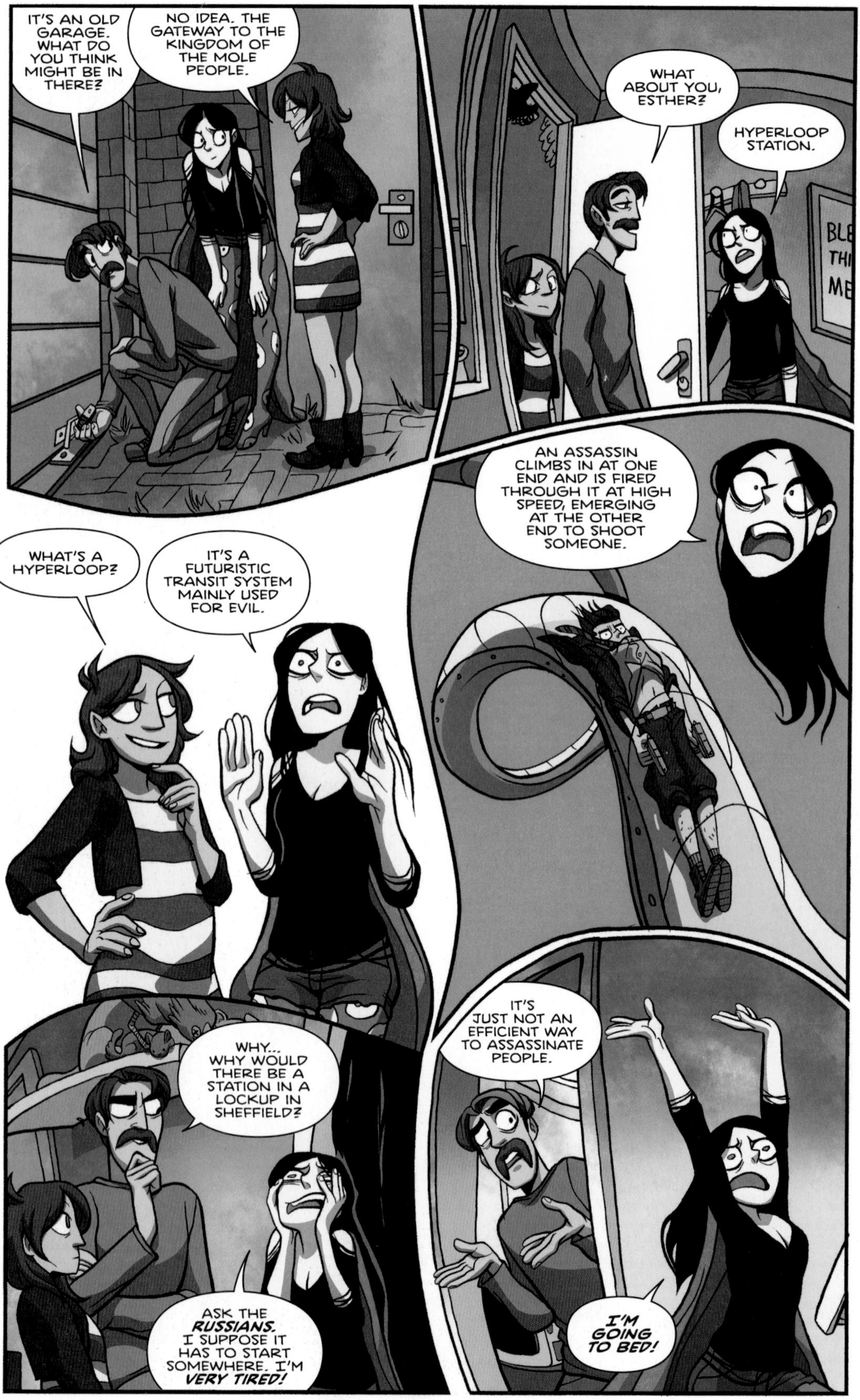
IT'S AN OLD GARAGE. WHAT DO YOU THINK MIGHT BE IN THERE?
NO IDEA. THE GATEWAY TO THE KINGDOM OF THE MOLE PEOPLE.
WHAT ABOUT YOU, ESTHER?
HYPERLOOP STATION.
WHAT'S A HYPERLOOP?
IT'S A FUTURISTIC TRANSIT SYSTEM MAINLY USED FOR EVIL.
AN ASSASSIN CLIMBS IN AT ONE END AND IS FIRED THROUGH IT AT HIGH SPEED, EMERGING AT THE OTHER END TO SHOOT SOMEONE.
WHY... WHY WOULD THERE BE A STATION IN A LOCKUP IN SHEFFIELD?
ASK THE *RUSSIANS.* I SUPPOSE IT HAS TO START SOMEWHERE. I'M *VERY TIRED!*
IT'S JUST NOT AN EFFICIENT WAY TO ASSASSINATE PEOPLE.
I'M GOING TO BED!

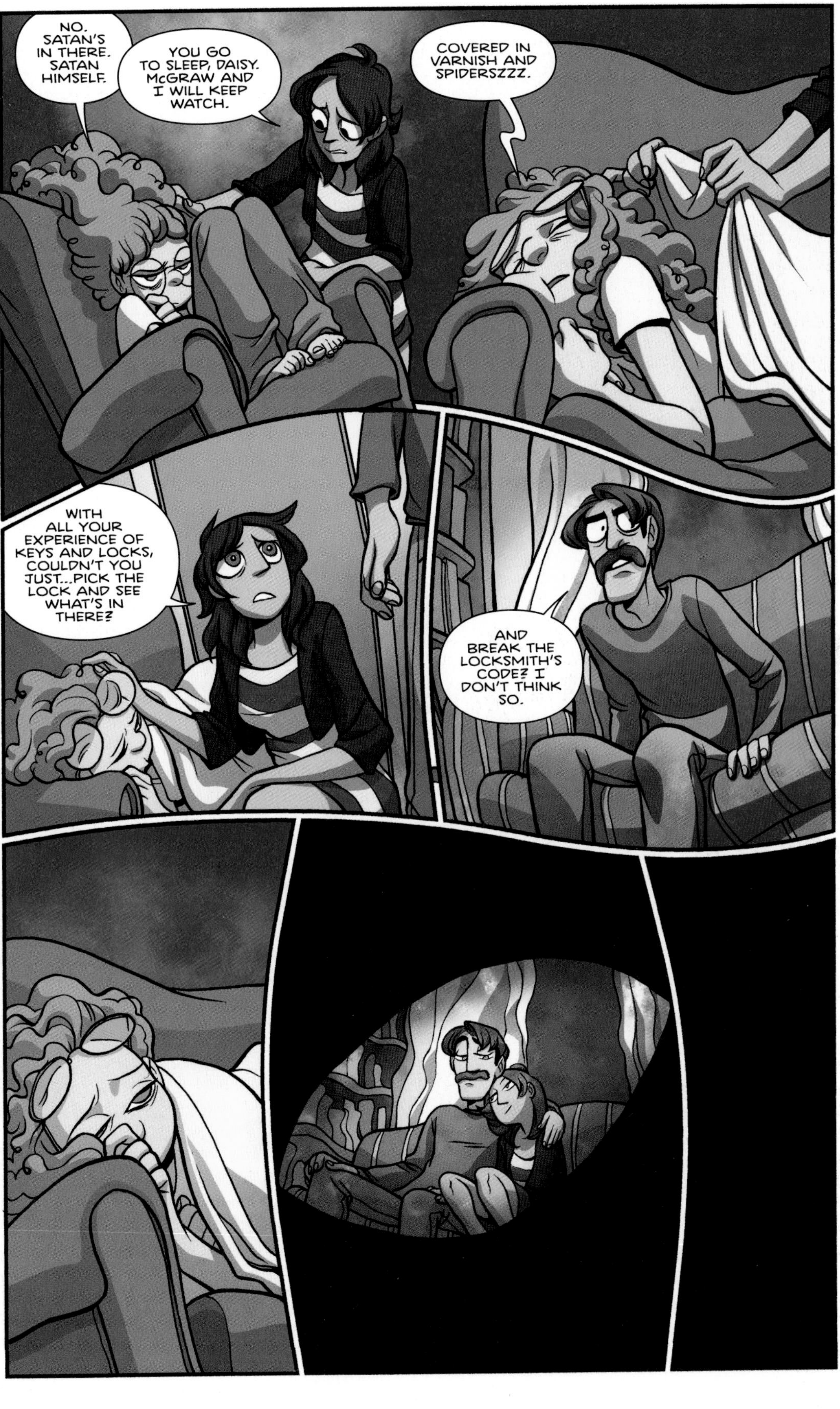
NO. SATAN'S IN THERE. SATAN HIMSELF.
YOU GO TO SLEEP, DAISY. McGRAW AND I WILL KEEP WATCH.
COVERED IN VARNISH AND SPIDERSZZZ.
WITH ALL YOUR EXPERIENCE OF KEYS AND LOCKS, COULDN'T YOU JUST...PICK THE LOCK AND SEE WHAT'S IN THERE?
AND BREAK THE LOCKSMITH'S CODE? I DON'T THINK SO.

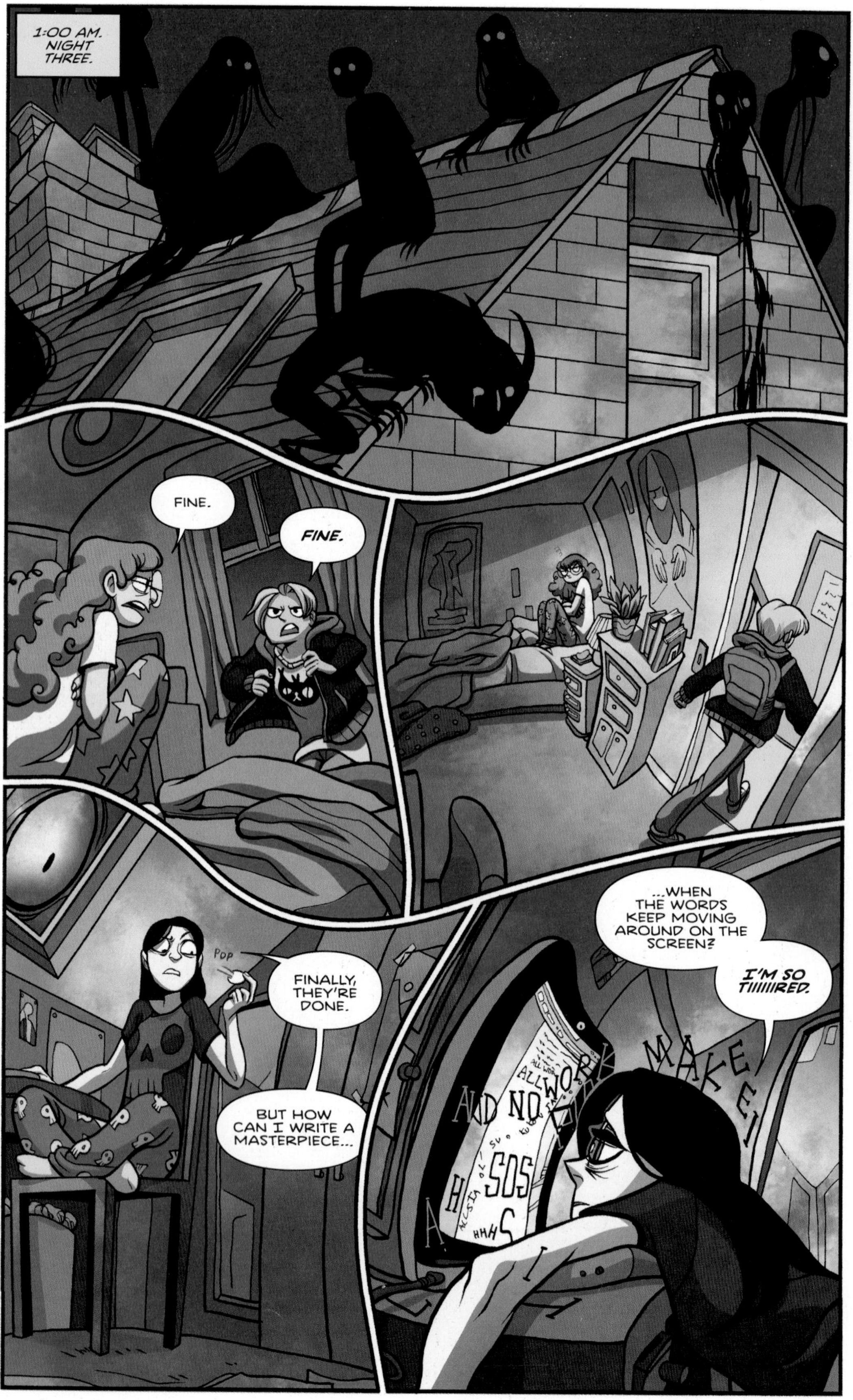
1:00 AM. NIGHT THREE.
FINE.
FINE.
POP
FINALLY, THEY'RE DONE.
BUT HOW CAN I WRITE A MASTERPIECE...
...WHEN THE WORDS KEEP MOVING AROUND ON THE SCREEN?
I'M SO TIIIIIRED.
ALL WORK
AND NO
MAKE
SOS

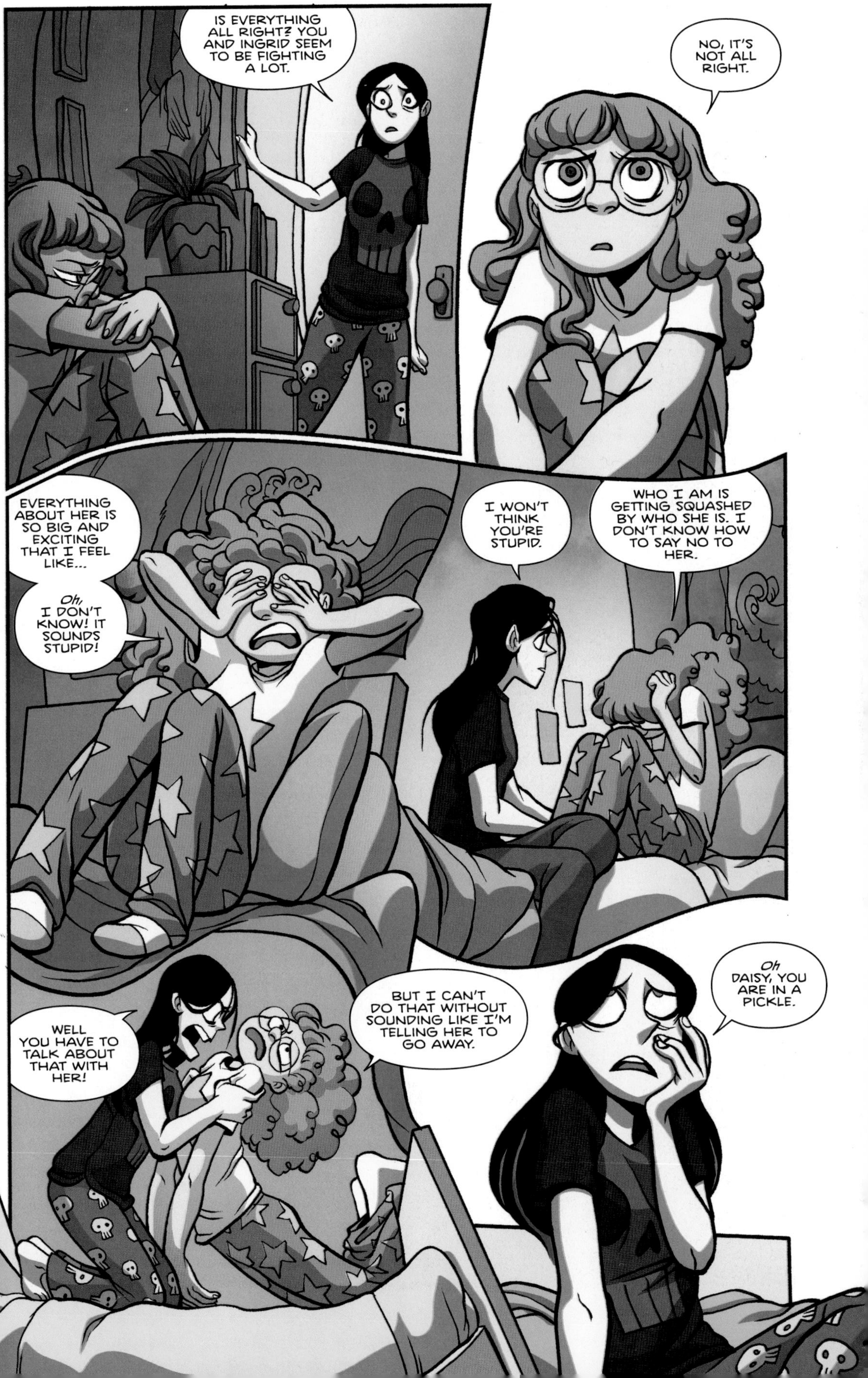
IS EVERYTHING ALL RIGHT? YOU AND INGRID SEEM TO BE FIGHTING A LOT.
NO, IT'S NOT ALL RIGHT.
EVERYTHING ABOUT HER IS SO BIG AND EXCITING THAT I FEEL LIKE...
Oh, I DON'T KNOW! IT SOUNDS STUPID!
I WON'T THINK YOU'RE STUPID.
WHO I AM IS GETTING SQUASHED BY WHO SHE IS. I DON'T KNOW HOW TO SAY NO TO HER.
WELL YOU HAVE TO TALK ABOUT THAT WITH HER!
BUT I CAN'T DO THAT WITHOUT SOUNDING LIKE I'M TELLING HER TO GO AWAY.
Oh DAISY, YOU ARE IN A PICKLE.

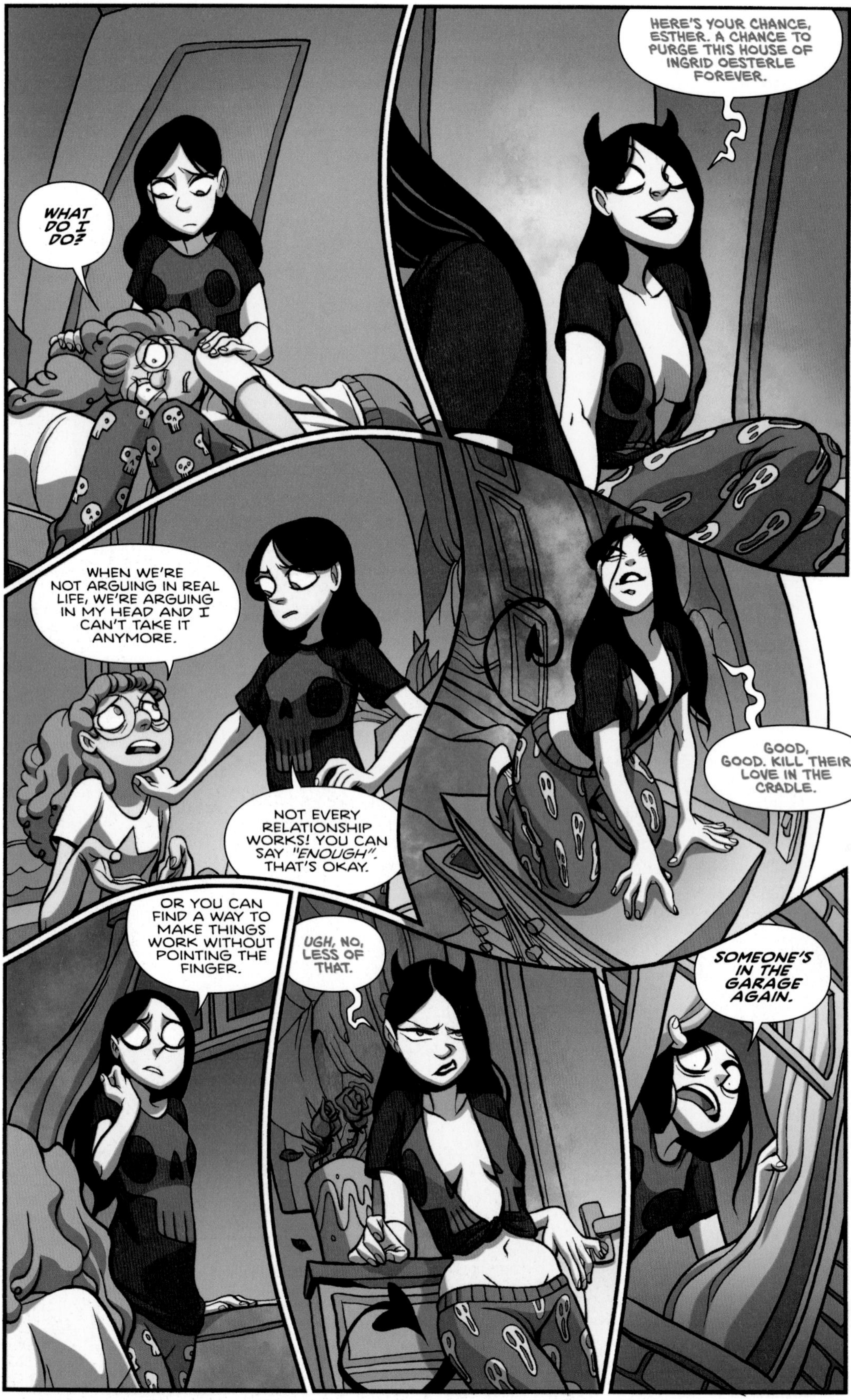
WHAT DO I DO?
HERE'S YOUR CHANCE, ESTHER. A CHANCE TO PURGE THIS HOUSE OF INGRID OESTERLE FOREVER.
WHEN WE'RE NOT ARGUING IN REAL LIFE, WE'RE ARGUING IN MY HEAD AND I CAN'T TAKE IT ANYMORE.
NOT EVERY RELATIONSHIP WORKS! YOU CAN SAY "ENOUGH". THAT'S OKAY.
GOOD, GOOD. KILL THEIR LOVE IN THE CRADLE.
OR YOU CAN FIND A WAY TO MAKE THINGS WORK WITHOUT POINTING THE FINGER.
UGH, NO, LESS OF THAT.
SOMEONE'S IN THE GARAGE AGAIN.

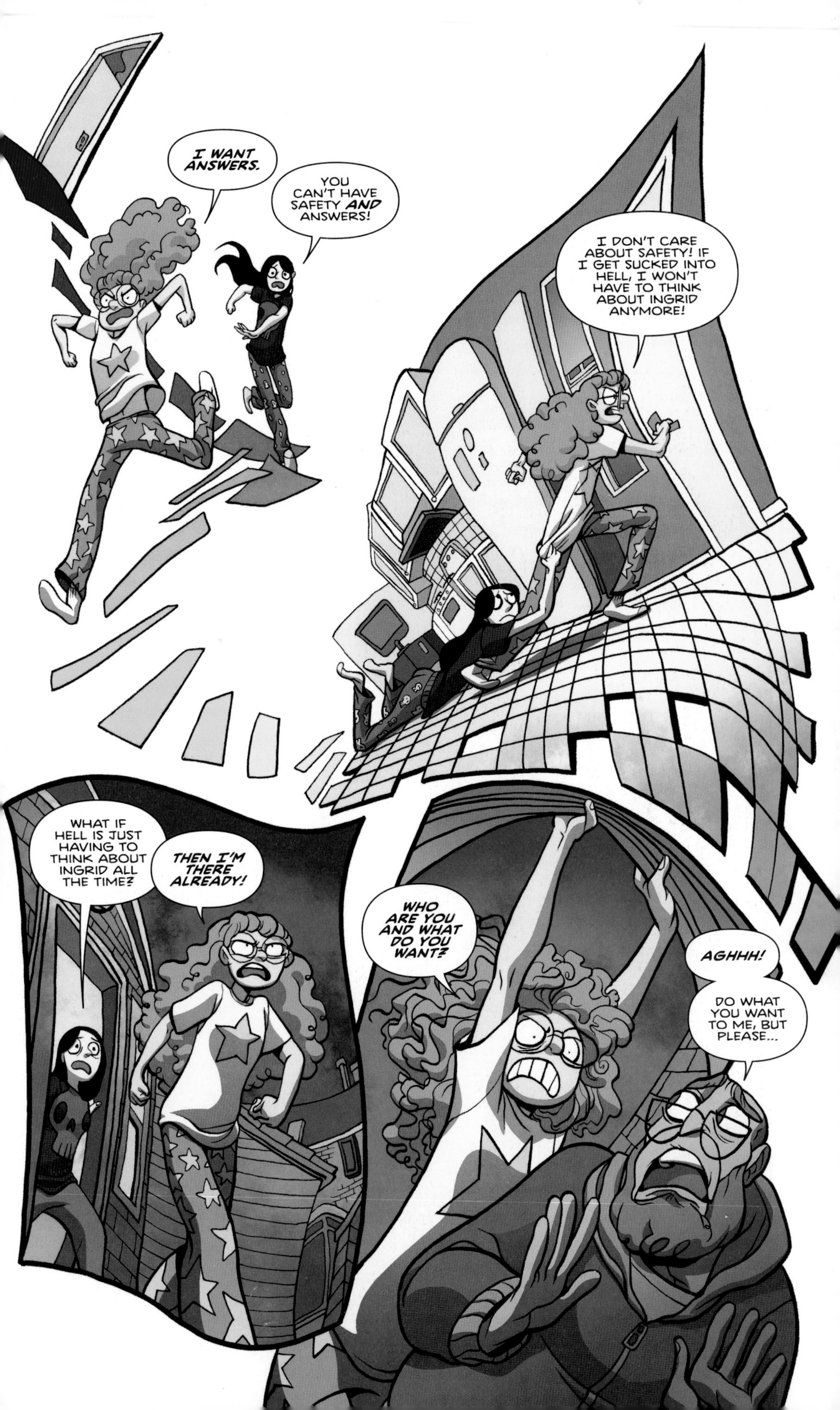
I WANT ANSWERS.
YOU CAN'T HAVE SAFETY AND ANSWERS!
I DON'T CARE ABOUT SAFETY! IF I GET SUCKED INTO HELL, I WON'T HAVE TO THINK ABOUT INGRID ANYMORE!
WHAT IF HELL IS JUST HAVING TO THINK ABOUT INGRID ALL THE TIME?
THEN I'M THERE ALREADY!
WHO ARE YOU AND WHAT DO YOU WANT?
AGHHH!
DO WHAT YOU WANT TO ME, BUT PLEASE...

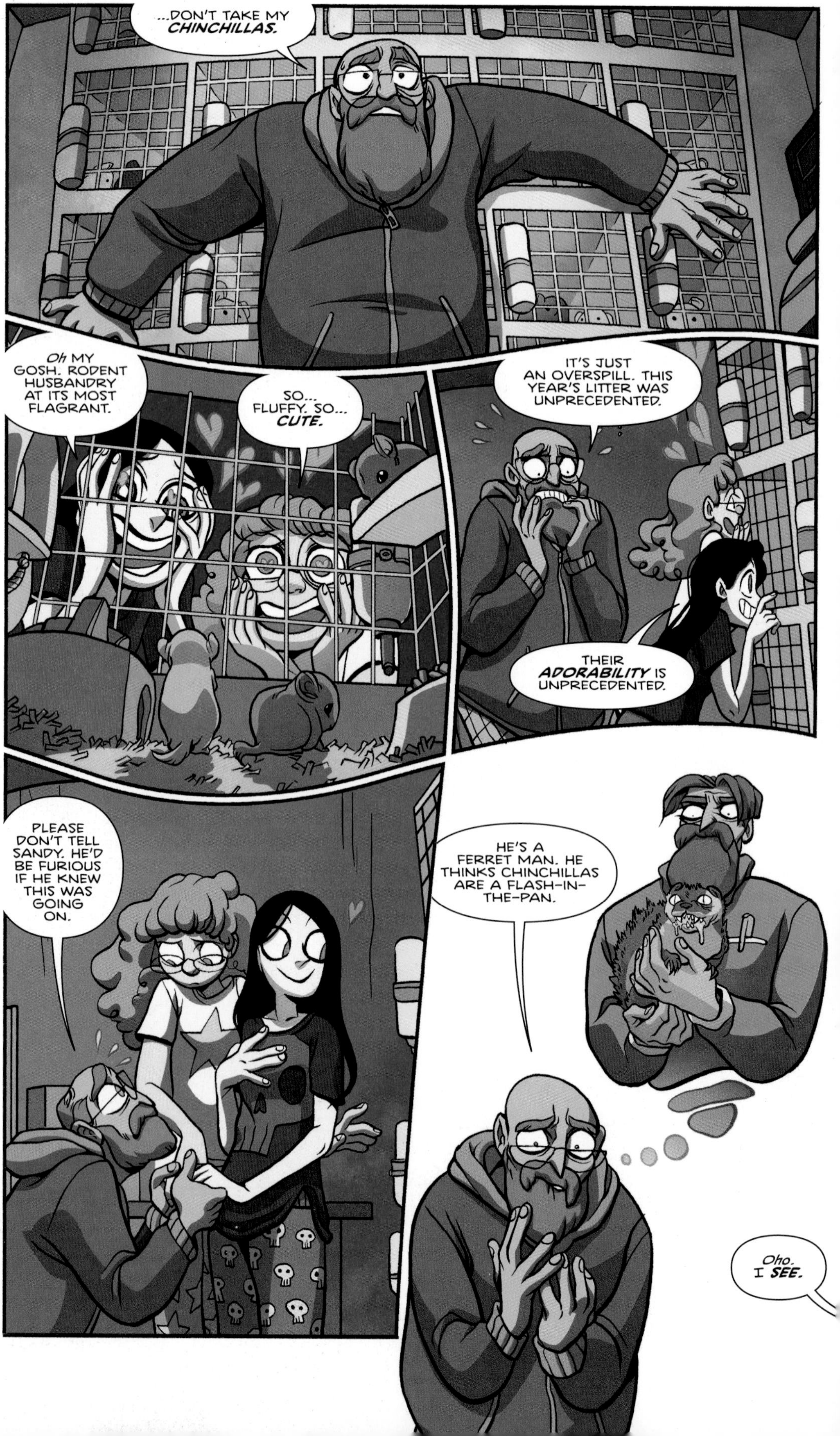
...DON'T TAKE MY CHINCHILLAS.
Oh MY GOSH. RODENT HUSBANDRY AT ITS MOST FLAGRANT.
SO... FLUFFY. SO... CUTE.
IT'S JUST AN OVERSPILL. THIS YEAR'S LITTER WAS UNPRECEDENTED.
THEIR ADORABILITY IS UNPRECEDENTED.
PLEASE DON'T TELL SANDY. HE'D BE FURIOUS IF HE KNEW THIS WAS GOING ON.
HE'S A FERRET MAN. HE THINKS CHINCHILLAS ARE A FLASH-IN-THE-PAN.
Oho. I SEE.

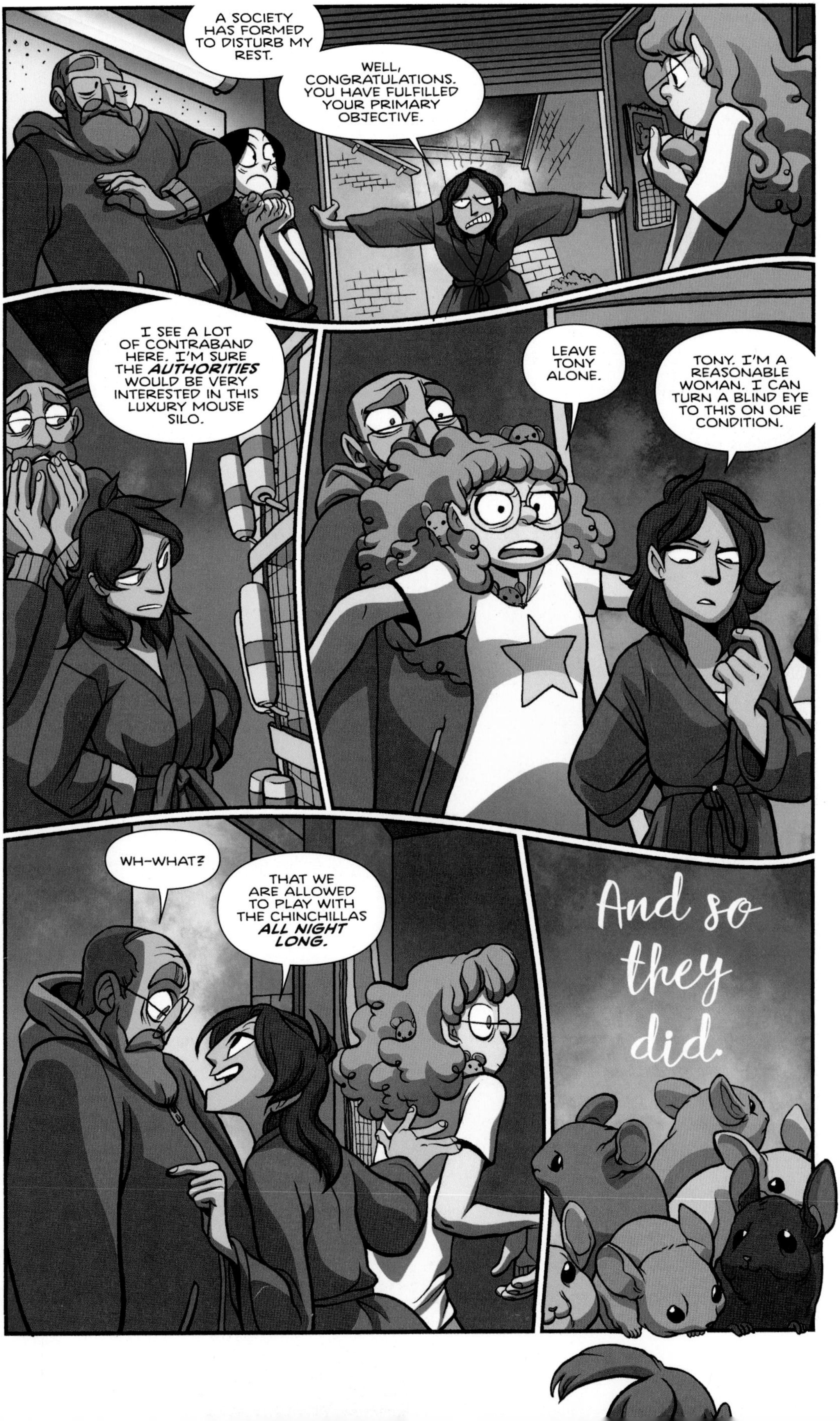
A SOCIETY HAS FORMED TO DISTURB MY REST.
WELL, CONGRATULATIONS. YOU HAVE FULFILLED YOUR PRIMARY OBJECTIVE.
I SEE A LOT OF CONTRABAND HERE. I'M SURE THE *AUTHORITIES* WOULD BE VERY INTERESTED IN THIS LUXURY MOUSE SILO.
LEAVE TONY ALONE.
TONY. I'M A REASONABLE WOMAN. I CAN TURN A BLIND EYE TO THIS ON ONE CONDITION.
WH-WHAT?
THAT WE ARE ALLOWED TO PLAY WITH THE CHINCHILLAS ***ALL NIGHT LONG.***
And so they did.

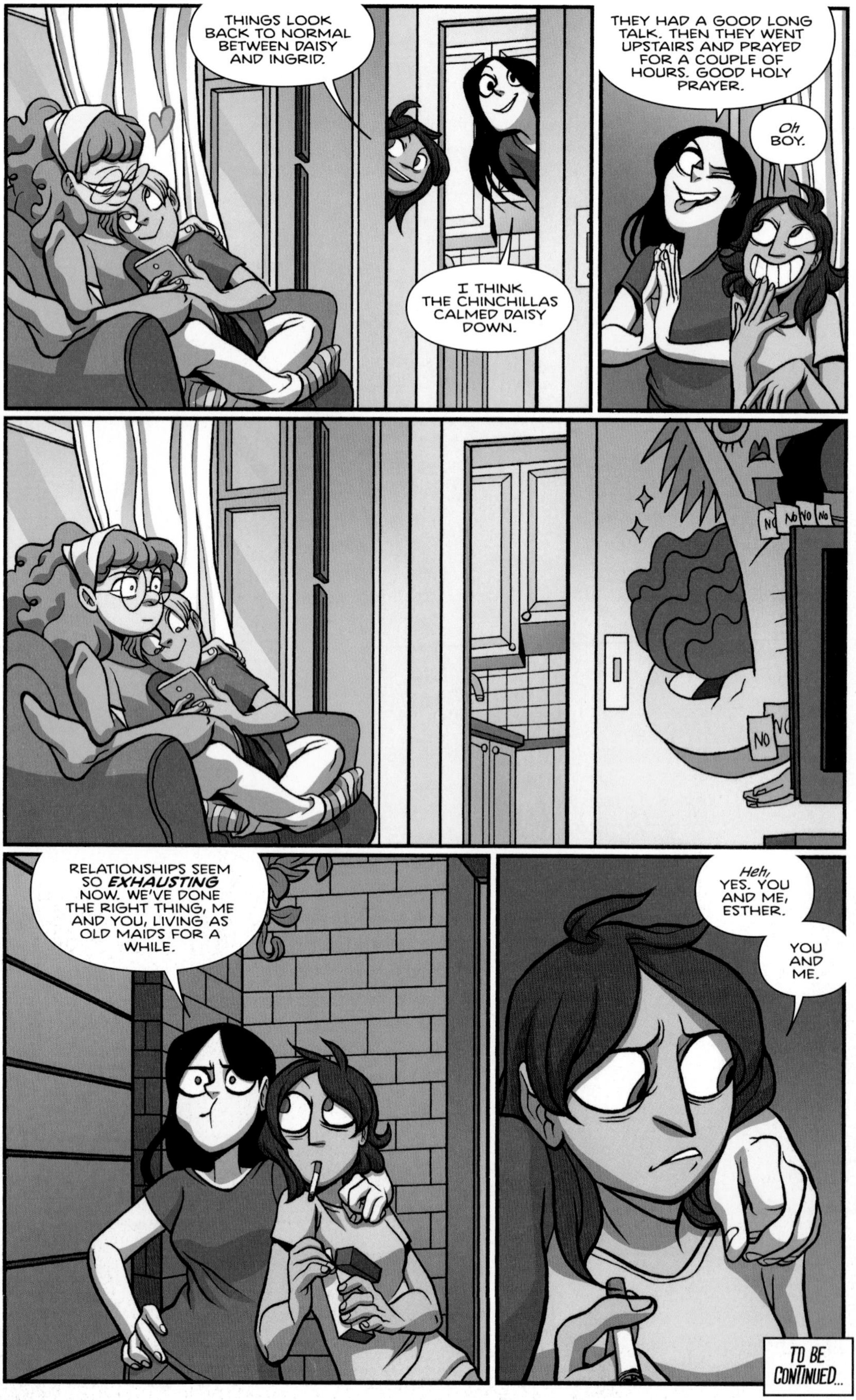

THINGS LOOK BACK TO NORMAL BETWEEN DAISY AND INGRID.
I THINK THE CHINCHILLAS CALMED DAISY DOWN.
THEY HAD A GOOD LONG TALK. THEN THEY WENT UPSTAIRS AND PRAYED FOR A COUPLE OF HOURS. GOOD HOLY PRAYER.
Oh BOY.
NO
NO
NO
NO
NO
NO
RELATIONSHIPS SEEM SO ***EXHAUSTING*** NOW. WE'VE DONE THE RIGHT THING, ME AND YOU, LIVING AS OLD MAIDS FOR A WHILE.
Heh, YES. YOU AND ME, ESTHER.
YOU AND ME.
TO BE CONTINUED...

COVER GALLERY

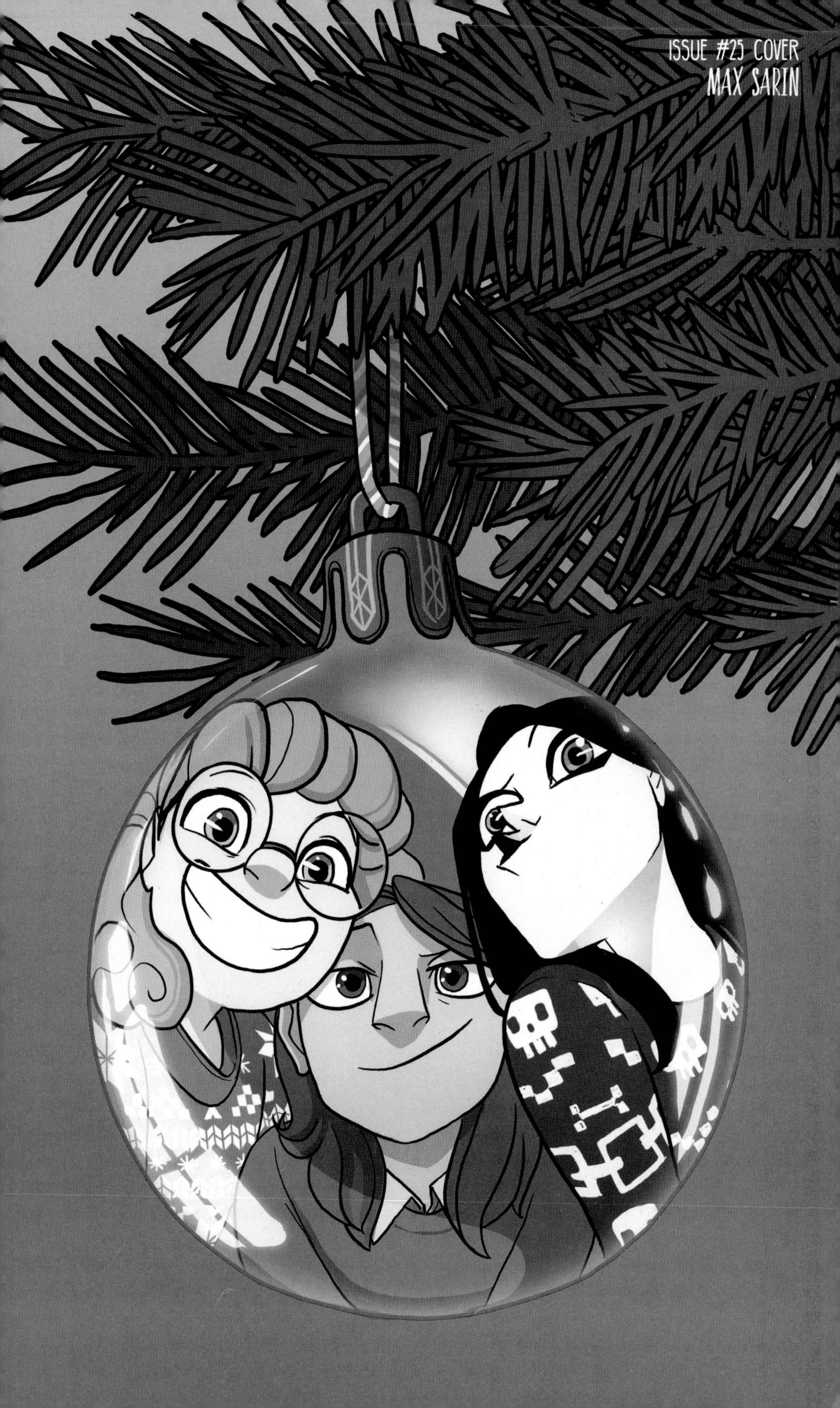

ISSUE #25 COVER
MAX SARIN

ISSUE #25 VARIANT COVER
MEREDITH GRAN
WITH COLORS BY HANNAH FISHER

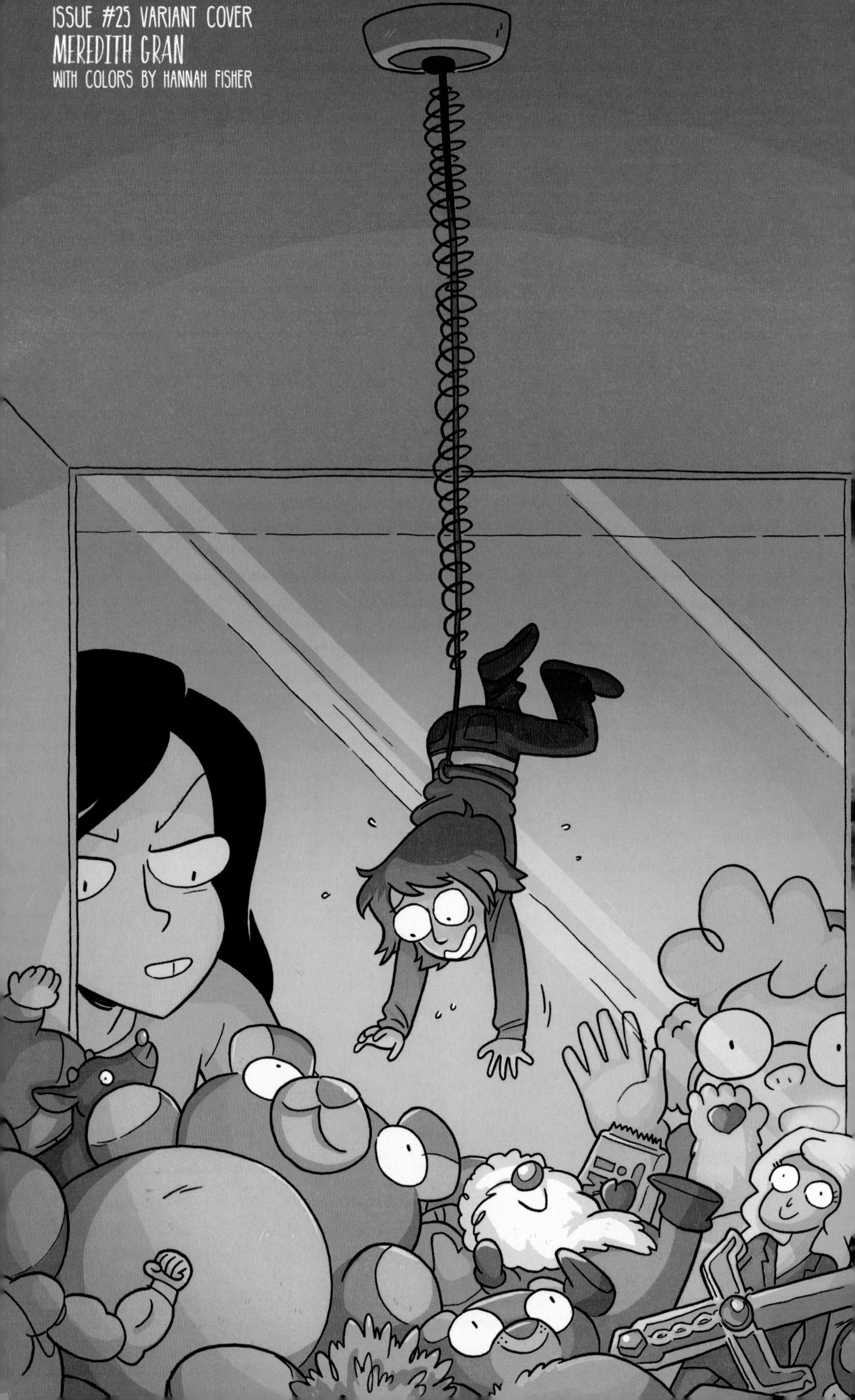

ISSUE #26 COVER
MAX SARIN

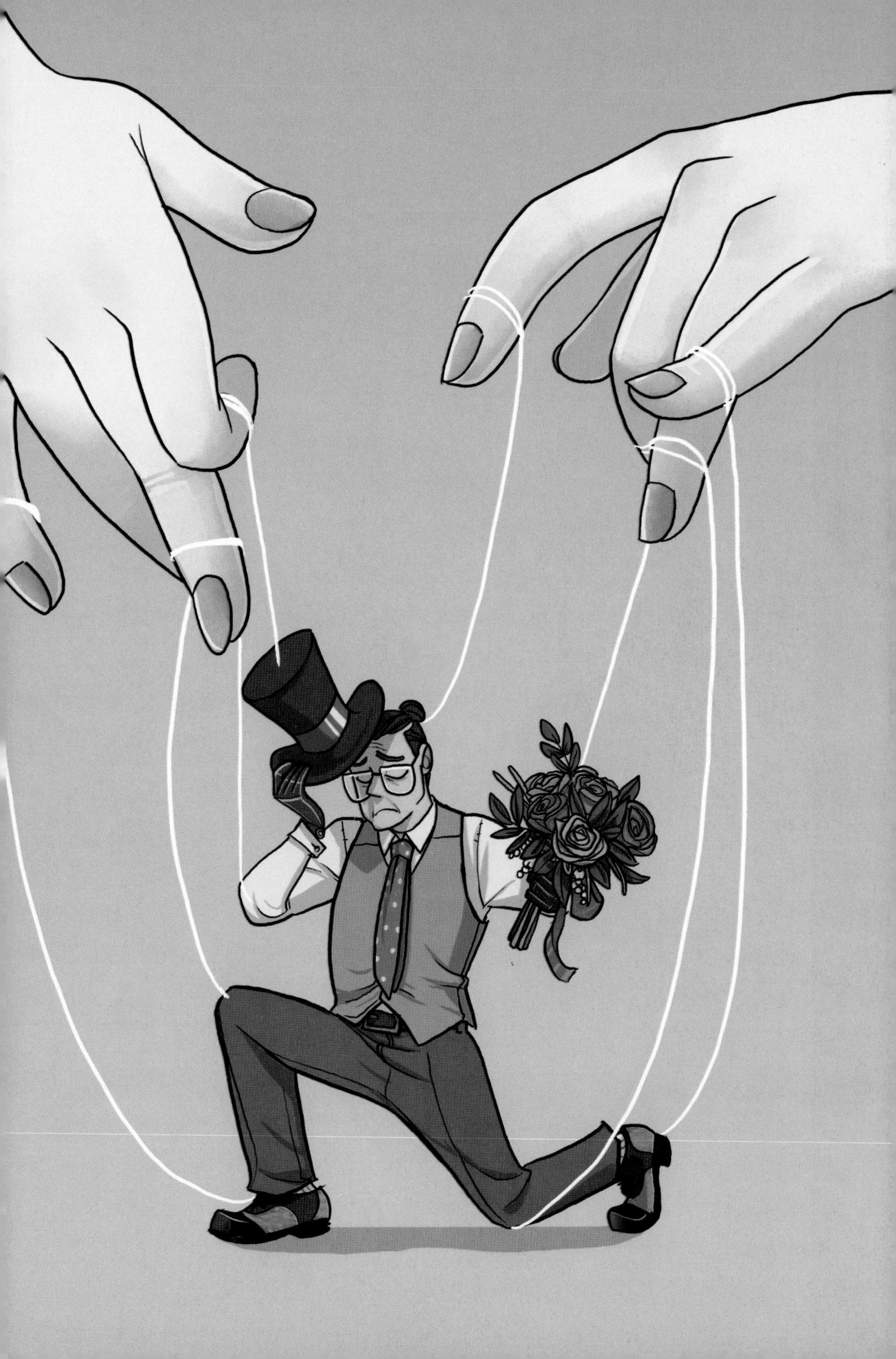

ISSUE #27 COVER
MAX SARIN

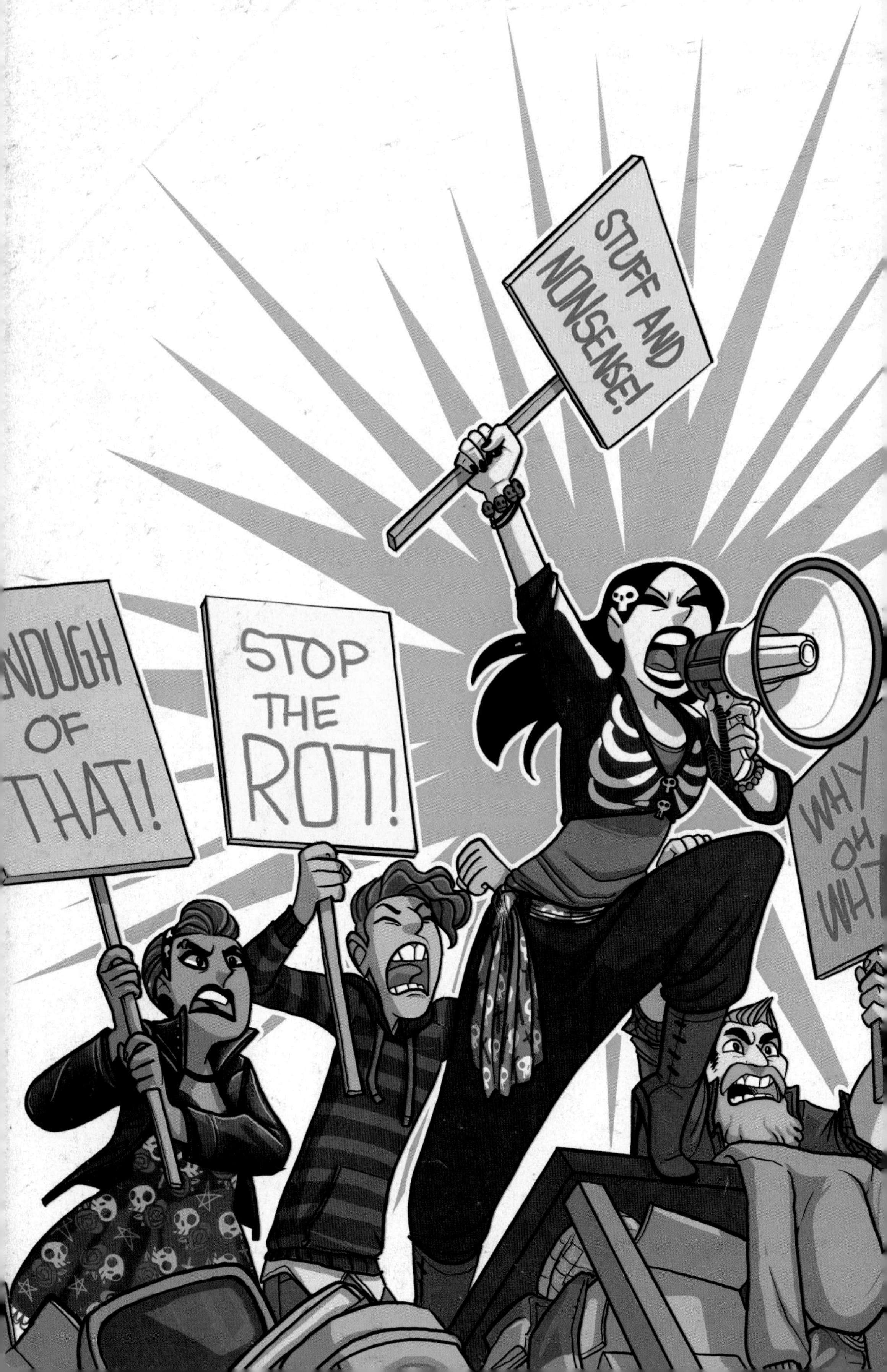
STUFF AND NONSENSE!
NOUGH OF THAT!
STOP THE ROT!
WHY OH WH

ISSUE #28 COVER
MAX SARIN

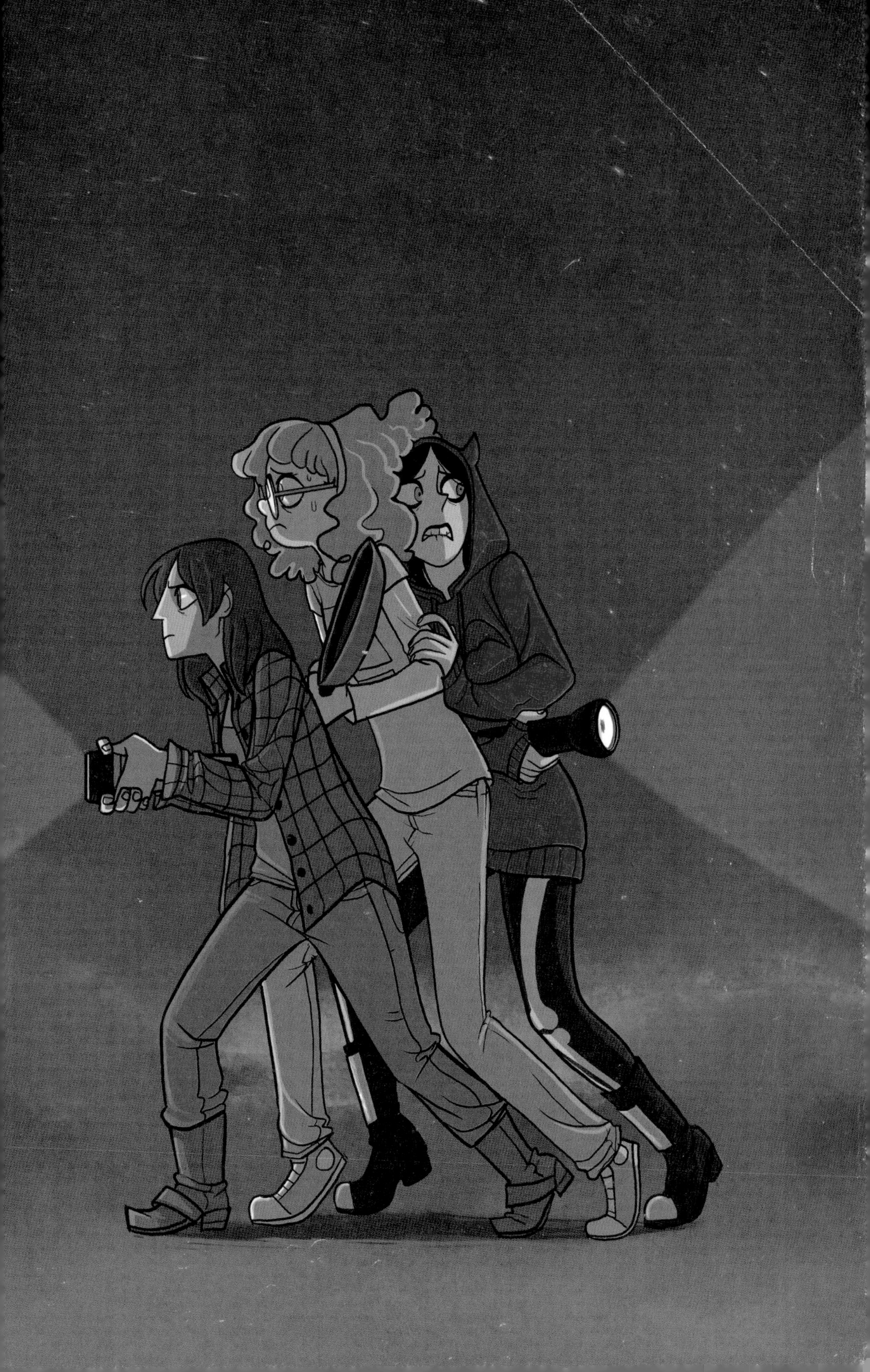

DISCOVER
ALL THE HITS

STEVENSON · ELLIS · WATTERS · ALLEN
LUMBERJANES
BEWARE THE KITTEN HOLY
NEW YORK TIMES BESTSELLING SERIES

Allison + Treiman + Cogar
GIANT DAYS
VOLUME ONE

RIBON · FISH · PEER
SLAM!
VOLUME ONE

Hope Larson · Brittney Williams · Sarah Stern
GOLDIE VANCE
Volume One

THE BACKSTAGERS

TYSON HESSE'S
DIESEL
IGNITION

BOOM! BOX™

AVAILABLE AT YOUR LOCAL COMICS SHOP AND BOOKSTORE

To find a comics shop in your area, call 1-888-266-4226

WWW.**BOOM-STUDIOS**.COM

Lumberjanes
Noelle Stevenson, Shannon Watters, Grace Ellis, Brooke Allen, and Others
Volume 1: Beware the Kitten Holy
ISBN: 978-1-60886-687-8 | $14.99 US
Volume 2: Friendship to the Max
ISBN: 978-1-60886-737-0 | $14.99 US
Volume 3: A Terrible Plan
ISBN: 978-1-60886-803-2 | $14.99 US
Volume 4: Out of Time
ISBN: 978-1-60886-860-5 | $14.99 US
Volume 5: Band Together
ISBN: 978-1-60886-919-0 | $14.99 US

Giant Days
John Allison, Lissa Treiman, Max Sarin
Volume 1
ISBN: 978-1-60886-789-9 | $9.99 US
Volume 2
ISBN: 978-1-60886-804-9 | $14.99 US
Volume 3
ISBN: 978-1-60886-851-3 | $14.99 US

Jonesy
Sam Humphries, Caitlin Rose Boyle
Volume 1
ISBN: 978-1-60886-883-4 | $9.99 US
Volume 2
ISBN: 978-1-60886-999-2 | $14.99 US

Slam!
Pamela Ribon, Veronica Fish, Brittany Peer
Volume 1
ISBN: 978-1-68415-004-5 | $14.99 US

Goldie Vance
Hope Larson, Brittney Williams
Volume 1
ISBN: 978-1-60886-898-8 | $9.99 US
Volume 2
ISBN: 978-1-60886-974-9 | $14.99 US

The Backstagers
James Tynion IV, Rian Sygh
Volume 1
ISBN: 978-1-60886-993-0 | $14.99 US

Tyson Hesse's Diesel: Ignition
Tyson Hesse
ISBN: 978-1-60886-907-7 | $14.99 US

Coady & The Creepies
Liz Prince, Amanda Kirk, Hannah Fisher
ISBN: 978-1-68415-029-8 | $14.99 US

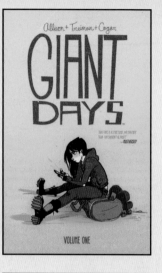